The Beat of Black Wings: Crime Fiction I...
Edited by Josh Pachter

Cover Copyright 2020 by Untreed Read.........g
Cover Design by Ginny Glass

"Marcie" by Ricki Thomas
"The Pirate of Penance" by Marilyn Todd
"The Gallery" by Christine Poulson
"Both Sides, Now" by Art Taylor and Tara Laskowski
"The Priest" by David Dean
"Big Yellow Taxi" by Kathryn O'Sullivan
"River" by Stacy Woodson
"Cold Blue Steel and Sweet Fire" by Donna Andrews
"Blonde in the Bleachers" by Carol Anne Davis
"Help Me" by Abby Bardi
"Free Man in Paris" by Brendan DuBois
"Shades of Scarlett Conquering" by Adam Meyer
"Blue Motel Room" by Edith Maxwell
"Talk to Me" by Emily Hockaday and Jackie Sherbow
"The Silky Veils of Ardor" by Greg Herren
"The Dry Cleaner From Des Moines" by Amber Sparks
"Man to Man" by Barb Goffman
"Dog Eat Dog" by Elaine Viets
"The Beat of Black Wings" by Josh Pachter
"Cherokee Louise" by Matthew Iden
"Ray's Dad's Cadillac" by Michael Bracken
"Sex Kills" by Alan Orloff
"Last Chance" by Sherry Harris
"Harlem in Havana" by Alison McMahan
"Taming the Tiger" by Mindy Quigley
"Bad Dreams" by John M. Floyd

ISBN-13: 978-1-94913-561-9

Also available in ebook format.

Published by Untreed Reads, LLC
506 Kansas Street, San Francisco, CA 94107
www.untreedreads.com

Printed in the United States of America.

Publisher's Note

This is a work of fiction. Names, characters, places, and incidents either are the product of the authors' imagination or are used fictitiously, and any resemblance to actual persons, living or dead, business establishments, events, or locales is entirely coincidental.

The publisher does not have any control over and does not assume any responsibility for author or third-party websites or their content.

THE BEAT OF BLACK WINGS

Crime Fiction Inspired by the Songs of Joni Mitchell

edited by Josh Pachter

Untreed
Reads

Contents

Introduction

As I write this introduction in February of 2020, Joni Mitchell—born Roberta Joan Anderson on November 7, 1943, in Fort Macleod, Alberta, Canada—is seventy-six years old. Her last album of new music, *Shine*, came out in 2007, more than a decade ago. Her website—*jonimitchell.com*—lists her last live performance as "a short set" at the end of a seventieth-birthday tribute held at Massey Hall in Toronto on June 19, 2013. Given the health issues she has wrestled with in the years since then—her ongoing struggle with Morgellons disease (which makes its victims feel like there are insects crawling beneath their skin), and a brain aneurysm in 2015—it seems unlikely that she will record or perform again...though hope, of course, springs eternal—and just a few days ago, James Taylor was quoted in *New York* magazine as saying that she "is planning a return to music."

Whether or not Joni writes or records or plays another note, her work—seventeen studio albums released over a forty-year period, beginning with *Song to a Seagull* in 1968, plus an assortment of live sets and compilations and other recordings—firmly establishes her as one of the most important singer/songwriters not only of her generation but in the history of popular music. Joni's legacy resonates. She is among the greatest of the great.

I came to Joni's music late in life. I knew "Woodstock," of course, and "Big Yellow Taxi," and "Both Sides, Now," and I thought every word, every note, on *Court and Spark* was absolutely brilliant, but that was about the extent of my familiarity with her until 1988, when I stumbled across *Chalk Mark in a Rain Storm* and fell head over heels in love. That record (remember "records"?) kicked off a ten-year streak of albums (remember "albums"?)—including *Night Ride Home* in 1991, *Turbulent Indigo* in 1994 and *Taming the Tiger* in 1998—that holds its own lyrically and musically against any body of work any recording artist has ever created.

Fast forward almost twenty years to 2017, when I took a break from simultaneously editing three anthologies of crime fiction to write a short story that appeared in my head on September 13, my sixty-sixth birthday. I called it "Killer Kyle," a name Joni aficionados will recognize from "The Beat of Black Wings," one of the songs on *Chalk Mark in a Rain Storm*. The first line of my story read, "It's funny how one thing sometimes really *does* lead to another," and that line could be an epigram for the book you now hold in your hands.

Because one thing led to another and, a month after I finished "Killer Kyle," I attended a crime-fiction conference called Bouchercon, which was held that year in Toronto, and sat in the audience at a panel honoring the Anthony Award nominees for Best Anthology of 2016, one of which was Jay Stringer's *Waiting to Be Forgotten: Stories of Crime and Heartbreak, Inspired by The Replacements* (Gutter Books).

A couple of weeks later, I wrapped up work on all three of the volumes I was editing—almost on the same day—and sank into anthology withdrawal. Trying to come up with a next project, I found myself thinking about Stringer's Replacements book and a couple of similar collections that had been released over the previous couple of years, such as Joe Clifford's *Trouble in the Heartland: Crime Fiction Inspired by the Songs of Bruce Springsteen* (Gutter, 2014) and *Just to Watch Them Die: Crime Fiction Inspired by the Songs of Johnny Cash* (Gutter, 2017).

And one thing led to another, and I found myself thinking it'd be fun to do something along those lines…and the songwriter who immediately came to mind was Joni Mitchell. After all, I'd already *written* one story myself, so all I needed was nineteen or twenty more and I'd have a book.

I started contacting authors, and it astounded me how quickly and eagerly people responded. Even those who turned me down—mostly because their plates were so full at the moment that they knew they wouldn't have time to participate—gushed about the idea and wished me well with it.

Joni's been in the news a lot lately, with David Yaffe's fascinating biography *Reckless Daughter* released by Sarah Crichton

Books in October 2017 and Susan Whitall's *Joni on Joni: Interviews and Encounters with Joni Mitchell* by the Chicago Review Press in the fall of 2018 and Ruth Charnock's *Joni Mitchell: New Critical Readings* by Bloomsbury at the beginning of 2019. And then of course there was the media attention paid to Yaffe's revelation that Joni was afflicted with the rare and bizarre Morgellons disease, and the subsequent death hoax, which went viral for about a week before the rumors were dispelled. Then there was the wonderful *Joni 75: A Birthday Celebration* at the end of 2019.

Anyway, one thing has led to another, and here we are: you hold in your hands a collection of twenty-six crime stories by a total of twenty-eight authors, tracking Joni Mitchell's songwriting career from *Song to a Seagull* in 1968 to *Shine* almost forty years later in 2007.

Some of the song choices (the big hits, like "Both Sides, Now" and "Big Yellow Taxi") were obvious, some (like Amber Sparks' selection of "The Dry Cleaner From Des Moines" and Greg Herren's of "The Silky Veils of Ardor") perhaps less so. What surprised me most were the songs that *didn't* get chosen. I mean, seriously, a book of Joni Mitchell–inspired crime stories that doesn't include "Raised on Robbery"? Come *on*!

There are two collaborative tales here, and each of them brings something extra special to the table:

- Individually, Art Taylor and Tara Laskowski are well known for their short crime fiction, and collectively they are a married couple raising a charming son. They've never before written a story together, though, and I was delighted when they accepted my invitation to tackle "Both Sides, Now." (This was the only time I paired song and writer. In every other case, the authors picked the songs themselves.)

- Jackie Sherbow and Emily Hockaday, on the other hand, *have* previously collaborated…but as co-editors, not coauthors. Jackie is the managing editor of *Ellery Queen's Mystery Magazine* and *Alfred Hitchcock's Mystery Magazine*, and Emily is the managing editor of *Asimov's Science Fiction* and *Analog Science Fiction and Fact*. In 2018, they put together *Terror at the Crossroads*, a collection of stories from those four publications, and it struck me that it would be interesting to see what they would come up with if they attempted to write a story together. They accepted the challenge, and their take on "Talk to Me" leaves me hoping they'll continue to work together on more stories in the future.

Les Irvin, who runs *jonimitchell.com*, recently emailed me the following comment: "Joni was once asked to explain one of her songs and replied: 'Who cares what I meant? What does it mean to *you*?' This collection perfectly embodies Joni's hope that her songs have inspired interpretation, improvisation and creativity in the minds of others."

Sure enough, the stories you're about to read were written as tributes to Joni Mitchell's talent and vision. The authors and I hope you will enjoy them—and will be motivated either to go back to the music that inspired them if you're already a fan or to explore it if Joni's work is unfamiliar to you.

May all your lights shine on!

Josh Pachter
Herndon, Virginia
February 22, 2020

Song to a Seagull

Released March 1968

"I Had a King"
"Michael From Mountains"
"Night in the City"
"Marcie"
"Nathan La Franeer"
"Sisotowbell Lane"
"The Dawntreader"
"The Pirate of Penance"
"Song to a Seagull"
"Cactus Tree"

All songs by Joni Mitchell.

Marcie
by Ricki Thomas

It's a lonely road to walk, the single life, with no one to hold when the nights are long, no one to confide in when the going gets tough. It's my fault I'm alone, but that makes it no easier. In fact, it makes it worse. One little mistake changed my life forever. I look at the handmade ornament his mother made for our engagement, and I feel sick.

Some days, I regret the way the past has unfolded, but then I remember how he'd don an exasperated expression and shake his head slowly, trivializing my fears and accusing me of being overdramatic. The disturbing memories happen less frequently as time passes, and I recall the happiness more and more. Time is a healer; it makes you forget the bad and replace it with rose-gilded good.

I didn't eat, at first, my sorrow so deep and guilt so great, but now I do nothing but, replacing the love we shared with chocolate, substituting our shared meals with mindless guzzling of unhealthy rubbish, trying to fill the void he left in me. The candy store feels like my only friend, its shelves littered with sugar-filled treats that boost my energy before I slump into a pit of despair. The only greens I consume nowadays are the sour candies that add excessive pounds of unwanted weight and twist my face as I wince against the bitterness. In the privacy of my lonely home, I fill myself with refined sugar, something I never did when we were together, but I suppose that's why I crave them. Then, I had no need of the comfort they gave, but now....

I watch the mailman walk by my gate, and once again there are no letters for me, impacting the loneliness within the four walls that were once a happy home. He won't send me those golden nuggets of love anymore, I made sure of that, and today I rue the emptiness I ensured with my rashness.

Once, in those delightful days, our two-up two-down was homey, our abundant clutter covering the floor and surfaces, our passion taking precedence over cleaning and preening, but now everything is spotless, scrubbed of dust and grime, for I fill my spare time with unnecessary housework to forget what has passed, the dull future I created.

The floor is free of dirt, the furniture shiny and polished, everything in its place. Faceless. A show home, with no personality or depth. An empty space I sleep in, weep in, a space I cannot leave until the day I die, lest someone unearth my darkest secrets and remove the memories that keep me going from one day to the next.

The curtains smell sweetly of their wash last week, but I remove them anyway—requiring a task to occupy my mind—and stuff them into the washer to needlessly freshen the material once more. They're looking worn now, the result of overwashing, but that won't stop my urge to reclean everything he might have touched when we were together and in love, to cleanse him from my soul.

After a lifetime, the cycle ends, and I hang the curtains out to bathe in the sun we used to make love under while the gentle breeze tickled our nakedness. The material flaps in the wind until they are dry, though my eyes are anything but. I remember when we bought the curtains with money hard-saved between us. Not from a department store or a chain of identical shops but a market stall that promised quality at a fraction of the price. Drapes that suited us, our personalities, that hung in pairs the same way we did, together against the cruel world.

Stop sniveling, I tell myself, wiping my tears on the shirt he wore the last time I saw him, soaking up his manly smell in the only way left to me. And I recall that final night, the vicious tone in his voice, fed up with my needy insecurity. With horror I realized that he was determined to move on. But how could I let him go? He was adamant our relationship wasn't working, insistent on dumping me on the scrapheap of childless spinsterhood. I retaliated in the only way I knew how, by sobbing my anguish and begging for another chance, a ploy that had worked a million times before. But he refused to compromise, with a firmness I'd never witnessed, and seconds later he was gone. Out of my life forever. I spray the dining table with polish and rub at it with his shirt—anything to remove the bitter scent that reminds me of our failure.

It's late, and I welcome the chance to end another meaningless day by succumbing to the one place that relieves me of my singularity, those eight hours in a world full of dreams, a million miles from reality. A hefty shot of whiskey ensures my slumber.

*

The weekend is here, two days of reminders within the deathly walls that house me, and again I wake to despair and sorrow. Saturday is the worst, enclosed by silence and regret, a prison of the unrealized dreams I once boasted of to the people I thought my friends, all of whom have long since deserted me. At least on Sundays I know that soon I'll have some work-filled hours to interrupt the chasm of my loneliness.

I make breakfast; too much, too fatty. Fried meats with oily eggs, drenched in baked-bean juice that does nothing to help my once-svelte proportions, the figure he openly admired both alone and in company, proud that I clung to his arm like a child to her doll. I clench one of the many rolls of overeating on my belly and lament my lack of willpower. But it doesn't matter now. No one else would want me, and I can't move on with baggage so heavy. I add several slices of thickly buttered bread and savor each comforting mouthful.

His absence drums deep within me as I try to fill the sink to wash my few dishes. But there's no water, and where once he would have taken a wrench or two and magically fixed the problem, I have to call a plumber at weekend rates to mend whatever it is that's broken. Not my heart, though. Nothing can help that. I find a number on the internet and make a call, and presently a jolly man arrives to complete a few minutes of work, explaining in alien terminology what the simple disruption has been. Eager to exclude him from my den of gloom, I pay cash and hurry him out the door.

Through a window, I watch him leave, and my eyes settle on the foliage beyond him, a myriad of color as flowers bloom and insects buzz, their kaleidoscope replacing the autumnal red tones that surrounded me when last I saw the love of my life. Although the sun beams relentlessly in the sky, it does little to cheer the misery that overwhelms me, a fly trapped in a web of deceit and lies.

Betraying the approaching autumn that will herald the anniversary of our end, patches of the scenery where the green is browning at the edges show me that almost a year has passed since he left my life and disappeared into heavens new. I remain in a state of limbo, dead to the world, my joyful existence executed and replaced with an abyss of nothing.

In the distance is the bay we used to walk along, him carrying a basket of food and drink, me a bag of linens and towels. We watched the ships on the horizon as we sat on our blanket, chuckling at silly jokes and grazing our picnic. Just us two, lost in a world of togetherness, oblivious to everything but ourselves.

That world is empty now, and I no longer traipse that path, unable to do alone what once enhanced our union. Would it help to revisit, I wonder? I open my all-but-empty fridge and search its shelves, eventually closing the door and grabbing a bag of candy. Yes, a walk might help. Reaching for the hook, I take my coat, the one I hinted for so blatantly that he gave it to me last year as an early Christmas present, to remind me of summer, its printed material resembling flowers on a spring day. I spent Christmas alone—my own fault, of course. Now it is summer, and I feel no better.

I keep my guilty head down as I hurry along the street to the coastline, the wind rippling the water and casting a chill in the air. Past moored yachts that live on the bay, vehicles littering the parking lots, over to the steep hill where we'd settle after a challenging climb, sheltered from the weather in a private cove that we honestly believed only the two of us knew. I fill my mouth with sherbet lemons, crunching their hardness to release the fizzy powder that tickles the back of my nose until a fit of sneezing threatens. They are supposed to be sucked, yet I chew my way through them as if they're gum.

But it's not the same. It will never be the same. The ocean no longer sparkles, the blue sky dulled through eyes that only see pain and despondency, and the destitution of my solitude is unbearable. I pour the final few sweets into my mouth, crunching them with sugar-coated teeth that have yellowed over the past year through lack of care, and scurry down the hill to the path that buzzes with other people's lives. Women I would once have seen as contemporaries in their skimpy clothes and strappy sandals I watch from beneath my hair with an edge of jealousy, aware of the weight I have gained amidst my anguish. Perhaps it's futile, a half-baked nod to the woman I once was, but I stop at a stall on the pavement and buy a bag of overripe peaches. Tonight, I'll try to eat them, leave the chocolate alone. A ridiculous façade, of course, but at least I'll have made some effort.

Close to home, I see the mailman and implore him to have something for me. Not bills or circulars, junk mail or rubbish, but a personal letter that will tell me I'm still loved—lovable—craved. A letter from the man I discarded so cruelly, all those months ago. He's gone, it will never happen, and I see the sympathy in the mailman's helpless expression. I shake my head and move on, desperate to be back inside the jail that devastates me yet holds an edge of comfort and belonging.

The anniversary of the death of our union passes painfully, the autumn fully fledged, and the sun turns to cloud, first bursting with rain that within weeks turns to snow. A landscape filled with white, both frost and delicate flakes piled high. Over a year under a shroud of doom and unable to see any future. I want to die, that's the only solution, but I want to be close to him, too. He was a seaman, sailing from one exotic shore to another, making his money by maneuvering the waves. Perhaps if I join him out there, feel the salty spray in my hair and suffer the temperatures icy or hot, dealing with Mother Nature as she throws out one surprise or another....

Donning three pairs of socks and some olive-colored boots, I again tread that painful path to the bay, avoiding out of self-preservation looking at the hill we used to climb, my mind resolved to the latest of my hair-brained plans to rid myself of this nightmare.

They laugh at me, the crew of the boat that's being prepared for its travels. "We can't take you," they say. "What good will you be on a boat bound for America?"

"I can help," I plead, ignoring my lack of fitness, due to my endless comfort eating. "I won't be any trouble."

"You'll eat us out of house and board," they smirk, hoisting thick rope from the mooring posts and curling it around their arms, freeing the trawler from its restraints. "Why not go on a cruise instead, far more appropriate for an overfed landlubber with nothing better to spend her time and money on?"

Disgusted, embarrassed, I hold my head high as I retreat, gazing at the shop windows as if this is what I'd truly meant to do, and eventually I decide. I know from the years I've lived here that the cruiser leaves at night, and I request a ticket to who-knows-where, eager to end this mire of loneliness.

Crying acrid tears, I return to the torturous jail that was once our home. Locking the door behind me, there's one place left to give me peace of mind. I unlock the back door and step onto the unmarred snow that so beautifully covers the garden he treasured. Feeling as close to my lover as can be, his presence seeping from my feet to my dizzy head, I stand by our heart-shaped pond, built with great struggle in the days when I had some energy.

Apart from lifting the hefty rocks that frame the edges, I didn't have to work too hard once I finished the foundations, and he did a lot of that before he departed. We'd designed the feature ourselves, a place for fish and frogs to breed in fresh water. He promised me when he first came up with the idea that we would listen to the fountain trickling at night, a calming, relaxing thrum to make love to, fall asleep to. I thought it would be too close to the house, worried it might be a hazard, but he reminded me it was *our* home and we had no little ones to be careful of. "Things should be the way we want them," he said.

So, come the spring before his departure, he took a shovel and dug deep into the soil, creating a mound of earth that he intended at some point to take to the dump. I worried the hole was too deep, mindful of the need to keep it algae free, but he dismissed my concerns, digging further as if out of spite. Then our plans were halted by an unexpected call from his employer: he was needed on a voyage to some distant land. I spent day after day, week after week, waiting for his return. And when the leaves turned russet and dropped from the trees, I realized that our fishpond would have to wait until the next year to be finished. No matter, though, as long as we were together.

He returned eventually, and we spent blissful days and nights catching up with each other's lives, fulfilling our needs and desires, loving each other in the way only we could. It was truly perfect until the green-eye crept through the holes in our relationship. I heard rumors from his fair-weather friends about his other love, a woman who'd borne his children in Malaysia—and, instead of taking it with a grain of salt as I should have done, I let envy take over and poison every moment we were together. I accused him, demanded to know her name, the names of their offspring. Why had he had children with *her*, though he'd claimed he didn't want them with me? Why wasn't I enough for him?

"Stop spouting rubbish," he would shout. His mates were practical jokers and none of it was true. But my insecurity wouldn't let me believe, and I nagged him relentlessly, woefully wondering why he'd needed to stray.

*

Until the day I crossed some invisible line. It was a Saturday, the weekend day I cherished, and I carped at him for hours, bleating my mistrust with vitriol, sarcastically picking on everything he said in self-defense. And finally, he uttered those fateful words: "I can't do this anymore."

I could have taken the hint, told him I was sorry, said I knew he would never be unfaithful, but instead I huffed about leaving him free to concentrate on his other wife, his Malaysian babe with no sexual hang-ups. He sighed with despair and took his keys from his pocket, dropped them on the coffee table and loped to the door.

What happened next was so quick I wasn't sure it was real. He was on the floor, a growing spillage of blood outlining his head. I stood motionless for what seemed to be hours, frozen by what I had done, while he lay equally motionless on the ground. Not a twitch, not a breath. He was dead, and I'd killed him.

In my hand was our ornament, the effigy of us as a couple carved by a sculptor as a gift from his mother when we'd become engaged, a symbol of our love and togetherness. And I'd used it to destroy us. I dropped it in disgust, fell to my knees, sat by his side as his blood seeped across the floor, wondering at how a split second could change our lives forever.

The pond will never be finished, I thought. *I'll be in custody for the rest of my life. Unless....*

That night, I drank until I slept. When the alcohol wore off, I awoke in a panic. His body was still on the floor, his blood staining the grout to forever remind me of my moment of foolishness. With strength I didn't know I had, I hauled him through the back door and pushed him into the hole he'd dug, the grave he'd unwittingly prepared for himself. Checking the neighbors' houses for signs of life, I trotted back and forth to the mound of earth, bringing bucket after bucket of wormy mud to the hole and tossing it over his lifeless body until he was covered. I unfolded the plastic sheet that would stop the pond from draining over him, treading it down and fixing it in place with the rocks we'd collected from our treks around the country.

I buried him maybe three feet down, and I worried there would be a smell—or, worse, that animals would scent his corpse and dig until they could rip at him, exposing for the world to see the death I wanted to pretend hadn't happened.

When friends and family asked of his whereabouts, I simply smiled and told them he was at sea. I hoped the day would never come when I had to tell the truth, which is why I have remained trapped in our house, ensuring no one will ever uncover the secret that lies beneath our pond.

Though my heart still beats and my lungs still breathe, I too am dead. I killed us *both* that day with my irrational act.

"Wait for me, Marcie," he used to say, each time he left on a voyage, and today his voice floods my head, chanting, whispering, ghostly echoes of the past haunting me.

It's time to join him, time to use my one-way ticket.

It's dark, and the boat sails at 4 AM. I await its departure, knowing I'll never reach its destination.

Once I'm overboard, drowning in a watery grave, I know I'll find him.

Waiting for me.

The Pirate of Penance
by Marilyn Todd

He can't take his eyes off the spiral metal staircase leading down from the street. The sign on the door at the bottom reads *Heaven's Gate*. No one cares. They only see the flashing neon sign: *NUDES*. He can hear the heavy beat of music through the thick gray metal door. He senses the excitement and looks around. Men in bowler hats and pinstriped suits, carrying briefcases just like his. Men in trilby hats and raincoats. Women in miniskirts and bright red lipstick, with prices chalked on the soles of their shoes. His heart kicks, his mouth is dry. He knows he shouldn't. Descends anyway.

*

She gives the distinctive knock-pause-knock-knock at the back, between the dustbins and the rats. *You're late.* Did he think she didn't know? Bleedin' bus didn't turn up, did it, which meant the second bus was packed. She ended up squashed among the smokers upstairs, and now she reeks of Player's Weights and Woodbines. *You're on in 10 minutes.* For Gawd's sake, she knows that, too! Gripping her fake snakeskin vanity case, she scurries to the dressing room. Halfway through changing, a bulb flickers twice, then dies. No matter, she can manage with just the one. On goes the eyeliner, the rouge, the false eyelashes thick as spiders. Three minutes later, there's her cue.

*

He's engulfed by a whirlpool of cigars, smoke and sex. Girls bump and grind to the hypnotic beat. They kick. They writhe. They flash a bit of leg, a bit of breast, was that a nipple? Too fast, they cover up. But with every sway and shake, every bend and twist and wiggle, their treasures are revealed. Ten-shilling notes litter the stage that's not a stage, just a cheap laminated board that runs the length of this seedy little club, where the lights are low and wooden seats (no tables) are spaced inches apart. The men come in alone, drinking but not drunk, bound by an invisible locker-room spirit.

Behavior that would appall them all as individuals becomes acceptable in this anonymous dark crowd. He looks at the sinuous objects of their leering, clapping and whistling. The girls' fixed smiles. Dead eyes. *There's got to be a better life for them*, he thinks.

*

Inch by inch, her clothes peel off, teasing all the way. Stockings always get the loudest whistle, coz they're usually the first to drop. She's not like the other girls. She keeps hers on. Even when there's nothing left and she's showing everybody Heaven's Gate, she keeps them on. Black fishnets, boy, that don't half get their juices goin'. Beyond the spotlight, she can see the surreptitious rubbing underneath their coats. No ten-bob notes for her. Uh-uh. They throw pound notes on the stage when she's performing. A whole quid, eh? Who'd have thought it? Just for a stupid pair of stockings. Her over-the-shoulder come-to-bed smile never falters as she wonders if she'll still be able to catch the last bus home and whether she can make the chip shop before it shuts. *There's got to be a better life*, she thinks.

*

All next day, he sits at his desk. Dullsville. Forms, reports, phone calls, faxes, meetings, poring over actuarial tables till his neck aches. No air. No windows. Just harsh fluorescent lighting and lunch in the canteen, where every day's predictable. Today, being Tuesday, it's sausage, mash and peas. His secretary is unmarried, fat and forty. Wouldn't know a smile from a fiver. His boss is plodding to retirement, not interested in anything except counting off the days and not rocking any boats. Stifled, bored, he knows he will be descending the forbidden spiral staircase after work.

*

She sees him, same seat three nights running, and her heart skips a beat. Could this be it? When she comes on stage, he leans forward, focusing on her and her alone. It could be, y'know. It could just be her ticket out of here. She shoots a smile straight at him.

Directs her striptease at him. Makes bleedin' sure he knows this performance is for him, and him alone.

He can't believe it. She's so beautiful. So young. Tumbling dark curls. Tempting dark eyes. And she's looking at him. Not through him. *At* him. Giving herself to him, and him alone.

She has him. She bloody has. He's hooked. She gives him extra special attention with her routine the next night. Whispers: *If you're interested, I'm off at midnight.*

He waits. Sweating. Midnight—midnight!—and he's escorting a drop-dead-gorgeous girl to dinner! Nothing like this has ever happened in his plodding, predictable life. "Tell me about yourself," she says while the waiter pours wine.

Is she mad? Actuaries have the knack of making accountants look exciting. He's done nothing. Been nowhere. But Jesus bloody Christ.

She's passing her little pink tongue over her little pink lips. Think, man, think. Say something. Do something. "I'm not a poet, not a pirate, just a pawn," he says with a lopsided smile, then does the single most stupid thing he's ever done in his life. He magics a pound note out of her ear, shapes it into an *S*, attaches two paperclips—the joy of clerkdom, you always carry spare ones in your pocket—jerks the note, and while the clips spring off and miraculously join together, he pulls that silly trick where you fold your hands over each other, twist and turn, turn and twist, and make it look like your arms are made of rubber.

She laughs. The laugh is genuine. This isn't what she expected. No pawing. No groping. No dirty language, no springing of the age-old question: *How much?* He's the perfect gentleman. OK, not Rock Hudson or Paul Newman or Elvis or Cliff. But she's not Jean Shrimpton, either. He tells jokes, does magic tricks. Corny, but the way he tells them makes her giggle. To her surprise, she looks forward to their next date.

*

Three weeks later, and he's been down the staircase every weeknight after work, once even trekking into town on a Saturday, when he should have been—who cares where? What matters is: he was here. With her. He watches the girls gyrate to the music, teasing off their costumes inch by precious inch. Of course he watches the other girls. But it seems to him the leers are cruder now when the girl with the fishnets comes on, the jeers are louder, the gestures more coarse. So far, he's only ventured a couple of quick pecks, first on the cheek, next on the lips. His dreams, though, are far from chaste, and all of a sudden he is jealous of these filthy animals who have no connection or compassion for the girl with the dark, tumbling curls. They just want to ogle her breasts and glimpse Heaven's Gate, all the while making vulgar gestures with their tongues. If they had the chance, the bastards would take her like she was meat. His face is set, but deep inside, he boils with rage.

*

She loves the way he performs card tricks on the restaurant table between courses. Especially the one where he lays the kings face up, the queens on top, then the jacks and then the aces, matching all the suits, puts them together, gets her to cut the pack three times, then, when he deals, out they come, all kings together, all four queens, four jacks, four aces. "I love you," he says, out of the blue. He feels silly, he adds nervously. It's so early in, but he does, he loves her, and he wants her to give up this seamy life. She spills her wine. Jesus. He isn't the Prince Charming she's dreamed of as a kid. His hair is starting to thin, he wears specs, he's the best part of twenty years older than her yet so bleedin' inexperienced, the only woman he talks about is his mother. But y'know what? He makes her laugh. He makes her laugh with his jokes and magic tricks and his impressions of everyone from Winston Churchill to Clint Eastwood to Laurel and Hardy. She invites him back to her bedsit on the Edgware Road. Gives herself to him.

*

He is walking on air. This lovely, lithe creature has opened her heart and her legs to him. He walks on air through phone calls and meetings, actuarial tables and reports. He catches himself whistling. Singing to himself. *He is in love.* For the first time in his pathetic, humdrum life, he is in love.

*

And so is she. Hollywood couldn't make this story up. The showgirl and the insurance clerk! Her young, him not so, her from the East End, him from Mill Hill, her lissome, him deskbound and pale. Oh, but what he makes her feel, though, in bed and out, is out of sight, babe. No one's ever put her on a pedestal before. No one's ever touched her the way he does, either, with tenderness and care. She's only eighteen, but, man, she's been putting it out for five years, has long since lost count of the number of men she's had and tears she's cried. Spellbound, she listens to the future he draws. "Two up and two down, nothing special," he says. "Two little girls, what shall we name them?" He'll build a rose bower in the garden, with a swing for the girls. She'll have his meal on the table when he comes home at night, she says—but only after he's taken her on it first! Oh, yeah. She'll be a good wife. The best wife *ever.* She'll cook and clean and scrub and polish. She'll have the sort of life she's always dreamed of. None of the raised voices, raised fists of her mother, or the uncles who used to come to her at night. He has saved her, and so what if the knight hasn't come galloping in on a white steed? Who wants drama when you can have magic tricks and silly jokes? So help her, she will love him with all of her heart for the rest of her life and beyond.

*

He doesn't understand. There's no pain, yet at the same time he can't move. His limbs won't move, his hands won't work, his vision is hazy and white. There is panic. He can't breathe. What—what's happening...?

"You lied to me," she hisses. "You said you loved me. You told me I was the only woman for you."

You are, he wants to say, *oh, God, you are,* but his mouth won't let the words out. Through the haze, he sees something sharp and bright and shiny coming down. Again, again, again.

"Then this sour-faced bitch collars me outside the club," she says. Her hands, her face, her clothes are wet with blood, she doesn't notice. "Calls me a tart, a slut and that's just for starters. Tells me to leave her husband alone, and I laughed, can you believe it? I actually bloody laughed. Told her to sod the hell off, I'm no home wrecker, me."

I'm sorry, he wants to say, *I'm so very, very sorry,* but he can't speak because of some weird gargling sound. Where's that coming from? For one silly, stupid moment, he thinks it might be him.

"Then she shows me these photos," she says, showering him with the prints that she's snatched. "You, the wife, two kids. Girls. 'What shall we name them?' At the beach at Margate. At the Tower of London. In your own bleedin' back garden. 'Two up, two down, nothing special.'"

The last thing he sees is a photograph. It's the rose bower that he built last summer. Funny, he could have sworn the flowers were white—but look, they're red.

Clouds
Released May 1969

"Tin Angel"
"Chelsea Morning"
"I Don't Know Where I Stand"
"That Song About the Midway"
"Roses Blue"
"The Gallery"
"I Think I Understand"
"Songs to Aging Children Come"
"The Fiddle and the Drum"
"Both Sides, Now"

All songs by Joni Mitchell.

The Gallery
by Christine Poulson

Maddie ripped open the padded envelope, and a CD clattered onto the kitchen table. She made a moue of disappointment.

"*Clouds*? Joni Mitchell? I didn't order this!" She looked at the address. "Oh, it's for you, Mum. Sorry!"

She grabbed her bag and swooped down for a kiss. "Got to go. Love you! Byeee!"

The door banged behind her, and the whirlwind that was Janette's teenage daughter was gone.

Janette was left staring at the CD.

Joni's self-portrait—cool blue eyes, long blond hair—stared back at her. When Janette blinked, she thought for a moment that the CD had actually moved. She gave herself a mental shake and reached out to touch it, the case smooth and cool under her fingers.

After all these years....

She picked up the envelope and shook it to see if there was anything inside. There wasn't. She looked at the handwriting: an elegant italic she didn't recognize. The postmark was North Wales.

The fortieth anniversary of Yvonne's disappearance was approaching. She had been half-expecting some kind of sign, she hardly knew what. In the local online newspaper that she looked at occasionally, she had seen that Yvonne's father had died. That too had gotten her thinking. But still, the arrival of the CD was a shock.

She stripped off the cellophane and went into the sitting room to put the disc in the player.

Joni's plangent voice filled the room: "When I first saw your gallery, I liked the ones of ladies...."

Janette caught her breath. The years dropped away.

She had saved up her pocket money for the LP, and they had played it over and over, her and Yvonne, lying on their backs on the floor in her bedroom—bodies at right angles, the Dansette record

21

player between them, the blond head and the dark one just touching.

They say that, as you get older, your memories of childhood become more vivid—but her memories of that summer of 1969 had never really faded....

*

Their favorite song was "The Gallery." They were fascinated by the lyrics and discussed them endlessly. Was it a kind of Bluebeard story about a man who collected and destroyed women? The refrain, "Lady, please love me now I am dead," was deliciously creepy. They subjected it to the kind of analysis they had been taught in their Eng. Lit. lessons. One thing seemed clear. The woman in the song was trapped. She had become just another picture on the wall, like all the other women in the man's life. The song was sinister, and yet it was so beautiful....

They were listening to Joni after school when Yvonne took the charm bracelet from her satchel and handed it to Janette. It had all the fascination of things in miniature: a little gold horseshoe, a tiny lock with a key in it.

"What's this one?" Janette said. "Oh, it's the Eiffel Tower. And—ooh, look!—a sweet little cat. It's fab! Where did you get it?"

"It was my mother's."

"Ah." Janette let out her breath in a sigh, for a moment envying Yvonne her tragic status and this precious relic.

It was something that set Yvonne apart, made her special. In their class of thirty girls, where everyone had two parents at home, Yvonne was the odd one out. Janette's mum said that no one died in childbirth these days, it was like something from a Victorian novel—but it had happened to Yvonne's mother. Her father hadn't married again. There had been a nanny and later a succession of housekeepers. Now it was just the two of them, and a woman came in by the day to clean and cook.

"You can wear it for a while. I wouldn't let anyone else," Yvonne said. She put the bracelet round Janette's wrist and fastened the clasp. "We'll always be best friends, won't we?"

"Always," Janette said.

And it was true that no other friendship had ever come close. She and Yvonne had never drifted apart, or fallen out, and no one had ever come between them.

Theirs was a friendship frozen in time.

*

"Who else could have known about that album? It was the soundtrack of our summer," Janette said.

Andrew frowned. "Joni Mitchell was the soundtrack of *everyone's* summer. I don't know…. Could it be someone who knew you both when you were kids…or maybe you accidentally ordered it via Alexa? Or Maddie did?"

They were in Andrew's kitchen drinking coffee. Though their marriage hadn't lasted, they were on good terms, and he lived in a flat a few streets away so they could share childcare.

She shook her head. "I can't think of anyone else who might have sent it."

"Well, it can't have been Yvonne. You *do* know that, right? So why are you haring off to North Wales?"

"It's time I went back."

"Facing your demons?"

She grimaced. "Something like that."

"If you're set on it, why don't I go with you? I'm owed time off."

She looked at him with an equal measure of affection and exasperation. He was still trying to take care of her.

"What about Maddie?" she asked.

"She's sixteen. She'll be fine. She can always stay with a friend."

"I'd rather do this on my own."

Their eyes met. She knew he was thinking that there was more to it than she had told him. And he was right. That was the trouble when you'd been married to someone for fifteen years. She still couldn't get away with much.

"Remind me," one of her friends had said, "why you and Andrew separated? I wish Don and I got on as well as you two do."

"It's *because* we're separated that we get on so well," she'd replied. But sometimes she wondered, too.

"I don't like it, Jan," Andrew said. "Promise me you'll keep your mobile on."

*

Back at home, Janette got out the one photo she had of Yvonne, a Polaroid taken by Janette's brother. Yvonne was wearing a chocolate-brown mini dress with a gold zip and a mandarin collar. Janette was in a burgundy corduroy trouser suit. Their makeup was modelled on Twiggy: spidery eyelashes and chalky lipstick. They both had a center parting and then a mound of hair swept up and backcombed to within an inch of its life.

Up in the northeast, they'd been a long way from the Swinging Sixties, from Carnaby Street and Biba and Mary Quant. But ripples from that glamorous world had reached them through the TV—*Top of the Pops*, watched every Thursday evening—and through Janette's copies of *Jackie* magazine, hoarded and endlessly reread.

Yvonne's father was strict, and her friends were vetted. Janette's house was the only one she was allowed to go to after school, perhaps because Janette's father was a vicar. The chocolate-brown mini belonged to Janette. Yvonne had to take it off and get back into her school uniform before she went home. The hairspray had to be brushed out and the makeup and silver nail varnish cleaned off.

Janette didn't like it at Yvonne's house, and Yvonne never seemed at ease there, either. Other girls' fathers, including Janette's, were benign, distant figures. Yvonne's father was different. Something about him made her want to shrink back. He was tall and broad, with a deep voice and a mouth that was always moist at the corners. The way he looked at her made her uncomfortably aware of her breasts. When she went to Yvonne's house, she didn't turn over her waistband to shorten her skirt, like she usually did after school.

*

"I'm not doing A levels," Yvonne said.

It was a few weeks before the holiday. They were on Janette's bed. Janette propped herself up to look at Yvonne, who was sitting with her arms looped round her knees. Her face was tucked into the crook of her elbow, and her voice was muffled.

Janette didn't understand. Of course, some girls were planning to leave school for jobs in banks or offices, but Yvonne was one of the cleverest girls in the class, always in the top two or three. The school was talking about Oxford or Cambridge for her.

"What'll you do?" Janette asked. *"Work in your dad's office?"*

He was a partner in a firm of solicitors in the poshest part of the city.

"I'm going to go to London. I'll get a job in a coffee bar."

Janette stared at her. Yvonne still wasn't looking at her.

"But — where will you live?"

"I'll get a bedsit."

"But — how can you?" This was so far outside Janette's idea of the scheme of things that she didn't know which objection to put forward first.

Yvonne went on. "I'm saving up my pocket money so I can buy a train ticket."

Janette was speechless. Neither of them had been to London or knew anyone in London. Yes, they would leave home for university one day, but they'd be eighteen and they'd be in a hall of residence. After that — well, they hadn't thought yet, but if Yvonne went so far away, what would happen to their plan that they would one day marry brothers?

Now Yvonne did turn to look at her. She was pale, and there were shadows under her eyes.

"Promise me you won't tell," she said. *"I hate it at home. Janette, you must promise to never ever tell anyone where I've gone! Cross your heart and hope to die."*

"But you won't really go, will you?"

"Promise!"

"All right! Cross my heart and hope to die!"

"No one at all!"

"No one at all."

"Not even your mum!"

Janette hesitated, but only for a moment. "Not even my mum. But when will you go?"

"I don't know. Soon. Sometime soon."

*

A week after the arrival of the CD, Janette drove into the little seaside town in North Wales.

The place was thronged with holiday makers, but she finally found a parking space in a huge car park on the front. That hadn't been there forty years ago. But why had she expected the town to be just as she remembered it? The wide sweep of the bay and the sandy beach were the same, but the place was more of a holiday resort now, with donkey rides and fish-and-chip shops. Back then it had felt wild and remote.

She got out of the car and felt the sun on her face. A salty breeze came off the sea.

As she walked through the streets, memories came back, like snapshots, vivid but disconnected: the excursion to Snowdonia, the climb up Cadair Idris, the early-morning dashes down to the sea, plunging into crashing breakers so cold they thought their hearts would stop.

It was their first time away from home, and what an adventure it had been! They had gone as a group by train. They had slept in dorms, Janette and Yvonne sharing with two other girls. There were outdoor activities, tennis and walking and games, but there was plenty of free time, too, and they were allowed to roam at will. It was on one of those wanderings that they came across the Gallery.

And now, all these years later, Janette turned a corner and there it was, or rather there was where it *had* been. It was a shop now, selling outdoor gear, camping equipment, walking boots.

*

"It's like the song!" Yvonne said. "And look, there are portraits of ladies, too!"

They peered through the window. There was no one in there. Just the pictures hanging on the walls—bold chalk drawings of women, some of them nudes.

"What do you think? Shall we go in?" Janette asked.

They had never been in an art gallery before. Greatly daring, giggling, jostling one another, they pushed open the door. There was a smell of fresh paint and sawdust.

"Look!" Janette dug her elbow into Yvonne's side.

Through an open door at the back they saw a man, outlined against the sun, naked to the waist, surrounded by small, barefoot children. The man's hair, his tanned chest, all were drenched in the raking sunlight. To Janette, it was if they had glimpsed a young god trailing cherubs.

The next moment he came through the door, and he was just a young man—though a good-looking one—and the cherubs were just ordinary children.

He introduced himself as Gareth. The girls were self-conscious, averting their eyes from his bare chest. He put them at their ease, explaining that the Gallery had opened only a week before. He was a sculptor and his elder sister, Aelwen, was a painter.

He invited them round for tea. They got permission from the hostel and went. It was a window into another world, a household unlike any that Janette or Yvonne had ever known. Aelwen was a beautiful, ethereal blonde, like Joni Mitchell on the cover of Clouds. The three children were hers, but no husband was in evidence. They were all vegetarians. Casual hospitality was dispensed...whoever turned up at mealtimes was fed. There were huge salads, wholemeal bread that Aelwen made herself, eggs from their own chickens.

Later, all this was to count against Gareth in that conservative Welsh community.

Of course they both fell in love with him. But, right from the beginning, Janette was sure it was Yvonne he was interested in.

*

The church hostel they had stayed in had long ago been sold and converted into a hotel.

Janette had booked ahead, and, when she let herself into her room, she realized that it had been carved out of the dormitory where she and Yvonne had slept.

For a moment, it all seemed too much. Her sense of the past welled up like water against a dam. It was almost as though the barrier could be breached and the past would come crashing in. Her head swam, and she sat down on the bed.

She took a deep breath. *You're not fifteen,* she told herself, *you're fifty-five, a respected lawyer, a mother with a teenage daughter of your own. You are fine, it'll be fine, whatever happens — and nothing will happen.*

She ordered room service and got into her pajamas and dressing gown. While she was waiting, she rang home, and a chat with Maddie steadied her. Maddie was a sensible girl. As far as sixteen-year-olds *can* be sensible….

*

"Shall we get the cards out?" Yvonne said, moving her lips as little as possible.

Friday night was their night for having a face pack — Yvonne's was pale green, and Janette's was white. It was important to stay poker-faced, to let the pack harden properly, so Janette simply nodded.

She got up and went to her bedroom door to listen, even though she knew the coast was clear. Dad always visited parishioners at the hospital on Friday evenings, and Mum was at her Mother's Union meeting. Her brother was out with his friends. Still, it was part of the ritual to check. Her parents didn't know about the Tarot and wouldn't have approved. That made it all the more fascinating.

The cards had been bought at a new shop in town that sold joss sticks and mahjong sets and books about the I Ching. Janette had wrapped the cards in an old silk scarf and hidden them behind some books. She got them out, along with the instructions for reading them.

They sat cross-legged on the carpet, facing each other.

"Three-card spread?" Janette mumbled.

Yvonne nodded.

Janette fanned out the cards face down, and Yvonne picked out three. Janette turned over the first card. It was the Tower, flames issuing from the top of the building, two figures tumbling. This was an unlucky card, representing disruption and trauma.

The next card was the King of Cups, upside-down, meaning a man who was dishonest and unscrupulous.

Something strange was happening. Janette felt the back of her neck prickling. Usually she needed to consult the book, but today the enigmatic symbols in their strong primary colors seemed to speak directly to her.

She turned over the last card.

It was the Ten of Swords, the unluckiest card in the deck.

Her eyes met Yvonne's. The impassive face, frozen in its pale-green mask, told her nothing, yet something leapt between them like a spark of electricity, and Janette heard herself say, "You're in danger."

Yvonne didn't speak. Her gaze shifted, so she was looking over Janette's shoulder. Her eyes grew wide. Janette turned. The door was slowly opening. For a heart-stopping moment, she had no idea who or what was about to come through it. Then Sukie, the vicarage cat, slipped into the room.

The girls gasped in unison. Janette bit her lip, trying to hold back hysterical laughter, but the more she tried to keep a straight face, the funnier it seemed. Her face pack was cracking. Yvonne's was breaking up, too, flakes fluttering down like plaster from a ceiling.

The sound of the front door opening sobered them in an instant. They scrambled to gather up the cards and get them back in their hiding place.

The next day, they left for Wales.

*

Room service arrived, and, after Janette had eaten, she went to bed. She fell asleep immediately, but it was a broken sleep with vivid fragments of disturbing dreams.

She woke with a start. Light was seeping round the edge of the curtains. It was early, but she knew she wouldn't be able to get back to sleep. She got up and pulled back the curtains, made herself a cup of tea and got back into bed.

It must have been about this time forty years ago, on the last day of their holiday, that something had brought her half-awake in the dim light of the early dawn. Yvonne was out of bed and pulling on a T-shirt. Janette muttered a question.

Yvonne laid a finger across her lips. "Go back to sleep," she whispered.

And Janette had. She had sighed, turned over and was gone, drugged by the long hot days of swimming and tennis.

It was at breakfast that Yvonne was first missed. When she didn't answer to her name for the register, a search began. By lunchtime, the police had been informed. Late that evening, Yvonne's father arrived. Janette's parents came the following day and took Janette home.

The police questioned Janette, but she didn't tell them there had been a day when Janette had had period pains and Yvonne had gone to the Gallery alone. Later, Janette had felt better and had gone to join her. As she walked through the Gallery, she'd seen Yvonne and Gareth deep in conversation in the yard. Yvonne was looking up at him, and the trust in her face and the tenderness in his made Janette catch her breath. She drew back, not wanting them to know that she had seen them. She slipped into the house to find Aelwen. Yvonne and Gareth soon joined them, and it was as if nothing had happened between them, but now Janette knew. They were in love.

At first she was afraid the police would find Yvonne and Gareth and bring them back. Janette would have died rather than betray them. She'd be like a heroine in a film about the French Resistance, silent under torture! She didn't even tell her mother, because she had promised not to. Decades later, when Maddie became a teenager, Janette worried. Because if she had kept a secret like that from her mother, what might Maddie be keeping from her? She knew she was overprotective, but was it any wonder?

The police thought of Gareth anyway. Their visits to the Gallery had not gone unnoticed, and he had left town on the day Yvonne had vanished. The police tracked him to London. But Yvonne wasn't with him, and he claimed to know nothing of her whereabouts. He had gone to London to visit a gallery owner who was planning an exhibition of his work. The police arrested him, but eventually they were forced to release him. No one had seen Yvonne with him, and his meeting with the gallery owner had been arranged long before Yvonne had even arrived in Wales.

Various local men had also been taken in for questioning, but they too had eventually been released.

Weeks went by, then months, then years.

Janette chose to do law and went to London University. She found herself haunting the coffee bars in the King's Road, peering into the faces of the waitresses. She searched for Yvonne in crowds, looked for her at sporting events and concerts.

She wondered if one day the phone would ring and it would be the police, or she would see a newspaper headline telling her a body had been found, and the search for Yvonne would be over. But she didn't really believe in either of those possibilities. One day, she was convinced, Yvonne would return.

The decades passed, and Yvonne was the shadow-friend who walked beside her, never growing any older, never changing, a figure Janette almost thought she almost glimpsed, standing at the back of the church on her wedding day or leaning over the crib to look at the newly born Maddie.

And all that time there was something Janette never told a soul, not even Andrew.

Yvonne had left her a memento and a message.

*

Janette got out of bed and went to the window. The sky was opalescent. The sea was far out. It was still so early that the sun had not yet risen above the mountains and the beach was in shadow. It was empty except for someone in the distance walking a golden retriever.

She hurried on her clothes and went down to the beach. The breeze was cool. She shivered and pulled her cardigan around her.

The dog walker was coming nearer: a plump middle-aged woman with gray hair.

As they passed, Janette gave a brief sideways glance—and halted. It was the eyes that did it. Her own jolt of recognition was reflected in the other woman's face.

And then they were in each other's arms.

They both pulled back at the same time.

"I didn't think you'd have a dog," Janette found herself saying.

There were tears in Yvonne's eyes, and Janette felt her own eyes smarting.

"Yvonne"—a thought struck her—"or *are* you still Yvonne?"

Yvonne shook her head. "I've been Grace for a very long time now."

"Where did you go that day?"

"I walked along the beach to the point where the road runs almost alongside. That was where I was picked up. Gareth and Aelwen had friends in a commune in Scotland, and one of them came down for me in a van. It was remote enough that no one was going to notice one more longhaired hippie. It was easier then to get a fake I.D. They applied for the birth certificate of someone who had died as a baby and used that to establish a new identity for me."

"And Gareth? I thought you were in love with him."

Yvonne laughed—and Janette caught a glimpse of the teenager she'd once been. "Perhaps I was, a little. Gareth turned out to be gay!"

"I know! I saw on the Internet—he has a husband now."

"We didn't even know people *could* be gay!"

"I'm sorry we didn't end up marrying brothers," Janette said.

"Yes. I don't suppose Andrew...?"

The years fell away, and they burst out laughing.

Janette said, "Just a sister, I'm afraid. So you know about Andrew?"

"It's easy to keep track of people these days. Yes, I know about Andrew—and about Madeline. I was thrilled when you had a daughter."

So Janette's glimpses of the shadow Yvonne who had accompanied her over the years had not been so far off the mark.

"What about you?" she asked.

"I've never married. There've been men, but...." She shrugged. "No one I wanted to trust with my story. As for babies, I've contented myself with other people's. I managed in the end to get to medical school. I'm an obstetrician."

"So you've had a good life? I'm glad."

"I've thought so many times about getting in touch, but they wouldn't let me. They said it was too dangerous. That he'd track me down. My father...he was a man who collected women. He slept with the nanny and the housekeepers and then, when the last one left, one night he came to my room...."

At last Janette understood that Yvonne hadn't been running *to* something. She'd been running away.

"I was ashamed," Yvonne said. "I thought it was my fault, and I didn't think anyone would believe me. I didn't know who to tell until I met Aelwen."

"We were such children."

The signs had been there, if Janette had known how to read them. But they had known so little. Scanty information gleaned from biology lessons at school, surreptitious perusal of a copy of *Lady Chatterley's Lover* that a friend had filched from her parents' bookcase: theirs was an innocence—or an ignorance—that was unimaginable now.

"He should have been punished," Janette said.

"He was. He never found out what happened to me."

"Now that he's dead, what will you do?"

"Nothing, I think. I've been the person I am now for so long. But I *did* have to see you again."

"And I had to see you. When the CD arrived, I knew that—" She cut herself off. "I nearly forgot—"

She delved into her bag and brought out a small black velvet pouch. She poured the contents into Yvonne's palm.

Yvonne's face lit up. "My mother's charm bracelet!"

She held out her wrist, and Janette fastened the bracelet around it.

Those many years ago, it hadn't been until Janette was unpacking at home that she'd discovered it in the inside pocket of her suitcase, along with a note: "Don't worry!!! I am going to be all right, but I can't take anything with me. Keep this until I come back for it and BURN THIS NOTE AFTER READING!"

Janette had done both.

Yvonne put her arm through Janette's. "We've got a lot of catching up to do."

The sun had risen over the mountains, and the shadows were retreating up the beach. The two women walked on into sunlight, the dog frisking around them.

It was going to be a beautiful day.

Both Sides, Now
by Art Taylor and Tara Laskowski

EXCERPTED FROM U.S. ATTORNEY'S MEMO:

Entered into evidence is the last-known correspondence between Anna Dunkin, 39, and Robert Dunkin, 46, a former financial consultant at Ketteridge Financial Services. Robert Dunkin was convicted of four counts of embezzlement, fraud, and money laundering, and at the time of these letters was serving a six-year sentence at East Gate Penitentiary in Lansing, Michigan.

*

January 7

Dear Anna—

Just a couple of weeks here now, but seems like months—years, honestly.

Who would've believed it? The slammer, the clink, the pen. From a junior executive suite in a high-rise office building to a 6 x 8 cell—when, before, cells were only fields on a spreadsheet.

Happy New Year. Hope your celebrations were better than mine.

I know I'm just repeating myself, but my mind still reels at the turn things have taken for me, for us. How quickly "hard-working" became "overworked," how quickly overworked turned to... inattentive? imprecise? A single digit wrong, and then an error repeated and...well, where that money went is as much a mystery to me as it is to them, but while I'm still racking my brain to figure it out, they clearly think they've found their man.

A 6 x 8 cell, when I pictured wider vistas. A beach somewhere, an ocean stretched out in front of it, moonlight on a summer night, you and your angel hair, a lifetime before us.

I know all that might seem out of tune for me, but I've been doing a lot of thinking. New Year's resolutions?

You've said that I keep things to myself too much. You've said I was always at work, always in my head, never opening up and letting you in. And it's true, I know it's true. Even after the arrest, even during the trial, I know I've...brooded and sulked and shut you out, time after time. Tried to handle this alone. It's who I am, I guess, and I'm sorry.

I never figured on a guilty verdict, I didn't.

Even here, I feel like I can't say the things I need to say, want to say—for different reasons now. They read every word of the letters going out, every word in. They're always watching—me, and you, too, I know you know. Just think of happier times between us, because we did have those: lazy weekend mornings, the two of us, drifting through the Sunday paper, doing the crossword together, or one of those puzzle books you used to get at the grocery store.

My *fourth* time writing this—*word* after *word*. I hope you will understand, really understand, what I'm trying to say here.

I keep on drafting and redrafting. I'm a poor writer. Should plan better how best to express myself, to get the words inside, out. In jail, I need...well, I thought money was everything, but from where I'm sitting, off for years, it sure lets me take account of my actions, access some new perspectives, find out how real security rests not in numbers of dollars but in you. Clearing the cloud in my head!

Yours,

Bob

*

January 15

Bob,

Funny you should mention clouds! Elliott and I were outside just yesterday—he's been so good about trying to ride without training wheels. The weather was unseasonably warm for January. The sky was clear and bright—if you were looking through a window, you'd swear it was June—and the clouds, well, Elliott was saying how they looked so puffy, like cotton candy. He said he wanted to eat them, and I knew what he meant. We lay on the ground in the backyard near Mama's gnome garden and looked up at them for ages. Found an ice cream cone, a castle, a caterpillar with a suitcase.

And before you get going on me like I know you will, Elliott's asked me to call him that. He says he just feels like Junior isn't right anymore, and, well, like you said, Bob, we've got to let him have some independence. To grow up and be a man. Like his daddy. So try not to say anything nasty that will hurt his feelings. He can sense these things.

I can tell you that we're all still feeling a bit blindsided by this whole thing. I believe you when you say it wasn't your fault, that it was a mistake, but still, Bob—to get caught up in something like this, after all we've built together? I won't lie and say that there was a long time that I felt hurt and betrayed. But I can either keep on shiverin' or jump in and take the plunge, as Mama says, and I think you're right that the best way is forward.

So I'm working on a lawyer for you. The Mendelsons—and yes, I know you don't like them, I can hear your voice in my head as I write this—"You mean the Meddlesons?"—have someone they think will be good. Someone who will get you out of there, Bob. And Peter's been so good with Elliott. He took him bowling the other day. And Patty brought over a casserole—so they aren't meddling so much as, well, saving me, Bob. Saving both of us, I hope.

I want you to concentrate on getting out of there. We will prove your innocence, darling. We must. So just remember to tell me everything and anything that might be helpful to your case. I need to know all the information. As soon as possible. To protect you and our family.

Forgive my messy writing. I'm not used to ink and paper. You know how long it took me to find this pen? I almost had to write to you with Elliott's crayons. Ha ha.

We hope to come visit soon.
With all my love,
Anna

*

January 27

Dear Anna—

Elliott. Yes, Elliott. I can see why he wants to be his own man—and to distance himself, I know that's it, too. I'll try to remember not to slip up and call him Junior when the two of you come to visit. I understand, I do. And I regret not having mentioned him in my last letter to you. He was on my mind—always, of course, even if things haven't always been easy between us. On my mind if not in the letter itself. My focus was elsewhere, as I hope you saw, trust you understood. Send a picture of him riding his bike next time. I'd like to see that.

I appreciate your reaching out to the Mendelsons, too. Whatever I think of Peter personally (meddler, windbag, full of himself), I'm glad that they've been supportive, that they're pitching in help to prove my innocence (though I don't expect much from their efforts, I'll be honest, again windbag). And I appreciate that Patty has been a friend when you've needed one, that last bit most importantly—and imagine she enjoys it too, you can tell how tired she is of Peter expecting her to fawn over him all the time. Please try to limit Elliott's time with Peter, though. I don't want his personality rubbing off on my son. (See, thinking of him here.)

Prison life has become…tolerable. I'd feared…the worst, as you know. But white-collar criminals aren't the hardened cons you see on television (everyone's innocent, just like me), and since it's minimum security, it's not just tolerable but would be livable, even, if I weren't separated from you, so far away.

The food is edible too—though not the restaurants we used to enjoy, the ones I'd looked forward to taking you to again, you and Elliott both. (See.)

Oh, and a *third* thing:

Can you believe this? The guards are friendly, can I possibly be so lucky? Bought me cigarettes. Need to reimburse—funds are tight!

My best for last. Pass along requests to Elliott: Come visit sometime through all this, OK?

Love,
Bob

*

February 9

Oh Bob—

What sort of food are they serving you? You say it's tolerable, but I can hear the short temper in your letter, and I'm sorry for it. Goodness, don't we both miss Theresa right now? She was always so good at editing your correspondence at the office, at striking out the unnecessary words that might make you look stupid or rude. I can see her red pen all over your "windbag" comments. Ha ha.

Speaking of, Peter is working hard to try to find an affordable lawyer for the appeal, honey, but it takes time—and money—and, well, right now we need to just figure something out. I'm resourceful, though, as you know, so don't worry too much about it. So is Peter, whatever you (and Patty) might think. Like the other day, he fixed the light in the basement that's been flickering like a horror show for years. You know the one. It was just a loose wire, how about that? Took him five minutes, and now it's bright as sunshine down there.

As for Elliott, he's doing fine with all of this. I mean, of course, he asks about you, and the kids at school are saying things—I don't know what, he won't tell me—but I just keep telling him to keep his chin up. He's a good boy. He's been trying to teach me this new game—it's a kind of code game, where you get a phrase—like, say, "survival of the fittest"—and you have to develop a kind of code to get your partner to guess it. He's quite good at it—he must get that from you—but I am terrible at it. I can't make my own codes to save anyone's life (!), but luckily I'm pretty decent at reading the code and guessing the message. So I guess that's something.

So, please, trust me. I know it's hard for you to place all this in my hands, my dearest, but have I ever let you down before?

I'm delighted that the guards are treating you well and hope we can treat them well, too. I will try to bring you some treats when we visit, if they allow that sort of thing? Blueberry pie (don't worry, no knives or chisels baked inside! Hahaha—oh, guards, I'm just teasing!) or my holiday nut bread. What would you most like, if you could have any food? (And no, the kalua pork from Helena's does not count—as I cannot fly to Hawaii...unless you can magically conjure up a pile of money for me! (Also a joke!))

Oh, I know I shouldn't tease, Bob. Please don't think I'm taking any of this lightly. Keep your chin up, baby! We miss you and love you and look forward to having you back once all this terrible injustice has been sorted out.

With all my love,
Anna

*

February 20

Anna—

Um...ouch?

I don't think my comments were, um, "stupid." Or "rude." I'd say they were pretty dead-on. And frank, which I pride myself on, as you know. And despite the way you make it sound, Theresa was never reining me in or directing things from behind the scenes. I made my own decisions, felt in control of what I said and wrote, was very precise with it, in fact—as you should know. I hope?

(Deep breath.)

...but maybe some of that's part of the problem, I recognize, reflecting on things here and our next steps—by which I mean, ceding some control myself to you, as you handle things on the outside. With Elliott, with the appeal, with everything. Putting things in your hands, as you said—our future in your hands. A little more give and take between us.

And meanwhile, I'm still in here, eating that food, killing time with my fellow inmates (a dull, unmotivated bunch), and trying to stay in good with the guards, building goodwill. Thanks for the deposit in my commissary account. I was able to repay the guard for his generosity with the cigarettes. Had tried a couple of times before, but couldn't do it discreetly.

Third time's the charm?

Please do pass along this word: That old fairytale Elliott loved, three years old, five years old? Fifteen lifetimes ago, for sure.

Well, *more directly*, the story itself. I've been thinking about it a lot—the meaning in it:

In Belize, on the banks of the Caye, a man named Richard Morgenstern found a shell, and it was a magic shell, that had a treasure inside, and it was a treasure he'd been dreaming about for a long time for his family and…. Well, you remember it, and then the happily ever after, like always.

I was gonna say tell Elliott that dreams sometimes come true, but really I want to tell you, too. Dreams and schemes, like the line from that old song you like so much.

Know that I love you—and trust you—always.

Yours,
Bob

*

March 20

Hi Bob—

Thank you so much for your last letter. It was very enlightening in so many ways.

Elliott's so good at the code game now. He's good at so many things. You should see him ride his bike! And climb trees! I can't keep up with him. It's funny how, as you get older, you understand yourself more—your weaknesses, for one, and also your true wants and needs. What makes you happy.

You also begin to understand how little one needs to be happy. How you can easily settle for small comforts. A little bit of savings, an easy job that doesn't require much thinking. A neighbor who pops by in the afternoons to check in on you, to see how you're doing, who might even sit on the back porch with you and chat—really chat, about everything, and who listens to you, too—and a boy growing up to be smart and sensitive.

It's funny, Bob. I've been thinking a lot about things—being reflective, I guess you'd say—since you've been gone. I had a dream the other night about our wedding day. Remember our wedding day? How long and loud it poured. Not even five minutes of sun the whole day, and everyone kept telling us that the rainstorms and hail were good luck. On our wedding day. I think it's funny how we pretend that terrible things are actually good fortune. Dog shit on your shoe. Bird shit in your hair. Lightning that strikes the dance hall right in the middle of the wedding toasts so that the DJ can't play music and the catering staff can't heat up the stuffed mushrooms and chicken kabobs. I wish I could say we can laugh about it now, but I can't. And I don't think it's good luck. I think it was an omen for us, Bob. An omen that we should've worked harder. That we should've made sure we were good at things like affection and love and communication.

Because these days, it feels like we aren't really hearing each other—don't you think? And that makes me pretty sad.

~A

*

March 28

Dear Anna—

I would say thanks for the last note—I was beginning to worry since it had been so long between letters, mine to yours, and I was glad to finally see it. But reading it now...well, suddenly I'm not feeling entirely relieved anymore.

I'd believed we were hearing one another clearly—trusted that we are. Still hope.

How are things going with all your efforts—like the appeal, I mean? Has Peter made any more progress finding someone? How's Elliott doing? Did you tell him about the fairytale I mentioned? That was important to me—to him and to you, too, I hope you know.

Look forward to hearing from you soon.

Love,
Bob

*

April 15

Dearest Anna—

It's been a few weeks now since I've heard anything, and so I keep rereading your last letter, trying to decipher what I'm missing between the lines.

Omens, troubles, sadness? Each time I work through it again, this cell feels a little smaller, the door more tightly sealed, the air thinner. Even the guards seem to be looking at me differently these days. Has something changed? Have I lost you somehow?

Too much in my head. Fears. Tears even, though I hate to admit it.

(Deep breath—again.)

You're my wife, my life, and without you….

Please, please, write again soon and let me know all is OK.

All my love,
Bob

*

May 5

Bob—

So sorry for the long silence. I've been waiting until everything was settled to fill you in.

You were right about it being lucky that you ended up in the prison you did. The guards are really wonderful there. It is too bad that we haven't been able to come visit you like we planned. I'm sorry about that. But, as you know, visiting hours end before my shift at work is over and before Elliott comes home from school, and with all this happening it's been tough to skip a paycheck. I couldn't really afford to do that.

But there were a few times when Peter picked up Elliott from school, so I was able to head over to Bailey's Brews just as some of the guards were getting off their shift. That's where they like to hang out, you know. That's where Jerry goes after his shift, after your conversations with him in the laundry room where he lets you sneak a cigarette or two.

Didn't you find it funny that he likes Merit Ultra Lights, just like you? A coincidence—a happy one, yes? And so nice to find a confidant on the inside, to feel like you can open up to someone, have a friend. To feel like you could confide in him your true plans, once you got out. Those plans that didn't include me, I'm afraid. But then again, your plans for the future never did include me—or Elliott—did they? Jerry was pretty clear on that point. I told him it would be worth his while to tell me everything you said, even the stuff that hurt. "She was a looker at one point" and "A man like me needs to be free, alone—not pinned down." Good work, Bob. You got what you wanted, right? A man. Alone. (Alhough I guess the "pinned down" and "free" part needs some work...haha)

And now that I see it for myself...well, I'll tell you, Bob, you're right once again. The world—life itself—looks very different from up high. I got a window seat, just like you always said. It is the best view. The world looks breakable from so high, doesn't it? So small and delicate. Like you can just pluck the houses and cars and trees right off the earth and move them, manipulate them, rip up roots and replant elsewhere. Start new.

Yes, I see this side now—and I have to say, I think I like the clouds best from above. Elliott loved when the plane just plowed right through them. He felt invincible. I can understand that. And Peter—well, he says that he prefers the aisle seat because he can get up to stretch his long legs. He didn't much enjoy take-off, but I think once he gets going, he'll be fine. Just fine. So I guess everyone's happy, yeah?

It might be awhile before we speak again, so I just wanted to leave you with this. I know you've been annoyed with my lack of communication. So I want to send you a poem from the *first letter* I ever wrote to you. Do you remember it? Maybe not. It's hard to tell what's real and what's fiction these days, isn't it? Anyway, I suspect you'll be able to glean the true meaning here, given your talent for hidden messages:

Yesterday, our unexpected
conversation about night
kisses inspired sensual sentiments.
My yearning
accelerates so sweetly.

With my very best wishes,
Anna

*

EXCERPTED FROM U.S. ATTORNEY'S MEMO:

On the morning of May 4, Anna Dunkin, Elliott Robert Dunkin, age 6, and Peter Mendelson, 41, boarded a flight for the Cayman Islands. Authorities had no cause to detain. On the same morning, prison guard Jerry Walters, 32, did not show up for his shift at work.

In the wake of these departures, scans of the correspondence between Robert and Anna Dunkin, made by correctional officers, were reevaluated and, in Robert's case, a pattern of skip codes was detected in specific paragraphs, signaled by an italicized number in a sentence preceding the coded passages. Based on decoded information, authorities were able to locate an offshore account at Caye International Bank in San Pedro, Belize, that Robert had set up in the name of Richard Morgenstern in the amount of 2.5 million dollars. However, by the time they discovered this account, it had been emptied of all assets.

Officials in the Cayman Islands lost track of Anna Dunkin, her son, and Peter Mendelson, who disappeared from a villa they had rented. It is suspected that they established new identities and have left the islands. Peter's wife Patty seems dumbfounded by her husband's disappearance; no contact between Patty and her husband has been detected.

Prison guard Jerry Walters was last seen driving a brand new BMW M4 convertible that he purchased with cash.

Robert Dunkin remains in East Gate Penitentiary. He is cooperating with authorities in trying to locate his wife, but has little useful information to offer.

Ladies of the Canyon
Released April 1970

"Morning Morgantown"
"For Free"
"Conversation"
"Ladies of the Canyon"
"Willy"
"The Arrangement"
"Rainy Night House"
"The Priest"
"Blue Boy"
"Big Yellow Taxi"
"Woodstock"
"The Circle Game"

All songs by Joni Mitchell.

The Priest
by David Dean

He had just returned to the table with his second whiskey when he saw her. Though she had managed to mask most of her face beneath a dark, wide-brimmed hat and wraparound sunglasses, he knew her. Despite the fifty-four years since their last meeting, years crowded with experiences and memories, travels and tragedies, he had never forgotten her, and the glass trembled in his hand.

Behind him, raucous laughter erupted from the bar, where a group of grinning Germans waited for the gale to blow itself out, happy, it would seem, with the progress of a soccer match on the widescreen. When he turned back from the distraction, she was looking at him from the entrance, her head tilted. He prayed she wouldn't recognize him in the dim lighting of the airport tavern.

Though he had so often longed for this moment, he had never believed that it would occur, and, now that it might, he was filled with dread. He was not even supposed to be in Frankfurt. His flight, like so many others, had been diverted here to wait out the weather that had swept in from the North Atlantic.

She began to walk toward him, maneuvering through the obstacle course of crowded tables without once glancing down, no smile on her face, eyes still hidden. He found himself rising from his chair, the multilingual chatter from the loudspeakers fading from his hearing, the bar gone silent to his ears.

Stopping in front of him, she removed the sunglasses. He had shaved often enough to know what she was seeing and couldn't imagine how she had recognized him.

"Facebook, John...social media," she replied to his unspoken question, smiling now. "You officiated at the wedding of one of my girlfriend's daughters a few years ago. She posted a photo of you with the bride and groom." She arched an eyebrow, studying his face. "I think I might have recognized you in any case."

Her gaze drifted down to his tie, and she added, "I was looking for the collar, though."

"We're allowed to travel incognito on vacation," he replied, his voice hoarse with disuse and emotion. "I see you do the same in your line of work."

Her disguise was hardly necessary, he thought. Though he could still see the slender girl he had known as a child beneath the thickened body, recognize the pale angularity of the young woman he had seen on dozens of record covers beneath the coarsening of age, he doubted many others would. They had both changed so utterly, yet were still visible to one another, a testament to...what?...love? They'd only been eleven years old when they'd last met.

"It didn't surprise me, you becoming a priest," she continued. "You were always easy to talk to." Taking the faded tartan tie between her long fingers, she remarked, "This looks like something your old man would've worn."

"He probably did," he quipped, reeling from the intimacy of her touch, her nearness.

Pulling his big head down with the tie, she kissed his stubbled cheek. "I'm not surprised you're so large...you were always a big boy. And you've still got all that curly hair." Releasing him, she asked, "May I join you, Father Athy?"

"I'd be crushed if you didn't, Caty Lovell."

Resuming his seat, he managed to catch the eye of the waitress. Young and too thin, she wore the dirndl costume of Oktoberfest though it was late February, the skirt quite short, revealing white stockings and bright red garters. "*Bitte?*" she enquired.

"Red wine, please," Caty responded in English. "Cabernet Franc, if you have it."

"*Danke,*" the harried girl answered, hurrying off through the refugee-like mob occupying her workplace.

"Are they afraid we'll forget we're in Germany?" Caty smiled, nodding at the departing girl, the dozens of tiny antlers mounted on the walls, the beer-festival décor.

"Why *are* you...in Germany, that is?" he asked, still not believing that she was there in front of him, that dozens of years and thousands of miles had been traveled to arrive at this moment. *God waits*, he thought.

"I was flying from Prague to my apartment in Paris," she explained. "We had a gig there. Nothing big…not like the old days. More of an intimate concert. Most of the audience was as old as we are." She smiled a little. "I'm a cure for nostalgia, John…or the cause of it, I'm not sure which. May I call you John, Father?"

He nodded his assent. "I wish you would."

"It was a beautiful rococo hall," she resumed, "and some people were in evening dress. Can you believe it? Over the years, I've gotten used to the finer things—I believe I wrote a song about that once."

"You did. One of your best, I think."

"Sometimes I can hardly remember when I didn't live like this, can barely recall the old neighborhood—but when I saw you, John, it all came flooding back."

"More's the pity," he answered, taking a sip of his Jameson. "It was an awful place in those days."

"Hell's Kitchen," she murmured. "They don't call it that anymore, do they?"

"No, it's called something else altogether…though I can't think what at the moment. I'm told it's a good address now." He shrugged. "Timing…."

Returning with Caty's wine, the waitress set the glass down on the table, sloshing some over the rim in her haste, then was gone once more to the clamor of other patrons.

"You said you were on vacation?" Caty asked, pausing to take a long swallow.

"A working vacation," John answered. "I was the spiritual guide for a pilgrimage to Medjugorje."

Laughing a little, Caty said, "I've no idea what that is, or where."

Smiling a little himself, he replied, "The tour company that organizes the pilgrimages pays for my airfare, room, and meals, in return for my officiating a few Masses and hearing confessions. As for Medjugorje"—the smile faded, and his face took on a thoughtful cast—"it's in Bosnia, the site of numerous purported appearances of the Blessed Virgin. I've been several times now. There's something there, Caty...something special. You wouldn't believe how many hundreds of thousands of people go there every year from all over the world—confessions are offered in twelve languages, and sometimes more." Turning a palm to the ceiling, he added, "I was on my way home...then this."

As if in answer, a dull tolling could be heard from outside, the basso profundo of the storm.

"I'll stick with Paris and L.A.," Caty replied. "As for confession...I'm long past that now. I wouldn't know where to begin." She regarded him for a moment, then sighed. "It's good seeing you again, John. I've missed you."

"And I you, Caty." His eyes caught her faded blue ones and held for a moment. "You were the first girl I ever kissed, you know."

Laughing, she said, "I hope that's not *your* confession. It wouldn't even register on the scale of my transgressions, and please don't tell me that I was also the last. I won't believe you."

Throwing back the remainder of his whiskey, John chuckled, "No, not the last. I had a few girlfriends in high school, several"— he paused and glanced at Caty with a bashful grin—"*lovers* in college. But I never forgot you, Caty. I loved *you*. I loved you from the first time you sang in the choir, when I was just an altar boy. I thought you looked like an angel and sounded like...like heaven itself. I was smitten. But you knew that."

"Of course I knew that. I loved you, too, you know."

He paused for a moment, making his decision, then asked, "Did you ever wonder why I didn't stay in touch after you moved away...never answered your letters or returned your calls?"

"Of course I did. But we'd been through a terrible trauma, John. Sometimes things like that don't draw people closer together but push them further apart. We reacted differently, that's all. We were just children."

"Yes, and that's why I have to tell you something I should've long ago, only I was too much of a coward. I probably never would've, if you hadn't found me here now. But if you're to love me, Caty—or, at least, the memory of me—you should know the truth. I don't want you to love a lie."

She took another long drink of her wine, then set the glass down. "If you must, John. If you think it will change anything, then I suppose you must."

"You remember that day on the roof?"

"Of course I do, I haven't gone senile. But I remember *many* days on the roof of our building, much better days than *that* one. The day you finally got up the courage to kiss me, for one. I remember the sound of the pigeons cooing and strutting in their coop behind us, the sky an Easter blue, even in those days of suffocating smog. I remember how we talked about all the places we would go, all the things we would do when we grew up and got married."

He reached across the table to clasp her hand. "And on one of those days, one of those rare golden days, you told me what had been happening to you...what your father had been doing. I think that was the first time I ever experienced real...anguish."

Caty sighed before taking another drink. "Didn't I say you were always easy to talk to, John? But I shouldn't have burdened you with that, you were too young."

"Me? My God, Caty, you were a child, too!"

"He was a mean drunk...and worse. A lot of men in the neighborhood were no better."

"But *that* day, Caty, when he staggered up to the roof and surprised us—I can still see it as clearly as if it happened yesterday—I remember the stench of booze on his breath and the stink of his clothes, his face full of rage and burst blood vessels. He seemed like the very devil to me."

"A bright red devil," Caty murmured.

"He thrust me aside as if I were nothing, small and spindly as he was, and I ran away, I was that frightened. I got as far as the door to the stairs when I heard him cursing and slapping you. You were struggling to escape, and he was calling you a whore—though we had only been kissing—and you slapped his face. I thought that was the bravest thing I'd ever seen anybody do. Then he reared back and punched you, and you went down as if you'd been struck dead. I thought you might be, Caty."

"Yes," she replied, "but that's when God intervened…at last…and he went over the parapet."

"He did," John agreed, turning his empty glass in his big hands. "Only it wasn't God who killed him."

"An *act* of God, then," she said softly. "In any event, the police thought so. They figured he tripped over me and fell…after all, he *was* drunk. And once they saw my face and talked to the neighbors, they closed their notebooks and went away. They knew him almost as well we did. He wasn't missed."

"You never told them I was there…was a witness. Why not?"

"What would've been the point? The police had everything they needed. It was over. I was free. And with the money from his insurance, Ma and me got a new start in the suburbs. I took singing lessons, went to college in L.A., and…well, you know the rest."

"Yes, but *you* don't," John replied, his breathing shallow and rapid. "I *didn't* go down those stairs, Caty. When I saw him hit you…knock you unconscious…something happened inside me. I saw red. No, not red. It was more like everything collapsing into a black tunnel connecting me to him, a passage I had no choice but to go roaring down. He was too drunk, I think, too focused on you to see me coming. And like you said, I was a big boy for my age, and he was a little man—I almost went over the wall, too, I slammed into him that hard."

There was a long silence between them.

"I can still see his face," he went on at last, "his expression as he stumbled backward toward the edge, somehow both terrified and sad in the same moment—he knew what was going to happen, yet he never made a sound. All I heard was the terrible thud when he struck the sidewalk six floors below, the sound of a side of beef slamming onto a butcher's table. I hear it sometimes still."

He paused to draw a ragged breath. "That's why I wasn't there when you came to, why I never got in touch after you moved away—why I couldn't talk to you."

She looked at him for several moments, her gaze level and unwavering, then said in a soft voice, "I was hoping you'd somehow forgotten these things, John. Kids do, sometimes—blank out really awful things in their lives and move on. I wish you had." She touched his face. "I know what happened that day. I wasn't unconscious, I was just pretending to be, hoping he was done and would leave me alone. I saw everything. But you were trying to protect me—who knows what you really *meant* to do? You acted out of love, and I've always been grateful for that."

"You *knew*...you always knew?"

"That's why I kept trying for so long to get in touch with you. I wanted you to know and not be alone with what happened. I never put it in a letter, because I was afraid someone else might see it. But when you never responded after all those years, I figured you had made your peace in your own way."

Taking both his hands in her own, she added, "If you hadn't done what you did, John, what kind of life do you think I would've had? I've made some bad choices—I don't have to tell you that, people like me have the sordid details of their lives splashed everywhere. There've been a lot of men in my life that I could've...should've done without. Things I should have avoided, not embraced. But there's been more good than bad—a wonderful career and an interesting life—and it's been *my* life, for better or for worse. *You* made that possible. My only real regret is that you've had to live with it all these years. I am sorry for that."

"You never told anyone?"

"Why would I? Why risk ruining *your* life when you had just saved mine. Did *you*...ever tell anyone?"

"Yes...my confessor."

"And you were forgiven."

"God's mercy is without limits, that's what we believe."

"Then you're wrong not to forgive yourself, John."

A buzzing came from within her purse, and she reached inside for her cell phone. Reading its screen, she rose. "It's my pilot. He says the storm is clearing. I have to go, John."

The priest also got to his feet.

"Want to go to Paris, Father?" she asked, arching an eyebrow.

John shook his head, smiling a bit. "I've got a parish in exotic New Jersey that awaits my return."

"I'm sure the ladies do, you big, handsome Mick. How they must love confessions on Saturday."

"Peace be with you, Caty Lovell," he said in reply, staring into the eyes of the eleven-year-old girl he had loved all his life.

"And with your spirit," she responded, giving him a chaste kiss on the cheek. Then, placing the sunglasses back on her face, she turned and threaded her way through the welter of patrons into a world wholly different from his own.

Watching until she had disappeared among the river of passengers surging through the concourse, Father Athy said aloud, "God waits. He always waits."

Then, with a shrug, as if suddenly waking, he threw some money on the table, snatched up his overcoat and went out to find his gate.

Big Yellow Taxi
by Kathryn O'Sullivan

Janet MacLeod yanked open the sash of her university office window and sucked cool October air into her lungs. Moments ago she had been enjoying a midmorning snack of organic apple slices and happily mulling over today's "Women Folk Singers of the '60s and '70s" lecture. Now, thanks to Stefano De Luca, she was battling an asthma attack and plotting a murder.

She closed her eyes and inhaled the faint smells of Long Island's North Shore: decaying seaweed, briny mud, stranded shellfish. She hadn't had an attack since her dissertation defense. She took another deep breath. The tightness in her throat eased—the residue from an old inhaler she had dug out from her desk doing its job. She opened her eyes, the danger over.

A breeze rustled the red leaves of her nearby cherished maple. Like the tree, Janet had planted deep roots at Three Village University, an elite institution nestled halfway between Great Neck and Montauk. She was a well-respected if not well-loved professor in the school's renowned music department. There she had intended to remain until they carted her out in a body bag— preferably mid-lecture. Thanks to Stefano De Luca, that plan was in jeopardy.

A leaf broke free and swirled in the wind. She had protested vehemently when the school's president announced the maple would be torn down for a parking lot. "Progress," he had called it. Over three decades, the tree had sheltered finch and cardinal nests and provided welcome shade from the afternoon sun while she graded papers. Tomorrow, her old friend would be hacked to pieces and replaced by twenty asphalt spaces. She closed the window and pushed the coming arboricide from her mind. Right now, she had a bigger problem.

Her computer monitor glowed with the email that had brought on the asthma attack. The communication was from Dr. Nussbaum, the department chair. Beginning in the spring semester and for the indefinite future, he "regretted" to inform her that her honors folk singers class was cancelled.

Across the hall, coins clattered in a can, a ball thumped against a wall, and students giggled. Janet's eyes narrowed to slits. She crept to the door, cracked it open, and focused on the office of Stefano De Luca, assistant professor of music, the source of the noise, and the reason for her course cancellation.

She had been excited—even, she hated to admit, smitten—when Stefano joined the faculty last fall. His publications on medieval folk music and his proficiency on the rote, an ancient stringed instrument from Wales, had impressed the discerning Janet. His resemblance to a young Marlon Brando was an added bonus. Others on the hiring committee had expressed concern that Stefano's resume failed to reflect "dedication to teaching." Janet had argued that he was simply early in his career. By the end of his first year on the faculty, she had seen the error of her ways.

More giggling followed more strange noises. The noise—and it *was* noise—was what Stefano had conned the administration and students into believing was "experimental" music. His so-called compositions didn't just ignore rhythm, melody, harmony and timbre, they defied them. It mystified her how Stefano, an accomplished instrumentalist, could create random sounds with found objects like trash cans, water balloons and squeaky chairs and declare them music. That Stefano threw away his talent on such garbage was an affront to the entire field, an affront to Janet, and a blemish on the department's fine reputation. But she could have lived with all that, provided her fiefdom remained intact.

Dr. Nussbaum had warned Janet that, if her honors course numbers dropped, the class would be cancelled. She had defended the decline as the result of a planning issue and requested Nussbaum move Stefano's course to a time not in opposition to hers. But the chair had a Darwinian idea of scheduling and refused. Today's email was the last straw. Time to silence De Luca and restore harmony to her world.

Her phone beeped. Class called, so homicidal musings would have to wait. She slid graded assignments into a tote, donned a tartan poncho, fluffed her spiky gray hair, grabbed her guitar and locked the door.

"Hello, Professor MacLeod," Stefano said, exiting his office with a trio of female students.

Janet forced a smile. "Good morning."

"Heading to class?"

"Yes, and I'll be late if—"

"I'll walk with you," he said, before she could finish.

"See you later, Old Man," one student teased.

"Bye, Stefano," said a second.

The third just giggled and retreated with her friends.

Janet shook her head. She'd never allow students to call her by a nickname or her first name. She hurried toward the stairs, her guitar case swinging at her side, and tried to avoid slipping on the polished marble floor.

"It's too bad about your folk-singers class," Stefano said, as they reached the steps that descended in a broad spiral to the first floor.

She squeezed the case handle. One swift, strong swing, and Stefano would go flying down the staircase, crack his head, and she'd be rid of him forever.

"Janet," he said.

She snapped out of her trance. "Oh, yes. My class. Disappointing." She scurried down the steps in an attempt to lose him.

"I'm surprised by your reaction," he said, right on her heels. "You love that class."

Please let him trip and break his neck, she thought. But the nimble Stefano glided down the stairs like a gazelle, and it was she who nearly tripped at the bottom.

"If you'd like tips on how you might increase your enrollment," he continued.

Janet screeched to a halt. "No!" Students looked up from their phones. She lowered her voice. "I appreciate the offer," she said, swallowing bile. "But your methods work for you. I'm certain they won't for me."

He flashed his pearly whites. "You're probably right. But if you change your mind, Dr. Nussbaum says I have enough students interested in my experimental course to offer another section. You could teach it."

Again, she resisted the urge to wallop him. Teach *his* class? What would she do? Empty her purse on the floor, smash a glass against the wall, crinkle paper and call it a symphony? She watched him strut away, certain of one thing. Stefano and his stupid course would soon be cancelled—permanently.

She entered her classroom. Her five loyal disciples had dutifully arranged chairs in a circle. How many professors could boast of such dedication and perfect attendance? So what if her classes no longer ran at capacity? Education was about more than putting butts in seats.

Her dark mood brightened as students discussed the works of Joan Baez, Judy Collins, Joni Mitchell. Her teacher's heart fluttered with delight when they debated which was a better protest song, Baez's "What Have They Done to the Rain?" or Buffy Saint-Marie's "Universal Soldier." Janet ended class performing a song of the students' choosing. Playing with her students built strong rapport. Inspired by a discussion they had had about climate change, her young scholars selected Mitchell's "Big Yellow Taxi." They sang a rousing rendition. Yes, her teaching methods were sound.

She hummed as she strolled from the classroom on her way to the cafeteria for coffee. She slowed behind a gaggle of students shuffling toward the exit.

"Did you hear? The dean cancelled Dr. MacLeod's honors class," said a woman Janet recognized as a junior piano major. "Now I have to find something else for next semester."

"You really wanted to take that class?" asked another student.

"Dr. MacLeod's cool, once you get to know her."

"Stefano says her music's from the Dark Ages."

The crowd pushed Janet out the doors and down the steps of Russo Hall. She stomped across the quad. The Dark Ages? No wonder her enrollment had dropped! At least what she taught was *about* something—the environment, civil rights, addiction, war. What was his noise good for? Absolutely nothing!

She crunched through leaves as she stormed toward the Student Union. Her mind whirled with ways to bump off Stefano. She didn't pack heat, so shooting him was out. The thought of touching him made her want to vomit, so strangulation was out. She left the quad and followed the brick sidewalk that led past the Russo Fine Arts Building.

Janet took great pride in having been high-school pals with Paul Russo. The Russos were prominent philanthropists and had paid for and overseen the construction of the university's music, fine arts, science and business buildings. Like most recipients of the family's generosity, the university had chosen to look the other way regarding the source of the Russos' money and their rumored ties to organized crime.

Janet passed the facilities and grounds supervisor spraying sidewalk cracks with weed killer. The words "put away that DDT, now" played in her mind. She marched up the Student Union's ramped entrance, slowed and stopped. She glanced back at the pooling pesticide and grinned.

She dashed into the Union. The facilities supervisor's lair was around the corner, near the service elevator. She was relieved to discover the door ajar and slipped inside. The workroom smelled of earth, chemicals and wet concrete. She had only been there a handful of times—mostly to complain about her classroom's chilly temperature. On one visit, the supervisor had regaled her with the potency of his pesticides. "That stuff in there is Schedule 7," he had bragged, pointing to a metal cabinet marked with a skull and crossbones. "Not your everyday over-the-counter mix. A few ounces could take down a horse."

Or an assistant professor.

She set down her guitar and scurried to the cabinet. The storage door squeaked. She scanned the industrial cleaning solutions and toxins and spotted a container with a picture of a rodent. She guessed she wouldn't need much. She retrieved an aspirin bottle from her tote, dumped out the pills, and unscrewed the rat poison's cap.

Footsteps approached. She poured liquid into the aspirin bottle, snapped on its lid, lowered it into her bag, and returned the jug to the cabinet. Seconds later, the supervisor entered.

"May I help you?"

Janet plastered on a smile. "I certainly hope so."

He glanced at the cabinet. "You have a rodent problem over at Russo?"

Yes. He's five foot ten with black, wavy hair.

"I saw a mouse," she said.

She'd never really have an innocent mouse killed. She didn't even like when her cat, Blue, left "gifts" on her stoop. But the explanation seemed a reasonable excuse for her presence, since mice often sought out warm buildings when the weather turned cool.

He locked the cabinet. "You should leave extermination to the pros."

"I'll keep that in mind."

He crossed to his desk. "Have you seen the mouse more than once?"

Every week for over a year, she thought.

"No," she said.

"Can you describe it?"

"Mousy?" she said, playing dumb.

He shook his head. She knew what he was thinking. Professors had book learning but no street smarts. But soon Stefano would discover just how "street" she was.

"I'll check it out," he said, dismissing her.

"You're a life saver." She grabbed her guitar and all but skipped from the room.

*

Janet spent the evening planning Stefano's demise. It would all go down during the team-building activity at tomorrow's faculty meeting. She usually dreaded Dr. Nussbaum's games, but the exercise would provide a distraction while she slipped poison into Stefano's favorite soda, Morning Mist. The drink's unnatural color and intense sweetness would mask the poison perfectly—or so she hoped. She transferred the toxin to a plastic travel bottle with a squeeze top. When the time came, she'd give Stefano's drink a squirt, and that would be that.

*

She arrived early the next morning and was relieved to discover the conference room adjacent to Dr. Nussbaum's office empty. She claimed a seat next to Stefano's usual perch, dropped her bag, and felt the poison bottle in her jacket pocket. Faculty trickled in. Then Stefano and Dr. Nussbaum entered, talking as if old chums. Stefano took his seat and placed his soda on the table. Operation Morning Mist was a go.

"Good morning, everyone," Dr. Nussbaum said. "You'll be pleased to know this will be a short meeting. Since many of you have complained about the team-building activities," he said, looking pointedly at Janet, "I've decided to discontinue them."

Several faculty members feigned disappointment, but Janet's dismay was real. Of all the times to stop his irritating games, he had to choose today? Janet only half-listened as Nussbaum droned on about university policies, admissions auditions and department updates. She needed a Plan B.

"Before we conclude, I'd like to congratulate Rich and Janet," Nussbaum said, snapping her back to the present moment. "As you know, they are in their thirtieth years at Three Village. They are our department's senior faculty—our institutional history, if you will."

She stole a look at Rich, who looked as insulted as she felt. *Senior* faculty? Institutional *history*? The chair made them sound like dinosaurs. Rich adjusted his bifocals and ran a hand through thinning white hair. She remembered when he had arrived, fresh out of graduate school, young and energetic. When had he turned into this tired old man? Self-consciously, she touched her own gray locks.

"Next spring, Janet and Rich will be honored with plaques and service pins at a ceremony for senior faculty," Nussbaum said.

Really? Again with the *senior*?

The group clapped. She forced a smile.

"I'd also like to commend Dr. Stefano De Luca. This morning, the provost approved expansion of his experimental program. Pending the board's approval, several rehearsal spaces will be redesigned into labs for Stefano's thriving courses."

Stefano grinned. There was no applause.

"What do you mean, 'redesigned'?" someone asked.

"So that we may offer our students rooms better suited to Dr. De Luca's innovative approach, some spaces will undergo demolition."

The room erupted in protest. The chair swiftly shut down the grumblings by pointing out that Stefano's classes had doubled in size while the rest had stagnated or declined. Janet felt sick to her stomach. She hadn't listened to her colleagues on the hiring committee, and now they were *all* suffering. Murdering Stefano was no longer just about her. It was about saving the department.

Nussbaum finished with a reminder about the fall get-together at his house this weekend and adjourned the meeting. Janet pretended to check phone messages until the room cleared. Perhaps she could still slip the poison into Stefano's drink. Unfortunately, he returned, grabbed his soda and joined Nussbaum in his office.

Then she saw Stefano's smoking vaporizer on the table. Of course. Why hadn't she thought of it before? Poisoning his drink would be lame. The vaporizer was much better. She suppressed a giggle, giddy with new hope. If she could get the pesticide inside the gizmo before Stefano returned, the next whiff he took would be his last.

She examined the box-shaped device. She knew nothing about vaping paraphernalia, but, if she could figure out how the thing worked....

"Your ideas will be integral to the design, Stefano," Nussbaum said from the other room.

She slipped the device into her tote.

Stefano entered. "Thirty years. Quite an accomplishment." He flashed a smug grin and exited.

Operation Final Puff was on.

She hurried upstairs to her office, locked the door and sat at her desk. She was about to type "How to use a vape apparatus" but stopped. The computer was university property. What if someone discovered her search? Better study the contraption without doing any research. After all, she disassembled musical instruments. How complicated could this doohickey be?

It took two attempts to remove the tank. She retrieved the pesticide from her bag, tilted the bottle, and imagined Stefano inhaling—the burning, wheezing, convulsing. She held the toxin over the opening. What was she *doing*? She wanted to kill the man, yes, but not torture him.

A knock made her jump. She pulled the poison away from the device.

She wasn't expecting students. Maybe whoever it was would go away.

A second knock, then a third.

Perhaps a colleague wanted to gripe about the rehearsal-room renovations.

She closed the still-full poison container, returned it to her bag, reassembled the smoking gadget and opened the door.

Stefano stood in the entrance, a buxom coed in tight pants behind him. "Have you seen my vape? I seem to have misplaced it."

"Your vape?"

"You know." He mimed smoking and rolled his eyes at Tight Pants.

Janet stole a look at her desk. Drat. She had left Stefano's vape in plain sight.

"There it is," he said, following her gaze.

"Oh, yes. I picked it up for you." She reluctantly returned the apparatus.

"Thanks. By the way, I told Dr. Nussbaum about my offer to help you with your enrollment. He's all for it. Said you should start by observing my classes for effective teaching strategies. I'm sure you'll get an email. Just wanted to give you a heads up." He saluted with the smoking equipment and disappeared down the hall with Tight Pants.

How dare he speak with Nussbaum about her and then mention it in front of a student? Observe his classes? Never!

Outside, a chainsaw revved. Her maple shook in protest. She had forgotten—or perhaps repressed—that today her tree came down. Anger over the tree's demise fueled her anger about Stefano. It was time to call in a pro.

*

Paul Russo sat across the booth from Janet and cocked his head. "You need help with *what*?" he asked.

"With getting rid of someone," she whispered. "You know—ice him, whack him, send him to the farm?"

"You find all that slang from a Google search?" he asked with a smile.

She stared at him hard. "I'm serious."

He studied her. "You are," he said, stunned.

She leaned forward. "So how does this work?"

He stole a look around the diner. "First of all, I'm not in the business of whacking people. Second of all, I'm not in the business of whacking people."

"I thought maybe, since I performed at your dear mother Sofia's funeral, you might want to do me a favor."

"You're trying to guilt trip me?"

"Is it working?" she asked, hopeful.

He pointed to his meaty, tan, expressionless face. "Does it look like it's working?"

She slumped back and stared out the window.

She and Paul had been friends for decades, but in all the years they had known one another he had never discussed his family's other "business." When she had played at Sofia Russo's funeral, the elder Mr. Russo had wept and said, "You're a good girl, Janet. If you ever need anything—I mean anything—you ask Paulie." She shouldn't have assumed "anything" included murder.

"So what did he do?" Paul asked, breaking the silence.

"Stole my students, offended my colleagues, hijacked our rehearsal rooms," she said, knowing how trivial it all sounded.

His brows furrowed. He removed a pen and pad from his pocket. "What do you mean, hijacked your rehearsal rooms?"

She perked up. It hadn't occurred to her that the Russos might feel protective of their buildings. "He wants to use them for experimental music."

Paul's pen hovered over the pad. "So?"

"So those beautiful rooms your family so lovingly built in your mother's name are going to be gutted, demolished, obliterated—for *this*."

She found a video of Stefano playing his "music" on her phone, increased the volume and pressed PLAY. Clanging, popping and screeching filled the air.

Paul hit STOP. "What's his name?"

For the next half hour, Janet relayed everything she knew about Stefano. The veins in Paul's temples throbbed as he scribbled notes. Finally, he had heard enough. He laid out a simple but elegant plan. The night of the fall get-together would be Stefano's last.

*

Janet's heart raced as she mingled with colleagues at Dr. Nussbaum's party. She had politely listened to teaching stories and university gossip, but her eyes had never left Stefano. To her surprise, he grabbed a fifth beer and headed her way.

"Quite the swinging hot spot," he said, gazing droopy-eyed about the room.

"Yes," she said, attempting to appear casual. "Dr. Nussbaum always has good food."

He leaned close. His breath smelled of beer and deviled eggs. "I know what you're up to. It's not going to work."

She swallowed. "What are you talking about?" she asked, keeping her voice calm.

"You're trying to get rid of me. But *I'm* going to get rid of *you*."

Her breathing became labored. She felt lightheaded. Now was no time for an asthma attack.

"You put the others up to complaining to the board," Stefano hissed. "But your rebellion won't work. I'm going to get those rehearsal rooms and become a permanent fixture on campus. Then I'm going to get you fired."

Janet's heart pounded. Her cheeks burned.

"Is everything okay here?" Dr. Nussbaum asked.

"Fabulous party, Dr. N," Stefano said. "But I gotta hit the road." He drunkenly searched his pockets.

The chair raised a brow. "I hope you're not driving."

Stefano found his phone. "I've called an Uber." He turned to Janet. "It's like a taxi."

I know what an Uber is, you twit, she thought, but bit her tongue. She didn't want to sabotage the plan.

Stefano's phone buzzed. "My ride."

He saluted Nussbaum, sneered at Janet, staggered to the door and exited. The screen door slammed behind him.

Janet watched Stefano approach a yellow SUV with tinted windows and open the back door. Her pulse quickened. Two shadowy figures sat in the front. Stefano hesitated. She held her breath. Then Stefano stumbled into the vehicle and out of her life forever.

*

Janet hummed as she placed two tropical bonsai on her office window ledge. *My little tree museum.* She eyed the freshly asphalted parking lot below and grinned. Paul's plan had worked beautifully. Assistant Professor Stefano De Luca hadn't been seen for two weeks.

She didn't know the particulars of Stefano's demise. Paul told her it was better that way—"plausible deniability," he called it. She had told Paul that Stefano was a devoted Uber rider when he drank and that he always drank at faculty parties. Paul had arranged for the SUV to be waiting a block from Nussbaum's house. When Stefano requested a ride, the SUV was the closest vehicle. The one detail Paul *had* revealed was Stefano's final resting place. She watched with satisfaction as the team of Russo Construction workers painted white lines to delineate the parking spaces. Stefano had been right. He *had* become a permanent part of the campus.

Her computer pinged with incoming email. Her heart skipped a beat. The message was from Dr. Nussbaum. Stefano's desertion had thrown a wrench into the chair's carefully planned spring schedule. Janet had been waiting for Nussbaum to decide what to do. Finally, she'd have her folk-singers class back, and the experimental-music courses would fade into oblivion.

She opened the email. Beginning in the spring and for the indefinite future, the chair was pleased to inform her that she would now teach...all the department's experimental-music classes! Janet inhaled sharply. Furthermore, Nussbaum would share Stefano's syllabi and assignments, so she could build on Stefano's strong foundation. There was nothing about the return of her folk-singers course.

Her throat tightened in an asthmatic spasm. She struggled to take in air. She fumbled with the desk drawer, grabbed the old inhaler and pressed. Empty. Her wheezing became more pronounced. She stumbled toward the door, bumped into a side table. The lamp smashed to pieces. She lunged for the phone's panic button and tripped. Phone, pencils and books crashed to the floor. Her first "composition," she thought, and snorted a chuckle. Her heart thumped as she sank to her knees. Then her cheek hit the carpet. As the room went black, she could almost hear Stefano laughing from his asphalt grave.

Blue

Released June 1971

"All I Want"
"My Old Man"
"Little Green"
"Carey"
"Blue"
"California"
"This Flight Tonight"
"River"
"A Case of You"
"The Last Time I Saw Richard"

All songs by Joni Mitchell.

River
by Stacy Woodson

The plane touched down on the tarmac of the Boston Logan International Airport and rolled toward the gate. First Sergeant Mick McCafferty was back on US soil. Normally, this would make him happy. But not today, not with the task that loomed in front of him.

"Welcome to Boston," the flight attendant said, too cheerfully. "The temperature is twenty-two degrees, local time is 1 PM."

Mick was alert, but he could feel fatigue pressing on him. Fatigue from two days of travel, fatigue from denied equipment requests, fatigue from a war that had raged for seventeen years and everything it had taken from him.

He shifted in his seat. The smells of desert and sweat floated from his Army Combat Uniform. But the women sitting next to him didn't seem to notice. They talked about Christmas, cutting down trees, hanging up reindeer decorations—a whole lot of superficial nothing.

He didn't understand how they could be so disrespectful, so disconnected from reality. Maybe they hadn't heard the pilot's announcement that the plane carried two fallen service members— or maybe they just didn't care, now that patriotism wasn't fashionable anymore.

Gone were the Stars-and-Stripes lapel pins, the yellow ribbons, the songs of war and peace. Soldiers fighting overseas were forgotten—forgotten like the two dead lying in the cargo hold.

Mick pressed his head against the window, tried to ignore the women and watched the taxiway slip by. Clouds, thick and ominous, cast dark shadows on the ground, the sky no different than the day Sergeant Jenny Waterman and her working dog Trigger had their final mission.

Their National Guard unit was assigned to the southern part of Helmand Province in Afghanistan, and it was their responsibility to

73

clear and secure a road for the Task Force. Intelligence reported improvised explosive devices buried in the area—twenty-gallon plastic drums filled with explosives made from fertilizer connected to motorcycle batteries. Technology existed that could detect IEDs, and Mick had sent multiple requests for support.

Each had been denied.

Congress had cut defense spending in an attempt to leverage the president into pulling troops from the Middle East. And there was no funding for new equipment—or so the story went.

Politics or not, Mick's mission hadn't changed. So he was forced to press on and use what he had: an MP canine handler and an IED detection dog.

Jenny and Trigger found the IED fifty meters ahead of their unit. Jenny marked the location, like she'd done countless times before, while they waited to proceed.

"We aren't getting any younger here, Waterman," he remembered Spanelli ribbing her.

It was constant during deployments, the ribbing. Among everyone, really. The only way to cope with the stress was to make light of it. And Jenny was just like the rest of them.

She glanced back at Spanelli, grin wide, middle finger extended. "Kiss my lily-white—"

Then: *Boom.*

*

He could still smell the sulfur, see the smoke, the mangled limbs, the bloodied road.

Jenny's empty face.

The women in the seats next to him laughed.

"Wait until Mary sees my ugly Christmas sweater," one gushed. "She'll die with envy."

"You'll win the contest this year, for sure," her friend giggled back. They continued to blather—about cocktails and manicures and favorite holiday dishes.

Their voices grated on Mick's nerves. He gripped his arm rests. But the pressure against his fingers did little to defuse the frustration building inside him.

Only a few more minutes, he reminded himself. *A few more minutes, and I'll be off this plane.*

He looked out the window again. Sleet pelted the glass. The plane turned and continued to inch forward, the terminal growing bigger in the distance. The two hearse drivers he'd hired and two baggage handlers were positioned near one of the gates. There was no color guard, no priest, no one waiting to offer their respects.

Just four people paid to be there.

Not that he'd expected anything different. Their National Guard unit was deployed, so there were no soldiers available for a color guard. And Jenny had grown up in foster care. She had no family and didn't believe in religion. But she believed in Trigger.

He taught her what unconditional love meant, she'd told Mick once. Her plan had been to adopt Trigger after the war, return to Boston and walk the dog along the Charles. It was on the river, after they were cremated, that Mick would scatter their ashes this evening.

The plane rolled to a stop.

"Folks." The PA system crackled again. "This is the pilot. We are at the gate. Please remain seated until the military escort on board can deplane."

Mick grabbed his backpack from under the seat in front of him, stood, smoothed his uniform, prepared to make his way to the door. But the women next to him didn't move. The one in the middle seat was on her cell phone, and the other one was in the aisle, trying to work the latch on an overhead bin.

Seat belts clicked. More people stood.

Mick glanced out the window. The belt loader for the caskets was at the plane, and the hearses, backs open, were positioned to receive them.

"Excuse me." Mick leaned forward.

Still nothing.

He tried again, this time using his command voice—a snap to his words, his tone direct, anything but polite.

The woman next to him glared, and then her eyes went wide. She pulled her phone from her ear and turned to her friend in the aisle. "Margery?"

Margery's focus was still on her bag. "Don't let Winona weasel out of picking us up from the airport. You tell her—"

"Margery!"

Margery finally looked at Mick, and her face flushed. "Oh!"

Both women cleared the row, and Mick headed for the door.

There were more passengers in the aisle.

More people ignoring the pilot's request.

Where was the flight attendant?

Mick pushed forward despite the congestion. Some passengers retreated to their seats. Others shot irritated looks but made room for him to pass.

Until he reached the bulkhead.

A man in business class stood sideways, blocking the aisle. His over-moussed hair nearly crested the bottom of the overhead bin. He wore a blue blazer with a Harvard alumni pin on the lapel, wool coat and tartan scarf looped over his arm. A roller bag rested on the seat next to him. The smell of scotch oozed from his pores.

"There's a Christmas party at the Crimson Club tonight. You should come as my guest," Harvard said to the flight attendant hovering in front of him.

She leaned against one of the seats, twirled a strand of her hair and giggled. "I might just do that."

Harvard unzipped the top pocket of his bag and tugged out a business card.

The floor under Mick's feet shuddered.

Baggage handlers inside the cargo hold.

They'd move Jenny and Trigger soon. He couldn't let them arrive without him.

"Excuse me," Mick said.

"Here's how to reach me, Nicole. It's Nicole, isn't it?" Harvard turned his back to Mick and handed Nicole his card.

Mick tapped his shoulder. "Hey, man—"

"Look, G.I. Joe," Harvard said, "the living have plans to make, places to go, people to see. Your friends—they're already dead. What difference do a few minutes make?"

Mick's breath caught. Blood rushed to his ears. He wanted to ball up his hand, crank his arm back and swing—hear the snap of cartilage, see the gush of blood, feel his fist drive deep into Harvard's face.

But he'd be no good to Jenny and Trigger locked up in Suffolk County Jail.

So he took a deep breath, tried to control the anger. He needed to push past Harvard, continue to the door, before he lost what little control he'd managed to muster.

But as it turned out, he didn't need to do a thing. The man was already on the move.

Harvard gripped his roller bag, ripped it across the armrest and dropped it onto the floor. Empty mini bottles, once filled with Glenlivet, rolled into the aisle. "Call me," he said to Nicole, in a breathy scotch-filled whisper, and then he stepped through the door onto the jetway.

Mick followed, forced to stare at the back of Harvard's head as he weaved his way to the terminal and finally rounded the corner, leaving a trail of trash in his wake: gum wrappers, business cards, more booze bottles.

A man in an orange reflective vest, one of the baggage handlers, approached Mick, picking up Harvard's discards along the way. The badge that hung around his neck said his name was Dale. "You the escort for the caskets?"

Mick nodded.

"I'll take you down to the tarmac," Dale said. "Got to make this quick. Need to turn the plane soon if we're going to keep our schedule. I'm sure you understand."

Mick understood, all right—he understood that old boy Dale was no different than the rest of the people he'd met on this trip.

He followed Dale through another corridor to a hall. At the end was a door with a keypad. Dale swiped his badge. The lock released, but the door didn't move. "Damn thing likes to stick," Dale explained. "Mind holding this?" He handed Mick the trash he'd collected and worked the door, again without success.

Mick shoved the junk in his cargo pocket and joined Dale. They both tugged, and the door popped open. Mick reached into his backpack, pulled out his fleece. A plastic bag with zip strips, duct tape and other deployment leftovers came with it. He slipped on the fleece, slung the pack back over his shoulder and descended the stairs behind Dale to the tarmac.

Jenny's flag-draped casket already inched down the belt loader. No one seemed to care that her military escort wasn't in place to receive it.

Thankfully, Jenny wasn't inside the hearse yet, and Mick could still do right by her and Trigger. He popped to attention, saluted. While he watched the casket continue its journey, his mind went to a memory of Jenny kneeling in front of a homeless man.

It was winter. Their unit had just returned from another deployment, and they'd stayed at their favorite bar until closing time. As they stumbled back toward the T, a homeless man sat huddled against a building, his body shaking from the cold. Jenny shrugged off her coat, draped it over his shoulders and called an Uber to take him to the nearest homeless shelter.

Mick was pretty sure she'd saved the man's life that night. He tried to submit her for a commendation, some kind of recognition for her decency, but Jenny wouldn't accept it. "Being decent shouldn't be exceptional," she said. "It should be *expected*."

It was a lesson that stuck with Mick, and he couldn't help but think the world would be a better place if more people were like Jenny.

After her casket was loaded, Trigger's was next. It was smaller, child sized. It had an innocence to it that Mick saw for the first time, and a lump grew in his throat.

Jenny and Trigger were finally home, victims of a war no one cared about. Mick wasn't sure which made him sadder, Jenny and Trigger or what his country had become.

After Trigger's casket was loaded, Mick climbed into the passenger seat of Jenny's hearse. He rode with her, Trigger in trail, to the funeral home.

*

Mick stayed until their bodies were cremated. Their ashes were placed in two plastic-lined cardboard boxes that fit inside Mick's backpack. It was hard to believe their footprint on earth had been reduced to something so insignificant.

He fished through Harvard's trash, still in his pocket, and pulled out his cell phone. He sent an email to his battalion commander, providing a status on Jenny and Trigger's remains. Then he reached for his wallet to settle the bill. But Sully, the funeral-home director, shook his head. "This one's on me, kid. Least I can do."

Mick was surprised by Sully's gesture, his kindness a sharp contrast to what he'd experienced earlier that day. And he was grateful.

Sully offered Mick a lift to his hotel. On the drive, Mick learned Sully was a Vietnam veteran, a Marine who'd fought in the battle of Khe Sanh. Mick told him about his flight, the indifference on the plane, the lack of respect.

"Folks forget about the troops overseas, just like they forgot the Vietnam vets," Sully said, his arthritic fingers curling tight around the truck's steering wheel—all except one, which was gone. "If it doesn't impact them in some personal way, folks don't seem to care."

Mick, sadly, had to agree with him.

After that, there wasn't much to say so they rode in comfortable silence. Soon they were in the Back Bay section of Boston, a block from Mick's hotel. Sully stopped at a light, and that was when Mick saw it.

The Crimson Club.

The colonial building was decked out for Christmas: wreaths on the windows, garlands of lights that cascaded from the top of the entrance. A stream of town cars pulled up to the curb. Couples spilled onto the sidewalk, some laughing, some stumbling, already filled with too much holiday cheer.

Mick's mind went to Harvard, the jackass on the plane. And then he thought about Jenny, Trigger and the countless others who had died in the war. Died so that these people would have the freedom to party, the freedom to enjoy their lives. And the anger he'd kept contained returned. He gripped the handle to the passenger door.

"Let me out here. I can walk the rest of the way."

*

Mick stood on a dock next to the Weld Boathouse. It was dark, but the moon was full, and he could see chunks of ice floating in the river below. The wind whipped, and the cold cut through him. He looped the tartan scarf around his neck, cupped his hands and blew warm air against his fingers.

"What do you want from me, man?" Harvard demanded. His hands were duct-taped to the armrests of an Adirondack chair at the edge of the dock, his feet duct-taped together.

It was good for Mick that guys like Harvard were predictable. It hadn't been hard to get him to the dock. Mick had Harvard's business card in his pocket—part of the man's airport discards. He'd sent a text to Harvard's cell from "Nicole," wondering if a tumble or two in the Weld Boathouse would rival the Mile High Club.

And Harvard had come running.

Mick used a sleeper hold to knock him out. Then he dragged the man to a secluded place on Weld's dock, where Mick ignored him now.

His focus was on Jenny and Trigger.

On the flight, Mick had considered what he would say before he scattered their ashes: a quote from the Bible, a line from a poem, some meaningful story from Jenny and Trigger's lives. But in the end, all he could think of was their military unit, the only family Jenny and Trigger had ever truly known. So he chose their unit motto. It was simple, meaningful—like the lives Jenny and Trigger had led—and he began his eulogy.

"Sergeant Jenny Waterman and her working dog Trigger made the ultimate sacrifice for freedom when they were killed in Afghanistan by an improvised explosive device. Both were dedicated soldiers and loyal friends." Mick's eyes began to mist. "*Facta Non Verba*—Deeds Not Words—our unit motto was how they lived their lives. May they serve as an example for others."

He scattered Trigger's ashes first, then Jenny's. Chunks of soot and pieces of bone caught the ice and skated along the current.

Mick thought about his own life, the soldiers he'd lost, the sacrifices they'd made for a cause no one believed in anymore.

And he wished he had a river he could skate away on.

"Well?" Harvard prodded. "Why am I here?"

Mick shook his head. He wondered if it was because the man was drunk or if it was just thanks to sheer arrogance that Harvard still showed no fear.

Not that it really mattered.

Mick didn't need Harvard afraid. In fact, it was better if he wasn't. This way, Mick would know if the message he wanted to convey got through to him.

"I wanted you to witness the funeral of two soldiers," he said. "To understand the sacrifice they made so that you can live your life the way you choose. So the next time you see someone who served their country, you'll remember this moment and show some measure of respect."

Harvard stared at him, wide-eyed.

And for a moment Mick thought, maybe, Harvard finally got it. Because if Harvard got it, then maybe, somehow, this country wasn't so bad off. And Mick could go back to Afghanistan and fight, still believing in the people he served.

But the moment was short lived.

Harvard tilted his head back and laughed. "Military people. You all have an overinflated sense of worth. You think you're special because you volunteered to serve—that somehow *this* makes you a hero. But enlisting to get your student loans paid and being on the wrong side of a bullet doesn't make you a hero. And I'm tired of people kissing your asses because of it."

Mick's breath caught. He wanted to argue. To hold onto the fragile thread of hope he'd created. But he saw the man's smug expression and realized it was useless. Harvard was too entrenched in his own self-serving world.

"Let's be real. If you wanted me dead, you would have killed me when I first walked into the Boathouse," Harvard continued. "So can we get to the part where you do the honorable thing—because I know you military guys get off on that—and let me go?"

Mick just stared.

Harvard sighed. "You've made your point, okay? I've learned my lesson," he sing-songed, like a child. "Does that make it easier for you to cut me free?"

Mick looked past Harvard to the river. Watched the chunks of ice drift by. Listened to the *slap, slap* of the current against the dock. He thought about Jenny and Trigger and others in his unit. He believed in them. Maybe he didn't need to believe in this country. Maybe believing in the people he served with was enough.

"For Christ's sake, I'm freezing my nuts off here. At least give me my scarf back—"

Mick's hands went to Harvard's scarf—still wrapped around his own neck—while the man continued to rant. He considered the temperature of the river, the effect it would have on Harvard's body. The shock of cold. The muscle spasms. The time it would take for death to take hold.

Jenny's words echoed in Mick's memory: *Being decent shouldn't be exceptional. It should be expected.*

Despite Harvard, Mick should do the decent thing, the honorable thing, and let the man live. Mick took off the scarf, his intent to return it and then start on Harvard's bindings.

"Hey! You listening to me, G.I. Joe?"

G.I. Joe.

Mick dropped the scarf and straightened. Blood rushed to his ears. The rage he'd felt on the plane came flooding back.

Jenny had been decent.

But Mick?

He just wasn't decent enough.

"How much longer are you going to make me sit here?" Harvard demanded.

"You're already dead," Mick said. "What difference do a few minutes make?"

He placed his hands against Harvard's chair and pushed.

For the Roses

Released October 1972

"Banquet"
"Cold Blue Steel and Sweet Fire"
"Barangrill"
"Lesson in Survival"
"Let the Wind Carry Me"
"For the Roses"
"See You Sometime"
"Electricity"
"You Turn Me On, I'm a Radio"
"Blonde in the Bleachers"
"Woman of Heart and Mind"
"Judgment of the Moon and Stars (Ludwig's Tune)"

All songs by Joni Mitchell.

Cold Blue Steel and Sweet Fire
by Donna Andrews

You glance in my direction, but you're not looking at me. You try very hard not to see me. I'm everything that scares you. Drunk, addict, homeless guy. Probably crazy, maybe even infected with something you could catch just from standing too close. So you don't even look at me, except with your peripheral vision, and you cross the street to get away from me and your footsteps get just a little quicker.

It's okay. I don't want to get close to you, either. You could be one of them.

You probably aren't, because my knife isn't warning me. It just lies in my pocket, inert, lifeless. If you were one of them, it would react. First a tingle, and then the chill, radiating out from the blade. Sometimes, if a very powerful one of them is nearby, the cold gets so deep it hurts to touch the knife, even through several layers of clothes, and the blade gives off an eerie blue glow, like witchfire.

It's pretty, that glow. Reassuring. And yet terrifying. Reassuring because I know it's protecting me. Detecting them and hiding me from them at the same time. And terrifying because it means they're nearby.

They're almost always nearby these days.

Most of the time I don't dare take out my knife to see the glow. Cops don't like homeless people waving knives around. Not even stubby little kitchen knives. *Only a little paring knife, officer. I just keep it to cut my food.*

But it's sharp. And the handle is steel, not plastic. Plastic damps the steel's power.

I think maybe plastic even attracts them. I stay away from it. That might be one reason why they haven't gotten me yet.

Who are *they*? Not sure it would help even I knew. I think it's a what, not a who, but I don't know. Sometimes I'm tempted to call them the Fae. I'm sure they're behind those legends. Elves. Fairies.

Not the cute little pocket-sized elves or fairies but the big beautiful scary ones with teeth. Iron was the only way to best them. Iron and steel. It's their kryptonite.

You don't believe in fairies? Fine. Neither do I. These things aren't fairies. That's just one of the ways they fool people.

The city's crawling with them tonight. No idea why. No idea if it's the whole city or just the parts where I can go. Maybe it's safe out there in the suburbs. Maybe all the trees and grass keep them away. Or maybe they got to the suburbs first. People there are soft, no street smarts. Maybe they've taken over the whole world except for the messy, dangerous parts like here.

No use worrying about that. No use and no time. Focus on the right-now problems. Like the Shelter Lady making her rounds. She's spotted me already. She's not one of them, I'm pretty sure. I think the beads have protected her, all those little metal beads woven into her braids, and both arms heavy with metal bangles. Not one of them, but she's helping them, all the same, even if she doesn't know it.

"Hey, Charlie," she says when she gets near enough. "You should come sleep inside tonight. It's going to get really cold after sunset. Down to twenty-eight."

"Think about it," I say.

"You wanna come now," she says. "Get there in time for dinner. Hot soup. You come later, we might run out before you get any."

"Okay," I say.

"Okay, you'll come?"

"Okay, I'll think about it."

She stands there looking at me, like she's trying to think what words will convince me. Or maybe she's just checking my pupils. What she doesn't say, because no one ever says it aloud, is that I should come hide in her shelter because someone's killing street people. She probably buys the story that there's a serial killer on the prowl. I know the serial killer story's just one of the ways they cover it up when they try to take someone and it goes bad. When they fail, you find the body. When they succeed, the empty shell keeps walking around with one of them in it.

"Maybe later," I say. Anything to make her go away.

"Okay," she says. "I'll look for you later. You think about it."

I nod and wrap my blanket a little tighter around me. Twenty-eight. Maybe I should find someplace to get out of the cold.

Not the shelter, though. It's underground. Church basement. You don't want to be down there after dark. In those dark hours when the powers of evil are exalted. Jail's better. It's all steel and concrete there in the jail. Safe.

Trouble is, stuff I could do to get into jail could also get me locked up in a psych ward if my luck's bad. They stay away from the jails, but they harvest the psych wards. You get thrown in a psych ward and you get sedated. It's for your own good. You'll feel much calmer in a minute. And when you're drugged out of your skull you can't fight them.

I need to keep moving. Stay warm. Find somewhere the Shelter Lady doesn't patrol. Somewhere they won't find me.

I pick up my bag and set out. If anyone is tracing my movements from above—and for all I knew they might be—they'll be puzzled. But down here on the ground there's a logic. I know where the good dumpsters are, and the mean dogs. I know which shop owners are going to call the cops if I lean against their building for a little rest and which don't care. And most important I know which streets are so thick with them that my knife will go crazy. The streets I choose, I get maybe a faint buzz now and then.

I find most of a Big Mac in one dumpster. I watch a cop hassle a panhandler and wonder which of them's setting off my knife. Maybe both of them. I move a little faster going past them.

Sunset comes a little earlier here among the tall buildings. The bright day is done, and we are for the dark. And they like the dark.

I spot Shelter Lady at the end of the street, and I'm tired. I've got no energy to argue with her. I need it all to stay awake and keep moving. So I step into an alley. Not a place she'd come looking for me. Not even a place she'd follow if she spotted me. She's brave, but she's not stupid.

I get a brief tingle off the junkie sleeping just inside the mouth of the alley. They're probably working on taking him over. Insert an invisible tendril, poke around, clear out a little of what's left of him. I'd wake him up if I thought it was any use, but he's already pretty far gone.

A little farther in is one of my hiding places. Bunch of trashcans under a fire escape. Always a few lumpy trash bags beside the cans. Overflow, or just some people can't be bothered to lift the lid. I slip in among them, and all you see is another bag in the shadows.

I can rest here for a while. Maybe even sleep a bit. I'm out of the wind, and the wall of the building's warmer than you'd expect. Somebody has their heat on tonight, and what leaks out will keep me from freezing.

Not sure how long I've been dozing when my knife wakes me. I can feel it trembling, and then it starts giving off waves of cold.

And above me the fire escape rattles slightly. Someone coming down. Stealthy, like they don't want to be seen either. Cat burglar, maybe.

My knife's so cold it almost burns.

He comes down the last flight of steps and crouches up there on the last landing. Then he swings down, hands holding onto the fire escape, until he lets go and lands on his feet. Light, like a cat.

I want to run away or pull back deeper into the shadows, but I know the only way I can stay safe is to keep still. And quiet, even though my knife hurts so much I want to scream.

Something rustles behind me. A rat, I think. The noise startles the burglar, and he looks under the fire escape.

I hear a soft hiss as he takes in breath. He sees me. He looks up and down the alley. Then he steps in closer to me.

He's holding a knife.

How can he be holding that? He's one of them; got to be, the way my knife is acting. It's not just burning cold—it's throbbing, and my head is throbbing with it. But they can't handle metal, not even coins.

Just having my knife in my jacket pocket right now is agony, so I pull it out. My first impulse is to drop it, even though I know the only way I can stay safe is to keep holding it. Hang onto it with a death grip, so even if they kill me they can't take me.

He reaches down and grabs my shoulder with his left hand. He's got his knife in his right hand. I can see it now—it's not metal—it's sleek and white. Plastic? Ceramic? No telling. Whatever it is, it's sharp.

Some long-forgotten instinct kicks in. I reach up, and instead of trying to fight him or push him away, I pull him toward me. He's not expecting that. He falls forward, and in the split second when he's gathering himself to pull back, I stab down with my knife. He goes rigid and collapses on me. I hear a clatter like someone dropped a plate. His knife, probably.

I heave him off me and turn him over so I can get my knife back. It's stuck in the back of his neck, right at the bottom of the skull. Brain stem injury, I think, and then I wonder how I know that. Did I read about it, a long time ago, before they came and made it impossible to think?

I pull my knife out and wipe it off on his clothes. It's still cold, even through my gloves, but not like it was. I tuck my knife back into my pocket. Then I reach over him and retrieve my bag.

I figure I should put some distance between me and him. My feet are starting to hurt. Frostbite, probably. I don't want to lose any more toes.

Only a couple of blocks to the church. When I get there, I have to bang on the door for a while. I can hear sirens in the distance. Plenty of reasons for sirens in this part of town, but something tells me they found the dead guy in my alley.

Shelter Lady finally opens the door.

"Charlie! You came!" You could actually believe she's glad to see me. Maybe she is.

"Got tired of walking," I say.

The room where we sleep is already dark. I let her lead me to a mat, and I lie down and pretend to go to sleep right away.

If you have to go into a shelter, the important thing is not to sleep too long at a time. You have to train yourself to wake up every hour or so. And change position every time, even if it's just a little, because if they're trying to take you that breaks it and they have to start over.

Staying awake shouldn't be hard tonight. My toes were numb when I came in, but now the circulation is coming back. First they start tingling and now they're burning. It feels like if I looked down they'd all be burned off, but it's okay. I'm not complaining. That's what coming back from frostbite feels like. Like your toes are on fire. But it's a sweet fire. A victory fire.

I lie still, with my eyes open just a crack, so I can keep an eye on the room.

I still don't like being in the shelter. Down in the ground where the dead men go. But I figure it will be okay tonight. I took out one of them. The universe owes me a little peace and quiet.

Blonde in the Bleachers
by Carol Anne Davis

I'm watching Jason as he watches the girls, casually selecting his next victim. He touches the hand of a teenager in the front row, and she grasps his fingers as he sings about quenching her desire. In reality, *he's* the one who ends up grunting and groaning on a hotel bed while his conquest lies mute. These girls dream of marrying their rock idol and living happily ever after, not of submitting to his increasingly misogynistic requests.

The band begins its encore, and I stare at the teenager, hoping that a caring mother or father will come to collect her. She appears to be on her own, but maybe there's an older sibling seated a couple of rows behind? She's probably eighteen or nineteen, which makes her legal in this state, but she looks far too starry-eyed for an egomaniac like Jason Jensen.

I'm still scanning the concert hall when he walks off stage. "Get me the brunette in the red dress." I know that her dress is actually maroon, but nuance is lost on my most successful client. I'm a thoughtful woman whose client is a Neanderthal man.

I deliberately walk past the teenager and smile instead at a twenty-something who follows us around from gig to gig. Jason's slept with her before—as have the guitarist, the drummer and most of the roadies—but he may well have been too drunk to remember. Hopefully he's gone straight to the shower, isn't watching my latest attempt to deceive.

"Jason would like to party with you backstage."

The twenty-something jumps from her front-row seat, looking as if she's won the lottery. I just don't get it. What lies will she tell herself about this sordid night? Oh, I can understand when the young actresses who sign up with my management agency chose to sleep with a top director to get a better part in his next movie, and can equally understand the young male models who become boy toys of the senior fashion editors. But Jason's groupies invariably go

93

home with jaw ache and personal membrane itching—and he never, ever phones.

He comes out of the bathroom, naked apart from a strategically draped towel, as we enter his enormous dressing room. I'm incredibly glad that I'm pushing fifty: he's never made a drunken pass at *me*.

"I wanted the brunette," he says loudly, as if he's ordering a burger.

"I did my best, but her folks collected her."

He looks the groupie up and down. "You'll do."

She reaches for his hand, smiling so widely I swear I can see her tonsils and adenoids.

It would be the end of my own career if I removed his adenoids by brute force and paid for her to have significant counseling. Sadly, these are choices I can't afford to make. If I only had to fend for myself, I'd simply get a job as a server in a wholefoods café and have a pressure-free life until retirement. But I need the money from my management company to pay for the butterfly farm.

Do butterflies need a *farm*, I hear you ask. (My hearing has always been exceptional.) Sadly, they do, as the Lepidoptera population has decreased by over fifty percent in the last twenty years, and we are heading towards a future that will be flutter-free. That's the collective noun for them, by the way: a flutter of butterflies. It's so much more appropriate than a grist of bees or a murder of crows.

I didn't know any of this, of course, when I took on the butterfly farm and its thousands of occupants. Oh, I'd seen my share of Monarchs and Purple Emperors, but that was as far as it went.

I was merely looking for a home and office when I viewed a sprawling property outside Los Angeles. At the time, I had several actors and models on my books, all of whom needed to be close to Hollywood. I had no idea that Jason Jensen and the Interceptors, the rock band I'd recently signed, would go stratospheric, and that I'd end up devoting most of my time to its loathsome lead singer.

I loved the house at first sight, and the layout was perfect. I could easily invite visitors into the reception rooms and have my living quarters tucked away at the back. There were additional bedrooms upstairs, ideal for when I had to accommodate visiting clients. As an added bonus, the asking price was compellingly low.

"Can I see the grounds?" I asked the world's thinnest realtor.

For the first time, she hesitated.

"I know about the outbuildings," I said. The man on the phone had explained that the current owners had a butterfly farm on the property, along with a tearoom and tea garden, all in various stages of disrepair.

"The owners are getting on in years, so they've let things slide a bit, but the place has enormous potential," she told me, sounding as if she was reading from a script.

I wondered if we'd find a desert strewn with tumbleweed, but instead we walked through the back door and found ourselves a mere thirty feet from an enormous wood-and-glass edifice. I'd assumed that the butterfly farm would be a large conservatory, but this was the kind of purpose-built building you might see in a zoo.

"Do you mind if I don't go inside?" the realtor asked, shuddering at the photograph of a cake in the tearoom window. "The humidity plays havoc with my hair."

"No problem." I went into the outer area and shut the door before carefully opening the smaller door to the inner sanctum. Immediately the heat enveloped me and I slipped off my jacket, glad that my T-shirt was exceptionally light. I admired the tangerine and yellow hues of what I would later learn were Question Marks and Jamaican Giant Swallowtails flitting between numerous Common Buckeyes. Although I was unaware of the demarcation at the time, I was in the room dedicated to butterflies native to the USA.

After opening and closing another door, I came to the area where the British butterflies were housed. Here there were Small Copper and Small Tortoiseshell varieties, and dozens of scarlet and black beauties that the placard on the wall identified as Red Admirals. There were also Brimstones (yellow) and Common Blues (take a wild guess) and Peacocks (which have large eye-like markings on their multicolored wings). The latter made a slight buzzing sound as they flitted nervously from plant to plant. As soon as I moved in, I went back to that room to hear the butterflies bombinating and soon grew to love that sound, the way a cat owner loves to hear a blissful purr....

Now I leave Jason to his latest conquest and drive myself home. In the lounge, I pour a generous glass of Jack Daniel's and take it out to the butterfly farm. I curl up on the chaise longue and watch my airborne tenants as I sip my bourbon before going to the adjacent kitchen to chop up some more apples and pears.

Most butterflies enjoy a liquid-only diet, sucking up the nutrients from nectar or rotting fruit or, less commonly, tree sap. They also appreciate a little sodium, so they often land on my sweaty skin. I can see how the previous owners struggled to run this as a commercial venture, constantly on the lookout for each day's corpses, since the public doesn't like to be confronted with illness and death. Fortunately, my income allows me to use the venue solely for charitable work.

I leave early the following morning, as the Interceptors' next gig is a six-hour drive away. Jason rides in the tour bus with the rest of the band: he loves the rock 'n' roll lifestyle, though part of my job is to get to the hotel in advance, to make sure they've laid on everything he needs. Oh, he doesn't want the snowy white kittens and bathtubs of asses' milk that some divas apparently insist on, but he likes a bar stocked with Jägermeister and a mini fridge filled with Giant Oreos and the ingredients to make a dozen BLTs. He also needs a George Foreman grill in his suite, as he detests room service. It's chilling how often the bellboys and waiters pass on gossip to the *National Enquirer*, and Jason gives them a lot to talk about....

That night, he attempts to go further than he's ever gone before in my presence, pointing out a girl who is certainly jailbait.

"Oh, Jason, no. She can't be more than fourteen."

"Her T-shirt says she's up for it."

She does indeed have his name and the words "I'll Do Anything For You" emblazoned across her crop top, but that is after all the title of one of the Interceptors' biggest hits.

"Girls that age are trying on their sexuality for size. She isn't ready."

"Get her," he says, and this time he watches me from the wings.

I don't get her, of course. Instead, I tell her to get out of here, because another concertgoer has accused her of pickpocketing. She starts to protest, and I hiss, "Just go. I don't want to start filling out police reports at this time of night." She flees, and I turn my weary eyes to the other stragglers, soon finding one who has seen it all before.

But this time Jason has seen it all as well, and he's livid.

"You didn't get the one I wanted."

"She lost her nerve, Jason."

"Bullshit. She was up for it."

"This is Donna," I say. She hasn't introduced herself, but it's tattooed on her neck, possibly in case she has a particularly early senior moment. As I leave, I hear the creak of his toy box as he opens the lid, and I fear that Donna is in for a particularly challenging night.

What to do? What to do? I go to my hotel room, but sleep eludes me. It's a cliché, I know, but I really am caught between a rock band and a hard place. If I do nothing, Jason will continue to commit statutory rape and ruin young life after young life, but, if I report him to the authorities, the Interceptors will be destroyed, and his three perfectly respectable band mates—all exceptionally talented musicians—will lose their careers.

I'll also lose my livelihood and have to give up the butterfly farm, disappointing the many life-limited children who visit during the months when the band is in the studio, recording. We have mobility aids and emergency breathing apparatus available, and it's so beautifully warm that even the frailest cancer patients can shed their hats without feeling cold. If you've ever seen a five-year-old girl suddenly straighten in her wheelchair and giggle as a three-inch Banded Orange Tiger brushes the sweat from her tiny fingers, you'll know why I spend all my free time down on the farm.

As an added bonus, I can afford to send my surplus stock to other butterfly farms, so as many people as possible get to view a selection of the 170,000 remaining varieties of Lepidoptera. They're not just eye candy, by the way: a world without butterflies would be a world with little to eat, as they pollinate so many of our food crops (alongside the bees, which are also in marked decline).

Suffice it to say that, after two hours of cogitating and three—okay, four—whiskeys, I make a phone call which I know will stop Jason Jensen in his designer-shod tracks. It's a call that will make him suffer, but it's also a call that will protect the nation's youth from his predatory ways....

*

The Interceptors play an outdoor gig later that week, and, at the end, Jason singles out a youngster who has rushed to the front of the stage. Hastily, I send her packing and turn my attention to the bleachers. I find a blonde who looks as if she's in her twenties and is wearing the world's shortest playsuit. It's cut to show off her tiny waist, taut buttocks and surprisingly substantial breasts.

I usher her backstage and into his dressing room.

"Jason, this is—"

He winks at her. "Tell your nipples to stop staring at my eyes."

She flashes a badge. "Jason Jensen, I am arresting you on suspicion of having sex with a minor." I hear her use other terms, such as "lewd and lascivious battery."

Jason turns to me, flushing wildly. "Oh, God. Can you—?"

I'm sure I can. I touch the woman's arm in a conciliatory gesture. "Look, these young girls throw themselves at him. They all say they're of age, and they often have the I.D. to prove it. Can't we make a donation to the police fund or something, and he'll be extra careful from now on?"

She hesitates, then stares, mesmerized, as I get out my leather-clad company checkbook.

"Are you attempting to bribe an officer of the law?"

"Not at all. As I said, you can pass the money on to the police fund. Or give it to charity. Jason loves to help others. In fact, he does charitable concerts every year."

She licks her lips. "How much?"

I name a life-changing sum. "I'll fill in the amount and leave you to fill in the name. Or make it out to cash, if you prefer. Really, we just want this to go away."

I can see the sweat running down Jason's face, and I also notice that his hands, clamped over his mouth in shock, are beginning to shake.

"Well, I'm a huge fan," she says in a softer voice. "But I'm obliged to—"

"We're all fans," I reassure her. "And, as you know, Jason has an exceptional talent that none of us wants to see go to waste."

"We could put on a show for your colleagues—free, of course," Jason stutters. "Anything you like."

"Anything?" Somehow, she manages to put a world of promise into that solitary word.

"Anything, ma'am." I can see Jason's confidence beginning to return.

She takes the handcuffs from the inner pocket of her jacket and his smile falters, then broadens as she murmurs, "You've been a very bad boy."

Which is my cue to return to the uncomplicated sanctuary of my butterfly farm.

*

I get to hear all about it a few days later, when Helena and I meet as arranged at a small wholefoods café. It's ideal for a rendezvous, not the type of place that a BLT lover like Jason would ever go. I eat here on a regular basis, so I know we're unlikely to be disturbed at this off-peak time. Helena, by the way, is the real name of the blonde in the bleachers, though I'm sure she introduced herself to Jason with a *nom de plume*.

"He's learned his lesson?" I ask.

"He's learned several lessons." She gives her familiar girlish giggle. Even in her office clothes you'd never guess that she's thirty-two years old.

"You filmed it?"

"Of course. I had the camera in my bag, set it down on his dressing table and got two hours of X-rated tape."

I watch the opening sequences on the handheld TV screen she's brought along, see Jason wearing the handcuffs, a mingled look of embarrassment and arousal on his face.

"You're going to do exactly as I say or face the consequences," Helena says.

He nods like a toy dog on the dashboard of a moving car, motivated to gratify this woman he believes is a detective and clear that displeasing her will lead to his arrest and a long prison term.

The video that follows is an extreme example of male submissiveness as she explores his well-stocked toy box and uses its contents in extremely inventive ways.

"I phoned him afterwards," she says, "and told him I've got it all on tape and will go public if he ever propositions an underage girl again."

"He still thinks you're the law?"

"Of course. I told him he could also be charged with attempting to bribe an officer and subvert the course of justice."

It's my turn to laugh. "Actually, it was me who did the bribing."

"Ah, but he was the one who persuaded you to get your checkbook out."

"How can I thank you?"

I see her swallow, eyes moistening. "What you did for my little girl was thanks enough."

I watch Helena leave the café and know that, given a couple of years, I could turn her into the household name she deserves to be. She really is a talented character actress. But she understandably gave up her career when her child became terminally ill.

That night I enter the butterfly house, clutching a smaller whiskey than usual. I feel calmer than I have in ages as I gently pick up eight dead butterflies, several the size of my palm. Some of these winged beauties only survive for three to four days, and the longest-lived are with us for mere months, but we are lucky to be touched by their gossamer brightness and to share their journey, for however brief a time.

Court and Spark
Released January 1974

"Court and Spark"
"Help Me"
"Free Man in Paris"
"People's Parties"
"The Same Situation"
"Car on a Hill"
"Down to You"
"Just Like This Train"
"Raised on Robbery"
"Trouble Child"
"Twisted"

All songs by Joni Mitchell
except "Twisted" (lyrics by Annie Ross, music by Wardell Gray).

Help Me
by Abby Bardi

The first thing I noticed about the black Mercedes was its diplomatic license plate, then the bright red lipstick on its rear window. I was a few car lengths behind, but I tried to catch up to read what it said. Someone was writing letters slowly, laboriously, and when I got closer I saw that the message was backwards but not hard to decipher: an *X*, then *E*, then *L*. As I sped up, I could see two hands bound together at the wrists with what looked like duct tape. They scrawled a *P*, then an *M*.

That's funny, I thought. It looked like someone trying to write "helpmate," or maybe it was "help me," with an *X* instead of an *H*. I happened to know that, in the Cyrillic alphabet, the *H* sound does not exist; the sound is *CH*, written as an *X*.

Finally, another *E*. *Xelp me.*

Panic shot through me. I floored my accelerator so I could get a better look, but a huge truck entered from an on-ramp and pulled in front of me, so I had to slam on the brakes. By the time I could pass, the Mercedes was nowhere in sight.

When I was able to stop and use my cell phone, I dialed 9-1-1 and told them what I'd seen. The operator sounded vaguely amused but took all my information and thanked me for being a concerned citizen.

The balconies in my building were already twinkling with holiday lights as I made my way to the one apartment that didn't have any. Holidays were torture as far as I was concerned. When I was working, I'd always gone back to Ohio to have Christmas with my parents, but since I'd quit my job, had a breakdown, gone on mental health disability and, just for fun, gained a hundred pounds, their faces no longer lit up at the sight of me. They no longer hung on every word as I told them wild tales—some made up, I admit—about my life as a spy, a word they liked to use, so I let them.

My sister had called a few times about holiday plans, but I hadn't responded to her messages. My plan was to eventually say I was coming, then at the last minute develop car trouble or a contagious illness. It wasn't that I didn't like my family, but I had trouble being around them—or, for that matter, anyone.

These were the things I was mulling over that day when I saw the writing in red lipstick, or thought I saw it. *Help me.*

No one had helped *me.*

*

A week later, I was on my way back from the liquor store and thought I'd drive past the Agency, just to see if it was still there. Normally I try to avoid that road, but every so often I feel like seeing the hodge-podge of hideous buildings and listening equipment and remembering my former life. I had loved my job, hanging out with a bunch of smart, weird people and listening to conversations through headphones all day. I had always been an introvert, but so was everyone else at the Agency, so we all got along. Eavesdropping is something introverts are gifted at, and it turned out I was pretty good at languages, too. I'd started in Arabic but switched over to Russian, which was easier and more fun. My colleagues and I would laugh about the crazy things "our" Russians said, though we weren't supposed to share what we heard.

On Friday nights, we'd hang out at a local bar. We weren't allowed to talk about what we did, exactly, but we were all intuitives and could easily guess what the others were up to. "I had Mink Man today," someone would say, and I knew that was the guy I'd heard the week before who kept trying to buy his mistress a fur coat on the black market. "Oleg and Tatiana are at it again," someone else would report, and we'd all groan, "Get a room!" I felt a pang now as I thought about my job, about the colleagues I no longer talked to, since they had sided with Bradley. I only barely remembered what it had felt like to have a normal life.

Just past the Agency, I saw the car again. I was pretty sure it was the same black Mercedes: I could tell from the diplomatic license plate. I wasn't sure what country the plate was from, since they were all encoded, but it looked like the same car. There was nothing written on the rear window, this time, but I followed it anyway.

*

Bradley and I had become friendly at work, though I hadn't noticed him at first. He was a nondescript guy with a long ponytail and wire-rimmed glasses, and he stayed up late every night playing videogames, he said, then came to work bleary-eyed and perhaps hung over. But he was a brilliant linguist and could put data together in ways that impressed our superiors, so after a few months he was promoted to supervisor. We reported to him, he did our evaluations, but he was just one of the gang. He seemed like a nice guy, but I didn't know him very well.

When I started getting weird anonymous emails, I had no idea who was sending them. At first they were playful, with remarks about my appearance—"u changed your hair. I liked it better before"—stuff like that. It occurred to me that maybe they were from someone at work, but everyone was so nice it seemed impossible. Bradley was the last person I would ever have suspected. He was always polite, respectful, slightly distant, as if he was thinking about important things and didn't have time for idle chitchat.

After a few weeks of sporadic, essentially harmless emails, the tone changed. "Cool Sailor Moon t-shirt. What would you look like naked?" This might have seemed funny to someone who was a good sport. That's the impression I got from my male colleagues when I mentioned it to them. I said, "Okay, guys, very entertaining. Now, whoever's doing this, please just stop it." But another email came the next day: "I want to rip your clothes off and make love to you." I replied NO THANKS, but the email bounced right back as undeliverable.

I immediately reported the two sexual emails to Bradley. He nodded thoughtfully and asked me to forward them to him. He said he would go to our IT people and pinpoint exactly where they'd been sent from. A week later, I asked if he'd found anything, but he said IT hadn't gotten back to him. Then, finally, he told me they'd reported that the emails were untraceable and had come from a Russian ISP address outside the Agency. There was nothing we could do about it, he said, but, if another one came in, I should let him know.

There wasn't another one.

*

The black Mercedes was speeding now as we turned north on the Baltimore-Washington Parkway. I hung back so the driver wouldn't know I was following, then finally managed to get my Yaris up to speed so I could pass. I got a good look at him: around fifty, square jaw, black felt hat, salt-and-pepper hair, black glasses, short pointy beard. He looked Russian, somehow—maybe it was the hat. He noticed me looking at him and veered into the next lane, then shot off the Parkway onto 895. I tried to change lanes to follow him and almost got broadsided by a minivan. When I got home, I opened a new box of wine and drank it for dinner.

*

The emails had stopped after Bradley's little investigation. I'd tried to forget them, but, that Friday night in the bar four years ago, I found myself eyeing my male colleagues and even some of the females suspiciously. Bradley had assured me the emails had come from outside the Agency, but what if they hadn't? How had the person known I was wearing my Sailor Moon shirt that day? It had been December and cold out, so I had on a coat when I left my apartment, and my neighbors couldn't have seen the T-shirt unless they'd been peering into my bedroom as I got dressed. I checked all my windows carefully, but there was no way to see in through my heavy drapes.

What made the email situation even more excruciating was the fact that whoever had sent them was obviously trying to mess with my head. It was nothing I could pinpoint, but there was always some underlying mocking quality to the messages' tone. *Why me*? I always wondered. The other women on my team were far more attractive. Even a hundred pounds ago, I was dumpy, pale, not terribly appealing. I'd dated off and on, but nothing special. That was fine with me—I was interested in the life of the mind, my job, my apartment, my cat (since deceased), and the small pleasures of a well-organized and routine existence. I was not looking for romance, and especially not the kind of thing my correspondent seemed to have in mind.

I had been afraid to tell my colleagues about the most recent emails because, although they all denied having sent them, I really had no way of knowing if one of them was involved. As we hung out in the bar that Friday evening, I felt like Bradley was giving me reassuring looks, as if to say *don't worry, it wasn't us*. He was unusually quiet. Though he sometimes held forth about gaming, or the dark web, or 4chan, on that particular evening he didn't say anything. Whenever I glanced over at him, he was watching me.

Finally he spoke: "I'll get the next round." A cheer went up—we knew he got paid more than we did, so we were happy to let him buy. I asked for a beer, since in those days I loved a good IPA, and he brought it to me. It tasted a bit strange, but I drank it, and, before I knew it, I was really, really drunk. Bradley offered to help me get home. He said I was too drunk to drive, so I got into his car.

I have only a weird, ghostly memory of what happened next. We were heading in the opposite direction from my apartment and I wanted to mention that, but somehow I couldn't talk. My eyes kept drooping shut, and the car seemed to be spinning. When I opened my eyes, I was lying on a bed, but it wasn't *my* bed, and Bradley was hovering over me. Then he raped me.

As he violated me, I kept saying the same words over and over: *Help me. Help me.* The words seemed to fly into the air and hover there like cartoon bubbles. He put a hand over my mouth to shut me up, but I kept saying it and saying it, or maybe I was just thinking it. *Help me. Help me.* Like that Joni Mitchell song, I thought later, though that was about love, and this was something else, something dark and fiendish and vile and wretched, something that would poison me forever and kill a part of me I could never get back. Even then, lying there helpless, weightless, like a dead person, I knew that.

Afterward, he left me there and I passed out. I think he took a shower. Then he came and lay next to me. I was still drugged—it's obvious to me now that he had put something in my beer—but I remember him putting his hand on my breast. I was still wearing the white cotton shirt I'd worn to work; he hadn't taken my clothes off except where they'd inconvenienced him. He leaned into my ear and whispered, "Admit it. Didn't it feel good?"

Didn't it feel good?

I vomited.

*

Of course I should have gone to the police. But I didn't. If I had it to do over again, I would have. But you have to understand, he was my supervisor. He was on my team. He was one of us.

This is why, when I finally told one coworker—who then told everyone else, though I'd asked her not to—no one believed me. One of them even laughed. "Brad wouldn't do that," she said. "He's not *like* that." Maybe she was dating him. Maybe she just didn't like me. By that time, several weeks later, my behavior had grown pretty strange. I was late to work all the time, or didn't come in at all, or when I *did* come in, I was still drunk from the night before. I'd switched to wine, because beer now made me sick.

Finally, I tried to file a complaint with HR. They asked for my medical records from the incident. I didn't have any. They interviewed me, and Bradley, and our whole team, and reached a verdict: it was a classic he-said-she-said situation, and there was nothing they could do. I stopped going to work. HR helped me get on disability.

My parents listened to my story with an air of sympathy—or maybe it was pity—when I went home for Christmas, but I could tell they didn't want to hear it. It wasn't that they didn't believe me—maybe they did, but they felt my going on about it was unseemly, and they were obviously shocked about what was happening to my career. My nephew had just been born, and they were thrilled that my sister had produced a boy. "Christmas is such a happy time," my mother said as she dandled him.

*

I tried not to think about what had happened. It was worse in December, even four years later, but I could handle it; I just bought as much wine as I could afford and tried not to go out, though I did have to see my psychiatrist for prescription refills. I focused on gratitude. I was grateful for my disability checks, meager though they were: I could not possibly have worked, given that I had trouble leaving my apartment. I was grateful for the few friends I had: I never saw them, but they phoned occasionally to check on me. Bradley had left the Agency soon after me, and, while they still didn't seem convinced he had done anything wrong, at least my few remaining associates purported to be agnostic about it.

I didn't think about any of this as I pondered the black Mercedes. At first I didn't know why it had resonated with me so strongly, but then I remembered the words on the back window. Had I imagined them? *Help me*—those were Joni Mitchell's words, of course, though her song placed them in a romantic context, but they were also my words. I thought of them as mine, though other people were free to use them.

I hadn't seen the person in the back seat of the car, but, because the writing was in red lipstick, I assumed it was a woman, and I imagined her as Russian because of that one Cyrillic letter. The driver had looked vaguely Russian, whatever that meant. (Don't get me wrong, I love Russia. I know they're supposed to be, if not our enemy, at least highly suspect, but I studied the language and culture during my training and I adore everything about the country—the food, the sound of the language, the alphabet with its twists and turns, the great novelists with their tragic outlook on life.)

When I closed my eyes, I could see those red words, scrawled crookedly on the back window of the Mercedes.

*

By January, I felt a little better; the difficult season had passed. On New Year's Eve, I drowned out the sounds of nearby parties with vodka shots and went to bed early. About a week later, I saw the Mercedes again. I was sure it was the same car, though it looked like there had been some damage to the rear fender and the diplomatic plate was bent. This time there was very little traffic, and I was able to pull up alongside. A blond woman was driving. She wore a black hat that looked like a man's, and her lips were bright red, the same color I'd seen on the back window. She didn't notice me staring at her as she drove, smiling, up I-95.

I followed her through the tunnel, past Baltimore, and maintained a discreet distance behind her for over an hour, changing lanes when she did, dodging the trucks that tried to come between us. As we crossed the state line into Delaware, I thought of turning back—my gas tank was almost empty, and who knew how far she was going?

Just before I gave up, she turned off the highway. I followed, a hundred yards back, and managed not to lose her as she pulled into a huge parking area next to a racetrack and casino complex. Instead of parking out front with all the other cars, she drove to the end of the long lot and pulled into a space beside a small grove of bare trees. I pulled into a space next to the casino, which seemed surprisingly crowded for late morning, and watched her step out of the car and walk the length of the lot, past me. She didn't see me, crouched behind my dashboard, but I got a good look at her: black hat, black fur coat, black leather gloves, and shiny heels the same bright red as her lipstick.

I was tempted to follow her into the casino but decided to have a peek at the Mercedes first. By this time, I'd forgotten how crazy this all was; I was on fire with curiosity about her, the car, her life. I recognized the feeling: it was how I'd always felt while monitoring people's conversations and translating their Russian into English. I had loved the way it made me feel to crack the code of people's private speech, without them ever knowing I was listening, and I missed it. I'd felt so alive, as if I were drawing vampiric energy from the messes of their lives.

It was with this same cocktail of curiosity and analytical hunger that I approached the car. I was right: the rear fender had suffered some damage, a fairly sizable dent, and one of the taillights had been shattered. The car was gleaming, as if freshly waxed, but on closer inspection looked worse for wear. I peered in the window. The tan leather interior was covered with detritus: oak leaves, loose papers, ballpoint pens, black notebooks, yellow legal pads, candy wrappers, vodka bottles, used teabags, a roll of duct tape. The back seat itself had a long, jagged tear, as if it had been cut by a knife.

Though I was afraid an alarm might go off, I tried the handle on the driver's side. The door opened, and I peered in. An empty Starbucks cup lay on the floor of the passenger side, a red lipstick stain on its rim. *This is insane,* I thought. I had broken into a stranger's car after following her for over an hour for no reason. My personal disintegration had now reached a new low.

But I couldn't stop—though something, some sixth sense, made me shiver. I glanced back at the casino but didn't see anyone coming. I got into the car—I was wearing mittens my sister had knitted, so I didn't worry about leaving fingerprints—and opened the glove box.

A purse-pack of Kleenex, a plastic wine glass and a gun.

I slammed the glove box shut and was about to turn and race back to my car, away from whatever this was, when I heard a sound. A groan.

I stopped breathing. Now I *really* wanted to run, but that same demented desire to crack the code froze me in my tracks. I stood beside the car and listened. The groan again.

With a sinking feeling in my stomach, I found the button for the trunk and popped it open. My heart was pounding as I inched toward the rear of the car and peered in.

In a vaguely fetal position, a man lay curled up in the wheel well. His face was so bloody it was almost impossible to recognize him, but I was pretty sure it was the same guy I'd seen on the highway. He had been vaguely handsome in his fast, expensive car, but now he was monstrous, cheeks swollen, eyes purpled, nose bleeding. He saw me and blinked, as if he could hardly believe it, and made another sound, not so much a groan as a death rattle. While his groans had been pathetic, a wounded animal's cries, this was menacing, even threatening. His shoes gleamed, polished and clearly expensive, perhaps from Paris. His gray trousers had perfectly pressed cuffs. His wrists and ankles were bound together with duct tape, and he seemed to be strapped to the wheel well, but he pounded his feet against the side of the trunk, demanding to be released.

I stared at him. Obviously I should free him, but he was so angry and menacing I was filled with terror. My therapist had worked on this with me, my tendency to go into freakout mode if a man even looked at me twice. This man did not seem happy, to say the least, and there I was, alone, a target. Even if I could get over the irrational part of my panic, I had no idea what he might do to me. He was yelling despite the duct tape, screaming something that sounded like "Help me!"

I was paralyzed with fear. What should I do? I could call 9-1-1, but I remembered the operator's tone during my most recent call: the same patronizing air of some of the people in HR I'd talked to about my rape, the same note of disbelief. What would the police think if I got involved in this? Would it end up in the papers?

I did the only thing I could think of: I slammed the trunk shut and made my way across the parking lot to the casino entrance.

It wasn't hard to find the blond woman: she was conspicuous in her red high heels, her black hat and gloves lying on the bar, hair loose and shining, the kind of hair some people thought was glamorous, though to me it seemed to be trying too hard. She was drinking something I was pretty sure was vodka and laughing with the bartender. They were speaking Russian.

I took the stool beside her and ordered a glass of wine. It wasn't quite noon yet, but, even on a normal day, I didn't have a problem starting early.

"So, you are Russian?" I said to her, in Russian.

She turned to stare at me. "Yes," she said, in English.

"I love the Russian language," I said in Russian. "I studied it in college." I took a long sip of my wine. It tasted cheap and acidic. That was how I liked it. "It is a beautiful language."

"It is shit language," she said in English. "What you want with me?" She didn't sound accusing or angry, just tired.

"Nothing. Just making conversation." I switched to English, since she seemed to prefer it. "I was just out for a little drive today. I think I've seen you before."

"You follow me." Now her eyes turned cold.

"No, no, but I saw you that day when you were writing on the back window."

"You are police?" Her voice turned to a hiss.

"No, I am your friend," I said in Russian. "And I understand. I think you were a prisoner in the back seat. I think that man in your trunk did something to you."

We locked eyes. She didn't speak for a long moment. Then she said, "Yes, he do something to me. So I do something to him. Now we are same. What you are going to do about it?"

I held up my glass and clinked it against hers. "Happy New Year," I said, in English, pronouncing the *H* as *CH*. "What did he do, exactly?" I asked this quite casually, as if it didn't matter.

She gave me a long stare. "I think you know what he do. What men do."

I didn't say anything for a moment. I took a big gulp of terrible wine. "So what's your plan? You're just going to take him for a ride around town?"

She threw back her head and laughed. I got a good look at her teeth: sharp, with pointed incisors, like vampire teeth. "This is good plan. Yes, ride around town."

"You know," I said in a low, confidential voice, "your car is kind of a mess."

"His car," she corrected me. "I am not keeping. I will leave somewhere."

"But—fingerprints?" I whispered.

She picked up a black leather glove from where it lay on the shiny bar and dangled it.

"But your lipstick. You must have left DNA all over."

"I have good friend." One corner of her mouth turned up. "He will fix. Is no problem."

I took a deep breath and held it. I considered never letting it out again, but then exhaled. It felt strange, as if I had never breathed before. "You must be very angry."

She reached over, grabbed my wrist and squeezed it, then squeezed harder. Just as I thought I might start yelping in pain, she let my arm drop and said in Russian, "'The darker the night, the brighter the stars.'" I recognized the line, from Dostoyevsky. "He spun me a web of glittering lies. He told me I was a beautiful goddess, a sylph, a nymph, then he trapped me in a box. I spent six months on the Baltic Sea. He made me do things—things I'd never imagined." She was speaking in lilting, beautiful Russian now, her voice like a melody I had heard before. I wondered idly if I'd ever eavesdropped on her. "Yes, I am very angry."

I stood up. "Me, too," I said in Russian. I took her hand and held it for a moment, then turned that into a handshake and walked away.

The gun was still in the glove compartment of the Mercedes, and the man in the trunk was still alive, though barely. It felt strange handling a firearm while wearing a thick, fuzzy mitten, but I managed. As I put the gun to the man's head, I thought I heard him saying something just before I pulled the trigger, but it was so faint I could barely hear it. I like to think it was *Help me.*

Free Man in Paris
by Brendan DuBois

Since Sloan's retirement, he has spent his fall and winter months in a remote villa in the village of Ilse-Sur-La-Sorgue in Provence in the south of France, and the spring and summer months in a comfortable and well-hidden flat in Paris. Even though he walks with a cane and when cold weather comes he's conscious of the shrapnel and bits of metal in his body, he is still fascinated by the narrow streets and avenues of the City of Lights. Once upon a time the great Samuel Johnson had said something to the effect that a man who was tired of London was tired of life, and Sloan knows the same can be said for Paris. There is plenty to explore and see, and he loves his walks and explorations. There is always a chance as he rounds a corner or slowly limps across an isolated park that he will see something new or amazing, like a hidden water fountain or some beautiful piece of near-forgotten sculpture.

In a way, he prefers London over Paris—no language barrier, a colorful history that he is more familiar with, and street signs he can easily read—but he chose Paris because of its more comfortable weather, and the food. Ah, the food! Sloan has traveled around the world a half-dozen times, has dined on everything from half-raw mutton to roasted grasshoppers to military rations, and in Paris he feels like he is making up for lost gastronomical opportunities. The flaky croissants, the still-warm baguettes every morning, the various sauces and soups—Charles De Gaulle once said, "How can you govern a country which has 246 varieties of cheese?"—and Sloan is fully prepared to taste every single one of those cheeses as long as he is alive.

Which is always a question, day to day.

*

On this day, Sloan limps to one of his favorite haunts, Café Travail Humide, which is at the intersection of Rue de Belleville and Rue Olivier Metra. Here the traffic is slow, there are lots of trees, and the café has outdoor seating. He goes to one of his favorite small tables and lowers himself, sitting with his back against a brick wall. In a moment, Jean-Paul, one of the older male waiters, comes out, dressed in the traditional black slacks, white shirt, and white apron that nearly goes down to his ankles.

He nods a greeting and there's a brief conversation, and, in a few minutes, Sloan's second breakfast of the day comes out: a complex cinnamon pastry, strong coffee and freshly squeezed orange juice. With a flourish, Jean-Paul unsnaps that day's copy of *The New York Times International Edition* and places it next to his second breakfast, and Sloan carefully reads the paper as he dines. Sloan is a world traveler many times over, and he still wants to call the newspaper by its old name, the *International Herald Tribune*, but one thing he has learned in retirement is to adjust to new things, new developments. One of the adjustments is how much time he now has. When he was active, mostly what he read were digests or finely distilled reports and interpretations of various news agencies. Now, he has the time to carefully read and examine the newspaper, and he is pleased that, on some days, it can take nearly the entire morning to go through the thin edition.

As he slowly eats, waiting for the coffee to cool down, Sloan glances around the small patio, recognizing most of his fellow diners. There's Zhukov, the Russian; two Chinese men who are always polite and whose names he always forgets; and the MacMillans, a retired British couple who smile a lot at each other, as if they are sharing a private joke, or are once again showing each other their pleasure in having survived to retirement and having each other's company in their remaining years.

Sloan possesses two ex-wives and no children, and he's gotten too old to worry about female companionship, though sometimes he does miss it. Truth be told, there's not much to worry about at this age, for he has a healthy pension and a fat bank account, and what really occupies his time is wondering if this is going to be the day when he will finally be killed.

Across the way a smart-looking female tourist—*American, probably*, he thinks—sits down at a table and starts leafing through a thick Fodor's guide to Paris. She appears to be in her late twenties, black hair, wearing tan slacks and a pretty red blouse and sunglasses. A heavy-looking large black leather purse is at her feet beneath the round metal table.

She stares and stares at the guidebook, not once looking back at the café and its morning customers. A few minutes pass, and the woman still hasn't turned her head.

Sloan takes his first sip of the strong Parisian coffee.

His killer is here.

*

When Jean-Paul returns to refill his coffee, Sloan talks to him in a low voice, and after slipping the man a hundred-Euro note, Jean-Paul goes over to the young woman's table and talks to her. The woman looks up, startled, and shakes her head. Jean-Paul leans down and tries again, and again.

The woman continues shaking her head, and then Jean-Paul, like Marshal Petain nearly a century ago, gives up and walks back, holding his hands out and giving Sloan a typical Gallic shrug. Sloan nods his thanks and waits a decent interval. Then he shoves himself up, leaning on the cane, and limps over to the woman.

Now she's attentive, and she whips up her head to take him in. She's attractive in the open American way, and seems to be a young woman out in supposedly Gay Paree taking in the sights, but the truth is, there isn't much to see in this part of the town. Plus her hands and forearms are strong and firm, meaning a lot of work has taken place to keep herself in shape.

"Come sit with me," Sloan says.

"Excuse me?"

He smiles at her puzzled yet concerned face. "Come, my dear. Do join me."

She attempts a smile that fails. Sloan knows there are lots of things going on in her mind. She's been briefed and re-briefed, has gone through drills and training, and Sloan is sure that having him come up and talk to her was never an envisioned scenario.

"I...do I know you?"

"I'm sure you do," Sloan says. "But still, come join me."

"I...I don't think so."

"You should."

"No," she says. "I don't think so."

Sloan nods, leans over so that only she can hear him.

"M'dear, if you don't join me, I'll kill you, here and now."

He limps back to his table.

When he gets there, he turns around and sees she's gathering up her belongings.

Sloan sits.

Waits.

The woman pauses, looks around, and comes his way.

She sits down and says, "I'm just doing this to appease your weird sense of humor. And you can buy me a cup of coffee as an apology."

Sloan nods, waves a hand at Jean-Paul, who comes over and takes her order, and then goes back inside.

"My name is Sloan," he says. "Yours?"

"Meghan."

"Ah, Meghan," he says. "A pleasure to make your acquaintance."

"I wish I could say the same."

"But you already know me so very well," he says. "You've been told of my upbringing, my service, my travels, my few successes and many blunders. And you were told that I left under dark circumstances, that some feel I was a traitor, that a subset of that group have decided I need to be killed."

"Oh, please."

Jean-Paul comes out and gracefully puts down two fresh cups of coffee and a small plate with flaky croissants, strawberries and sliced cheeses.

Sloan gestures to the plate. "Will you join me?"

She says, "Do I have a choice?"

He picks up a slice of cheese—even now, he can't tell which kind of cheese it might be—and places it into his mouth, along with a fresh strawberry.

"You have many choices," he says, enjoying the tangy and sweet taste combination on his palate. "You can leave and tell your superiors you've failed. You can kill me now, in front of these witnesses. Or you can depart and hope to find me at my pension— but, in doing that, you run the chance of missing me. I may be old, but I know how to hide where I live and to keep myself safe there."

Meghan says nothing, and Sloan adds, "Or you can stay here and enjoy this morning with me."

Meghan picks up a croissant, tears off an end, and says, "You're a piece of work."

"An old and damaged piece of work. But one with a functioning mind, which is a threat, isn't it?"

"I don't know what you're talking about."

"You certainly do," he says. "I can tell you're trying to deceive me, and you're failing. Your hands are quivering, just a bit. You can't look straight at me, and your eyes are flickering just a little. M'dear, those are all signs of deception."

"You—"

"And deception is something that exists in all cultures, in all parts of the world. Trust me, when you're alone and deep in the mountains near the Khyber Pass, carrying an AK-47 over one shoulder and a duffel bag full of hundred-dollar bills in the other, you have to read the face of the tribal leader who's sitting across from you. And you have to puzzle out if he's going to take your money and grant your request, or just take your money and slit your throat."

Meghan eats another piece of the croissant.

"But I'm sure you already know that, don't you?" Sloan says.

She picks up a cloth napkin. It drops to the stone terrace, and she bends over for it. Her face is red with embarrassment.

"An accident," he asks. "Or a signal?"

"What?"

"Young lady, your hearing is perfect, otherwise you wouldn't be here," he says. "The napkin drop. Was it an accident, were you signaling an observer that you are close to performing your mission, or were you telling him or her that it is falling apart?"

She wiped her fingers, took a breath. "You seem like a nice old man, but a bit paranoid."

"Even paranoids can have enemies."

"And why would you have enemies?"

"Because I'm an outlier," he says. "I survived, I retired and I've kept my mouth shut. No TV appearances, no op-ed columns in the *Post* or the *Times*."

"How does that make you dangerous?" she asks.

He stirs some sugar into his cup. "I've kept my mouth shut. Does that mean I'll keep it shut forever? Or does it mean that, at some point, I will give up what I know for a nice payoff?"

Meghan takes another tear from her croissant. "And you think...that makes you a target?"

"I do."

"Because of what you know?"

"Absolutely," he says. "You know what Stalin once said about problems: 'Death solves all problems—no man, no problem.'"

"And now *you're* a problem?"

Sloan smiles. "No, I was always a problem, as I'm sure you know. Never made it as a station chief or director because I preferred to be in the field, working hard, and not filing BS field reports."

Meghan stops eating. Then she looks at her coffee cup and takes a slow sip.

Sloan leans in. "So how are you planning to do it? A quick stiletto to my ear? A spray of nerve gas to my face? A signal to a sniper on the roof that all is well, and that the shot is permitted?"

Meghan puts her cup back down on the table. "Let me make this as clear as I can," she says. "I don't know what you're talking about. I'm a grad student from Columbia University in New York. I'm here to do some research on medieval architecture for my thesis. *Finis*. The end."

Sloan says, "Please do excuse me," and he suddenly grasps her right hand, runs his old fingers along her young fingers, and then traces up her wrist. She recoils, as if a grumpy male gynecologist with ice-cold hands was examining her.

"What the hell is this all about?" she demands.

He releases her hand, nods. "My apologies. Sometimes touching reveals more than seeing...and my touch finds a very muscular wrist, very strong right hand, and calluses along your first finger and the web between it and your thumb. Meaning a right hand that is used to a lot of physical labor. With those calluses, I'd guess shooting a weapon, over and over again."

Somewhere a clock chimes. Sloan says, "Marines? Army? Special Activities Division of the CIA?"

Her face falters, and Sloan knows that at last he's found a chink in that very cool and professional armor.

"My apologies, young lady, but it seems you've failed in your mission," he says. "I'm still alive, and your cover has been blown. So there are just two options available for us. Shall I go on?"

Meghan says not a word. Which makes sense. If she's wired for sound, or if there's a shotgun mike being used in her direction, she won't admit a damn thing.

But there's the slightest movement of her chin.

"Options?" she asks.

"That's right," he says. "Option one is that you leave now, and tell your superiors to leave me the hell alone. I've kept my mouth shut all these years, and I intend to keep it shut for a long time to come."

She attempts a smile. "While not admitting a damn thing, that's not an option that's enforceable, now, is it? I could leave, but what you're asking for…how would you know that it ever happened?"

"I suppose I would just have to rely on your word as an officer and a lady. Or an NCO and a lady. Or a former member of the armed services and a lady."

Her smile widens. "And what's option two?"

"If you don't agree to option one," he says, "you'll be dead within the next fifteen minutes."

That certainly gets her attention, and the hand that is bringing up a piece of croissant drops to her lap.

"You've got one hell of a nerve, threatening me like that," Meghan says.

"I never make threats," he says. "Only promises. And I promise that you will be dead…well, in about *ten* minutes, unless you agree to depart and tell your superiors, in no uncertain terms, to leave me the hell alone."

She reaches down for her bag, her chair scrapes back, and he says, "Note that I didn't say you'd be shot. Or stabbed. Or strangled."

"What?" Meghan asks, eyes wide.

"I just said you'd be dead," he says. "That's all."

Her eyes are still wide, and she looks down at her half-eaten croissant and almost empty cup.

"Very good," he says. "Death doesn't have to be violent, now, does it? It can be quiet, undetectable…something that won't be revealed in an autopsy. At some point, a Parisian forensics team will just shrug their shoulders and say, *death by natural causes.*"

"You poisoned me," she says.

Sloan shakes his head. "No. *We* poisoned you."

She slumps back in her chair. "Who the hell is *we*?"

He points up at the café's sign. "Can you translate the name?"

Meghan looks up. "Café Travail Humide. Something to do with work. Correct?"

"Not bad," he says. "It's not the best translation, but it roughly means Café Wet Work. Do you get the reference?"

His guest shakes her head.

Sloan says, "Tsk, what they're teaching you young'uns nowadays."

"Please," she whispers.

He takes pity on her and says, "From the early days of the NKVD, the KGB and FSB, the Russians have always had a special bureau for assassinations and political murders. The nickname for this type of job was 'wet work,' because when you kill someone up close and personal, you can get blood on your hands or shoes."

Off in the distance, he hears the pulsating siren of a French police car. He goes on. "The name of our café...it reflects who owns it, who frequents it. You see, at all points in their lives and careers, field agents like me look forward to retirement. But what kind of retirement? Sitting quiet and alone in a senior citizens' community? Taking up golf? Or bridge? No, not that...but here, we can ensure a financial future for ourselves and have a place where we can gather, reminisce, and make friends with old enemies."

She looks around, and he says, "That's right. We're all here. Chinese, British, Russian, Bulgarian...."

"But...why?"

He shrugs. "After years of working in the field, following orders, lying and killing for our countries, we few, we unhappy few, we realized that we had more in common with each other than with our respective fellow citizens. They could never understand who we are, what we did."

Meghan says, "Please…I'm sorry. Is there—?"

"An antidote? But of course. Yet you must realize—"

"The first option," she says. "Please. I'll do it. Honest."

Sloan turns and catches the attention of Jean-Paul. He waves his hand, holding up one finger. Jean-Paul nods and briskly walks into the café.

"He'll be along shortly," Sloan says. "No worries. There's plenty of time. Will you allow me to quote you some music?"

She bites her lower lip, then slightly nods.

"Years ago," he goes on, "Joni Mitchell released a song, 'Free Man in Paris.' Lovely title, don't you think? It sounds like something from World War II, perhaps, about the Resistance or something similar. But no…it was a song about her friend, the music producer David Geffen. They were spending time together in Paris, and Geffen was pleased that he was in a place where he could feel free, with no phone calls, no messengers, nobody bothering him."

Jean-Paul emerges from the café, carrying a small round serving platter, with a small glass balanced in the middle, filled halfway with a clear liquid.

Sloan says, "But there are four lines that have always stuck with me. Would you care to hear them?"

She nods.

He quotes:

"I was a free man in Paris, / I felt unfettered and alive. / There was nobody calling me up for favors, / no one's future to decide."

Jean-Paul lowers the platter and Meghan grabs the glass and downs the liquid in three quick gulps. She makes a face as if she's just swallowed cod liver oil and whispers an obscenity.

Sloan smiles. "So here we are. Free men and women, living in Paris, no longer asked to do foul things. Do you understand now, Meghan?"

She glares at him, picks up her bag, and quickly walks away.

A few minutes later, Jean-Paul sits down across from Sloan. "So," he says, in clear English, for Jean-Paul is not French, but French-Canadian, and is retired from the Canadian SIS. "It went well?"

"Thanks to you, my friend."

Jean-Paul slowly gathers up the dishes from Meghan's breakfast. "Do you think it will work?"

"She's alive," he says. "And she will deliver the message."

"Are you sure?"

Sloan picks up his coffee cup, takes a warm and satisfying sip.

"We'll never be *quite* sure, now, will we?" Sloan says. "But one thing will always be certain."

"Which is what, my friend?"

He smiles. "We're all free men, at least for today."

Jean-Paul smiles. "Until tomorrow."

"Always until tomorrow," Sloan says, picking up his newspaper, looking forward to the rest of the day, however long it might last.

The Hissing of Summer Lawns

Released November 1975

"In France They Kiss on Main Street"
"The Jungle Line"
"Edith and the Kingpin"
"Don't Interrupt the Sorrow"
"Shades of Scarlett Conquering"
"The Hissing of Summer Lawns"
"The Boho Dance"
"Harry's House/Centerpiece"
"Sweet Bird"
"Shadows and Light"

All songs by Joni Mitchell.

Shades of Scarlett Conquering
by Adam Meyer

Even for a Wednesday night, things were slow at Sonny's Video Emporium. I was just about to pick up my trigonometry textbook— my parents had warned me I'd have to cut back my work hours if I got another C—when Nathan came up behind me, holding a stack of videotape boxes to be shelved.

"Babe alert at ten o'clock," he whispered.

Turning, I saw a woman dressed in skin-tight jeans and a long black sweater, her blood-red nails raking the spines of the brightly colored VHS boxes spread across the clearance table. At that angle she looked pretty enough, with her wavy dark hair and her sharp cheekbones, though her nose was a shade too long and her eyes too far apart. When she turned, however, and her piercing green eyes locked on mine, my heart stuttered. This woman, whoever she was, was the most beautiful creature I'd ever seen in Sonny's—maybe in my entire life.

"Can we help you, ma'am?" Nathan asked.

"I certainly hope so." Her gaze shifted from me to Nathan as if she was trying to decide which of us was less likely to disappoint her. "I've been looking around, but I can't seem to find your classic movies section."

She had a hint of a southern accent, the "I" coming out sounding more like "Ah." Leaning in, I could see faint lines around her eyes and realized she was older than I'd first thought—maybe mid-thirties—but that didn't take the edge off her beauty. In fact, it probably added to it.

"It's, ah, right behind you," I said.

"That?" She put one hand on the strap of her big black designer handbag and waved the other dismissively at the thinly covered shelves. "That's barely even a taste of what's out there. Where's *Vertigo,* or *Double Indemnity,* or *The African Queen*?"

I was quiet, because I'd never even heard of those movies and didn't want to show my ignorance. Fortunately, Nathan—a few years older than me—had taken a couple cinema classes at SUNY New Paltz.

"You like Bogart," he said, eyes lighting up. "We've got *The Maltese Falcon*."

"Completely overrated. Bogart practically sleepwalks through the whole picture."

I'd never heard anyone call a movie a *picture* before, though at least I knew who Humphrey Bogart was.

"I totally disagree," Nathan said, puffing out his chest a little, the way he did when he was about to lecture someone on the French New Wave or the genius of Kubrick. "I think the sepia-toned palette really reflects the sense of ambiguous morality that—"

"Nonsense, the movie's just plain dull." The woman shifted her laser focus back to me. "What do *you* think?"

"I, um, I haven't—"

She shook her head. "You wouldn't know Peter Lorre from Peter Fonda, would you? How unfortunate."

With that, she turned on the heels of her shiny leather boots—the kind that would do little against the punishing snows coming in off the Hudson River in another month or two—and spun away. I figured that would be the last we'd see of her at Sonny's, and I'm sure so did Nathan. Neither of us took our eyes off her as she walked out.

"What a know-it-all," he said, grabbing a tape from the counter and heading off to shelve it. I glanced out the window—the woman was still visible, making her way across the strip mall parking lot—and I felt a sense of urgency I've only experienced a few times in my life. Some part of me knew, just *knew*, if I let her walk away without doing something, I'd always regret it.

I waited a moment, looking down at the countertop, then up at Nathan. "Hey, you mind if I take a quick break?"

If Nathan looked at me, surely he'd see it all written on my face: the fear, the desire, the uncertainty. But his eyes were trained on the wall labeled NEW RELEASES, as he tried to find a place for *Die Hard* on the crowded shelf. "You're closing, right?"

"Yeah."

"Sure, go ahead. Just be back by six-thirty, okay?"

I hurried out to the lot, glancing quickly at the bruised blue-black sky. For a moment, I thought the woman was gone. But then I saw her beside a shiny red sports car that had as many curves as she did, one arm reaching into her oversized bag. Her eyes flicked up at me, dismissive and suspicious, and immediately I felt deflated, abandoned by whatever confidence had propelled me this far.

"What's your name?"

"Glenn."

She pursed her dark red lips. "I'm Scarlett. And I hope that someone gives you a real movie education someday, Glenn."

"Me, too, I guess."

As she reached into her bag to pull out her keys, I spotted a couple of the yellow stickers we put on our clearance videos. She adjusted the bag to hide the tapes and looked directly at me, daring me to call her a thief. I didn't. I was too shocked to say a word, and also faintly aware that she was judging me as much as I was her.

"Goodnight, Glenn." She jabbed her key into the door lock, then turned to face me one more time. "By the way, do you know anything about VCRs? The picture on mine's gotten a bit fuzzy. Maybe you're handy with that sort of thing?"

"I—"

My mouth hung open like the register drawer when I'm trying to figure out the correct change on someone's late fees.

"Never mind. See you around."

As she tossed her bag with the stolen videos into the car, I finally found my voice. "Have you checked the coaxial cable? If it gets loose, that can sometimes—"

"Honestly, I don't know what you're saying. But perhaps you could look at it for me."

I couldn't tell if this was a question or an order. "You mean come by?"

"I live off Davenport Road." She gave me the address. "I'll be around all day Saturday, but I'm not an early riser."

A moment later, she was peeling out of the parking lot. I just stood there and watched her go, hands shoved in my pockets, starting to shiver in the evening breeze.

*

Scarlett lived in an old frame house that had once belonged to the town librarian. When I turned into her front drive, her Trans Am was angled toward the front porch, and a shiny new Buick was tucked away on the far side of the house, out of view from the road. I climbed the porch steps and looked at my reflection in the door glass, smoothing down a piece of stray hair I could never seem to tame. Giving up, I knocked.

"You came," Scarlett said, holding the screen door open. She wore black stretch pants and a Duke University T-shirt. Her makeup was freshly applied, and she smelled of bath gel.

"I'm not too early, am I?"

"It's after two. I'd hardly call that early for any decent person." I looked around her living room. I'd been here a couple times when Mrs. Wilkerson owned the place, but it was unrecognizable now. The curtains were red silk, the furniture big and old and satiny, the walls covered with movie posters: *Gone with the Wind*, *The Lady from Shanghai*, *Suddenly Last Summer*.

"Here you go, the TV."

The big boxy thirty-five-inch Sony rested on a low wooden chest, surrounded by videotapes. Most of the titles I didn't know, and there were black-and-white images on their covers. But scattered among them I saw two with yellow stickers, the ones she'd taken from Sonny's.

"There's a tape in there already," she said, nodding at the VCR. "Go ahead."

I turned on the TV and, reaching for a bulky remote control, pressed Play. A man stood in a dimly lit room, smoking a cigarette, pacing back and forth. Black and white, of course. The image was slightly warped at the top and bottom, and scratchy white lines ran across the screen.

"This might just be the tracking," I said, jabbing at the remote. A minute later, the image was pristine. The man was looking at a blond woman in a coat, both of them acting jittery, nervous. I looked over for Scarlett's approval, but she had already left the room. I heard a toilet flush upstairs.

Waiting for her to come back, I sat on the edge of the couch and watched the TV. Normally, I only see black-and-white movies if I poke my head into my father's den while he's watching old Westerns. This seemed different, though. Seeing these actors slide in and out of the shadows, I felt like I had discovered a portal into a forgotten world.

"It's good, isn't it?" Scarlett had appeared in the kitchen doorway, an open bottle of beer in her hand. "It's called *Double Indemnity*, and the story—well, I don't want to ruin it for you. Why don't you take it?"

"Home, you mean?"

"Unless you're too busy watching *this* nonsense." She grabbed one of the movies she'd swiped from Sonny's, holding it out like a dead fish. "I couldn't get more than twenty minutes through this one. The lead actor has some charm, but not enough to carry it."

"You don't like Mel Gibson?"

She shrugged, as if she had little opinion of the most famous movie star in the world. "I'd rather watch the classics than subject myself to what they call pictures these days. We'll see if you agree."

She hit the eject button on her VCR and handed me the tape.

"I'll have it back in a few days."

"Take your time. I've got plenty to watch." She gestured at a bookcase in the corner. There were a couple of paperback novels on the shelves, but mostly they were packed with videocassettes. "What do you think of my collection?"

With the weight of Scarlett's eyes on me, I wanted to say something wise.

"It's, ah, pretty cool."

Scarlett laughed, a sound that shredded the last of my confidence. But her eyes sparkled. I was trying to think of something clever to add when a deep voice boomed. "Hey, darlin'?"

A man lumbered down the staircase. I recognized Gerald Crosby instantly, though I was used to seeing him in suits, not jeans and a pullover sweater. A former football star at Shadwell High, he was best known as a lawyer who starred in his own local commercials, which featured Crosby behind a desk telling people, "Don't settle for less." I had seen him around town from time to time, with his wife and two little blond daughters.

"Oh," he said, looking at me.

"He was just leaving," Scarlett said. "See you around the video store."

"You work at Sonny's?" Crosby asked, smiling. "Anything good come in lately?"

Before I could answer, Scarlett replied, "Please, he's got terrible taste. I'm trying to do something about that, but we'll see."

I felt a flutter in my belly—the hint of invitation in her words was intoxicating—but when I looked back she had draped herself around Crosby.

"See you around," I said, tucking the copy of *Double Indemnity* under my arm. I headed out just as Crosby touched Scarlett's cheek, her dark eyes looking past him, focused on the blank TV.

*

I watched *Double Indemnity* that night and, after a brief bathroom break, watched it again. I was captivated from the opening sequence, when a sweaty, shaken Fred MacMurray records his murder confession, all the way to the closing, when he slumps down in the doorway of the insurance office and gets a light from Edward R. Murrow. Sure, the slow pace of it took some getting used to, as did the slightly mannered acting style, but there was something about it that captured me. The all-consuming passion that takes hold of Fred MacMurray. Barbara Stanwyck in those tight blouses. The way she manipulates him into doing exactly what she wants and needs.

The whole time, I kept thinking of Scarlett.

The next morning, I drove out to the edge of Davenport Road, pulling over onto the shoulder and studying Scarlett's house. I hoped I might catch a glimpse of her through one of the front windows or on the porch, but she didn't appear. I walked in a little from the roadway but didn't see Crosby's Buick there, either, so I assumed she was alone. I imagined going up to her front door, the VHS of *Double Indemnity* in hand. "Did you like it?" she'd ask, and pull me close, curling those blood-red nails into the nape of my neck as she kissed me, lips pressing so hard I couldn't breathe.

I let that fantasy play and replay in my head, like a tape on a loop, as I watched and waited. Finally I started the car and drove away. I didn't want to be late for work.

It was a Sunday, and I had the noon-to-six shift at Sonny's. I found myself spending the whole day wondering if Scarlett would show up. Noticing my constant glances at the front door, Nathan said, "Forget it, she's not coming back."

"Who's not coming back?" I asked, going around the counter, straightening videotapes. I always find it easier to lie if my hands are moving.

"That lady who thinks she knows everything about old movies."

Bet she knows a lot more than you do, I thought, but said nothing. Nathan's ego can be fragile, especially when a woman is involved.

"I asked around about her a little," he said.

That caught my attention, but I was careful not to seem too eager. "Hear anything interesting?"

"Her name's Scarlett, Scarlett Dupree. She's from Durham, North Carolina, her father owned a movie theater there when she was a kid. Place closed down years ago, after her parents were killed in some kind of car accident. Her grandmother raised her, she moved away, moved back, got married. She had some kind of admin job at Duke, worked there until about a year ago. She quit soon after her husband died."

The word that seemed to stick in my brain was *husband.* I thought back to Scarlett's living room, tried to remember if I'd seen a wedding photo, or any family photos at all. But I hadn't.

"Seems like he left her pretty well fixed, so she took some time off. Then, a couple months ago, she took a job working as the assistant to the humanities dean at Bard and moved up here. Seems like a long way to go for secretary work. Plenty of schools down south."

I shrugged. The idea of moving far away from home made sense to me. Then again, Nathan was twenty-four, old enough to go anywhere he wanted, and he had chosen to stay where he was.

"Maybe she just wanted a change," I said, trying to keep my voice neutral. Like I didn't much care about Scarlett's situation, one way or the other. "A fresh start."

"Maybe." Nathan sounded skeptical. "Or maybe she was running away from something."

*

Three days later, Scarlett showed up at the store again. We didn't get much foot traffic on Wednesday evenings. People who had rented movies the weekend before had already returned them, leaving us in a kind of midweek lull. Nathan was in the back, doing inventory, and I was behind the counter, poring over my trig book for a test the next morning. As Scarlett came in, I smacked the book closed, watching as she made her way toward me.

"Favorite scene?" she asked, her lips turning up in the faintest hint of a smile.

"I, ah—"

I had been preparing myself for this conversation for days, but now my mind seemed to have turned to mush. "The one where he says he's not going to help her kill her husband, and he storms out of the house. But we know better, even if he doesn't, not yet."

She nodded her approval.

"A reasonable choice. I like the one where he confronts her, tells her he knows what she's done, and why she's done it."

"That's a good one, too."

I remembered the scene. "We're both rotten," she tells him, trying to shift the blame.

"Only you're a little *more* rotten," he says, and she doesn't deny it, just looks at him with that unique mixture of defiance and pride.

Scarlett turned up her chin, studying me closely. "You seem to have an appreciation for the classics. Would you like to see more?"

The word "yes" was only one syllable, but my mouth had a hard time saying it.

"Come by my house Friday night. There's something I want to show you."

She left. Her words were still ringing in my head when Nathan came out of the back room.

"Who was that?" he asked.

"Scarlett." Just saying her name left me a little breathless. "The lady who—"

"What was she looking for this time?"

I stuck a scrap of paper in my trig textbook, set it aside. "She was just browsing."

"You sure?"

Feeling the pressure of Nathan's gaze, I looked away. "What do you mean?"

"Rumor has it she was caught shoplifting from the Price Chopper the other day. And I noticed we're a couple titles short on the clearance inventory. If she comes in here again, keep an eye on her."

I had no trouble telling the truth this time. "Absolutely, I will."

*

That Friday night, when my parents asked me where I was going, I said I was heading out to a movie with some friends. Even though my mom and dad would never have stopped me from going to Scarlett's, I didn't want them asking a bunch of questions, either. Besides, I've always liked having secrets.

I knocked at Scarlett's front door and waited, then knocked again. Finally, hearing no answer, I walked in. The first thing I noticed was that all the lights were off. I moved carefully through the almost-dark, finding my way by the glow of the TV screen. The smell of burnt popcorn hung heavily in the air. I inched forward, holding a bouquet of flowers I'd bought on the way, feeling both foolish and anxious.

"There you are," she said, stepping out of the kitchen. She handed me a glass bowl full of popcorn. "I burned it a little. You'll have to pick through to find the ones that aren't black."

"Um, thanks."

"And what's this?" She took the flowers with an amused look. "Why, thank you, Glenn. You're a true gentleman. But I hope you don't think—"

She shook her head at me, her long dark hair shimmering. "I should have been more clear about my intent, shouldn't I?"

"No, I just...my mother taught me never to show up at someone's house empty handed."

"A well-raised boy." She brought the flowers to her nose, inhaling deeply. "You remind me a little of Jimmy Stewart, you know."

Was that a compliment? I'd seen him in some of the old Westerns my father liked so much. I'd always thought he looked like a pushover, with his oversized ears and his expression of perpetual confusion.

"Maybe it's just that earnestness, that sense of goodness, that comes off of you. Sure, you like the idea of being a rebel, but beneath it all you're a good kid, and someday you'll be a good man, the kind who always does the right thing."

Was Scarlett right about me? I hoped so. I followed her to the kitchen, where she set the flowers on the counter beside a scattering of blackened popcorn kernels. A faded photo hung on the wall. It showed a teenage girl in a green silk dress, her hair pinned up, her chin raised to expose her graceful neck.

"That's me," she said, filling a crystal vase with water. "A million years ago."

"You look—"

A sudden hardness in her eyes stopped me. Would she be upset if I told the truth, that she looked stunning, luminous, impossibly young?

"—happy," I said, watching her reaction closely.

"Do I?" she asked, setting the vase on the counter. "I'd like to think I was."

I looked around the room, then blurted, "You don't have any wedding pictures."

"Who said I was married?"

"Well, I—"

She waved a hand. "I understand: it's a small town, and people gossip. Louis and I were never very happy. Is it wrong of me to say I'm not sorry he's gone?"

I felt a lump in my throat, too big to swallow. "What did he die of?"

"Excessive pride. And a heart attack. At least that's what the doctors said...even after an autopsy, they couldn't be sure. I've had some problems with the estate, which is how I met Mr. Crosby."

"Are you going to marry him?"

She flashed me an amused look. "As you can imagine, Mrs. Crosby might object to that. Besides, a woman must have everything, and while Mr. Crosby offers certain pleasures, that's not enough for me. It never is. I like a certain amount of...freedom, I suppose." She picked up a wineglass and took a long sip. "Now, any other questions before we start the movie?"

Soon I was sitting on the couch, perched on the edge of the cushions, aware of the faint scent of her perfume even more than the popcorn smell. She was less than two feet away, one hand on her wineglass, the other at her chin, her eyes glued to the TV. I tried to keep my gaze there, too, but it kept drifting to Scarlett, as if there was some magnetic force inside her that pulled my eyes from the screen.

The movie was another James M. Cain adaptation, *Mildred Pierce*. I found this one slower and more plodding, although the performance by Joan Crawford was good, and the relationship between her and her daughter had a kind of spark to it. Still, I could barely follow the plot. I was aware at every moment of Scarlett beside me, shifting so her legs were beneath her, leaning in ever so slightly toward me, the faint warmth of her breath on my cheek.

Halfway through the movie, she hit Pause and turned to me. "You haven't fallen asleep, Glenn, have you?"

She sounded like she was teasing, but there was an edge of accusation underneath, as if she felt I wasn't giving the movie its due.

"Absolutely not," I said.

She reached for her wineglass, realized it was already empty. "This is a test, you know."

"Of what?"

"Of how interested you really are. *Double Indemnity*, now that was easy. But this one…its charms aren't so obvious to the casual viewer. I want to see what kind of audience you are. Because my tastes, they can be a little unorthodox."

"Mine, too, sometimes."

She looked at me then, her dark eyes fixed on mine, and I moved toward her without thinking. Her lips were soft and her skin was warm and the powdery scent of her was so strong I felt like I was drowning in it. I'd kissed girls before, but it had never felt like this, with such a peculiar rush of excitement and danger flooding through me.

"Glenn, please—"

It took a moment for the words to register, as if they were beamed from a distant radio signal. But Scarlett's face showed a mixture of worry and disappointment, and I knew I'd made a mistake.

"I better go."

I stood up so quickly my right knee banged the coffee table, Scarlett's wineglass wobbling on its surface.

"Hold on, Glenn." She patted the couch beside her. "Let's at least watch the rest of the movie."

She reached for me, but I backed away, feeling a twinge in my knee.

"Maybe another time," I said.

Scarlett turned on a lamp, and I blinked against the brightness, needles jabbing my eyes. She put a hand on my arm as if to keep me there. Her touch was both steely and gentle, and I hated the way it set my nerve endings on fire.

Still feeling the tingle of Scarlett's lips on mine, I felt my body hum. "Gerald Crosby's wrong for you. You deserve better."

"There's something you should know about me, Glenn. I'm not a good person. But I've always gotten what I deserve." She touched my cheek with her hand and smiled so gently I felt she might fade away into the gloom, like an image from one of her favorite movies. "And I hope that, someday, you will, too."

*

I watched *Double Indemnity* again that night, studying it as though there were clues to Scarlett hidden somewhere in its grainy images. Maybe there were. The next couple days at the video store, I looked up every time the front door pinged, hoping it would be her. At night I drove to Davenport Road and watched her house, trying to get up the nerve to approach.

Finally, I couldn't take it anymore. On a drizzly Friday evening, I parked in front of Scarlett's house and knocked. I waited for her to answer, but she didn't. I'd seen her moving through an upstairs window, so I knew she was home. I knocked again, harder this time, feeling the door shake beneath my fist, didn't stop knocking until my hand was sore.

Then, turning away, I saw a wineglass on the arm of a wicker chair on the porch. There was a curve of bright red lipstick on its rim, a residue of dark wine at the bottom. I could imagine her sitting here, staring off into the darkness, her long legs stretching out before her as she sipped from the glass, brooding.

The rain had become a deluge by the time I got back to my old Malibu. I slid behind the wheel, as cold and wet as a dog left out in the yard.

I only drove as far as the edge of Davenport Road, where I pulled into the brush and turned off my headlights and waited, staring back at the house. I'd told my parents I was going out with some friends to a movie and dinner, so they weren't expecting me for a couple hours. I didn't have to wait that long. The Buick pulled up half an hour later, again parking behind the house, out of sight of the road. I watched Crosby hurry beneath a wide black umbrella to the safety of the porch. A few minutes later, a light went on in the bedroom upstairs. I drove away.

Back home, I got my father's hammer from the toolbox on the pegboard wall in the garage. I set *Double Indemnity* on my dad's workbench and smashed it. I pounded it again and again, watching the case shatter, yanked the thin ribbon of tape out like a black plastic tongue and hammered some more, then finally threw the whole mess into the trash.

*

Two days later, the telephone woke me. My parents were early risers and had gone to church, and I was in the house alone. I would've let the call go to the answering machine, but I had an idea who might be on the line.

"Glenn? It's me. Scarlett."

"What's wrong? You sound upset. Are you okay?"

"I'm fine, it's just…it's Gerald. Mr. Crosby."

I worked hard to keep my voice neutral. "What about him?"

"Last night, he stayed late at his office, called his wife about nine o'clock and said he was on his way home. He never made it."

"What happened?"

"He's missing. The police think…well, whatever happened, they think I had something to do with it." Her voice broke, the sound of her crying coming across the line. "They're wrong, Glenn. I'd never lay a hand on him, I swear. But the police, that's not how they see it."

"I don't understand."

"The cops—they need someone to blame, I suppose. The thing is, I was scared, and I told them I was with you last night. I said we were here, watching movies, and that you left a little after midnight." Her voice was unsteady. "I know it's a lie, but they were coming on strong and I panicked." She paused for a moment. "Where *were* you last night?"

"I went to Kingston to see a movie. Alone."

"Perfect. If you say you were with me, no one will know the difference."

"You should tell them the truth. There's no reason for them to think you did anything wrong."

She took a long pause before going on. I waited. I would've waited forever to hear her voice again.

"There's something I haven't told you about my husband," she said carefully. "He did die of a heart attack, but the Durham police—they thought it might have been induced by poison. I was under investigation for a time. In the end, they cleared me, of course. But that's why...I hope you'll back me up here. I know it's a lot to ask, but, please, Glenn—"

"You want me to lie for you?" I could hear my voice rising in pitch. "I mean, what if you really *did* do something—?"

I didn't say the word *criminal*. I didn't have to.

"Glenn, I haven't done anything wrong. You have to believe me."

Of course I would give her what she wanted. I had no choice.

"Scarlett, I'm just not sure—"

"Please, Glenn, say you will. I need you to do this for me."

That word caught in my brain. *Need*. No woman had ever needed anything from me before. No woman like Scarlett, anyway.

"Yes, of course, I'll say I was there. But people thinking you had a teenage boy at your house...it won't make you look very good, will it?"

"No, but at least it's not a crime." Scarlett sounded perfectly calm all of a sudden, as if she had never been upset at all. "Besides, maybe the police will find Gerald at some motel in Kingston or something, with a hooker and a serious hangover, and I won't have to worry about this anymore."

"I sure hope so," I said.

*

Scarlett was wrong. A day later, they found Gerald Crosby along the banks of the Kingston River, his head bashed in with a rock, his pants pulled down to his ankles, his face gnawed at by coyotes. At least that was the rumor, which the police wouldn't confirm or deny, even when I was sitting with a detective named

Clarence Williams in a conference room at the station, my parents sitting nervously in the corridor outside.

"How well do you know Ms. Dupree?" Detective Williams asked, leaning in. He had a gentle manner and a tuft of silver hair that he kept pushing back into place across his steep forehead.

"Like I said, I met her at the video store. She'd invite me over to watch movies sometimes."

"Did you ever see Mr. Crosby there?"

"Once," I admitted.

"Do you know what the nature of their relationship was?"

I shrugged. "I didn't think too much about it. None of my business."

"But you must've had some ideas."

"I could guess. But we didn't talk about that kind of thing."

We went around and around like this for a while, and finally Detective Williams slid his chair around, trying to get closer. For a moment I thought he was going to put his arm around me, the way my father sometimes did when he wanted to lecture me about something.

"You're a good kid, you got your whole life ahead of you. But I want you to understand, this woman's dangerous. You shouldn't try to protect her."

"I'm not."

"Do you know what kind of car she drives?"

"Um, a red sports car."

He leaned back in his chair, studying me, trying to weigh something. Finally he said, "The night Gerald Crosby disappeared, someone saw a red Trans Am idling outside of Mr. Crosby's office a little before nine. That's the same kind of vehicle Ms. Dupree drives."

I opened my eyes wide, looking shocked. "That doesn't mean anything. Did anyone see Mr. Crosby get into it?"

"No, they didn't. But as you can see, the case against your friend here—"

"—is purely circumstantial." I cleared my throat. "I don't think I want to answer any more questions."

Detective Williams looked at me and shook his head. "Whatever you think she's going to give you, son, it's not worth it."

"Who says she's going to give me anything?" I asked, doing my best to look like Jimmy Stewart, innocent and confused, maybe just this side of naïve. Detective Williams backed away from the table and stood up in defeat.

*

For the next month, I stayed away from Scarlett, waiting to see what happened with the investigation into Gerald Crosby's murder. I'd heard that the cops were looking closely at her, and of course the rumor mill was churning, with all the locals convinced she was guilty. But no charges were brought, and I breathed a sigh of relief. No one thought she was innocent, but that didn't make her guilty.

One night, I drove out to her house and parked around the side, out of sight, where Gerald Crosby used to leave his Buick. I wore the same chinos as the night I came over to watch *Mildred Pierce,* and I had put on a new blue button-down shirt I'd picked up at Macy's. I'd even splashed on some of my father's cologne, dabbing it behind my ears and across my forehead, just the way I'd seen him do on date nights with my mom.

I knocked softly and Scarlett answered right away, looking as if she'd been expecting me. She wore a simple white blouse and a green skirt that reminded me of the color of that silk dress in the old photograph. Her face was puffy as if she had been crying, but there was no sound of grief in her voice, only hardness.

"Hi, Glenn."

"Aren't you going to invite me in?"

"I don't think that's a very good idea."

I pushed past her anyway, into the living room. The TV was on, the image frozen. I recognized Joan Crawford, though she looked younger than she had in *Mildred Pierce*. More innocent.

"*The Bride Wore Red*," Scarlett said. "You should see it some time."

So she wasn't inviting me to stay. That was all right. I wasn't there to watch movies, anyway.

"The police think I did it," she said.

"But they haven't arrested you. There's no evidence."

"No, but they believe someone lured Gerald down to the river, probably someone he knew. And they got a call from a concerned citizen saying my car was seen outside his office the night he disappeared."

I smiled. People around town had talked about the red Trans Am outside Crosby's office, but no one seemed to know the "concerned citizen" had been an anonymous caller. I thought it unlikely the detectives had told Scarlett this. She must've put the pieces together and figured it out for herself.

"What have you done?" she asked.

"What's it matter," I said, reaching out for her.

She slapped my hand away. I frowned. I'd imagined telling her everything, starting with the squirrels and raccoons I'd started targeting when I was about thirteen. I used to knock them out of trees with rocks, then pull them apart to see what their insides looked like. A hunter had caught me in the woods about a year ago, and my father had sat me down and told me I had to stop, so I did. But I still felt the urge sometimes. Killing Gerald Crosby hadn't been all that different. I'd lured him down to the riverbank by telling him Scarlett was going to be there and wanted to see him, and, when he realized it was all a ruse, he'd tried to fight me. He still had some of that old football-player strength, but I had a stockpile of rocks and my aim was true.

I didn't tell her any of this, though. All I said was, "Just like Fred MacMurray, right?"

"But that was only a movie."

"Not to me."

She turned away, folding her arms across her chest, and glanced across the room at the telephone.

"Careful, Scarlett," I said. "You're off the hook for now. But what if police find something you left behind in the woods…a piece of glass with your fingerprints on it or something."

Her eyes narrowed. She'd probably never noticed the wine glass that had disappeared from her front porch. But I'd picked it up with the sleeve of my jacket so as not to leave my own prints on it, and I'd kept it in the glove box of my car. Just in case.

"You're sick," she said, seething.

"Isn't that what the cops said after you killed your husband?"

She looked away, dropped her eyes, and I knew in that moment that she had done it. Killed her husband. *We're both rotten*, I thought, *only you're a little* more *rotten than me.*

"You'll never get away with this," she said.

"Why not? I'm a good student, I've lived in this town my whole life. You're the kind of woman who'd poison her own husband, steal someone else's man and take advantage of an impressionable teenage boy." I took Scarlett by the hand, her fingers were cold. "Besides, I didn't do it for myself. I did it for us."

"I never asked for this."

"Of course you did. You just never said the words."

I started to pull Scarlett upstairs, but she pushed me away. I moved back in, grabbed her by the arm, twisted until she yelped. When she finally looked at me, there was something I'd never seen in her eyes before. Defeat.

*

I had a late shift at Sonny's the next day, so I slept until noon. It had been a long night, but I felt good. Refreshed. I was whistling when I came into work, but the look on Nathan's face stopped me cold.

"I guess you haven't heard," he said.

"Heard what?"

He told me the news about Scarlett. The police had gone out to the house to talk to her again, and had found her dead on her living room floor. She'd apparently taken too many sleeping pills.

"Not surprising," Nathan said, "after what she did to Gerald Crosby."

"You don't really believe she killed him, do you?"

Nathan looked at me with pity, as though I was hopelessly naïve. "They were lovers, Glenn. She got jealous of his wife, she wanted him to leave her, and he wouldn't. They fought about it, and she killed him. She couldn't live with the guilt, so she killed herself."

"Sounds like something out of one of those—what do you call them?"

"Films noir," Nathan said, and he launched into an explanation of how the genre was really an extension of German Expressionism. To be honest, I wasn't listening too closely. I was thinking of Scarlett, the way she'd looked near the end, her bluish-black eyes tinged with fear, the last pill going in between her ruby red lips. "A woman must have everything," she'd told me, and, in the end, that's what she had: a young man who loved her with all his heart, and the freedom she couldn't live without. With all that, she must've died happy.

At least I like to think so.

Hejira

Released November 1976

"Coyote"
"Amelia"
"Furry Sings the Blues"
"A Strange Boy"
"Hejira"
"Song for Sharon"
"Black Crow"
"Blue Motel Room"
"Refuge of the Roads"

All songs by Joni Mitchell.

Blue Motel Room
by Edith Maxwell

Who in hell thought blue was a good color for a motel room? Blue walls, blue bedspread, even blue institutional drapes. I glance around and shake my head. *Oh, well. I'll be moving on from Savannah soon.* I pull the door shut and head out to my housecleaning job.

It doesn't take me more than two hours to clean Gloria Lee's already spotless condo, which is elegantly furnished in a minimalist style. I finish in the bedroom, pulling the snowy white bedspread taut and smooth.

My daddy was an incorrigible crook. As I use his Zen-and-the-Art-of-Safecracking method to quietly open the strongbox set into the bedroom wall, I miss him with a pang as sharp as the switchblade I carry for insurance. I hear his voice telling me: *Listen for it, Robin. Feel it. Become the lock.* I become the lock, even through my blue cleaning gloves.

Works every time. I pull open the heavy door, expecting to find a diamond bracelet, the emerald necklace I'd read about, the fabled silver stein that had been found in a cave on a Greek island. Me, I'm after only a minor bauble, something small I can pawn. A trinket the owner won't miss for a while. Diamond earrings, maybe. I'll take the money directly to the Savannah homeless shelter and then hit the road for another state, where I'll find another housecleaning job and commit another petty crime. I am my daddy's daughter, after all. Stealing from those who can well afford to lose a valuable keeps my skills from getting rusty. And when I give away the cash, I get that warm-flannel feeling.

I stare. There's the stein, protected by a clear box. Behind it sits an assortment of boxes from Tiffany and several from Savannah's own Harkleroad. I do not reach for the smallest box stamped with the gold diamond in a fancy *H* setting.

Because in front of all the treasures rests a desiccated hand, palm up in supplication, as if asking me to reattach it. As if begging me to find the person who separated it from its owner's arm. The skin is dark and stretched over the bones. I swallow down bile. Who keeps a hand in their safe? And why?

A creak sounds in the hallway. I whirl. The cleaning agency said the homeowner wasn't supposed to be back until hours from now. My heart's an effing jackhammer. I wait. But no one materializes. It's a beautiful hundred-year-old mansion that was condo-ized. Old buildings creak.

I move like sludge to face the open safe again. The hand's still there, sitting atop a white business envelope. I imagine the mummified appendage whispering to me: "Help me. Solve this. Avenge me."

I can't, I think. *I'm a traveler, a thief. I'm not a detective.*

Still, I snap pictures with my phone, a close-up and one from farther back, so the shot includes the furniture and the framed photograph of Gloria Lee on the wall. I can get the pictures printed and mail them to the Savannah police. With no return address, of course.

Gloria gazes at me from the photo, a steely-eyed woman in an expensive-looking gray suit and black Louboutins, if I'm not mistaken, an emerald necklace her only adornment. She's posed in front of a boxy building identified as Lee Enterprises. Who *is* this woman with a hand in her strongbox? She hasn't been here the previous three times I've cleaned the condo. I haven't seen any pictures of children or a husband around, so maybe her work is her life.

I shake my head. On with business. Steeling myself, I reach over the hand and select the smallest box. A quick peek shows earrings made of sparkling starlight. Into my apron pocket goes the box.

"Bye, hand," I say. I close and relock the safe. "I'll see what I can do."

*

Back in my room, I slump on the depressing blue bedspread with its black-rimmed cigarette-burn holes. I gaze at the blue drapes, my mood bluer than the walls. All I see is that severed hand.

I stopped in the pouring rain at a drugstore on my way back and printed the damn photographs. Right now I should be packing my roller bag. I should be loading my bourbon, peanut butter, crackers and dark chocolates into the cooler. I should aim for the next state west, find a housecleaning agency in a tony Montgomery, Alabama, neighborhood, lean over the manager's desk and lie once again: "I'm writing a novel featuring a cleaning lady, and I need firsthand experience to make the story authentic. I need to inhale the solvents, endure the abuse of homeowners, feel the tired muscles and joints from scrubbing and vacuuming for a living. Won't you help me?" My references are glowing, even though they were faked by girlfriends back in Los Angeles. And I actually *have* written a couple of nonfiction books on the sociology of employment, earlier in my life while I was still denying my true calling. So I'll be good in case they Google me.

I let out a big sigh and switch on my laptop. I owe it to the hand to type up an anonymous note to the cops about the pictures. But first to dig up the Savannah police location. I put on gloves to address an envelope to Habersham Street and affix a stamp, supplies I always travel with. I'm old-fashioned that way. I like to write my guy real letters from the road. Brett doesn't write in return very often. He's too busy, with all those pretty girls coming around.

Once I get the note printed and mailed, I can leave town. Would I prefer the refuge of the road, nonstop, all the way back to L.A.? Sure. Does Brett want me back? I can't say. I have two dozen road maps—I'm old-fashioned that way, too—and I plan to take my time. I suppose I should worry about my compulsion to steal as I go. Since I no longer have Daddy, I chalk it up to honoring his name— and his skills. I never profit from my takes, anyway.

I get sidetracked digging deeper into Gloria Lee. Before I took the job, I'd only searched on her treasures, assisted by my purloined copy of Harkleroad's customer list. Maybe I can find a clue online about the hand. I know she likes a classy shoe with a red sole. I narrow my eyes at the screen. The Lee Enterprises website, just as understated and elegant as Gloria and her home, identifies it as an investigation and protection business, whatever that means. *Huh.* Must be a pretty high-end enterprise for her to have such expensive taste. Is she a fancy private detective, or does she supply bodyguards for celebrities? Maybe both.

A shudder ripples through me. She could have a connection to the Mob. Cutting off someone's hand is the kind of thing you read about them doing. Searching gets me nowhere, though. No news reports of a missing hand. No crime reports about an arm being hacked off above the wrist. I let out a creaky groan and, duly diligent, type the note.

When I step out of my room at 6:30, thumb drive and envelope in my bag, the now-light rain's a balmy whisper on my skin, the palm trees slick black cellophane under the streetlight. And it's nearly dark. *Damn.* I like being on the freeway after the glare of the sun is gone, but driving will have to wait a bit. I chance an inquiry at the front desk. No, they can't print my letter for me.

Leaving an office store twenty minutes later, stamped letter in gloved hand, I tuck my crazy-curly red hair firmly into my beret, turn up the collar to my coat and slide on shades, despite the darkness. I don't want to run the risk of a camera spotting me at the post office around the corner. Daddy taught me well.

I walk up to the mailbox. The heavy blue pull-down door shuts with a satisfying thunk. Now I can hit the road.

*

"Ms. Robin Rousseau?"

Outside my blue motel room, I whirl at the voice. My car is packed, and I'm about to reenter the room for one last check, to make sure I haven't left anything behind.

My questioner is Gloria Lee, live and in color. *Shit.*

"Yes?" I feign innocence.

"I understand you've been cleaning my condominium recently." Up close, she looks older than in her picture. Fine lines crack the skin on the outer corners of her eyes and around her perfectly made-up lips. Her light cap of hair is expertly streaked to cover the inevitable gray. She's shorter than she appeared, too, despite the heels, coming only up to my shoulder. But then I'm five foot ten and look down at most women.

"I have." I struggle to keep my voice calm. I've never been caught before. "I was there this morning. Did I miss an area?"

"It's what *I* am missing that concerns me." She stresses the personal pronoun. "I know you were in my safe." Her gray eyes bore into mine.

I swallow. What an idiot I've been. I worried about security cams at the post office, but I never checked for one outside her condo. I close my eyes for a second. She's still there when I open them. She's a private investigator. Of course she has security on her property, and she knows exactly when I went in and when I left.

"The earrings, please." She holds out her palm.

"I don't have them." I can't deny I stole them, though. "Listen. I can explain."

"I really don't want an explanation." She drops her hand.

"I didn't take them for myself. I pawned them and gave the money to the homeless shelter, the one on Arnold Street." I shrugged. "It's what I do."

She blinks. The hint of a smile plays with the corner of her mouth. "Where did you pawn them?"

"At Cash America."

"Who taught you to break into safes?"

My smile is a wistful one. "My father. My late father." A truck bumps and rattles over the road. Two teen girls slouch by in pajama pants and flip flops, both staring at their phones. The air smells of Fryolator oil and diesel exhaust.

Gloria nods.

I've been honest with her. Maybe she will be with me. "What's with the hand?"

"I knew you'd ask." She gazes at the palm trees before answering. "It's my late brother's." She addresses the top of my right ear.

She's lying. I'm sure of it.

"Do you know what my company does?" Gloria lifts a single eyebrow.

"Something about investigation and protection."

"Yes. Did that worthless agency tell you?"

Not so worthless. They obviously informed her about where I was staying. "No. I Googled you. But your website is kind of vague."

"We like it that way. Some of our clients have a rather intense need for privacy." She tilts her head. "I've checked you out, Ms. Rousseau. Your talents are wasted on housecleaning. How would you like a job?"

Whoa. I didn't see that coming. "Me? You employ petty crooks?" She must have checked me out pretty quickly.

"We need all types. And we'll pay you enough to upgrade your, ah, housing." She gave the side eye to my cheap-ass motel's neon sign. "Belle's Beds. Sounds like a whorehouse."

"Hey, the price was right." I clear my throat. "You know, I'm kind of a tumbleweed right now. I appreciate the offer, ma'am, but I get antsy if I stay too long in one place." Well, unless Brett wants me back.

"I get it. How about you stick around for a month? We'll train you on a trial basis. Paid, of course, with an advance. If it goes well, you can work remotely."

The money would be nice. I might acquire some useful new skills. Should I tell her the teensy-tiny detail about mailing a picture of the hand to the police? *Nah.* Not now, anyway. I nod slowly, and send up a message. *Hey, Daddy. I'm going legit.*

*

I gaze at the sunset outside the window of my room. Gloria recommended one of those extended-stay places, but my blue motel room has grown on me. The manager at Belle's Beds was happy to have me stay on, and I could save more money this way. I sip my bourbon and wonder about the guy who came in to the office today. The dude with the hand prosthesis.

I've been in the thick of training for two weeks now, learning the fancy secret databases and search engines Lee Enterprises has access to, getting one-on-one self-defense instruction from a big square-headed bodyguard named Tug. Gloria even wants me to learn to shoot. The thought makes me a little queasy, but I suppose it's a good idea. That's on the schedule for tomorrow. I haven't seen any evidence of the police checking into Gloria, so maybe they discarded my anonymous note and pictures. Or maybe they don't care.

Twice now, an older gentleman has come to see Gloria. His neatly gelled dark hair is threaded with silver, and his suit didn't come off a Macy's rack. She introduced us when I encountered them in the hall today.

"Robin, this is Mr. Davies," Gloria said.

"Nice to meet you, sir." They're all big on using "sir" and "ma'am" in these parts. I'm definitely not in California anymore.

"James." Gloria turned to him. "Robin Rousseau, my new employee."

He shook my hand, giving a little bow. "Enchanted, Miss Rousseau." His deep brown eyes looked haunted, though they were edged with smile lines.

I tried not to stare at his left hand. It was made of something artificial, a gray tint staining the supposed flesh tone.

Gloria cleared her throat. "I'll be back in two hours." They disappeared out the front door. Gloria's affect with him was cool and crisp, not like he was a dear old friend or a former lover, so it must have been a business lunch.

Of course I went straight to the secret search engines. If it's his hand in her safe, what kind of leverage does she have over him?

But I got no satisfaction. Lots of men are named James Davies. A Welsh rugby player. A Canadian professor. A British electrical engineer. Even a novelist. I couldn't dig up a single story about one who'd lost a hand.

Gloria returned to the office alone.

"How was your lunch?" I just happened to waylay her as she headed to her corner office. "I'm looking for good restaurants around here."

"The Olde Pink House is an excellent choice. Pricy, but worth it."

"Thanks."

*

Now I sip and muse in my temporary home, where I barely notice the blue décor anymore. The man with the artificial hand isn't Italian, so he must not be part of the Mob. Unless James Davies is an assumed name. He does have dark hair and eyes, not that that means much. Maybe he's one of the clients the agency investigates for and protects.

I'm seized with a need to know. I owe it to the hand. But no way I'll be able to tail Gloria or snoop in her office. The woman is good. She'd find out. I could try to worm the story out of Tug, but he's truly the strong silent type and super loyal to Gloria. I have some pretty sharp hacking skills, but *nah*. She must have her personal accounts locked tighter than a nun's knees.

My gaze lands on the maps next to my blue bed. Two more weeks of training before I can hit the road again. My hands itch to hold the steering wheel, to have the vibration of the road in my feet. But I have to solve this mystery first.

What would Daddy tell me to do? His soft baritone echoes in my head. *Be one with the problem, sugar. Feel it. Become it.*

*

We all post our schedules on the Lee Enterprises proprietary app. When I check in at work before hitting the firing range the next morning, I see Gloria has added a lunchtime appointment for tomorrow, which is Friday. She's blocked off 12 to 2 and added "JD" in the Notes area. I block off 1:30 to 3:30 for myself and enter "Doctor Appt" as a note. If anybody asks, I'll tell them it's female stuff. They won't want details.

I'm thinking it's time to come clean with the boss about the letter and picture I sent the cops. Better she hears about it from me. I knock on her door jamb. She glances up.

"Ms. Lee, I took a picture of your open safe last time I was there cleaning." I clear my throat. "And I, uh, sent it to the Savannah police. I thought you should know."

She nods once and taps an envelope on her desk. I try not to stare at the police shield in the return-address corner.

"Not a problem, Robin." She gives me a cool smile. "Thank you for letting me know." She swivels her chair away, clearly dismissing me.

All righty, then. Looks like she has an in with the local police. I guess I'm not surprised. Just last week, I read a news article about how corrupt the department is.

Tug and I spend the rest of the morning at the Quickshot indoor shooting range, him teaching me firearm safety and how to aim and shoot. I surprise myself with my accuracy. I just go inward and do Daddy's Zen trick, becoming both weapon and ammunition.

"What do you know about Mr. Davies?" I ask Tug in the car on the way back to the office. I figure it's worth a try.

"Acquaintance of the boss." He keeps his eyes on the road.

"What happened to his hand?"

"Accident."

"What kind of accident?"

When I'm greeted with silence, I give up.

*

At 1:45, I'm lurking behind a column in the parking garage across from the Olde Pink House. I've gambled that's where Gloria and Davies eat lunch. A petty thief like me is nothing if not a weigher of the odds, and this particular bet pays off. Gloria clicks neatly down the front steps of the old pink mansion alone and enters the garage. Two minutes later, she drives out in a silver Jaguar. Not a red one, not a convertible, just a very fine—and expensive—automobile.

But after five minutes, James Davies still hasn't appeared. That's too long if he's just using the restroom. Has he adjourned to the bar, or did he depart before I arrived? I saw Gloria leave the office with him at a few minutes past noon, so he must have been here. I'm about to go retrieve my car when he emerges through the heavy front door of the restaurant. *Bingo.*

He turns right toward the corner and heads across the street into leafy Reynolds Square. I follow at a discreet distance. People eat lunch on the stone benches, an elderly couple strolls hand-in-hand down a path. When Davies, today sporting an ivory-colored brimmed hat, pauses in front of the statue of John Wesley, I casually move next to him and look up at the founder of Methodism as if I haven't recognized him.

"Miss Rousseau?"

I glance over in feigned surprise. "Oh, Mr. Davies. This is a lovely square, isn't it?"

"Indeed it is."

"We don't have such lush greenery in Los Angeles, where I'm from."

"This is quite a change for you. Are you enjoying the work at Lee?" He has that soft southern accent that always sounds gracious, no matter who is speaking.

"Yes, sir, very much. I had a doctor's appointment and got out early, so I thought I'd grab a sandwich and check out a little local scenery." I gaze at the statue of a man who'd lived three hundred years ago, another thing we don't have in L.A. "Do you live around here?"

"Yes, ma'am, just a few blocks down on East Bryan." Gloria's friend points with his ghostly artificial hand. "I enjoy walking to restaurants and such, and this is about as centrally located as one can get."

"Do you have a condo? I was wondering about the price of living downtown."

"No, it's just me in my big green house, but I need the privacy." He tips his hat at me. "Good day, Miss Rousseau."

*

Sunday finds me lurking outside a big green house on East Bryan at 8:00 in the morning. My hair's tucked into my beret again, and I'm wearing my huge sunglasses. I'm dressed in dark jeans and a long-sleeved *T*, an entirely different look from what Davies has seen me wear at the workplace. I keep my head down and apparently focused on my phone, like just about everybody else in the known universe these days.

After I returned to work Friday, Gloria called me in to say my performance in the first two weeks was excellent and she was upping my access to the client database. She gave me an assignment to check out some dude in Nebraska and who his enemies were. While I was doing that, I paged through the database of our protection clients. Protection, I'd learned by this time, meant everything from providing home security systems to assigning bodyguards. James Davies wasn't on the list.

Yesterday in my blue room, I dug up his exact East Bryan address. With that one additional tidbit of information, I learned Mr. Davies is a stalwart at the Wesley Monumental Methodist Church, only a mile's walk from his home. Their website shows a huge ornate mother church, with worship at both 8:45 and 11:00. Davies even teaches Sunday school, which takes place at 9:45. But I couldn't find a thing about his past, his work history, his personal life.

That's going to change as soon as he leaves the house this morning. Problem is, I don't know if he frequents the 8:45 church service or the 11:00. Whatever. I'm on the track of the hand now—at least I hope I am—and if I have to wait an hour and a half, I will.

I luck out when he exits his house at 8:15 on the dot. Today he wears a snappy linen suit and a different light-colored hat trimmed with a green ribbon. I wait ten minutes before moseying across the tree-lined street, where a locked metal gate is no match for me and my picks. Neither is the front door.

Inside, I stand and absorb the house for a moment. It smells of rich old wood with a faint overlay of lemon polish. The silence is interrupted only by the distant tick of a clock and a muted car horn outdoors. The gleaming floorboards in the foyer are worn smooth around the edges of an antique oriental rug. I scan for security cameras. I don't spy a single one. *Whew.*

"Hello? Cleaning service," I call out, just in case he has a cook or a housekeeper. Nobody hurries in wiping her hands on a dishcloth. I figure I have at least until 11:00, but the sooner I can clear out, the better.

A staircase on the left leads straight up to the second floor, and the hall next to it stretches to the back of the house. I aim that way first, so I'll know where the back door is. In case I need it.

I return to the study I passed on the right, my fingers itching to find the safe. A dude like James Davies simply has to have one. As I pull on my blue nitrile gloves, I scan the walls. I check out the floor-to-ceiling bookshelves and the heavy maroon drapes. I peer behind a couple of fat upholstered chairs. Cabinet doors halfway up from the floor are set into the paneling on each side of the fireplace. I open the one on the right to see bottles of expensive liquor. Behind the door on the left, a lovely old-fashioned safe door with a spinning combination lock greets me. *Bingo.*

Two minutes later, I stare at the paper I've pulled out of an envelope I found in the safe. I spread it smooth on the wide desk. The typed heading reads "Contract." The next line is "Parties: Gloria Lee and Jimmy Buccarelli."

A click breaks the silence. I whip my head toward the hallway. Front door? *Shit.* My throat threatens to close. I start to fold the contract.

The long-case clock in the hall gongs once. A giggle burbles up. Those clocks always click before they chime. It's 8:30. I'm good.

As I return my focus to the paper, my eyes are drawn to a framed picture on the desk I paid no attention to before. It's a younger Mr. Davies, hands in pockets, with a younger Gloria Lee's arm tucked through his. Across the corner is signed, "Ever yours, Jimmy B."

Got it. No wonder I couldn't dig up the dirt on this James Davies. He *is* Italian, as I'd guessed. I read the rest of the contract with eyes wide. The gist is that Jimmy hired Gloria to cut off the hand of the guy who hacked off his. She must be hanging onto the hand as proof, leverage, something. At the bottom I see "Copy one of two," with "GL" handwritten after it. So Gloria has her own copy, no doubt in the envelope under the hand in her bedroom lockbox. I guess the hand wasn't asking for my help, after all.

Wait. The envelope holds another folded paper. I wouldn't have thought my eyes could get any wider, but they do. I stare at a list labeled "Subsequent Lee hands" and inhale with a sharp rasp. Under it runs a *Who's Who* of Mafia family names, more than a dozen of them, with a date next to each. My nostrils flare, my mouth pulls down.

I quickly lock the safe and shut the paneled door. I gotta go.

*

I glance around my blue motel room once more before shutting its door for the final time. Funny how the color has grown on me over these weeks of calling it home.

I don't mind going legit when it involves surveillance. Online research is fine, maybe even a little hacking. Certainly picking locks and opening safes. But sawing off people's hands? I don't want to be anywhere near Gloria Lee, or her name-changing friend with the Mediterranean looks and the courtly manners who keeps tabs on her subsequent mutilations. I don't want that kind of work to grow on me. I know Daddy would agree.

Five minutes ago, I sent her an email:

Dear Ms. Lee:

I find the new job isn't working out for me. Thank you for the opportunity to work with your firm. I've deleted any links to your databases and am sure you will change my passwords, anyway. I'll be traveling for the foreseeable future.

With best regards,
Robin Rousseau

Gloria might try to find me. I've deployed my alternate I.D. and credit cards, though, and I'm betting she won't know to look for Maddie Day. When I get back to town, Brett might even think my having a new name is a turn-on.

In the car, I smooth out the map of Alabama on the passenger seat. Two dozen other maps wait neatly folded beneath it. They'll take me from this coast to the other one. To Brett and L.A., where I belong.

Next to the Alabama map sits the envelope from the safe. I touch it, as if it were a talisman.

It might be good to keep it close at hand, so to speak.

Don Juan's Reckless Daughter

Released November 1977

"Overture/Cotton Avenue"
"Talk to Me"
"Jericho"
"Paprika Plains"
"Otis and Marlena"
"The Tenth World"
"Dreamland"
"Don Juan's Reckless Daughter"
"Off Night Backstreet"
"The Silky Veils of Ardor"

All songs by Joni Mitchell.

Talk to Me
by Emily Hockaday and Jackie Sherbow

Lucas slouched on his side of the therapist's couch. As when sharing the queen-sized mattress at home, he and Jenna each staked out their space and stuck with it, week after week.

"Let's begin," Dr. Havermeyer said, "with where you see yourselves in five years."

"Like a job interview," Jenna laughed, doing what she always did, trying to make a connection. She folded her hands together, and Lucas felt his own hands tense up.

"Right," the therapist agreed. "It's good to know what you want from a job, and it's good to know what you want from a relationship."

"I'm flexible," Jenna answered. Was she trying to get good grades? Lucas didn't think that was how therapy worked. He also doubted Jenna's sincerity. Flexible? She ate the same breakfast five times a week.

"We can get to compromise later," Dr. Havermeyer said. "Why don't you both tell me what you want."

"I want Lucas to *talk* to me," Jenna responded. "When I ask him about the future, he has nothing to say. Does he want to stay here in the city or move to the suburbs? Does he want kids? A dog? These should be easy questions. If we aren't going to take it to the next step, what's the point in staying together?"

Jenna was perched on the edge of the couch, head tilted. She had stopped the hand wringing and now held her paper Au Bon Pain cup between her thumb and middle and ring finger, daintily, as though it were a glass of Scotch. Lucas pinched the bridge of his nose and studied the tray of succulents on the table in front of them. He couldn't identify whether the plants were living or wax. They looked very lifelike.

"Can you answer any of these questions, Lucas?"

The therapist was looking at him, and he focused on the pale, freckled skin of her throat, imagined the two women turning to stone and never asking anything of him, ever again.

"I like how things are," he responded. "Whatever Jenna wants is fine with—"

"But I don't *want* 'whatever.'" Jenna was tugging on a strand of hair. "I want us to decide *together*. I tell you all the time how I feel about kids versus no kids, the suburbs versus Queens, and you just shrug and nod, and I have no idea how you *feel!*"

Her voice became shrill, and she leaned back and pulled in some air. He knew this move. When she spoke again, she would be calm. She knew about control—she hadn't lucked into being a junior partner by thirty.

"You were always quiet," she said. "That's part of what drew me to you. Mr. Mystery." The corner of her mouth nudged up, as if tugged by a string. "But it's different now, and when I try to come up with solutions, you either get mad or you shut down. You let me spiral, and you never say anything."

Lucas concentrated on her hands, clasped in her lap, and her wrists, imagining her pulse. One, two, three....

Jenna, giving up on him, turned to Dr. Havermeyer. "He doesn't finish conversations. He doesn't see things through. Lately, after sex, he rolls away before I can even grab my vibrator."

Lucas felt his face change, though he tried to freeze it. He didn't want to seem like a prude. The therapist raised an eyebrow, and it was then he realized they were ganging up on him.

He could feel Jenna watching him from the side. He took a breath. "This isn't even *about* me," he said, more urgently than he meant to. In his mind, Lucas shuffled through confidences Jenna had offered him over the years, like some kind of desperation slot machine, until he settled on one. He knew, even as he was saying it, that it wasn't true, but he couldn't stop himself: "Some guy in high school—a friend?—pressured her until she slept with him. Rape, basically." He felt both ashamed and triumphant. "And she never talked to him again. That's what this is about."

The look on Jenna's face was not what he expected. Bemusement, confusion.

"That's…*nothing*. It happens to every girl. Woman. I want you to talk to me because I want you to talk to me. That's what a relationship *is*." She let out one exasperated laugh and gave the therapist a look that said: *Do you see?*

Lucas thought of his own youthful experiences—how liquid consent could be, how little he'd cared. He was surprised by his disappointment. Had he liked believing she could break—that women were so easily breakable?

"Lucas," the therapist said, "this is the kind of intimacy a lot of partners want. Tell me this: where do you see yourself living in five years?"

It was as though he hadn't spoken at all. But he had, hadn't he? He looked from one woman's face to the other and saw hope and disappointment, one moon rising while another set.

*

Outside, the sky was overcast. Jenna arranged the items in her bag—phone, keys, MetroCard. Taking stock, as she habitually did before leaving or entering a space.

Lucas stuck his hands in his pockets and peered uptown into oncoming traffic to see if they could cross against the light, and Jenna looked at him, narrowing her eyes. The light changed, and he was a few steps into the intersection before he noticed that she hadn't followed.

"I have to be back at the office in an hour," she called from the corner. "Are you headed home? I'm hungry, and I could use a drink…."

McCail's—an old pub and a neighborhood favorite—was just around the corner, in the shadow of Grand Central. He and Jenna had been there on one of their first dates, and over the last ten years they had broken up there once and made up there plenty of times.

A drink would be nice. He *needed* a drink.

*

Though it was Wednesday, the bar had a healthy crowd, so they ended up on two stools in the corner near the jukebox.

"Is any of this because I've been with more people than you have?" she said at last. She peeled the edges of her Corona Light label, not looking at Lucas, as the bartender cleared their plates. "If you need to get something out of your system," she said, "I could look the other way." Her fingers spun the bottle on the bar top, leaving a wormhole of condensation rings. "Maybe we could even find someone together."

Lucas drank his tequila soda quietly. After all these years, Jenna was still keeping score, controlling the game. He had no idea what to say.

Even at the start of their relationship, under the initial well of words, there had been a flat plane of nothingness within him. An expanse of ice. He could see it now: he had dug all the way through what he had to offer, and there was nothing left. Beneath the ice was only more ice.

His hairline began to tingle. He was drowning. He had to get out of there.

"Lucas? You considering it?" Jenna wore a wry smile, but her eyes were shrewd. Was she joking? Alarm rippled through his muscles. Now that they were in therapy, they were *always* in therapy. He had never before felt so *taut*.

Jenna moved around his stool to stand between him and the exposed brick wall, placing her hands on his knees. "It could be fun." Her edges were taking on a pink hue: the corners of her eyes, her hands, her cheeks. A blush crept along the nape of her neck.

How did she manage to make everything so hard? He felt trapped, and suddenly he was on his feet, pushing her away, her body hitting the wall. Dazed, he realized he was holding her there.

She looked at him as if he were a stranger. With fear. The chatter in their corner of the bar had faded, and he sensed the focus on him. He released her.

"I'm sorry. I just"—he held his hands out—"no, that's not what I want."

Jenna was edging away, rubbing her shoulders where he had pinned her.

"I have to go," she said, tearful. "You don't have to be such an asshole."

Someone stopped her on the way out, mouthed something too quiet to hear over the music. She gave a calculated *It's nothing* headshake. Lucas turned back to the bar, letting fresh anger course through him. *He* was the asshole?

He switched from tequila sodas to shots. Salt, tequila, lime. They went down easy. People came and went in the seats beside him, and the bar chatter grew to a dull roar.

"Did you see they remade *The Kid*? They animated it and made it cool."

"Nobody has any original ideas anymore."

"Do you have some change for the jukebox?"

"Hey, did you see what happened at the border?"

"What are you reading? Really, Willy the Shake? In this day and—"

He couldn't stand it.

He leaned to unhook his jacket from where it hung below the bar, and under the foot rail something caught his eye. Seafoam green leather. A wallet. He bent down to grab it and flipped it open.

Staring back at him was a driver's license photo: Samantha Colt. DOB 5/10/1994. Restrictions: B (corrective lenses). Brown-eyed. Brunette.

Suddenly the bar seemed quiet, cool, cavernous. Folding the wallet shut, Lucas slipped it into the back pocket of his jeans. He headed for the door, clearing it just as the bartender yelled, "Hey!"

He'd forgotten to pay their bill.

*

Lucas looked up at the constellations set into the expanse of Grand Central's vaulted ceiling. Below it, a crowd funneled into tunnels. He had taken the Metro-North only once before, on a weekend hiking trip with Jenna. This time, he boarded a New Haven train. Sitting next to a window in a red vinyl booth, he reached into his jacket. Gloves, keys, wallet. And Samantha's wallet. He didn't take it out, but he could feel it there, pressing against his side. Pulling out his round-trip ticket, he slipped it into the seat pocket for the conductor and pulled on his hood, looking out the dirty window.

What was he doing? He wasn't sure, but all the same he hadn't fought the impulse that put him here, watching rivers and estuaries unfold underneath the rail bridges as he headed north. His thoughts drifted back to the day before, which he'd spent at the public library. Inside the wallet, he'd found a student I.D., indicating Samantha Colt—Sam—was a grad student in Connecticut. Google Maps put her a mile from the train station, in a rundown building close to campus. A woman in a neighborhood like that might really need her wallet returned, might really be grateful. That's all this was about, right?

If you knew how to navigate the web, it was easy to find everything about someone, and there she was, in a local paper as a high-school student with a volunteer group, graduating from college, on a dating site: *No roommate. ;)*

This wasn't a girl who overthought things, and, though Lucas knew it was dangerous to advertise living alone, he appreciated her free-spirited nature. Samantha wasn't looking for anything *intense.* She was *laid back, casual.* She didn't need to hash everything over or learn every detail of a person's inner thoughts. He could tell by her profile tags that she accepted people as they were. Suddenly, Lucas was glad he'd felt compelled not simply to drop the wallet in the mail.

*

Stations flitted by, and passengers appeared and disappeared like ghosts.

Would she answer the door? Would she be relieved to have her wallet back? What if she wasn't alone? Would he have to talk to her?

Finally, the train approached Guilhaven. Lucas kept his eyes lowered and got to the door just as it opened.

Only a handful of others got off at the stop. He busied himself looking at a billboard of local items: photos, want ads, dog walkers, tutors, house-sitters, events at the university and local high schools. Once the train's lights disappeared down the track and the parking lot emptied of the recently disembarked, he set off.

It was a fifteen-minute walk. The town and its streets, houses and stores were on the faded, slightly shabbier side of old New England charm, but there *was* charm—and he smiled at the quiet. No horns honking, no music, no sirens. Many of the front walks had deflated Halloween windsocks—cats, pumpkins, ghosts—still hanging, a few weeks late. Some had Christmas decorations already, though they might still be there from the year before.

The small detached rental's white paint needed a touch-up, and the grass in the tiny yard was fading in the fall weather. The tree out front had lost almost all of its leaves. A pair of green rain boots stood outside the screen door. Jenna had the same boots in black.

It was easier than he'd thought it would be to walk up to the door and knock. After all, he was just returning a wallet.

He heard movement inside, and the interior door opened. Samantha, the face from the driver's license and dating profile. A little taller than he'd expected, but her.

"Can I help you?" she asked, not unfriendly—but she didn't open the screen door.

"Hey—it's Samantha, right?"

Her smile faded a bit. "Do I know you? Are you in the econ program?"

Lucas felt he had to widen his own smile to compensate. He had a trustworthy face.

"No, I...." He trailed off, then tried again. "I think maybe we were in the same bar. I found your wallet." He opened his gloved hands in a gesture of goodwill. "You did lose your wallet, right? In Manhattan?"

Samantha visibly relaxed. "I did. So stupid. I started replacing some of the cards, but the DMV is killer." She looked at him expectantly. Over her shoulder, he could see down a hall that framed a doorway showing a slice of dingy yellow kitchen. Something hot was on a table. Coffee?

Why didn't she seem more grateful?

"Do you mind if I come in for a minute?" he asked. "My wife wants to move out of the city, and we've never checked out this town. I'd love to hear about the neighborhood."

"Oh, sure, um...it's a nice place. I need to study, but I did just make some tea. You can come in for a bit, I guess. Warm up with some caffeine and conversation." She flashed a smile that Lucas suspected she had been told was charming. "I have a minute to talk."

To talk.

Something inside his chest snapped like a broken guitar string.

*

On the train home, Lucas sat backward, the shadows of trees and buildings surprising him, seemingly coming out of nowhere, prophesying the approaching landscape. He felt vaguely lightheaded, and his mind raced.

It was too bad what had happened to Samantha Colt. But bad things happen in transient neighborhoods.

As the train rattled along the rails, the weight Lucas had carried since Jenna insisted they go to therapy melted away. He felt free.

He found that he was eager for their next session. He had so much to say. He knew where he wanted to live—parts of Guilhaven were in a great primary-school district.

And maybe they *should* get a dog. He and Jenna would have to talk about that.

The Silky Veils of Ardor
by Greg Herren

The elevator doors opened. Cautiously, her heart thumping in her ears, she stepped out into the hotel lobby and took a quick look around. At the front desk, a young woman in uniform was checking in a couple. They didn't look familiar. But it had been so long since she'd seen any of them…would she recognize anyone?

She didn't notice she was holding her breath.

She walked across the lobby to the hotel bar entrance. A reader board just outside said WELCOME BACK BAYVIEW HIGH CLASS OF 1992!

The black background was faded, the white plastic letters yellowed with age.

The urge to head back to the elevators and punch at the UP button until the doors opened, get back to her room and repack her suitcases—everything she'd just carefully put away neatly in drawers and hung in the closet—was strong. She resisted, recognized the need as irrational, closed her eyes, clenched her hands until she felt her ragged bitten nails digging into her palms.

You can do this you can do this you can do this you can do this….

A dull murmur came from the hotel bar, laughter and talking, the rattle of ice against glass, the whir of a blender. From where she stood, she could see the bar was crowded, cocktail waitresses in too-short black skirts and white blouses with trays balanced on one hand maneuvering expertly around groups of people.

Maybe no one there was from the reunion. Maybe she was early. Maybe—

You can do this!

She'd always had social anxiety. Had never made friends easily, couldn't make small talk, sometimes said the wrong thing, alienated people without even knowing what she'd done. Parties and dances had always been agony. Even with friends, people she felt relatively certain actually *did* like her, there was always the irrational fear

183

she'd say the wrong thing, forget a birthday, commit some horrific social faux pas that would turn them against her, show them what a damaged, worthless person she actually was. She'd started seeing a therapist after college, years after she should have, but her parents thought therapy was all touchy-feely mumbo-jumbo for the weak and all you had to do was suck it up and forget about it, not worry, lock it all away in some dark corner of your mind and move on.

But she always worried, never able to relax, be honest with people, be herself, share her secrets.

You can do this. You can. You can do anything. You've come back to Florida and survived so far, haven't you?

The Xanax had made the airport and cross-country flight from California bearable. But it was wearing off now, and she didn't want to take another. Dr. Silverman had been so happy, so thrilled, when she told her she wanted to come to her twenty-fifth high-school reunion. "I'm so proud of you," Dr. Silverman had beamed. "This is such a huge step."

You can do this.

"Lany? You *are* Lany, aren't you?"

She smiled hesitantly at the short woman in the mom jeans and ugly beige knit sweater with sequined cats appliqued to the front. There was something vaguely familiar about her, but Lany couldn't place the face. She'd considered studying the faces in her senior yearbook, just to be safe, but had put it back on the shelf. It had been twenty-five years. She certainly didn't look like the Lany Taylor they remembered anymore—if any of them remembered her at all—and there was little chance any of them would look like their air-brushed and carefully posed senior pictures. But this hesitant, short, round woman in an ugly sweater had recognized something of Lany's teenaged self in her face.

The woman smiled more broadly, stepping closer, looking at her over the top of her silver-rimmed glasses. "You don't recognize me, do you?" She laughed, a musical sound that carried Lany back to memories of little cardboard boats of skinny French fries and chocolate milkshakes, cafeteria noise and whispered confidences, plastic trays and cellophane-wrapped plastic tableware, rough white folded paper napkins that didn't absorb anything.

"Allyson...Bates?" It couldn't be, but it was, somehow. The eyes, they were the same, despite the dark circles and the lines radiating out from the corners.

"You *do* remember me!" Allyson threw her arms around Lany, who fought her instinct to stiffen, struggling with her own uncooperative arms until they were around Allyson's wide back. She was soft and warm. "I know I don't look anything like I did when we were kids, but I was so hoping you were going to come!"

Lany hadn't sent the RSVP back in the mail, hadn't answered the e-vite or clicked *Attending* on the Facebook event page, wanting to be able to back out if she changed her mind. She hadn't even gone back to the event page after that first visit, when Tiffany Stewart-Malcolm had sent her the invitation to join, afraid somehow they could tell she'd been there, that some electronic notice had been sent to someone: *Lany Taylor visited your event page, would you like to send her a message?* She'd bookmarked the website Tiffany, apparently still as Type-A as ever, had created for the reunion, making sure she had the hotel discount code and the dates right, resisting the urge to go back to the Facebook page to see who was coming and who wasn't, to read all those posts and comments about *the best times of our lives* and *remember when* and *oh, it seems like just yesterday* and *where did all the time go?*

"I didn't think anyone would care whether I came or not," Lany replied.

Don't be self-deprecating, Dr. Silverman said in her head. *Why wouldn't people want to see you? Why wouldn't people care? You've created this monstrous high-school experience mostly in your head, you know.*

"Oh, don't be silly! I've really missed you! I haven't seen you since graduation." Allyson tucked her warm hand through Lany's arm. "I've thought about you a lot since then. I've *missed* you." She adjusted her glasses with her free hand. "I don't know about you, but I could use a drink." She tugged at Lany's arm.

It was a hotel bar, like so many other hotel bars, showing signs of wear and tear, badly in need of renovation. Worn-out vinyl seats and half-empty bottles, harried bartenders of both sexes filling orders, cocktail waitresses doing their little dance with their trays, avoiding brushing against the tiny round tables and the drinkers perched on the bar stools. She didn't recognize anyone, but Allyson would interrupt her running chatter to say hello to someone, say, "You remember Lany?" to a face that smiled politely and nodded hello before they moved on. Allyson rarely stopped talking, even to breathe. Lany had never needed to speak when Allyson was around. She'd always been grateful for that. She was one of those girls who did everything, joined every club, auditioned for every play, was elected class secretary every year, sang in the choir and played flute in the marching band. Everyone knew who she was, and no one disliked her, not even the burnout kids or the Goths with their white makeup and black eye liner. You couldn't not like Allyson…but girls like Allyson never got picked to be a cheerleader or Homecoming Queen or asked to prom by the hot guys.

Allyson was always a little boy-crazy, wasn't she, or was she remembering that wrong? Her memories lied to her sometimes. But she could remember a string of crushes, and boyfriends who never seemed to stick around for long, and obsessions with Patrick Swayze and Emilio Estevez and Tom Cruise. The walls of Allyson's pink-and-blue bedroom were covered with posters of young movie stars, yellowing tape at the corners.

"Is—?"

She had to ask, but somehow couldn't get the name out, couldn't bring herself—even now, after all these years—to say his name out loud.

Allyson kept talking, leading her through the crowded bar, past people whose faces told their stories, past graying hair and wrinkles and potbellies, hearty laughs and voices stained with the weight of the years, past colognes and perfumes, the smell of stale smoke and sour sweat and alcohol. She didn't recognize anyone right away, tried not to meet anyone's eyes as they looked at her and quickly away. She, too, looked different than she had all those years ago, and no one had ever really noticed her or paid attention to her, had they? She might as well have been invisible, carrying her books clutched to her chest as she dodged her way from class to class, hoping someone would see her and say her name, someone, anyone, would say, "Lany! Don't you look pretty today!"

No one ever did.

Except that one time.

"Here! I knew there'd be a free table somewhere!" Allyson presented the table with a flourish, as though she'd accomplished something. She'd always done that, Lany remembered, acted as if anything she did was an accomplishment. "What a terrific parking place!" she'd said that day they went to Bayside Mall, even though it was a long walk from the Macy's entrance and an even longer walk to the Claire's just on the other side of the food court. Allyson wanted to get another ear piercing, and Lany hadn't been doing anything else that day, and her mother had pushed her to go, hadn't she? Told her she needed to get out of the house more, maybe if she did she might find a boyfriend.

The table needed to be cleared, sweating glasses of melting ice and wet cocktail napkins scattered about, the fingerprint-smudged bowl of salted nuts already picked over. Lany gratefully slid onto the banquette, her back against the cracked brown vinyl worn through in places, took a deep breath, overlooking the hordes of people from her vantage spot.

If he comes, I'll see him from here. Then I can decide.

He probably wasn't coming.

He wasn't the type to come to a reunion.

Or maybe he'd changed.

She'd come, hadn't she?

Allyson used one of the napkins to wipe the table down, stacked the empty glasses. "I'll just take these up to the bar," she said with a warm smile, always so eager to please. That hadn't changed in twenty-five years, had it? Allyson had always wanted everyone to like her.

Don't be such a bitch.

"I'll grab us a couple of drinks while I'm there," Allyson was saying. "What do you want? Should we be daring and have Cosmos?" Her eyes glittered with excitement, as if she never dared drink ordinarily—and maybe she didn't. Maybe this reunion was her chance to get away from her life and kick up her heels and do things she wouldn't ordinarily do.

Maybe I shouldn't judge.

"A glass of Chardonnay," Lany replied, reaching into her purse for her wallet, feeling the little bottle nestled against it in the bottom of her purse, wondering if this was the weekend she would finally use it. If she had the nerve. If she had the guts.

That's why you're here, isn't it?

"No, no, this one's on me!" Allyson replied, waving her off. "It's the least I can do." Her voice dropped a register as she said it, a look of something—pity? concern? apology?—crossing her face.

What do you have to be sorry for, Allyson?

Allyson disappeared into the crowd, and Lany found herself staring at the men, peering at their faces, trying to decide if any of them could be him.

Colby.

His name was Colby.

They'd gone to different elementary schools. It wasn't until seventh grade and junior high they were walking the same halls, sometimes in the same class, the same lunch period. He was so good looking, she remembered, that first time she saw him—was it the first or second day of school? She couldn't remember, and her memories often lied to her, anyway. But she remembered him, with his thick mop of blondish-brown hair, the curls and waves hair-sprayed and gelled into place, the dagger earring hanging down from his right ear, the tight jeans torn open and frayed at the knees, the tight Black Sabbath T-shirt hugging his chest and shoulders.

That memory was true, was real, she'd recorded it in her diary exactly the way it happened, the way she caught her breath when she saw him coming down the hallway toward her, the casual, self-aware strut of a guy who knew every girl who saw him wanted him, the way the veins streaked down his forearms, the way his nails were polished black, the way his mismatched eyes—one green, one blue—focused on making eye contact with a slight smirk on his thick lips. That moment, the girlishly pretty boys of Duran Duran and Wham ceased to exist for her. She tore their posters down from her walls that night, or maybe it was the next weekend. But she knew, she knew then, that this guy, whatever his name was, would change her life.

Just the sight of him had awakened something in her. Desire, an almost animalistic feeling she was too young to wrap her mind around, but girlishly pretty androgynous men weren't enough for her anymore.

Colby had made her ache in places she didn't know she could ache.

She knew she would know him if she saw him now, even after twenty-five years.

She watched as a waitress emptied her tray at a table, black skirt sagging a bit in the back, sensible black flats a little worn at the heels, a small hole in the back of her black hose. She looked young but tired, bags under her eyes from too many hours carrying trays of drinks and dealing with the advances and tired come-ons of drunks traveling on business and bored, miles from their wives and families, where she had to play the game of being flirty enough to get a tip but not so flirty as to get groped, not make the gentleman in his cups angry when she didn't take the room key he offered.

Not every *man*, Dr. Silverman would say.

The waitress, whose name tag read KAYLEIGH, squeezed herself through the crowd and used a wet towel to wipe the rings away from their table. "Something I can get for you?" she asked, expertly flipping a cocktail napkin down, picking up the dirty nut bowl, and slipping her tray under her arm in one fluid motion.

"My friend went to the bar," Lany smiled. "But some peanuts would be nice, yes." She fumbled in her purse, her fingers brushing the bottle again, opened her wallet and slid out a bill. It was a five, and she slid it across the table.

Kayleigh smiled a genuine smile, slipped the five into her apron and said, "I'll be right back with the peanuts and an appetizer menu."

There was something about Kayleigh that was familiar, but it danced away when she tried to grasp it.

Lany could see Allyson slowly working her way through the crowd, trying not to spill the drinks, smiling and chatting as she walked, the way she always had. She'd always envied Allyson, the easy way she had with people, how she could talk to anyone about anything at any time. She'd never been able to do that, always fumbling awkwardly for something to say that wouldn't sound embarrassingly stupid and always, *always*, failing.

"That girl looked familiar," she said, as Allyson cheerfully handed her an almost-too-full glass of wine.

"What girl?" Allyson collapsed into her chair with a loud exhausted exhale, as though she'd somehow run a half-marathon, and sipped from her Cosmo.

"The cocktail waitress."

"Kayleigh?" Allyson smiled and pulled her compact from her purse, carefully checking her lipstick and hair. "She should. She's Janna Melgren's daughter. You remember Janna, don't you?"

Janna Melgren.

Who could possibly forget Janna?

No matter how much she'd tried over the last twenty-five years, Lany hadn't been able to. She'd spent many nights as a teenager wondering what she'd ever done to Janna to deserve her hatred, her scorn, her insults. Janna was effortlessly beautiful, or so she'd seemed at the time, with her reddish-gold hair that fell in perfect waves down her back, her big full breasts she wore low-cut tops to show off, her slender waist and long legs. Every boy at Bayview High wanted Janna Melgren, and she knew it. Crowds parted to let her pass by with whomever she deigned to walk the halls with, whichever boy she chose to date for a moment before getting bored and moving on.

None of the girls liked Janna, who went to college parties on the weekends and drank, who always had a joint in her purse, who set style trends for the other girls without knowing or caring. She was a mean girl, years before the movie made the term recognizable, her wide-open green eyes always sparkling with malice, always looking for a sign of weakness, and always managing to find one. Sometimes her eyes would fall on Lany, her lips curl up in a contemptuous smile, and she would say something horrible, something cruel, something that felt like a whip crack slap across her face—but Lany couldn't respond, couldn't say or do anything, couldn't let Janna smell blood in the water. She hated Janna, oh, how she hated her, prayed every night for her to die.

Janna.

She owed Janna quite a debt.

"Janna got pregnant that summer after graduation," Allyson said, not even trying to pretend she wasn't enjoying telling the story, and Lany remembered Allyson had her own reasons for hating Janna. "The boy wouldn't marry her. It was—you know." She snapped her fingers. "Colby Lockhart."

"Colby?" She managed to keep her voice calm as she reached for her wine glass, managed to get it to her lips without spilling. The wine was cheap bar wine, but it would do. She set the glass down, marveling at how steady her hands were, her voice. No one would know just by looking at her. "Colby got Janna pregnant?"

Lany had left after graduation, had never looked back, never come back. She'd gone to stay with her grandmother for the summer before college, that long boring summer in the wet heat of rural Alabama, slapping at horseflies and sticking to the vinyl furniture. Her father had applied for a job in Houston and got it, and they'd sold the house and moved. She'd never had to return to Florida, for any reason, and after not returning phone calls or answering letters she'd been forgotten, gone from their lives like she'd never been there in the first place.

"He said it wasn't his." Allyson made no attempt to hide the malice now, and Lany wondered what had happened to change her. Allyson had never had anything bad to say about anyone, could always find something nice to say, always had some reason for excusing even the most inexcusable conduct. Hadn't she always found excuses for Janna's cruelty, even when she'd been its target? Or had the malice always been there, kept hidden like a treasure from the rest of the world? "He wouldn't marry her. He said she slept around and he wasn't going to tie himself down to some tramp."

That sounded like Colby.

Her left hand dropped to her lap.

"You still…live here?"

Allyson sipped her Cosmo. "I sure do. I'm secretary of the Alumni Association."

Of course you are.

"I thought Tiffany planned the reunion?"

"She's a good organizer, isn't she?" Allyson looked around the room. "And that woman can track down anybody. She found you, didn't she?" She laughed her little laugh again. "She ought to be a private detective. She managed to find everyone."

Everyone?

But she couldn't make herself ask.

"Janna's been married a few times," Allyson was saying. "Has a lot of kids. She's no better than she should be, if you know what I mean." She winked. "Put on a lot of weight, too. Although I'm one to talk." She patted her ample sides. "I never bounced back from my first. I keep thinking I'll join a gym, but who has time? Maybe once the girls are grown."

"Do you think Janna...do you think she'll be here?"

Allyson frowned. "She might. Let's ask Kayleigh." She twisted around in her chair. "Where is she? I don't see her...Janna RSVPed, but just between you and me"—she leaned across the table and lowered her voice—"I don't think she wants people to see how far she's fallen. Remember what hot shit she used to think she was?" Her voice dripped scorn, her eyes flashed. "She's a cashier at Publix now."

Lany looked at her, picked up her glass of cheap wine and took another sip. Had Allyson always been this...this *nasty*? This wasn't how she remembered her old friend, but her memories...her memories *had* lied to her before. Maybe she just hadn't noticed. Maybe she'd been too wrapped up in her own drama to notice. Maybe it wasn't....

Maybe it wasn't an accident they'd gotten separated that day at the mall.

She'd stopped at Macy's to look at some sunglasses she could never afford, tried them on and examined herself in the little mirror, smiling and wishing she could somehow swing a pair. But when she turned around to ask Allyson what she thought, Allyson was gone. She took the glasses off, put them back, smiled an apology to the woman at the counter and tried not to panic as she looked around for Allyson. Allyson was her ride, she'd have to take the bus home if she couldn't find her. There was nothing worse than the bus, but she knew Allyson was getting her ear pierced at Claire's, so she could just go there and wait for her to turn up. So she was by herself when she ran into Colby and his best friend Trav, both looking like sin in blue jeans and their sleeveless black tank tops, both smiling in what she'd thought was a friendly way.

It wasn't until later she'd realized their smiles had been predatory.

"No, she won't show," Allyson went on, giving up on locating Kayleigh. "I mean, it's bad enough the way she's let herself go, right? Everyone remembers her as the sexy girl, the one all the guys wanted. And now her daughter is waitressing here for the reunion weekend. Funny how that turned out, isn't it?"

"Almost…almost like it was planned that way."

"Almost."

She heard herself asking the question: "And Colby? Is he coming?"

She'd been in love with Colby since that day in the seventh grade, but never got up enough nerve to actually talk to him. She used to watch him whenever she could, dream about him asking her out, write stupid schoolgirl fantasies in her diary about what it would be like to kiss him, how it would feel to have his thick arms around her, his skin pressed against hers, how he would smell. He was a secret she didn't share with anyone, watching him get involved with other girls over the years, as he got taller and his shoulders wider and his muscles thicker, the hair poking out from the neck of his T-shirts, the way his pants rode down a bit when he kneeled to check the air in the tires of his car so she could see the smooth dark skin of his lower back, the pale skin where the muscles started to curve outward above the waistband of his BVDs. Her heart ached every time she saw him with his arms around another girl, caressing her, looking deep into her eyes before he kissed her. She knew who Trav was, of course, his ever-present best friend, not quite as good looking or sexy but attractive in his own way.

That afternoon in the mall when she ran into them right outside the Miller's Outpost and they smiled and said hello, she wasn't sure how to react, her heart racing so fast she could hear it in her ears, all thoughts of finding Allyson gone from her mind because she'd never been this close to Colby before, close enough to smell his Fahrenheit cologne, his musk and sweat beneath it.

"Hey, Lany," he'd said, that mesmerizing smile drawing her in, that tantalizing slightly crooked tooth in front, "want to grab a hot pretzel with us?"

"Colby?" Allyson was giving her a strange look. "You don't know, do you? You never answered my letters—did you even read them?"

Her palms were sweating as she picked up her wine glass, looked into Allyson's glittering eyes.

Focus, don't go there, don't think about any of this, it's not important, what's important is you're here and you know what to do; there's Xanax in your purse and you know how to recognize the signs now, so you can get out of here and go back to your room if it gets bad.

"Colby died the year after we graduated, driving drunk," Allyson was saying, toying with the diamond ring on her left hand, fused with a wedding band. "But you just ran away, and you never looked back, never thought about us again, did you? Your parents wouldn't even give me a number where I could call you. I missed you. You were my best friend."

"He's *dead*?"

The relief! She felt tears coming to her eyes, fought them down, wiped at her eyes with a cocktail napkin. All this time, he was *dead*.

Dead.

"Are you all right?" Allyson finished her Cosmo, tilted her head. "I know, it must be a shock. You really had a thing for him back in high school, didn't you?" She clucked her tongue, patted Lany's hand. "It's too bad things didn't work out." She winked. "But you know, sometimes it's just as well."

"Things...didn't work out?"

"That day at the mall." She pushed her chair back. "Remember?"

Oh yes, I remember.

It was taking all her self-control to avoid shaking. Somehow, she managed to choke out the words: "That...day at the mall?"

"Yes." Allyson's smile never wavered. "I think I'll get another drink. Can I bring you some more wine?"

Lany nodded, watching as she got up and walked through the crowd, smiling and saying hello to almost everyone. Allyson. Her parents asked her, when they called, if she wanted Allyson to have her phone number, if she wanted to talk to her, but she always said no. Those last few weeks of school had been so hard, so rough. She hadn't gone to graduation, hadn't talked to anyone, just kept her head down and went from class to class, wandering through the halls with her books clutched to her chest, staying away from anywhere she might have seen Colby, bumped into him, not trusting herself to not start screaming or shaking or crying, to not melt down.

After getting pretzels, they'd invited her out to the parking lot to smoke a joint, and hadn't she been so happy to go with them? Didn't she feel cool, didn't she feel smart, didn't she feel sexy, when Colby took her hand and held it all the way out to Trav's van, parked near the JCPenney? Oh, yes, she'd gone, willingly. She took a hit from the joint and coughed, felt weird and queasy, and when Colby started to kiss her, hadn't she kissed him back? Hadn't it been what she'd always wanted, written about in her diaries year after year after year, dreamed about in class? It was her own John Hughes movie come to life, the sexy cool bad boy finally seeing the quiet mousy girl for what she was, and, when he put his hand on her breasts, hadn't she let him?

Hadn't she?

Hadn't she asked for it?

"You have to stop blaming yourself," Dr. Silverman told her. "Having a crush on a boy and having him show you some attention—that wasn't an invitation."

Words. They were just words. She agreed with her therapist, nodded, made mental notes not to go on shouldering the blame. But that voice was always there, inside her head, whispering *you asked for it, you have no one else to blame, you wanted it.*

Kayleigh swooped in with another bowl of peanuts, offering her a tired smile. Lacy could see Kayleigh's mother now in her face, and...and traces of Colby, too, the mismatched eyes, the shape of the mouth. She choked down a sob, fought past the irrational nausea and fear, reminding herself *you came here to confront your past.*

Allyson was coming back now, carrying another Cosmo and another glass of wine, a man at her side.

"Look who's here!" Allyson said. "This is my husband Trav. You remember Trav Martin, don't you?"

Lany looked up at the man with the receding hairline and a few hairs growing out of his nostrils, beaming down at her with his red face and expanded waistline. He was wearing a white shirt and tie, sweat beads on his forehead and dampness at his armpits. But she looked at his sunken brown eyes and the crowned ridge of bone above them, and it was him.

It was him.

The last lie she'd carried for twenty-five years broke in her head.

"Trav," she said, her voice barely audible over the roar of the crowd, yet strong, secure. "How could I forget?"

He leaned down and kissed her on the cheek, his lips wet and slick.

"So nice to see you again."

That afternoon at the mall, in Trav's van.

Trav with his headphones on, listening to his Discman. She could hear the Beastie Boys over her own weak, begging sobs for Colby to stop what he was doing, even after it seemed like she'd left her body and it was happening to someone else. Trav, in the front seat, acting like he didn't know what was going on in the back, what was happening to her, as her fantasies of living happily ever after with Colby, of going to prom with him and loving him and having his children came to a sobbing, broken end in the back of a van in a mall parking lot on a spring weekend afternoon.

She smiled as Trav pulled up a chair, snapped his fingers at Kayleigh and ordered a beer, made small talk about her life in San Francisco. The two of them blathered on and on about his work at the car dealership and their kids, and she put her hand inside her purse and felt it there, her little bottle, her escape plan, and smiled at them.

"Lany didn't know about Colby Lockhart being killed," Allyson was saying, as Lany picked up her glass.

"Such a tragedy," Trav shook his head. "He always thought he was invincible."

"Did he?" Lany's voice sounded far away, like it was coming from the far end of a long tunnel.

Trav laughed. "Yeah, he was always doing things, you know, taking risks. Back then, I thought it was so cool...now I can't believe we made it through high school alive."

"Risks?" Lany asked, somehow keeping the smile on her face.

"I always thought he'd settle down if he found the right girl." Allyson shook her head, sipping her Cosmo, reaching out to squeeze Lany's hand again. "I thought for sure...you know. I thought, that day at the mall...."

The realization hit Lany like a fist.

You left me at Macy's on purpose!

"...and he seemed interested, seemed to think you'd be right for him. I thought for sure, you know, the two of you would hit it off and become a couple and we'd all double date." Allyson was smiling at her. "I was so sorry it didn't work out."

It didn't work out.

Maybe Allyson didn't know. Maybe Trav didn't know.

Maybe...maybe she was remembering wrong?

She closed her eyes.

She could feel Colby's breath on her neck, the tears on her face, the tinny sound of the Beastie Boys coming from Trav's headphones.

Her memory wasn't lying this time.

Maybe they didn't know.

Maybe they didn't want to know.

In either case, it didn't matter.

It had happened, and it was *their* fault.

She wanted to throw her wine in Allyson's face, scream at her, at both of them.

But no—no, that wasn't nearly enough to make up for what they'd done to her.

The night was still young, and there was plenty of time for her to empty her bottle of poison into their drinks.

There would be enough for both of them.

She raised her glass in a toast, and they all clinked glasses.

"To old times," she smiled at their beaming faces. "I'm so glad I came."

Mingus
Released June 1979

"Happy Birthday 1975 (Rap)"
"God Must Be a Boogie Man"
"Funeral (Rap)"
"A Chair in the Sky"
"The Wolf That Lives in Lindsey"
"I's a Muggin' (Rap)"
"Sweet Sucker Dance"
"Coin in the Pocket (Rap)"
"The Dry Cleaner From Des Moines"
"Lucky (Rap)"
"Goodbye Pork Pie Hat"

All lyrics by Joni Mitchell.
"Happy Birthday 1975," "Funeral," "I's a Muggin',"
and "Coin in the Pocket" raps by Jazz Workshop, Inc.
All music by Joni Mitchell
except "Happy Birthday 1975 (Rap)" by Mildred J. Hill
and "A Chair in the Sky," "Sweet Sucker Dance," "The Dry Cleaner
From Des Moines,"
and "Goodbye Pork Pie Hat" by Charles Mingus.

The Dry Cleaner From Des Moines
by Amber Sparks

In Las Vegas, the woman had found the kind of luck she liked best. Her best luck involved invisibility, the kind that allowed people to overlook her sticky fingers and her quiet dine-and-dashes. She was tan and brown and beige and gray, plain and unobtrusive as backdrop. It had been a source of some small pain in her youth; she would wonder if she'd ever find love, ever cash in her virginity. She wasn't offensive or even unattractive. Just the one person in the bar you'd pass over as you scanned the pickings. The one you couldn't I.D. in a lineup. Eventually, the disappointment of loneliness gave way to a kind of exhilaration, the understanding that she alone possessed a sort of superpower. She was invisible, and as long as she was careful and committed only small crimes and carried a little luck with her, she could do more or less as she liked.

When she ordered drinks, she chose what was on tap and didn't linger long—she kept her face blank and drank briskly, though not quickly enough to arouse attention. She sidled off the barstool and strolled out calmly, and often the empty glass left behind was the only way anyone knew she'd been there. In stores, she could pocket things and walk right out—even when they had camera footage, she was so nondescript the police just shook their heads. She looked, they said, like anyone's mother. How on earth would they find her? She moved around a lot, never stayed in one neighborhood long. It was always cities, because there she never stood out; so many invisible people haunt the shops and strip malls of suburban America. And now she found herself in Las Vegas, unwilling to leave though she'd surely outstayed her welcome by now. Her luck had just been too good; the takings too plentiful.

She was, she thought, the only person in Vegas who wasn't there to gamble or drink or marry. Or, she corrected herself, to do business; Vegas these days had a whole sideline in conventions and meetings, full as it was of large, cheap hotels and plenty of diversion. She was also, she thought, the only person who actually liked the Strip, but not because it was the Strip. She liked it because of what she became inside it. The grandiose, improbable casinos, competing with one another for pomp versus circumstance, flashing marquee desire versus plaster Paris and Rome. It was all so impossibly large and complex and so well-oiled that a person like her could disappear inside, a plain little pinball pinging around inside a neon nerve network.

She spent her days wandering the false streets of Venice, the plaza of Rome, the Eiffel Tower. She sat with a drink sometimes, watched countless strangers win and lose more money than she'd ever have—sometimes skillfully, sometimes not. Luck, she thought, featured into most winning, but there was also a small group of almost invisible people—invisible like her—who you'd never know to see them, but they were the real geniuses at winning. At poker. At blackjack. Some even worked the slots. They were never flashy, or loud, or overconfident. None of them looked like James Bond. They wore sweatshirts, jean shorts, reading glasses, cropped hair. They were quiet, and she knew their secrets only because she'd seen them winning, again and again and again. She noticed the special little privileges they had: large sums advanced to them, access to special rooms, drinks and deference from the casino staff. All of it small, unobtrusive, hushed as aristocracy and real, serious money.

If she'd been a different sort of criminal, she'd have tried to become one of them, imitate or impersonate them. But she couldn't; there was nothing to grasp, no detail substantial or solid. The regulars were like ghosts. They haunted the places reliably, but beyond their scheduled appearances they were silent and secretive, and anything left of their lives before had been buried.

One late afternoon, she was pocketing soap at a fancy bath store in the Venetian, and a shadow fell over her shoulder. She was ready; she arranged her face in blank, neutral confusion. She turned. It was one of the regulars, a shorter man in a blue polo and khaki cargo shorts. His hair was in a graying brown ponytail. His face was so unremarkable it was almost a blur. Just like her. She thought she'd seen him winning big at the craps tables at the MGM Grand. Yes? she said.

If you want to cheat, he said, go high stakes. It's Vegas! Why steal bath bombs? His voice was louder than she'd expected it would be.

She raised one eyebrow. I'm not stealing anything, she said. You must be mistaken. He reached a hand in her jeans pocket (her front pocket, the *nerve*) and pulled out a thirty dollar soap shaped like a scalloped cupcake. She raised her other eyebrow. The store clerk started toward them and she took it to the counter, furious. The bath she took with this strawberry scented soap might be perfectly pleasant, but it would not be worth thirty dollars. Her hands shook as she counted out bills, saw the gambler was still standing there, watching her. She was even angrier. She was usually cool as milk.

I've seen you, he said, walking out, following fast on her heels. MGM Grand. Harrah's. Caesars. I've seen you pretending to play the slots. What are you really doing here? Not just petty theft, I assume.

You've never seen me, she said, walking faster. How had he seen her? No one sees her. Her heart fluttered and people stared. Her face felt flooded with spotlight.

I used to be a dry cleaner, he said. From Des Moines. But I see everything. I notice everything. Always have. That's how I came to be a gambler instead of a dry cleaner. I had a talent, followed my heart, came out here. What's your passion? I'm staying at the Venetian. I like it here—I like the way the ceiling is a sky, how you can think you're somewhere cool and breezy. I like the gold things, everywhere. I like gold. They call me Midas at the MGM, I've won so often. What's your name? Where are you staying?

Nowhere, she said, frowning. She reminded herself to be a blank. She was staying at the Mirage and that was much too close to him, just across the street—and anyway she'd have to skip town tonight, get on a bus and bail. She was even angrier at the thought. She *liked* Vegas. She wanted to *stay* here. Her sensible, invisible shoes clacked loudly on the Venetian walkway tiles, and she glared at the gondoliers who seemed suddenly poised to offer her a ride. Who was this man and why had he ruined her superpower?

Let's get a pizza, he said, and grabbed her arm. Or a cookie. There's a great Hawaiian cookie place. I want to talk to you. I think you're fascinating. I'd love to sleep with you.

She stopped.

I'll turn you in, he said playfully, then put his hand over hers.

This was the second time he'd touched her, and it was a sensation she was utterly unused to. Her insides curled.

The long con, she thought. He'd be such a perfect mark. She could take, and take, and take, and one day disappear. But she wasn't made for the long con. She was made for minute-crime, for in and out and gone. She was supposed to be invisible. What would happen if he could see her, even just for a night? Would it break some spell? Render her features more distinct, her outline suddenly pulled into a fixed shape?

On the Greyhound to Reno, the man next to her mumbled to himself for a while and fell asleep. He smelled like whiskey and sour smoke. The teenager behind her hit her with his rucksack, and seemed surprised to be apologizing to no one at all. The bus driver tried to focus on her and failed, squeezing himself behind the wheel and dreaming about his shift end, Netflix and a cold Bud Light. She leaned back in her seat and sighed. She called the police on the burner phone, told them where to find a lot of recently stolen goods—a thief in room 1205. Venetian luxury suite. Hurry, he's probably still asleep. How did she know? She didn't want to say. He might be dangerous, careful now.

She'd be more careful from now on. Her luck was made, not found; this she now knew. She tossed the phone out the window and waited for the bus to grind on out of this McDonald's parking lot, gravel spitting, wheels rolling toward the next big town to take her out of focus.

Wild Things Run Fast

Released October 1982

"Chinese Café"
"Wild Things Run Fast"
"Ladies' Man"
"Moon at the Window"
"Solid Love"
"Be Cool"
"(You're So Square) Baby I Don't Care"
"You Dream Flat Tires"
"Man to Man"
"Underneath the Streetlight"
"Love"

All songs by Joni Mitchell
except "(You're So Square) Baby I Don't Care"
(music and lyrics by Jerry Leiber and Mike Stoller).

Man to Man
by Barb Goffman

It's strange that two people could be married for a decade only to realize they'd never truly understood each other. Take David and me. I married him for his money and his promises of fun. He married me for my body and sparkling personality—or so I thought. Rich man, younger trophy wife. It's an old story.

So imagine my surprise when I realized that David actually loved me. And thought I loved him. It left us in an awkward position, especially since he just told me that we're broke.

"We're not broke, Cecelia," he said in a soothing tone. "Don't overreact." The lines in his forehead, almost hidden beneath his tousled gray hair, hinted otherwise. "If we were broke, we wouldn't be eating here."

Here was our favorite steakhouse in downtown Chicago. It had white linen tablecloths. A fabulous view of the river. Sometimes you'd see a celebrity across the room. This was the life David had promised me—the life I'd given up my security for. After my first husband was killed in a tragic accident in my early twenties, I'd been set financially, with a nice monthly settlement income, but only as long as I remained single. I'd had fifteen great years of that life, including scores of gentleman callers. Then I gave it all up for David—well, for his promises of fun and lots more money.

Not for poverty. That, of course, was out of the question.

"Stop hinting around," I said. "Spell it out. Where do we stand financially?"

A gal's gotta know these things, especially a gal in her late forties. If I had to start looking for a new man, I'd need to get some work done. A nip there. A tuck here. And maybe some new boobs to complete the package.

"We have to tighten our belts on the bigger-ticket items for a while, until the market picks up."

"Meaning…?"

"Well, we should put off buying that beach house in St. Thomas, for starters. And the trip to Europe should wait. And maybe...."

"Maybe what?"

He shrugged. "Maybe we won't get new cars next year. And maybe you should cut back on your shopping."

I took a large gulp of my wine. The beach house and the trip, okay, those were expensive. We always traveled first class. But no shopping? No new cars? New luxury vehicles didn't cost that much. We always got new cars every three years. If David wanted to put those purchases off, we surely were in far worse shape than he was willing to admit.

"Hey," David said. "Perk up. We're fine." He patted my hand. "We have the apartment. We can still go to Manhattan next summer. And go see the kids."

The kids? I tried to smile, but couldn't even muster the energy. My son Eric lived in Seattle. David's daughter Liza and her family lived in St. Louis. If we couldn't travel to those places first class, why bother going? Not that Eric and Liza weren't lovely people, but neither of them were a barrel of laughs. Eric always droned on about computer stuff. And Liza was all about her kids, who liked to call me mee-maw. No, thank you.

"We can dine out whenever we want, within reason," David continued.

This proposition at least had merit.

He leaned toward me, his slate-blue eyes soft and kind. "And we still have each other."

Oh, goody.

As I fought not to roll my eyes, the waiter brought our first course. David dug into his charred octopus salad, nodding toward the wall of windows with the grand view. "We live in one of the best cities in the world. We can find loads of things to do right here in Chicago without dipping into our savings. And once the market rebounds, we'll have our play money again."

He'd better be right. The thought of ending up worse off financially than before we'd married made me shiver. And I couldn't count on finding a new man to marry, not at my age. Not if—I realized now—I couldn't afford the nip and the tuck and, especially, the new boobs.

"We'll get it all back," David said, picking up his glass. "Have a little faith. And patience. Our luck will change."

"You're right. Of course it will," I said, pushing myself to smile. The economy would rebound, and so would our portfolio. I just had to be patient.

*

Patience, of course, wasn't my strong suit. Six weeks later, David came home from work to find me sitting in the dark in our living room. I blinked and squinted as he turned on the lamp.

"Cecelia, are you all right?"

I glared at him. *Just peachy, Sherlock.*

"What is it?" he said. "Clearly something's wrong."

What was your first clue? My swollen eyes or gray sweats? I hadn't worn sweats in years—I'd dug them out of the back of my closet—but they fit my mood.

"I've been snubbed," I said, my lower lip trembling as I fought not to cry again.

"What?" David sat beside me on the couch.

"Pamela Falenwolfe asked me to give up my seat on the museum fundraising committee today. Asked, as if I could say no."

"Why would she—?"

"Because it wouldn't look right to have a committee member who can't buy a table for the fundraiser!" David laid his hand on my arm. I shrugged it off hard. "Everyone was expected to give a check for twenty-five thousand today, and I had to decline." Hot tears escaped my eyes. "I was humiliated."

"Honey, I'm sorry."

A lot of good that did me. *Sorry* didn't make up for the way they'd all looked at me. I didn't know what had been worse, the *friends* who'd stared with pity or the ones who'd turned their heads away, as if I was a beggar on the street, best to be avoided.

David clutched my shoulders. "Things won't be this way forever."

I pushed him away. "Are you kidding? Of course they will. Even if you turn things around, what happened today will always be remembered. I'll always be the woman asked to step down from the board. I'll always be less than them."

"Then you don't need them."

My eyes rolling, I half laughed. "That's easy for you to say. You go to the office every day. Your world hasn't changed. But mine has. The invitations have already slowed down, even before today's fiasco."

"Well, what about Bonnie and all your old friends? Call them."

The women I ghosted after I moved up the social ladder by marrying David a decade ago? For a smart man, he really could be clueless.

"Maybe I'll do that tomorrow. For now, I'm going to go to bed."

"So early? Are you sure?"

"Yes."

"Can I get you anything?"

A do-over would be nice. But since that wasn't possible, I merely shook my head and walked away.

*

By the time November arrived, I'd practically become a hermit. Nowhere to go. No one to go with. My mood was as dour as the Chicago sky.

It was ten o'clock on a Tuesday morning, and I was in my bathrobe, staring out the bedroom window, watching people on the street below. Everyone was in such a hurry. They were probably heading to important jobs or fun outings. I wished I had somewhere exciting to go.

The phone rang, jolting me from my melancholy. It was probably David. But it didn't matter who it was. At this point, I'd talk to a wrong number. Or even a telemarketer.

"Hello," I said, forcing myself to sound cheerful.

"Hi, Mom."

Eric usually called every other Sunday. A middle-of-the-week call couldn't be good. "Is everything all right?"

"Everything's fine. Better than fine, actually."

"What's going on?" I could tell from his tone—he had news.

"You know my friend Shelby?"

"Yes," I said, though I didn't really *know* her. I only knew *of* her. She and Eric had been dating for over a year. Since they both lived in Seattle, I'd never had the chance to size Shelby up. When David and I last went to visit, Shelby had been conveniently out of town.

"Well, things have gotten pretty serious. She wants me to go home with her at Thanksgiving to meet her parents."

My stomach dropped. Eric was supposed to come here for Thanksgiving. It'd been the only good thing on my horizon—someone other than David to talk to and do things with, even if it was Eric. Liza and her family were going to her mother's for the holiday, but Eric was supposed to come here.

"Mom, did you hear me?"

I reined in my irritation. "Yes, I heard you."

"I'm sorry. I know you were looking forward to me coming home, but this is important."

"Sure. I get it." Showing my disappointment wouldn't help matters. Men needed to feel understood, even when they didn't deserve it. "This is a big step. I'm happy for you, sweetheart."

He sighed. "Thanks for understanding."

"Can you come home for Christmas?" I said, without missing a beat. The best time to ask was when he felt guilty.

"Ummm, you know the end of the year is always busy for me at work."

"Right. Sure." Why should he make time for his mother? I was just the person who bore and raised him.

"Mom, don't be like this."

"Like what? You're busy. I get it. You know, I'm busy too. Lots of things to do. My charity work is keeping me hopping, so I have to go now. But we'll talk again on Sunday, all right?"

"Sure, Mom."

"Okay. Bye now."

I clicked off before I could say another word, afraid my façade would have cracked. As I set the phone down, I focused on a framed photo of David and me on the nightstand. He was smiling in that way of his that aggravated me so. Smirking, really, like he had a big secret.

Without Eric at home, it would just be David and me at Thanksgiving. I'd have to stare at that annoying smirk for four days. There'd be no company to break up the monotony. No Black Friday shopping to add to the festivity. Nothing good or fun. Just David and me.

And knowing him, he'd want to talk. But what would we talk about? All he was interested in lately was work, since he'd been putting in so many hours, trying to earn a promotion. But I didn't care about that. And what would I have to say? I had nothing happening in my life. No social groups. No events. No trips I was planning. I could barely pay attention to what was on television. No one ever called me, and I had no one to call.

It felt like I was in solitary confinement. Sure, I was in an upscale high-rise, but the isolation was overwhelming. And things didn't get better when David came home at night. He made me so angry sometimes, I wanted to scream.

This was all his fault. *Your fault. Your fault. Your fault.* The words ran through my head whenever I saw him, like tickertape. I'd had a fine life before I married David. Friends and activities. A series of boyfriends who took me out. Now I had nothing. Heck, worse than nothing, because David had shown me what I'd been missing and then he'd taken it all away.

He kept saying I should have faith. Be patient. The market would rebound. But there was no guarantee of that. David had made his money by taking big risks. We couldn't count on a repeat performance. The only thing I could count on was endless days with nothing to do and nowhere to go. And the anger rolling around my stomach. That seemed to always be there lately. And it was growing.

*

At 7 PM on New Year's Eve, I stood in my closet, stepping into the silver pumps that looked perfect with my beaded black gown. It wasn't new, but hopefully no one would notice. I didn't know where we were going, but David had said to dress up. It had been so long since we'd gone anywhere exciting or elegant. Maybe things were finally turning around.

"Knock knock," he said.

I looked up to find David leaning against the doorframe. I felt kindly toward him for the first time in ages. The gray beard he'd recently begun growing had filled out, giving him a distinguished air. I'd be proud to have him by my side tonight. "You certainly know how to wear a tux."

He smiled. "And you, Cecelia, know how to wear everything. You're dazzling."

My heart melted a little. I'd been so cold to him these past few months, especially because the market had improved for some people, but not for us. Except for our three-day visit to Liza's family for Christmas, I'd cocooned in the apartment. Here I was safe from the raised eyebrows of former friends whose charitable contributions I no longer could match and whose shopping trips I no longer could join. Sure, a couple of them had reached out to me over the past few months, but I avoided them. I didn't fit into their world anymore. I didn't fit in anywhere.

Still, I longed to be out among people, so I was beyond excited about tonight.

"Where are we going?" I asked, for perhaps the tenth time.

"All will be revealed. But first...."

He reached into his pocket and pulled out a velvet jewelry box. I licked my lips. It had been so long since he'd surprised me like this. One of his big gambles must have finally paid off.

"For you, my love," he said.

"Thank you." I breathed deeply as I took the box. Not wanting to appear eager, I forced myself to open it slowly. Inside I found...a thin white-gold necklace with a small dark-blue sapphire pendant. I blinked.

This was it?

It was lovely but so common.

"Do you like it?" David said.

Nodding, I searched for words, ultimately settling on the trite. "It's beautiful."

"Let me put it on you."

He wrapped the chain around my throat, then stood back and gazed at me with a grin. He seemed to actually think this was a great gift. Had the man lost his mind? He'd given me something far nicer than this on the first Valentine's Day we'd spent together— and we'd merely been dating then.

David grabbed my hand. "Are you ready to go?"

I guessed so. "Let me get my purse."

"You don't need your purse."

What? "Of course I need my purse."

"Not where we're going."

He tugged me through the bedroom and into the hallway, where a delicious aroma caught my attention. Confused, I followed David to the dining room, where two place settings had been arranged. Our china and crystal. A man in a waiter's uniform stood beside the table. I took a few more steps and peeked into the kitchen, where a chef was working.

"We're eating here?" I said.

"Surprise," David said.

"But—"

"Why go out on a cold night when we can have everything we want right here," he said. "It's perfect, isn't it?"

Perfect? My mouth dropped open. I had another word for it.

For months I'd been practically a recluse. How could he think staying home tonight would have any appeal? I wanted to be out among people. I was sick to death of being only with him.

"The salad course will be ready in a few minutes," the waiter said.

"That gives us just enough time for a dance," David said.

I noticed for the first time the soft music coming through the speakers in the walls.

David reached out a hand. "Shall we?"

He had no idea I was furious. How could the man be so dense?

I let him lead me to the living room and hold me close. He seemed content as we swayed back and forth. But me? His fingers on the small of my back burned like a bee's sting. I didn't want to eat at home. Dance at home. Be at home. I wanted to go out into the world, show off my beautiful gown, and go to a magnificent gala.

It would have been one thing if I'd never known how wonderful it was to have real money. But now I did know. David had shown me the good life. And then he'd yanked it away. He'd conned me, God damn him!

As David leaned in for a kiss, the hatred in my stomach bubbled over. I was done with waiting for things to turn around. And I was done with him.

I knew what I had to do.

*

Two Fridays later, David returned home to a chicken dinner—one of my usual, if boring, meals—and a chocolate ganache cake with vanilla frosting.

"Surprise," I said happily as I brought out the cake. I didn't have to fake my cheerfulness. Over the past week I'd gotten out in the world again, and I felt so much better. More energized. Of course, I also was happy because I wasn't waiting any longer for our luck to change. I was taking steps to make it happen.

Well, I was going to make *my* luck change, anyway.

"What's the occasion?" David asked. We didn't usually have dessert.

As I reclaimed my seat, I said, "I made a New Year's resolution to get out of the apartment more, so last week I signed up for an intensive baking course at that pastry shop a couple blocks over. All day every Monday, Wednesday and Friday. And this"—I waved my hand over the cake—"is the result of my first week's classes."

He beamed at me. "I'm happy for you, honey. Thrilled you're finally trying to make our new reality work."

Finally? *Screw you, David.*

But I didn't let my ire show. Instead I smiled back at him. He didn't need to know how angry I was deep down. Just like he didn't need to know that I already could bake, although my skills were rusty. My grandmother had taught me as a child. I'd never told David about it. I'd wanted him to see me as someone to be chased and won. A woman in an apron wouldn't have enticed him. And once we married, why would I have baked?

"I promise things won't be like this forever," David said.

I'd heard that before. "Would you like to do the honors?" I handed him the cake knife.

David sliced up two pieces and dug into his. "This is great. So rich and moist."

"Thanks. Before you know it, I'll be able to make that king cake you rave about each year. The one from...."

I tapped my finger against my lips, waiting for him to supply the store's name.

"Luscious Lagniappes?"

"That's right." *Thank you, David.*

King cakes are a New Orleans specialty. They're doughy bundt cakes with gold, green and purple sugar icing, and cream cheese, chocolate or cinnamon filling, as well as a tiny plastic baby squeezed inside the cake as it cools. Whoever gets the piece with the baby in it is supposed to have good luck for the coming year. You can buy them year-round, but they're most popular at Mardi Gras. David and I took an amazing trip to New Orleans shortly after we met, and I had my first taste of king cake there. I'd decided it would be my good-luck charm now. Someone in David's department at work did business with a company in New Orleans, and every year on Mardi Gras the owner sent a thank-you king cake from that Luscious Lagniappes place. Apparently David's colleagues drooled over it as much as he did.

"Wow, just mentioning that cake makes me hungry," he said. "If you can create that cake, I will die at your feet."

Or at someone's feet.

"I hope I'll be able to do it," I said. "I always was a good student."

It helped that the shop owner's daughter, who was teaching my class, really did know her stuff. I felt confident that, before the course was over in six weeks, I'd have learned everything I needed to in order to complete the final steps in my plan.

In the meanwhile, I'd have to keep up appearances. So I smiled once more at David and ate a forkful of the chocolate ganache cake before pushing my plate aside. It *was* pretty good, though packed full of calories. That didn't bother David. He quickly finished his slice and the rest of mine. His penchant for sweets would work in my favor.

"Not that I'm complaining," he said. "But I must admit, I'm surprised by this choice of hobby. You always eat like a bird."

I laughed. "True. But I'm in this for the creativity. Sifting. Measuring. Making something from nothing. That's what interests me."

Like what you used to do with money, David. But now you've left that job to me. So....

"I'll leave the eating to you," I said.

*

A week later, while David was away on a business trip, the king cake I'd ordered from that New Orleans bakery arrived at the pastry shop for me. Well, it arrived for Pamela Falenwolfe, the name I'd given to both the bakery and the pastry shop. It gave me a little thrill to involve that witch from the museum in my plan. And for the amount I was paying for the course, and in cash no less, the pastry shop owner was happy to accept a delivery for me, especially after I explained it was a surprise for my husband.

Having the cake delivered there and using the fake name were key parts of my plan. If the police ever investigated whether I played any role in the tragedy to come at David's office, our apartment building's front desk would have no record of a delivery for me from a New Orleans bakery. There'd be no trace of a king cake here in the apartment. Or the tiny plastic baby I'd already bought. Or the antifreeze, either. I'd get rid of all the evidence in advance. And if the cops somehow made it to the pastry shop—and really, how would they?—no one there knew me by my real name.

I brought the king cake home after class in its wonderfully plain and unmemorable brown box. The time had come for me to see what all the fuss was about. And to practice duplicating the recipe. I had to be sure it would taste exactly right so that, when my poisoned version of the cake arrived at David's office a couple of days before Mardi Gras—in this box from that New Orleans bakery they all loved—everyone would eat it.

It did bother me that the antifreeze I planned to add to my dough would take out a bunch of David's colleagues. Hey, I'm not a monster. But it was the only way I could think of to ensure that

David would die without anyone suspecting he'd been the target. He was simply an executive in that department. Just a poor innocent bystander who loved king cake. And I'd be a poor widow with a big payout coming.

*

When the big day finally arrived, I woke up happy. I was eager to finish the plan—not only because I wanted the mid-seven-figure check from David's life insurance, but because I would feel better with him gone. I could take the money and move somewhere amazing, with exciting people and lots of interesting things to do. Somewhere no one knew about my humiliation, where I could start fresh, without the anger David always inspired lately.

Maybe I'd even have some romance again, but I didn't plan to remarry. David had been a mistake. From now on, the dating life was for me. When I got tired of one man, I'd be free to move right on to another. As a rich woman, I wouldn't have to worry about being alone.

But first I had to implement the final step of the plan. I put on glasses and a wig and dressed as a typical nondescript package-delivery person. I timed my arrival at David's office for shortly after noon, when the receptionist on his floor went to lunch and her desk was left unmanned. I knew from prior visits that lunchtime was busy there, with people coming and going. No one would pay any attention to me as I left the cake on the receptionist's desk. Once she found the box with David's colleague's name on it, the cake would be delivered to him, and in minutes everyone would gather in the conference room to dig in.

The delivery worked like clockwork. I could have sworn I saw David walking into a fancy restaurant a block from his office with a group of men while I was on my way with the cake, but it couldn't have been him. He was watching our pennies. But I didn't have to anymore. So I took myself out for a celebratory lunch at a fancy restaurant where no one knew me. I splurged—how I'd missed splurging—on a delicious if pretentious shrimp and cauliflower dish. No dessert. I had that waiting at home. One last piece of my final practice king cake. I'd hidden it a few days before in the freezer. This morning I'd moved it to the fridge so I could eat it this afternoon while I waited for word of the catastrophe at David's office. My own little festivity.

I paid in cash for lunch so not to leave a trail, and I headed off to do some shopping. Nothing hard-core. I had to pay in cash for this, too. But I'd deprived myself for months. No more. I hit my old haunts and wandered around, salivating at all the goodies. Even the air smelled better in the high-end stores. I bought myself a little trinket—some luxury soaps I could enjoy during my mourning period. And I discreetly threw away my wig and glasses before I made my way back to the apartment.

I opened the front door. The air seemed to smell better. Of course it didn't, not really. But being out in the world, back in my old element, had done wonders for my spirit. I dropped my purse on the counter and made my way to the fridge for my celebratory piece of cake. I pulled it out and dug in. Mmmm.

My grandmother would be really proud of this cake. It was light and buttery with a strong cinnamon flavor and a silky vanilla glaze. Blissful, I began walking around the apartment with the plate, luxuriating in each bite as I took in my apartment—mine, all mine. For now. Once the police finished their investigation, it would go on the market. I'd be far too distraught to live here anymore.

I'd nearly finished the large slice when I wandered into my bedroom—and stopped short. "What the hell?"

David was lying on the bed asleep. Or was he dead?

He answered my question when he stirred. "Cecelia." He blinked his eyes open, pushed himself up against the headboard, and smiled.

So, not dead. Not yet, anyway. "What are you doing home?" I said.

"Oh, good. You found the cake."

"What?"

"I'm getting ahead of myself." He grinned. "Honey, it took several months, but I did it. I got the promotion. Senior vice president. It comes with a bigger salary, bigger office, a ton of stock options and other perks."

My eyes widened. "That's fantastic." I hoped it came with a larger life insurance policy, too. Would that have kicked in yet?

"I would have waited to tell you at dinner. It normally wouldn't look right for the new senior vice president to take the afternoon off. But my boss insisted. You remember that delicious king cake we get every year?"

"Yeah...."

"Well, it came today. And just as I slid my fork into my slice, I felt pushback." He reached into his pocket and pulled out a tiny plastic doll, which he held up between his thumb and index finger. "I got the baby!"

You could have fit a huge piece of king cake in my mouth, considering how much it was hanging open.

"It's supposed to signify good luck," David continued. "So each year the head of our division tells whoever gets the baby to take the rest of the day off. He said I especially deserved it because of the promotion. We'd just gone out to lunch to celebrate, so I hadn't gotten much done today, but he told me to go anyway. So here I am. Home to celebrate with you."

Of course he was. No matter how much I hated him, he seemed to love me even more.

David sighed happily. "When I got home and you were out, I ate that slice of cake in the fridge. And then I decided to take a nap until you came back."

"You ate the cake in the fridge?" That didn't make sense. *I* had just eaten the cake in the fridge.

He jumped from the bed, took the plate from my hand, set it on the dresser and hugged me. "Between my promotion and getting the baby, we're on a roll, honey." He pulled back, looking lovingly at me. "Thank you for being patient. I told you our luck would change."

Uh huh. Until his kidneys began shutting down.

"So how was that cake from New Orleans?" I asked. "Your slice with the baby in it?"

"You tell me." He glanced at the dresser. "That's it. I brought it home to share with you."

I staggered back, kicking myself. I should have seen this coming. Of course he'd saved the poisoned cake to share with me. The idiot loved me.

Dog Eat Dog
Released October 1985

"Good Friends"
"Fiction"
"The Three Great Stimulants"
"Tax Free"
"Smokin' (Empty, Try Another)"
"Dog Eat Dog"
"Shiny Toys"
"Ethiopia"
"Impossible Dreamer"
"Lucky Girl"

All songs by Joni Mitchell.

Dog Eat Dog
by Elaine Viets

The first time I tried to kill my husband, I failed. Miserably. I gave him a little push at the top of the stairs, and Colgate tangled himself in his walker and fell down the twenty-seven marble steps, just as I'd hoped. He cracked his head—but not hard enough.

Now he's in a coma. The doctors say there's still brain activity and he could wake up at any time, so I can't pull the plug on him. He might go on forever this way. As I sit by his bedside, watching the fluid drip through his IV, I imagine each drop is a dollar. Even his immense fortune will eventually drain away.

I want desperately to finish him off, but I don't want to get caught.

I'm the fourth Mrs. Colgate Osborne, and I'm determined to be the last. And everything was going fine until that damned preacher—the Reverend Joseph Starr, mega-millionaire pastor of the *Starr in the Heavens* TV congregation—came along.

I go by the name Tish Osborne now. Sounds classy, doesn't it? I've been cleaned up quite a bit since I was eighteen-year-old Tiffany Yokum, a clerk at the Sav-All Hardware and Bargain Barn in Festus, Missouri. Colgate was a randy seventy-two when he spotted me behind the cash register, falling out of my tank top. He practically drooled when I rang up his order, but I had that effect on most men.

I quickly realized Cole wasn't the usual redneck contractor. His hair was too well cut, and his Cartier tank watch was real. He had nice hands—the nails were manicured and buffed, with no motor-oil stains on them. When he handed over his American Express Platinum card to pay for his new flashlight, well, that was proof he was loaded.

"I hope you'll come back next Monday, sir," I said and smiled. "We have a special on light bulbs. The kind that last *extra long*."

I gave those last two words an illicit little oomph.

"My favorite kind," he said.

I blushed becomingly. Being a fair-skinned nearly natural blonde, that was easy to do.

"May I have your phone number, sir?" I asked.

"Only if I can have yours," he said.

We swapped numbers, but I didn't write his on the store receipt. I kept it.

Next Monday, he came in at noon for those light bulbs and asked about my lunch break. "I have half an hour in ten minutes," I said.

I thought we'd go to the McDonald's down the street—it was the closest place to the Sav-All—but Cole had brought a picnic, with cold chicken, chocolate cake and champagne—*real* champagne, with a cork in it. It sure beat the peanut-butter sandwich I had stashed in my locker. We ate in his car, a vintage Bentley with leather seats, and the time passed quickly.

As we ate, Cole told me he loved hardware stores: the scents of oil and rubber, the aisles of shiny gadgets, the rows of fresh-cut wood. I feel the same way, and we talked happily about the CT-15 Multi-Square. "It's like a Swiss Army knife for wood workers," I said.

I knew men liked presents, and so I decided to prime the pump. Next time we met, I gave him a Leatherman Style multi-tool with a knife, scissors, nail file, two screwdrivers (flat and Phillips) and tweezers, all on a little key chain. It was only twenty bucks, and I got my employee discount, too.

He showed his appreciation with a Tiffany bracelet, and I showed my appreciation...well, never mind how. But I was very appreciative, and the old goat was very happy.

We were married two months later, and he whisked me down to his winter home in Fort Lauderdale, Florida, which was to be our permanent home.

I never went to college, but I'm not stupid. I knew that, now that Cole and I had tied the knot, my struggles had just begun. My new husband was very classy, and I had to fit in with his wealthy set.

So the first thing I did was make friends with his housekeeper, Mrs. Anderson. She'd been with Cole for twenty years and three wives. I slipped her a little extra out of the mad money he gave me, and Mrs. A advised me where to shop on Las Olas—the local Rodeo Drive—and which saleswomen to make appointments with. She also recommended I ditch my fake nails and get a refined French manicure, then sent me to a salon where I had my long hair tamed into fashionable waves and its color became "not so blond," as the tactful stylist said.

The other problem I faced was Cole's two kids. Actually, both "kids" were in their mid-thirties and unmarried, but I didn't want any trouble. Cole could be a bit tight with his money, and I convinced him to spend it generously on his children. When Trey (from Wife Two) wanted a new Mercedes, I encouraged Cole to buy him a snappy red convertible. And when Bitsy (from Wife Three) wanted to vacation in the Seychelles but Cole objected that the Caribbean would be just as good and a lot cheaper, I suggested he go ahead and send her to her fancy Seychelles resort for the "trip of a lifetime." Soon Trey and Bitsy were my good friends, which neutralized me as a bone of contention with both children.

I helped Cole entertain, too. Actually, Mrs. A did all the work, but she guided me to the right charities in Fort Lauderdale, and I gave a fabulous dinner for the library's Literary Fest. I enjoyed talking to the writers and reading their books. Many of them wrote mysteries, my favorite genre, and soon I had a big library of signed first editions.

Then there was the music. We supported the symphony and the opera, of course, and I can't tell you how many long, dull evenings I sat through in our private box. At least I got to wear pretty clothes and fabulous jewelry. I perfected the art of appearing wrapped up in the music: eyes closed, hands clasped. While the sopranos howled like sirens in another language, I listened to my favorite album on invisible ear buds. It wasn't country music, like you'd expect from a Festus girl. No, I loved Joni Mitchell, especially her *Dog Eat Dog* album. I had somehow landed in a dog-eat-dog world—even more of one than the trailer park where I grew up—and the title song described my new life perfectly:

> *Where the wealth's displayed*
> *Thieves and sycophants parade*
> *And where it's made—*
> *The slaves will be taken*
> *Some are treated well*
> *In these games of buy and sell*
> *And some like poor beasts*
> *Are burdened down to breaking*

I was the well-treated slave, and I'd sold myself into slavery, but I knew that. One misstep, and I'd be one of the poor beasts, working again at the local hardware store or greeting people at Walmart. I had a prenup that would give me a measly hundred thousand dollars if we divorced, but, if I could hang on until Cole died, I'd get half his fortune.

I knew exactly what I had to deliver to enjoy my gilded cage: sex. Most guys Cole's age are alike: a blow job and a couple of pumps, and it's over. I told him his prowess was "positively presidential," and he strutted around our bedroom like a rooster. Good thing he didn't read those stories about Stormy Daniels.

Sex with Cole was no big deal, pun intended. In exchange for making him feel manly, I got to live in an oceanfront mansion, wear beautiful clothes, eat the best food and drink champagne. He wasn't bad looking for an older man—he had thick white hair, a tan hid most of his age spots, and he dressed well.

As I entered my mid-twenties, I had to work harder to keep my girlish figure. My trainer was worse than a drill sergeant, and I endured endless runs on the beach. Awful as it was, it beat standing on my feet all day on a concrete floor, running a cranky cash register for nine dollars an hour. When Cole got to be about seventy-five, he started taking Viagra, but that was okay. It did most of the work for me. About eighty, the sex tapered off totally, except for an occasional grope. When he was eighty-three, he began using a walker. I relaxed a little, then—he couldn't chase the fifth Mrs. Osborne on a walker. I made sure his nurses were burly men. By now, he had Type 2 diabetes, but he handled it well and took his insulin faithfully.

I thought I would sail smoothly along into Cole's sunset years and collect the cash when he went to his reward. But then that damn preacher showed up: the smarmy Reverend Joseph Starr, mega-millionaire pastor. Cole was flipping channels one Sunday morning, trying to get the baseball game, when he accidentally lit on Starr's show in mid-sermon.

The reverend was pounding the pulpit and exhorting his followers: "Have you laid up your treasures in Heaven? Have you atoned for your selfish, evil ways? Heaven is your next stop, brothers and sisters, and you should prepare your soul to meet your Maker."

Cole was mesmerized by Starr's performance. He finally switched over to the game, but it was too late: Cole knew he was due at the Pearly Gates soon, and he had begun to brood on his immortal soul.

"I've committed many sins, sweetie," he said to me at dinner that night. We were having chicken marsala, his favorite.

"Me, too," I said.

"But not on my scale," he said, and smiled at me. "I've done grievous wrongs—I've bribed people for land deals, I've destroyed the environment, I've built shoddy homes that couldn't possibly survive a hurricane."

"Nobody's perfect," I told him, and patted his liver-spotted hand.

"I'm hoping the Lord will forgive me," he said, and went back to his chicken.

"I'm sure he will. Look how much you've given to the library."

"But I need spiritual guidance. I'm going to talk to that preacher, Reverend Starr. I need his advice."

"He lives in Orlando," I objected.

"He's flying down tomorrow to speak to me. He has his own plane. Please have something nice for our lunch."

I was so upset, I couldn't finish the rest of my chicken. What kind of preacher has his own plane? One who needs lots of money, that's what kind. I recalled Joni's warning in "Dog Eat Dog" about "snakebite evangelists and racketeers." Starr would work on Cole's guilt and milk him for every dollar—and my husband was one big cash cow.

The next day, Reverend Starr arrived in a long black limousine, right at lunch time. He was slick as a used-car salesman, from his carefully oiled dark hair to his thousand-dollar suit. And the diamond pinkie ring! Big enough to make Satan's eyes sparkle. He carried a black leather briefcase.

Mrs. A had prepared a sumptuous spread of caviar, cold lobster salad, chocolate mousse and the best Kona coffee. I pretended I was interested in the word of the Lord, and asked if I could stay for their after-lunch conversation. Then I listened as my fool husband confessed his sins, mostly dealing with his construction company. (Really, in any state but Florida, Cole would have been indicted years ago. I thanked God the authorities here are lax and prayed that the statute of limitations had expired.)

"Oh, my brother, your sins are many," Starr said. "But God will forgive you."

"Really?" Cole looked hopeful, as I tried to bury my alarm.

"But you must atone, and atonement requires sacrifice."

"Anything," Cole said.

"What would you think of a carillon to ring out the praises of the Lord?"

"A bell tower?"

"Not just any bell tower: the Colgate Osborne Carillon, largest in the United States, with one hundred bells." He spread his hands in such a way that the bell tower seemed to spring from them. "People will come from all over the world to hear its beautiful music. It will be part of the Starr in the Heavens complex. My flock will sing your praises, long after you've gone to glory in your Heavenly home."

I was horrified, but Cole was interested. Way too interested. Reverend Starr opened his briefcase and brought out the plans for the tower, and he and Cole pored over them for nearly an hour. At four o'clock, Starr jumped up and said, "Is it really four? I must return home to write my Sunday sermon."

Reverend Starr kissed my hand, and then Cole wrote him a check on the spot and I kissed a million bucks good-bye. I didn't protest. I couldn't. All I could do was hope this was just a passing fancy.

But the reverend flew down week after week, and each time he had bigger and better plans for the Colgate Osborne Carillon, and each time Cole wrote him another hefty check. When the total hit ten million, I realized Starr was determined to bleed us dry.

"How much longer are you going to keep seeing the Reverend Starr?" I asked.

"He brings peace to my soul," Cole said. His hand shook slightly as he talked.

"But at what price?"

"What shall it profit a man," my husband said, "if he shall gain the whole world and lose his own soul?"

I didn't like the sound of that. Not at all.

"I understand, sweetie, but you've invested a lot of time"—and money, but I didn't say that—"in the carillon project."

His next words chilled me to the bone: "As the Lord said, 'Go, sell all that you have and give to the poor, and you will have treasure in heaven.' My sights are set on Heaven, Tish."

"But how will we live?" I asked.

"The Lord will provide," he said.

But not in the manner to which I'd grown accustomed. So that's when I decided Cole had to die. His sense of balance was growing steadily worse. It would be easy to give him a little push and send him down those steps.

But I dithered, until the Saturday when Cole arranged a shopping spree for me at Tiffany's in Bal Harbour during another of Reverend Starr's visits—this one in the company of a lawyer, who was tagging along for some unspecified purpose. Cole even sprang for a chauffeured limo to take me to the store. "I can't go with you, my darling, but you buy yourself something pretty," he said. "I've scheduled a salesperson to help you, with a limit of fifty thousand. I'm sure you can find something nice for that amount."

You bet I did: a diamond ring that had to be delivered by Brink's truck. Fifty thou isn't really all that much for a Tiffany ring, but it was a start.

By the time I returned, Reverend Starr had left—and so had the lawyer. I suspected now that Starr would get at least half the estate, and the children and I would split what was left, if anything. Just thinking about it made me mad. I'd given ten years to Cole—the best years of my life—and now this preacher comes in and cuts me out?

So when I saw Cole scooting down the hall toward the steps, being held up by a walker with tennis balls on its legs and slightly tipsy from his luncheon glass of Chardonnay, it was easy to smile and give him that little push. He toppled down the stairs, all tangled up in his walker.

I screamed. Mrs. Anderson came running. Someone called 9-1-1, and, the next thing I knew, Cole and I were in an ambulance. Cole was unconscious, and the doctors said he was in a coma. They admitted him to the ICU.

I played the perfect wife, spending hours at his hospital bedside, holding his hand. I called his children, who came to see him. I made friends with all the nurses and sympathized with their complaints.

Really, twelve-hour shifts were barbaric, I told them. Even I never had to work those. I brought a big box of Godiva chocolates for them and had lunches delivered from the best local restaurants to the nurses' station. They liked me and kept me informed about Cole's condition.

They weren't quite so crazy about the reverend. He visited every Saturday, stood there in his exquisite suit, oily and arrogant, as if he expected them to drop everything and swoon. Instead, they ignored him. He gave them lectures about modesty and humility, which they also ignored. He caught one nurse smoking in the stairwell and said, "Tobacco is the Devil's weed, Sister." She told him, "I'm not your sister, and cigarettes aren't mentioned in the Bible. Beat it."

When he came to Cole's room, Reverend Starr made a big show of the laying on of hands. He'd rest his palms on Cole's scrawny, sunken chest and say, "Oh, Lord, heal our brother, and let him finish his mission on Earth. And if that is not Your will, please call him home to glory."

I always said amen. Especially to that last part.

Cole never moved. A ventilator helped him breathe, and he had so many tubes and IV lines I could hardly find him amidst the medical paraphernalia. He'd lost weight, too, looked very old and very frail. I was tempted to put a pillow over his face, but I'd read enough mysteries to know about DNA on pillowslips and the telltale petechiae from smothering.

So far as I could tell, the laying on of hands didn't do one bit of good. After three weeks of being the faithful, worried wife, sleeping every night in an uncomfortable chair and wandering around the ICU floor like a ghost, it was time to end this charade—and the Reverend Starr was going to help me.

The next Saturday, I dressed like a woman in deep grief: a simple black pantsuit, modest low heels, black gloves. My long blond hair was in a tight bun.

When Starr arrived, I said, "Reverend, I do believe that the laying on of hands is helping Cole. Last week, I thought he tried to communicate with me after you left, but then he lapsed back into unconsciousness. Would you do me the favor of blessing his medication, and laying your hands upon it to make it more effective?"

The swellheaded fraud smiled at me and said, "Of course, Mrs. Osborne. Where is it?"

"Right here," I said, pointing to Cole's IV drip.

Reverend Starr put both hands on the bag and said. "Oh, Lord, we ask you to let this medication heal our brother, Colgate Osborne. You can do it, Lord. You have the power to perform the miracle that will bring him back to his loving wife."

I kept my head bowed and bit my lip to keep from laughing during this charade.

"Thank you, Reverend," I said softly. "And now this."

I handed him the black 200-unit Humalog KwikPen, which looked like a fountain pen. Colgate used them for his diabetes, and we had a supply at home. Reverend Starr took the pen in his hands and blessed it, too. Now I had what I wanted. The reverend laid his hands on Cole's chest and asked the Lord to save him.

When he finished, Reverend Starr asked me, "What are the doctors saying?"

"Let's go outside to the family room," I said.

In the family room, I told him, "I'm losing hope, Reverend. I'm afraid he's never coming back to me." I shed a few tears—not enough to mess up my makeup, but still effective.

He patted my gloved hand. "There, there," he said. "What you need is rest. Why don't you go home, and I'll pray over him? It's only three o'clock. I'll stay until four."

"That would be wonderful, Reverend," I said. "You've been so good to him."

He patted my hand again and walked me out the door. I waved good-bye to all the nurses and went for a drive. After an hour, I stopped at a gas station and changed into green scrubs and put on a brown wig, and stuffed my black outfit into a tote bag. I drove back to the hospital. No one noticed me. I was just one more nurse.

Cole's room was empty, except for my ailing husband. I slipped on nitrile gloves from the box on the wall, took the "blessed" 200-unit Humalog KwikPen and injected it in Cole's IV injection port. Then I left it by the bedside, retreated to a bathroom, dumped the wig, scrubs and gloves and got back into my black weary-wife outfit. As soon as I left the bathroom, I heard the frantic Code Blue announcement and followed the stampede of hospital personnel to Cole's room.

The nurses wouldn't let me see him. Ten minutes later, the doctors told everyone to stop. They'd given up.

The nurses came out, brought me coffee and told me how sorry they were. I asked for a moment alone with my husband, and they said, "As soon as we clean him up a bit, Mrs. Osborne."

Half an hour later, I was alone in the room with Cole. All signs of the recent battle to save his life were gone, but the tubes were still in his arms. He looked peaceful.

I rang for a nurse. "What can I do for you, Mrs. Osborne?" she asked.

"Why is that here?" I pointed to the Humalog KwikPen. "Cole used those at home, but he didn't need them in the hospital. You handled his insulin for him."

The police were called, and Cole's sudden death was ruled a homicide. I explained that the Reverend Starr had been alone in the room with Cole. The reverend's fingerprints were all over the injection pen that had killed my husband. The police found out that Cole had recently made a new will, leaving everything—everything!—to Starr.

The reverend was arrested for murder in the first degree. That means the crime was premeditated. And Florida is a death-penalty state: the sentence for first-degree murder is either life in prison or death, and it would be worse for the reverend, because my husband was eighty-three, making his killing a felony murder, or "aggravated abuse of an elderly person."

The Reverend Starr is rich and powerful, and so are his friends. So the "snakebite evangelist" got away with reduced charges, convicted of third-degree murder and sentenced to fifteen years in prison, plus another fifteen years' probation—all the while protesting his innocence.

But no one believed him, especially not after word got out about Cole's will.

Because the reverend was convicted, though, he can't inherit Colgate's money. The children and I will get the considerable remains of Cole's fortune, just the way he wished it: one half to me, and the other half split between Trey and Bitsy.

Of course, even if I hadn't inherited a dime, I was prepared.

I'd had copies made of my jewelry and sold the originals in New York. I'd sent my barely worn dresses and purses off to consignment shops. I'd skimmed money from my household budget.

In the end, I had accumulated a nice little nest egg—even without my inheritance, it would have been enough so I'd never have to work again. I bought a one-bedroom condo by the sea. Up the coast from Fort Lauderdale in a quiet little town.

Where life isn't quite so...dog eat dog.

Chalk Mark in a Rain Storm

Released March 1988

"My Secret Place"
"Number One"
"Lakota"
"The Tea Leaf Prophecy (Lay Down Your Arms)"
"Dancin' Clown"
"Cool Water"
"The Beat of Black Wings"
"Snakes and Ladders"
"The Reoccurring Dream"
"A Bird That Whistles"

All songs by Joni Mitchell
except "Cool Water" (by Bob Nolan with revised lyrics
by Joni Mitchell)
and "A Bird That Whistles" (traditional, generally called
"Corrina, Corrina").

The Beat of Black Wings
by Josh Pachter

It's funny how one thing sometimes really *does* lead to another.

You take Audrey Monaghan, for example. Audrey wasn't what you'd call a "hippie," not exactly. She was only fifteen during the Summer of Love, born not *in* the Age of Aquarius but right smack on its cusp, and, two years later, when she was between her sophomore and junior years of high school and working for her dad at his stupid drugstore on Long Island and dying to hitchhike up to Bethel for the Woodstock Music & Art Fair, he wouldn't give her the weekend off. Then, the next week, he actually handed her a cardboard box and the keys to the truck and told her to deliver some stupid prescription to a regular customer who was on vacation way the hell upstate in Bethel, only two and a half miles from Max Yasgur's farm outside White Lake, and on the way up she stopped at the farm to take a look, but all that was left to see by then was an ocean of mud where, five damn days earlier, Sly and the Family Stone had taken the more than four hundred thousand attendees higher, and Carlos Santana had told them they'd got to change their evil ways, and Janis Joplin had begged them to try just a little bit harder.

So one thing led to another, right, and the next year Audrey bought the single—remember singles?—of CSNY's hit version of the song and pretty much wore it out on her turntable. "By the time we got to Woodstock, we were half a million strong, and everywhere there was song and celebration." And the paper label told her the song had been written by "J. Mitchell," so she asked around and found out about Joni, who she'd somehow managed to miss up till then, and she bought *Ladies of the Canyon* and *Blue* and *Court and Spark* and wore *them* out, too, listening to "Big Yellow Taxi" and "This Flight Tonight" and "Free Man in Paris" over and over and over again until her dad told her to turn the goddamn noise *down* already.

After a while, Audrey sort of outgrew Joni, but one thing led to another and, in 1988, when she was pregnant for the third time—the first two times, at seventeen and nineteen, she'd terminated with extreme prejudice, no rugrats were gonna tie *her* down, but in 1988 she was thirty-six years old and *married*, can you believe it, to Tommy Wilkerson, the proverbial boy next door (except he'd grown up two doors down and not literally next door)—she was ready and she really *wanted* the baby.

Anyway, Tommy brought her home this new Joni Mitchell CD (remember CDs?)—*Chalk Mark in a Rain Storm*—one day about two months in, and it was totally different from the old days, really rockin', you know what I mean?, and Audrey just absolutely dug it. She played it so often she would have worn it out, if you could wear out a CD, which apparently you couldn't.

Her favorite track was "The Beat of Black Wings," man, that song just *got* to her, you know how a song can crawl under your skin and just *live* there, am I right?

> *I met a young soldier*
> *His name was Killer Kyle*
> *He was shakin' all over*
> *Like a night-frightened child.*

So in the dead of one night along about the middle of her second trimester, when the baby started to kick, Audrey patted her belly tenderly and shushed him, "It's all right, Kyle, don't be scared, go back to sleep." She and Tommy were convinced the baby was a girl, and they actually had the conversation one morning over coffee, could you name a girl child Kyle?, but then after a twelve-hour labor that had her screaming despite the epidural and the breathing exercises and all the rest of it, the baby had come out a boy after all, so "Kyle" it was and no worries about could you or couldn't you.

And one thing led to another, the way it does, and Kyle grew up. I would like to say that he grew up tall and proud, "Killer Kyle," captain of the football team in high school, king of the prom, admired by all the boys and the heartthrob of all the girls, but that would be stretching the truth just a—well, actually, it would be stretching the truth pretty much all to hell and back.

Kyle Monaghan was a dumpy little boy and, this has to be said, not all that smart. He didn't walk till he was fourteen months old, didn't say a word till he was almost two, and when he finally *did* start walking and talking, he didn't have much of anyplace to go or anything to say. Audrey loved him, in her own way, but she was so caught up in Tommy's ongoing alcoholism and drama that she never had the time or, frankly, the energy to give her son the attention and encouragement he needed.

By the time he got to high school, Kyle's face was bubbly with acne and he was two years older than the other kids, having been left back once in the fourth grade and again in the seventh. He didn't make the football team—hell, he didn't even bother trying out. He *did* approach a girl in the cafeteria one lunchtime and stammer out an invitation to the prom, but Jane Blaine—who was called "Plain Jane" behind her back and generally acknowledged to be the least attractive girl in her class—laughed at him and said she'd rather not go at all than go with a loser like him. (In fact, she didn't go—and neither did he.)

Nobody ever called him "Killer" Kyle, not one time. Not even Audrey.

At nineteen, a junior in danger of being left back for a third time, Kyle gave up on school. One afternoon, without a word to his mother—Tommy was in prison by then, doing a nickel for an attempted robbery he'd bungled so badly even the judge had to suppress a smile as he sent the graying rummy off to the joint—Kyle walked into the Army recruiting station downtown because there was a "Help Wanted" sign in the window and he thought maybe he could pick up some cigarette money sweeping the floors or something, and walked out again in a daze, a stack of enlistment papers in his hands.

At least *they* wanted him, they needed him, they trained him to kill. They gave him a gun, they gave him a mission, they sent him off to Kuwait for two weeks to get as used to the desert heat as anybody ever got, then trucked him and a hundred other grunts up to the Iraqi border to keep the world safe for democracy, which was a laugh, because everybody knew it was *really* all about protecting the flow of oil.

And eventually his tour was over and he came home, only Audrey was shacked up with some dude only four years older than Kyle by then and they didn't have room for him in the double-wide, so he rented himself a little shitbox apartment and got himself a nothing job at Costco, worked his forty hours a week and spent his nights and weekends playing Mortal Kombat and sucking down PBRs and shopping online.

And then finally one day he checked into a hotel downtown and carted three duffels full of hardware and shells up to the suite he'd reserved with a credit card no one would ever pay off.

And you know what happened next. I don't even want to write it down. I *can't* write it down, not now, maybe not ever. It's too soon. It will always be too soon.

Which brings us back to Audrey Monaghan. They had her on the *Today* show the morning after the massacre, sandwiched in-between some NRA loon mansplaining to Savannah Guthrie that guns don't kill people and a sitcom star who—I swear to God—was hawking her new cookbook. Audrey had on a demure black miniskirt, her long hair streaked with gray and tied back with a scrunchie. She sat knee to knee with Hoda Kotb—and at sixty-four years of age her knees still looked pretty good—trying to hold in the tears as she told the country what a sweet child her Kyle had been and how she couldn't understand what had *happened* to the precious little boy she'd raised all on her own, taking tissue after tissue from the box Hoda held out to her and wiping smears of mascara from the corners of her eyes.

Audrey's precious child is burning in hell now. At least I hope he is.

This was his story. It was a tough one for me to sing. Hard as the squawk and the flap, and the beat of, the beat of black wings.

Night Ride Home

Released February 1991

"Night Ride Home"
"Passion Play (When All the Slaves Are Free)"
"Cherokee Louise"
"The Windfall (Everything For Nothing)"
"Slouching Towards Bethlehem"
"Come in From the Cold"
"Nothing Can Be Done"
"The Only Joy in Town"
"Ray's Dad's Cadillac"
"Two Grey Rooms"

All songs by Joni Mitchell
except "Slouching Towards Bethlehem" (lyrics adapted
from W.B. Yeat's poem,
music by Joni Mitchell) and "Nothing Can Be Done"
(lyrics by Joni Mitchell, music by Larry Klein).

Cherokee Louise
by Matthew Iden

From the floor, my brother Harley squinted up at me where I lay on the couch, idly fanning myself. "Tadpoles?"

"Gross."

"Rock hunting?"

"Too hot."

He chewed his cheek. "Archie and Jughead?"

I huffed, caught out. It had been a long, lazy summer and, for once, Harley had picked something that caught my interest. But I'd already set up a pattern of denying him and, as an older sister, I knew it was critical not to give in. "I told you, Harley, that's kid stuff."

He frowned. "Wasn't kid stuff before."

"That was then," I said, using a line our father was fond of when we had him on the hook. "This is now."

"C'mon, Ginny."

"I'm not a kid anymore, so leave me alone." My voice ended on a high note, making me sound like I was whining as much as my brother, so I tacked on a "Jesus, Harley" for emphasis. I felt daring for using it.

Harley's face puckered like the top of an old peach, and I almost apologized—he looked ready to bawl. But he kicked the corner of the couch instead and stalked from the room, muttering as he banged down the hall, through the kitchen, and out the back door: "Jayzus, Harley. Jayzus, Harley. *Jayzus*, Harley."

I gulped and swung my feet off the cushions to follow. If Daddy caught us swearing, he'd whip us both…and me twice as hard, since he'd know exactly who had taught his son to cuss.

Or maybe he'd whip me anyway. Daddy and I hadn't been getting along that summer—or, really, since Mama passed the year before. More than once, as the three of us gathered to watch *Holiday*

Ranch on our new black-and-white TV, I'd glance over and catch him staring at me, a worried look on his face. From where I sit now, I understand what was on his mind, but at the time I felt as if my existence offended him. Often he'd simply turn his head and scowl, but sometimes he lost his temper and yelled at me for no apparent reason. I'd stomp to my room in tears while he snapped open the evening edition of the *StarPhoenix* and pretended to read.

I was still deliberating whether to chase after Harley when Daddy pulled up to the house in his cruiser. I quailed a little, hoping he wouldn't see the guilty look on my face. But when he came inside, he smiled broadly as he spied me sitting on the couch.

"Hello, sugar." He made a show of looking around. "Where's your brother?"

"He just ran out back," I said, not volunteering why.

"That's too bad," he said, looking glum. "And here I was going to take everyone out for ice cream."

I leapt to my feet and raced to the kitchen, hollering for Harley, and in ten seconds flat we were bouncing up and down in the cruiser, heading for Dairy Queen. Daddy let me sit in the front seat, where I put on his peaked cap and fiddled with the radio, and Harley sat in the back, his fingers and thumbs clutching the security grate like a crook on his way to the slammer.

I got a simple vanilla cone, my favorite. Daddy got a Klondike bar, nibbling carefully so he didn't get chocolate on his uniform, wincing once when he bit into the foil by mistake. Harley got a snow cone but, in his excitement, squeezed it so hard that it shot rocket-like toward the sky before hitting the ground with a *plop*. Daddy raced to get another before Harley pitched a fit.

The line had grown long, and my father wouldn't allow anyone to let him cut, despite the offers. Harley glared at me as I attacked my ice cream, and I really hammed it up, giving long, lingering licks from near the bottom of the cone, rolling my eyes and making yummy noises. But after a minute or two, I felt something like heat on the side of my face. I looked to my left.

Two men sat together at a nearby picnic table, grinning at me. They were probably only in their twenties, but of course they seemed old to me then, with days-old stubble and brows that hung over dark eyes like a shelf.

"Don't stop on our account," one said. The other guffawed. A feeling of shame and excitement ran through me at the intensity of their gaze, the rough invitation in their laugh. I flinched as melting ice cream trickled over my knuckles.

A shadow fell across our table, and I heard my father say, "Everything all right here?"

I turned, but Daddy wasn't looking at me, he was staring at the men. He gently handed the new snow cone to Harley, then told us to wait for him by the car. We scampered to the cruiser, but I peered over the hood to watch.

My father walked to the men, leaned over, and placed the palms of his hands flat on the picnic table. His face was inches away from theirs. Their smirks had vanished.

Daddy wasn't a big man, but he made others seem small by his presence. He spoke quietly for a minute, never raising his voice. The two men, nodding and pale, scrambled off the bench and down the street, cringing.

Daddy returned to the car. Ignoring Harley, he addressed me. "Those boys say anything to you?"

I shook my head. "No, sir."

His pale eyes kept me pinned. "You're certain?"

"I'm sure, Daddy."

He held my gaze for another second, then his eyes flicked over my clothes. "When we get home, go through your mother's things and find a sweater that suits you. You wear it from now on, any time you leave the house, understand?"

"A sweater?" I gawped at him. "Daddy, it's damn near ninety—"

"Don't swear at me."

"I'm not swearing *at* you, I'm—I'm just...*swearing*. You want me to wear a wrap? In July?"

"Ginny, I won't tell you again," he said. "You want to leave the house, you cover yourself. End of discussion."

We drove back home in a tense silence, the only sound Harley happily slurping away at his replacement snow cone. When we got there, I asked if I could go out, and when my father reminded me about the sweater I complained again about the injustice of his demand. He said I wouldn't be leaving the house that day or the next or the one after if I didn't learn some respect.

My anger chilled to ice, and I spent the rest of the afternoon locked away in my room reading. By five, I was bored senseless and slunk down to join the others. I took my customary spot on the couch without giving Daddy so much as a glance. My plan to torture him with my silence short-circuited, however, when I heard other kids walking past our house, chatting and singing, their laughter fading down the street like a missed opportunity. I stomped my heel in frustration.

Her father looked up from the paper. "What is it now?"

I opened my mouth to let him have it, but the sound of crunching gravel and the growl of an engine told us someone had pulled into our driveway. Daddy put the paper and my tantrum aside and moved out to the porch, closing the door behind him, though not before I got a peek outside. A patrolman had stepped out of his cruiser and was walking toward the house, his face twisted as though it hurt to think. Harley and I crept to the nearest window.

"Evening, Chief," the policeman said. "Sorry to bother you at home."

"Tom," my father greeted him. "What's going on?"

"Well...maybe nothing."

"Tell me." I couldn't see him, but I knew my father had gone into his listening stance: slight frown, feet spread wide, hands in back pockets.

"You know Betsy Groggins, on 11th?"

"Terrible gossip, but yes."

"She called me at home a few nights ago. Said there was trouble at Ben Aaberg's place."

I felt a tingle run through me, from the crown of my head to my ankles, and Harley turned to me, his eyes round as eggs. Mr. Aaberg was my best friend's daddy—not her *real* one, she was always quick to point out with a gesture at her dark, coffee-colored eyes and long black hair—only her foster father. But still. Harley started to whisper a question, but I shushed him as my father continued.

"What kind of trouble?"

"Drinking. Hitting his wife."

"That's a family matter, Tom, not really something for us to get involved with. Even if she came in to register a complaint."

"That ain't going to happen."

"Why's that?"

"Betsy said Donna Aaberg up and left yesterday, hat on head and suitcase in hand."

"Problem solved, then, wouldn't you say?"

"Normally I would, Chief, but I went over there anyway to check and, well, it's just a feeling I got, but…."

I heard a shuffling of feet, and Tom's voice went quiet, out of range. Daddy lowered his voice to match and we heard nothing of the conversation until a few minutes later when my father said, "All right, Tom. I'll have a talk with Ben tomorrow."

"Careful, Chief. He's an ornery bastard."

"He's a drunk and a bully, you mean." He paused. "Maybe I'll chat with Betsy first."

Tom cleared his throat. "Can you not mention I told you, Chief? She asked me to keep this on the q.t."

"I'm sure she did," Daddy said, his voice so dry you could mop a spill with it. "I imagine you're only the tenth person she's told today."

Tom laughed and said that was probably true. And then he wished my father a good night, got in his car and pulled away. We dashed back to our spots—I snatched up a six-month-old copy of *Life* magazine while Harley went back to waging war with green army men. Daddy came through the door and looked us over, then spoke to my brother.

"Young man, would you do me a favor and fix my pipe?"

Harley's eyebrows climbed to his buzz cut. "Really?"

"Use the stool and do it over the sink, so you don't make a mess, all right? Set it on the end table when you're done, and I'll smoke it after my bath."

"Gosh, you bet!"

Daddy watched him go, then turned to me. I looked back at him, suspicious. Harley might not know when he was being cleared out, but I did. Our father sat at the end of the couch and pinched the bridge of his nose.

"Ginny, you're friends with the Aaberg girl, aren't you? What's her name?"

"Louise," I said cautiously. "And she's a foster, not an Aaberg."

"Fine, a foster child. Have you seen her lately? Gone to her house?"

I chewed my lip. It had been a while, actually. A year ago, we'd been inseparable, but ever since she turned thirteen she'd seemed listless, barely acknowledging me the few times we'd seen each other. I missed her, I realized. "No."

"Let's keep it that way."

"Why?"

"That is your favorite word this year," he said, peeved. "Could you do what I ask for once? Without questions?"

From two rooms away came a clatter that sounded a lot like a pipe being dropped in a sink, followed by a muffled, "*Jayz*us, Harley." Daddy frowned and glanced toward the kitchen.

I poked him with my toe. "Is Louise in trouble?"

"Trouble?" He turned back to me. "No. No, I don't think so."

"Can I talk to her if I see her on the street? Can we see a movie together? Can she come to our house?"

"I...." He looked uncomfortable under the barrage. "It'd just be better if you didn't, all right?"

"You still haven't said why."

"You don't need to know why," he snapped. "Just do as I say, Ginny!"

I huffed and raised the magazine, big as a billboard, between us. He sat for a moment, then sighed and stood. I resolutely refused to acknowledge him.

Daddy started up the steps, then paused. "Ginny?"

I lowered the magazine and granted him an arch glance. "Yes?"

"*Life* is a lot easier to read right side up." He proceeded upstairs without another word.

It certainly wasn't the worst row we'd had or would have, but something inside me exploded. Anger at my father's seemingly arbitrary rules merged with a pent-up confusion and discomfort over the changes happening in my body, my mind, my place in life. I wanted to run down the street with my hair on fire, scream bloody murder, smash all the dishes in the house. Anything to break the sense of a net being slowly drawn close, suffocating me.

Thirteen-year-old girls everywhere in every time feel these things, of course, but there was something about being a policeman's daughter in that era that made it worse. People talked in those days, and, no matter what they tell you now, it was no Golden Age, without vice or meanness or sin. Opinions mattered, and reputations determined entire futures. I had to watch what I did and said, who I spoke to and how, even more so than the other poor girls who were trying to find themselves after the War and before the Pill.

I was tired of it. Life, I felt, was unfolding around me, and I was missing it, pinned in my place like a butterfly in a specimen box.

Well, I thought, *that's going to end tonight.*

Above my head, the bath water gurgled through the pipes and into the tub. With a thrill running through me, I slammed the magazine down, slipped my sneakers on, and headed for the door.

"Where you going, Ginny?"

I froze. Standing in the archway connecting the living and dining rooms was Harley, Daddy's pipe cradled in his hands.

I swallowed. "I'm going out."

"Out? Where?"

"Just out," I said impatiently. Impulse does not appreciate being questioned. I jerked the door open and clattered down the steps. Harley called out something about Daddy getting mad. *That's why I'm doing it, dummy,* I thought, surprising myself at the clarity of the realization.

I set a brisk pace up the street, having no idea where I was going, simply happy to be free of the house. Summer twilight was still two hours away and, overhead, the sky was a gentle lavender fading to orange. In the distance, the Broadway Bridge—anchored on the far side by the elegant lines of the Bessborough Hotel—linked our boring suburb with the more thrilling downtown. I headed in that direction, though my stomach quivered at the thought of crossing the bridge, something I had been absolutely forbidden. My stride slowed as temptation warred with prudence.

I didn't need to go that far, I decided. I wanted to teach Daddy a lesson, not drive him crazy. He had to see I was no longer a little girl; I could take a risk or two and be okay.

I would go to Louise's.

The Aabergs lived in the direction I was already going, so it seemed fated and, my mind made up, I stepped up the pace. I knew that the minute my father found out I'd left against his wishes, not only would he come looking for me, but Tom and the entire police force would be on the lookout, too. I had to reach Louise's before I got nabbed and hauled back home in shame.

I knew where she lived, naturally, but I'd never spent much time there. No slumber parties or afternoons talking about boys or sharing pot roast dinners with her family. We'd found our fun on the go, swinging in the trees in Friendship Park or throwing pennies on the CN rail line or rambling along the river where it passed under the Broadway on its way north.

Saskatoon didn't really have a *bad* section of town, not the way I understand it now, but where the Aabergs lived was about as bad as it got. The cottages were just a little more ratty, the yards a bit more down in the mouth. With the sun still visible in the sky, I felt invincible, but I knew in a few hours I'd rather be almost anywhere else.

Folks were out on their porches, enjoying the summer, moving gently on gliders and swings to an invisible rhythm. I whistled and swung my arms as I walked down the street, trying to act like I would if I were heading for my own home, but I felt the itch of eyes following me.

Tucked in tight between two shacks, the Aabergs' house was not much wider than the space required for a window, a door and a broken porch swing. I swallowed, then stepped lightly up the stairs. Flaking paint crunched under foot and the boards sagged as I approached the door.

I knocked softly. "Louise?"

I heard a noise from inside—a low, rhythmic sound, like a dog coughing—but no one answered. It was dark through the grimy window.

Flummoxed, I scowled at the door. My great act of defiance would go up in smoke if Louise wasn't around. Well, I hadn't come all this way just to slink back home. I skipped down the stairs and went around the side, following the cracked cement walk to the back of the house.

Hanging on a line was laundry that I knew wasn't dry because the sun never reached the tiny, muddy yard. Two shirts and a pair of knickers had fallen to the ground, becoming indistinguishable from the dirt. A car battery held up the rotting steps leading to the back door. Garbage, gathered haphazardly in a bag, had spilled across the miniscule landing.

Egging myself on, I crept up to the porch. The back door was open, and the screen lolled wide from a broken latch, screeching softly as it swayed in the sluggish breeze. From inside the house came the low, rhythmic sound I'd heard before.

Dumb as I was, I slipped inside, convinced I'd find Louise asleep on the couch or washing dishes. I'd wake her and we'd head for the streets. Or I'd help her finish the dishes and tell her all about the stupid hoops Daddy was making me jump through. We'd have a grand time, like before.

"Louise?" I made my way through the mudroom, past a rusty toolbox and yellowed boots and overalls covered with grease. A saloon-style louvered door separated the mudroom from the rest of the house.

I pushed the door open and froze.

I was in the Aabergs' meager kitchen. They had a woodstove and the kind of icebox you only saw in old-timey movies. Dirty cups were piled high in a tub, and a tower of plates perched on the edge of a butcher block. The dingy green linoleum floor had peeled upward in places, exposing black gum underneath.

Ben Aaberg was leaning against the stove, his drawers and underpants around his ankles. On her knees in front of him, in a filthy white dress, was Louise. His fist had a handful of her hair and he was forcing her to...do things to him. From his mouth came the strange, low grunts I'd heard from outside.

I gasped, and that simple noise broke some kind of spell. Aaberg raised his head, and his eyes focused blearily on me. Louise pushed away from him and tumbled backward onto the floor. When our eyes met, I saw the same dead look she'd given me each time we'd met that summer.

The man laughed, a sound like sheet metal tearing, and he lurched across the room. I hesitated for one terrible instant—*Run!* I wanted to scream at Louise, but she hadn't even budged from her spot on the floor—then, as I turned to flee, he grabbed my long hair as it fanned out behind me.

He was horribly strong and yanked me off my feet, dragged me to him like he was reeling in a net. I screamed and clawed long, bloody marks down his arm, but he only laughed and wrapped me in a clumsy hug, his erect penis jabbing at my thigh and his wet, starfish mouth searching for mine.

With a yell, Louise came off the floor and jumped on his back, pounding him around the ears and neck, hollering at him to leave me alone. My fingers, slapping at Aaberg's face, found one of his eyes. I pushed.

Aaberg roared, and the three of us wheeled around the room, knocking the stack of plates to the floor, where they shattered. One-handed, he reached back and threw Louise against the tub, smashing the cups there. Then, with blood streaming down his face, he pushed me to the floor, his hand squeezing my throat. Broken bits of ceramic ground into my back.

Black spots filled my vision. I squirmed and fought for breath, which seemed to excite him. He panted as he pawed at my shorts. I swam in place desperately, scattering dirty plates and silverware and cups like I was making a snow angel out of broken glass.

He'd gotten my shorts over my hips when my hand found a long, moon-shaped shard of plate. Ignoring the edges cutting into my palm, I brought it down in an arc with both hands. Five inches of broken glass sank into his neck just above the collarbone.

He gave a high-pitched screech and bucked off me, reeling and tripping over his pants and falling to the floor, where he thrashed like a fish. Blood sprayed from the wound, painting the wall scarlet.

Coughing and choking, I backpedaled, scattering the debris on the floor, then scrambled to my feet and fled. I ran in a straight line without looking back, leaping the backyard fence like a deer and sprinting through the neighbor's yard to the street beyond, not caring where I was going as long as it was away.

I remember peering constantly over my shoulder. I remember bending over and vomiting in the street. I remember rubbing the spot where he had clutched my throat, though by some miracle I had none of his blood on me.

Hours passed in a blur. At some point, evening slid from twilight to darkness.

My father found me a block from our house. He stopped his cruiser in the middle of the street, gumball flashing, headlights pinning me in place. I had stopped shaking by then, but the sight of him leaping from the car caused tears to well in my eyes. He scooped me into his arms, holding me for long minutes.

As happens to parents, anger followed fear. Holding me at arm's-length, he shook me in time with his words.

"Ginny, where the hell have you been?"

I mumbled something about being mad and wanting to teach him a lesson.

"You picked a fine night to show your independent streak."

"What?"

"Didn't you hear the sirens? Your friend Louise stabbed her foster father. Tom said the Aabergs' looks like a goddamned slaughterhouse." His eyes narrowed. "You haven't been with her tonight, have you?"

"No, sir."

"Do you know where she might be?"

"No," I said carefully. "We haven't really seen each other since last summer."

His hands squeezed my shoulders. "You wouldn't lie to me, would you, honey?"

His eyes held me. *I'm giving you a choice*, they seemed to say.

I opened my mouth.

Looking back, I can't blame myself for wanting to avoid the truth. In most of the ways that counted, I was still a child. The instinct to save myself from the things I'd just witnessed and done—the thing that was almost done to *me*—was human and understandable.

But I knew, whatever I said, my father would believe... including a blatant, outright lie. A lie that would hurt just one person, the one who deserved it the least.

Louise.

I started to sob. He pulled me in for a hug and a shudder ran through him, shaking me. Burying his face in my hair, he whispered, "Tell me, honey. We'll make it right."

So I told him.

*

When I got home this evening, I changed out of my uniform and strolled across the street. My father raised a hand from his porch, where he sat reading the paper and puffing away on his pipe—some things hadn't changed after his retirement and hopefully never would. Climbing the steps, I pecked him on the cheek and brushed a hand over his steel-gray hair.

"How's work, Chief?" he asked, with a twinkle in his eye.

"The Prosecution Office would like me to slow down, or so I've been told," I said, leaning against the porch railing. "Louise loves it, of course. She puts the crooks on the docket as fast as I nab them, but her fellow attorneys don't seem to appreciate our work ethic."

"They have a point. If you and your sister don't slow down, there won't be any crime left in Saskatoon to stop."

I shook my head ruefully. "I don't think we have to worry about our job security."

"No, probably not." He lowered the paper and looked into the distance. It was a long, lazy summer evening, and the sun was still hours from setting. He was quiet for a long moment. Then, his voice thick, he said, "I think about that day a lot. What nearly happened to you. The terrible things Louise suffered. The trial, your acquittal. What I could've done differently...."

"Dad." I put a hand on his shoulder. "That was then, and this is now. Nothing happened to me, we saved Louise, and we gave her a family she could trust." I squeezed. "Now she and I are out there making sure it doesn't happen to anyone else. Just like you did."

He shook himself and looked up at me, his eyes glistening. "I'm proud of you, honey. Proud of you both. Then and now."

A lump started in my throat. I laughed and said, "Hey, what do you think about grabbing an ice cream while it's still light out?"

"You paying?"

"I drive, you pay, that's the rule," I said. "Now get your wallet before I cuff you and put you in the back."

Ray's Dad's Cadillac
by Michael Bracken

On the first Saturday in January, 1959, Ray's dad paid cash for a brand-new Wood-Rose Cadillac Sedan de Ville and drove it straight home from the showroom floor. As Ray and I stood in the driveway, admiring the giant pink fins and twin bullet taillights, Ray's dad said, "You drive up in a car like this and people notice you. They don't see what you do or where you live. They just see what you drive, and a car like this says you *are* somebody."

Ray's dad taught math at the high school Ray and I attended, and he and Ray lived in a run-down two-bedroom ranch just like my mother and me. We didn't even have a car—my mother rode the bus everywhere she couldn't walk—and I wondered what our means of transportation said about us.

"The Barber made me wait a week for my money," Ray's dad continued. He'd bet on the outcome of the twenty-sixth NFL Championship game, and, when the Baltimore Colts beat the New York Giants 23-17 in sudden death overtime, he'd found himself flush with cash for the first time in his life. "The Barber wanted to hold my money, but I wouldn't let him."

Ray's dad's gambling habit was a secret, one I only knew about because Ray kept no secrets from me. His dad usually won small and lost small, but his big win on the NFL Championship game changed him in ways we didn't realize at the time, and he was still admiring his new Cadillac when Ray walked me the three blocks home and followed me inside.

Four years after my father's heart attack, my mother was still the grieving widow. My father's badge, the American flag that had been draped over his coffin, and a framed photograph of him in his uniform the day he graduated from the police academy had been arranged on the fireplace mantel where everyone entering the house could see them. His uniform—the one he wasn't buried in—hung in my mother's closet, and his service revolver and throwdown lay hidden in the bottom drawer of her dresser, beneath her corsets.

I genuflected toward the mantel, a reflex more than the sign of respect it had once been, and followed the smell of fresh-baked chocolate-chip cookies into the kitchen.

My mother noticed Ray behind me and asked, "How's your dad doing?"

"Floating on air," Ray said. "He just bought a new car."

"That old DeSoto of his finally give out?"

"No, ma'am," Ray said.

Before he could continue, I blurted, "Ray's dad bought a Cadillac."

My mother's eyes widened. "A Cadillac? Your dad must be stepping up in the world."

"Yes, ma'am," Ray said. "He certainly is."

*

Ray showed me his dad's notebooks, the pages filled with equations far beyond my ability to comprehend. As I flipped through them, Ray explained that his dad believed gambling was applied mathematics, and that if he gathered enough data and developed the correct formulas, he would win every bet. Until the Colts beat the Giants, Ray's dad had lost more than he had ever won, but as winter turned to spring Ray's dad found himself riding a months-long winning streak that convinced him he had finally perfected his formulas.

That spring also marked a change in my relationship with Ray. We had been friends since grade school, but the Spring Dance marked our first official date—we rode to the dance in style in the rear seat of Ray's dad's Cadillac—and soon after we declared to our friends and parents that we were going steady. This came as no surprise to anyone.

Our dates were limited to our neighborhood until the release of *The Diary of Anne Frank,* a movie not available at our local theater, so my mother allowed us to take the bus downtown.

On the bus, we held hands and pointed out interesting sights—the old woman walking six poodles, the young girl twirling three Hula-Hoops, the hot rod filled with teenaged boys passing the bus. Halfway to the theater, Ray nudged me and pointed to a nondescript barbershop. He whispered in my ear, his warm breath tickling me, "That's my dad's bookie."

I knew what a bookie was. "How do you know?"

"Before my mom left us, he made us wait in the DeSoto when he went inside to conduct his business."

*

That summer, Ray turned eighteen and Ray's dad allowed him to drive the Cadillac. Every Saturday night for the rest of the summer and into the fall of our senior year, we listened to rock 'n' roll as we cruised through town past the roller rink and the record shack, and then we drove out to Love Field to watch the planes. That isn't all we did. Sometimes Ray let me drive around the field, and we often took advantage of the Cadillac's roomy rear seat, making love and making plans.

That fall, I found myself in Ray's dad's sixth-period algebra class, trying to comprehend how to deduct a number from a letter and wondering when I would ever need to.

Three weeks after the semester started, Ray's dad held me after class. "If you don't pass algebra, you won't graduate."

My math skills were good enough. I could balance a check book, measure ingredients to scratch bake a cake, and count the days between Aunt Flo's visits. I had my sights set on marrying Ray, having babies, and taking care of my family, and I said as much.

Ray's dad shook his head. "You're smarter than that. You could accomplish so much more."

"How?" I asked. "I'm not going to college like Ray. The best I can hope for is secretarial school."

*

When I arrived home from school that day, I discovered that my mother had come home early and my father's things were no longer on the mantel. They had been replaced by fall decorations.

I asked her about it, and she said, "I've been grieving long enough. It's time I moved on with my life."

"What about me? Maybe I'm not ready."

My mother took my hands and looked into my eyes. "It's been four years."

"Where did you put his things?"

"In the closet with his uniform."

"And what about—?" I stopped myself as I stared back at my mother. I realized it would be best if she didn't know everything my father had taught me.

*

Ray's dad's winning streak began to sputter at the start of the school year, and his losses began to accumulate. I knew because Ray told me, and he told me that his dad spent even more time poring over the formulas in his notebooks, looking to replicate his win the previous December but only falling further behind.

That October, the Los Angeles Dodgers met the Chicago White Sox in the World Series, and we watched NBC's broadcast of each game with Ray's dad. He seemed confident at first, but he was a nervous wreck during Game Six. He started pacing when the Dodgers went up in the top of the third inning. He became more agitated when they extended their lead at the top of the fourth. He calmed a bit when the Sox picked up three runs in the bottom of the fourth, but when neither team scored another run for the next four innings, he began to swear.

"What's wrong?" Ray asked.

"I have the Sox in seven," Ray's dad said. "I did the math. They're a lock."

The Dodgers picked up another run in the top of the ninth, and we ducked out of the house when Ray's dad began throwing things at the television. Game Six ended with the Dodgers winning 9-3 and taking the series four games to two.

*

The following Saturday night, Ray and I lay together in the afterglow of our coupling. The roar of a Boeing 707 coming in for a landing drowned out the Motown playing on the radio and drowned out the sound of a car pulling into the farmer's field behind us. I was trying to decide if I should tell Ray that Aunt Flo was two weeks late when the door jerked open and a mug with a face like a bruised thumb shouted, "Get out of the car!"

He grabbed my ankle and dragged me out of Ray's dad's Cadillac. I squirmed and kicked and tried to keep my skirt from sliding up to my hips because my underwear lay on the floor mat, and when my bare butt hit the ground, I scrambled to cover myself before I realized he wasn't interested in me.

As someone watched us from the driver's seat of the car parked behind Ray's dad's Cadillac, Thumb-face reached in and grabbed Ray. "Get out of the car and give me the keys."

Ray fought harder than I had, but to no avail. Thumb-face dragged him out and dumped him on the ground beside me. Ray scrambled to his feet. "I'm not going to let you take my dad's car."

"I ain't stealing it, kid," Thumb-face said. "Your dad's a welsher. He bet a bundle on the Sox and lost, so I'm collecting it as payment of his debt."

Ray put up his fists.

"This ain't about you, kid," Thumb-face said. "Don't make it about you."

Ray threw a punch at the man and missed. Then Thumb-face drove his fist into Ray's face, smashing his nose and dropping him to the ground.

I screamed, "You didn't have to do that!"

No longer concerned with flashing anyone, I tried to push Thumb-face off of Ray. He was too big, and my efforts only irritated him as he rifled Ray's pockets. He found the keys, slipped behind the wheel of the Cadillac, and started the engine. He threw my purse out the window and drove away. The other car followed.

I watched until both cars reached the road. When I returned my attention to Ray, he had peeled off his button-front shirt and his T-shirt, and was using his T-shirt to dab at his bloody nose. When the bleeding stopped, I took his face in my hands and examined its new shape.

I pressed my right thumb against the left side of his nose and asked, "Does this hurt?"

He winced.

I shoved hard and pushed his nasal cartilage back into place, something I had seen my mother do for my father. "You'll be okay."

Ray put his button-front shirt back on, I collected my purse, and we began walking.

"My dad thinks he's so smart because he teaches math. He says he plays the odds, but I think he plays for the rush, especially after last year's big win," Ray said as we walked through the darkness. "He's never lost this much before."

I let him talk, lost in my own thoughts.

"There's no money in being a gambler. The money's in being the house and taking a rake off every win and every loss."

"That means you can't ever win."

"Not over the long term," Ray said. "You have to know the odds, and you have to quit when you're ahead."

We had reached the road by then, and we walked in silence while I contemplated the gamble *we'd* taken. I finally said, "I'm late."

"Late? Of course we'll be late."

"No," I insisted. "*I'm* late."

Maybe the pain from his broken nose made Ray think more slowly than usual, but a moment later he said, "We've been using protection."

"Maybe it didn't work."

He stopped, took both my hands in his, and looked into my eyes. "Then we'll get married sooner than we planned."

*

We walked a long way before we found a bus stop, and we had to transfer twice before we reached our neighborhood. We walked directly to Ray's house and were surprised to find my mother there and Ray's dad in far worse shape than Ray.

"Two men were here," my mother said.

"They wanted my car," Ray's dad said. "I wouldn't give it to them."

Ray told him, "They took it anyhow."

"They said Ray's dad owed his barber some money," my mother said, and I realized then why Ray's dad always let Ray take the Cadillac on Saturdays. He was making time with my mother. "Why would he owe his barber money?"

"Not *his* barber," I explained. "*The* Barber. His bookie. Ray's dad bet on the World Series and lost. He didn't have the money to pay, so they took his car."

She didn't understand. "Took his car? *You* had his car." For the first time since we'd walked in the door, she took a good look at us, saw Ray's broken nose and my general state of dishevelment. "What happened?"

We told her about the thumb-faced man taking the Cadillac.

"That car was all we had," Ray's dad said. "Without it, we don't have anything."

Ray's dad wasn't the only one who lost something special when the Cadillac was taken to pay his gambling debt. Ray and I had lost our secret place, the place where we made love and made plans and saw the future's endless possibilities.

"I wish your father were here," my mother said. "He would know what to do."

*

The four of us spent Sunday together, my mother and I nursing Ray and his dad. My mother tried to explain to me why she was with Ray's dad, but I didn't listen. She thought I was angry with her for trying to find love again, but I had other things on my mind.

The next morning, after my mother left for work, I prepared for my day. First I telephoned the school and, impersonating my mother, let the office secretary know I would be home with a stomach virus. Then I retrieved my father's throwdown, a cheap Saturday Night Special that better fit my small hand than his service revolver. I cleaned it carefully, even wiping down the bullets before I loaded it, and put it in an otherwise-empty old purse. I dressed in blue jeans, a simple white blouse, and flats. I stuck some money in my pocket.

I rode the same bus that Ray and I had ridden to see *The Diary of Anne Frank,* but I exited at a stop one block from the barbershop. Ray's dad's Cadillac was parked at the curb in front, looking none the worse for having been taken from us.

When I stepped inside, I found Thumb-face standing behind one of the barber chairs. He wore a short white jacket with a comb protruding from the chest pocket. He did not recognize me. "You lost, miss?"

"I want to see the Barber."

"I don't do women's hair."

"Not you," I said. "*The* Barber."

Thumb-face eyed me up and down. "Why would he want to see you?"

"We have business to discuss."

"Him and you? You're nothing but a kid."

I planted my feet and glared at him.

A deep voice came through the open office door. "Send her in."

Thumb-face motioned me toward the back and I stepped into the office, a room barely big enough for the massive desk behind which sat Ray's dad's bookie.

The Barber looked me up and down and asked, "What can I do for you, little lady?"

"I came to get Ray's dad's Cadillac back."

He laughed.

"I want you to put the keys and the title on the desk."

He laughed again.

I reached into my purse and removed my father's throwdown. I cocked the hammer and pointed the business end at the Barber.

He licked sweat from his upper lip. Then he nodded to the left. "They're in the drawer."

"Take them out slowly. I don't want to see anything but the keys and the title."

I watched him reach into the drawer with his left hand and remove Ray's dad's key ring and the title to his Cadillac. I should have been watching his right hand, too, because, at the same time he was getting Ray's dad's things, he leveled a revolver at me.

Thumb-face burst in, startling both of us. My shot drilled the Barber between the eyes. His grazed my blouse and blew through Thumb-face's chest.

My ears were ringing and I was shaking, but I knew I had a limited amount of time. I pressed my father's throwdown into Thumb-face's hand and scooped up the car keys and title. I walked out of the barbershop, slipped into the driver's seat of Ray's dad's Cadillac, and drove away.

After I parked the Cadillac in Ray's dad's driveway, I retrieved my underwear from the floor mat, put the keys and the title in the mailbox, and walked the three blocks home to burn my clothes.

I was showering when Aunt Flo finally came to visit, and I knew then that everything would be okay.

*

I never grasped algebra and still don't understand it, but I graduated with the rest of my class. I married Ray that summer and supported him through college. He now teaches math at the junior high school our oldest attends, and we live in a nice house.

We don't gamble, but we still find romance in the back of Ray's dad's Cadillac.

Turbulent Indigo

Released October 1994

"Sunny Sunday"
"Sex Kills"
"How Do You Stop"
"Turbulent Indigo"
"Last Chance Lost"
"The Magdalene Laundries"
"Not to Blame"
"Borderline"
"Yvette in English"
"The Sire of Sorrow (Job's Sad Song)"

All songs by Joni Mitchell
except "How Do You Stop" (by Dan Hartman and
Charlie Midnight)
and "Yvette in English" (by Joni Mitchell and David Crosby).

Sex Kills
by Alan Orloff

A sixty-foot supermodel towered over Times Square, jeans-clad ass taunting the people of New York as she tossed a come-fuck-me grin over her shoulder. Buy my jeans and you, too, can get whatever you want! Money, fame, power, me, me, me!

The lure of sex ran rampant. Buy our products, pump up your sex appeal, live the beautiful life. Who could argue with those millions of pulsing lights on the digital displays soaring into the air? Or the slick and glossy covers of the fashion mags with one-word titles? Or the dancing pixels on every screen you owned?

Want to fuck me? Want to get fucked? Buy my products!

Erin Rose slumped in the back seat of the taxi, barely glancing at the kaleidoscopic ads illuminating the night sky. Twenty years ago, that had been *her* very fine ass plastered on billboards and magazine covers across the country.

Across the world.

The sexiest supermodel selling the sexiest products to the sexiest consumers. *Sex sells!*

And after Erin's time at the top had passed, her daughter, Sierra, had enjoyed even greater fame. So much fame that people everywhere just pointed and whispered *"Sierra"* when she strutted by. No need for the *"Rose."*

Until a year ago. Then Sierra had become known as the supermodel who'd ODed and wasted a fairy-tale life bursting with unbounded promise.

Erin tried to forget the past and push her grief aside, but like every other time, she failed. How could you ever hope to put the death of your child behind you?

Especially when it had been your fault.

She hadn't supplied the fatal drugs, but she might as well have, for all the nature/nurture she'd given her daughter. She'd been

Sierra's mother, the supermodel, instead of Sierra's mother, the role model.

Big, big difference.

The light turned yellow, and the taxi driver leaned on his horn, just one in a growing taxi horn concerto, as traffic slowed to a stop. He pulled up next to a big black Escalade on Erin's left, with personalized plates—"JUST ICE"—and bootylicious rap lyrics booming from its speakers. *Sex sells!*

The guy in the passenger seat glanced over at Erin, then looked away, uninterested. If he'd spied her twenty years ago in the back seat of a Town Car, that guy would have stared, eyes wide. Twenty years ago, she would have licked her ruby red lips and tried to make the gawker come in his pants.

Erin hadn't looked in a mirror in almost a year. With good reason. While her body had stayed in good shape—a few added pounds merely accentuated her generous curves—the drugs and booze from the endless party days had taken their toll on her once-flawless cover-girl face. Wrinkles, permanent bags, two plastic surgery efforts gone awry. Grief had only accelerated the process. She knew her face appeared now as a puffy, distorted version of itself, like a faded photocopy of a faded photocopy of a once-gorgeous original work of art.

The damage to her psyche had been far worse. In her twenties, she'd popped pills to stay skinny. In her thirties, she'd snorted coke to stay relevant, shot heroin to stay cool.

Since Sierra died, she'd stayed drunk to stay numb.

Drugs kill! Booze kills!

*

The taxi dropped Erin at her destination, a nondescript building halfway down a nondescript side street far from the frenzy of Times Square. No dazzling billboards here. Just trash piling up on the curbs and the nauseating smell as it decomposed.

Working-class New York.

When she got out of the cab, she transformed into an anonymous diva out on the town—scarf over her head, big designer sunglasses, another scarf around her neck. Luxe accessories topped off a shimmery, form-fitting silver gown she'd squeezed into, slit all the way up one side. Six-inch stilettos boosted her height to over six and a half feet. America liked its supermodels long and strong and sexy. She might have put on a few miles since she'd cavorted as the Most Beautiful Girl in the World, but she still commanded the attention of every man in every room.

She stood out, all right, especially in this neighborhood. With her face mostly covered, though, she wouldn't be identified.

If anyone still remembered her at all.

Erin poked the button on the security panel and was buzzed right in. Took the stairs—carefully, on her skyscraper heels—to the second floor, found Unit 212. Rapped the cat-shaped knocker. Stood back and waited.

She heard some fumbling from within, and then the door opened. A stocky guy in his thirties with a gleaming shaved head stared up at her a beat before speaking, pupils dilating. He wasn't short, but she still had about eight inches on him. "Come in. Come in. Any friend of Jackie's is a friend of mine. You can call me Ace." He swung the door wide. She glided in. "Have a seat."

He gestured to a stained sofa with sagging cushions. Two brown tabbies occupied one end.

"That's okay. I'll stand. This shouldn't take long, right?"

"Uh, sure. No problem." Ace disappeared from the room, down a hallway into the rear of the apartment, then returned carrying a space-age aluminum briefcase. He squinted at her, cocked his head. "Do I know you?"

"I don't think so."

"You look familiar." His face brightened. "I know, you're Erin Rose, the model!"

"I wish." Erin faked a chuckle. "She probably lives the life, huh?"

Ace chuckled back. "Well, you fooled me. When I was a teenager, I had her poster tacked up on the ceiling—over my bed. The one where she's sitting on a stool, legs spread wide, wearing thigh-high boots and a see-through blouse. She helped me pass many lonely nights, if you know what I mean."

After the first fifty times, Erin was no longer surprised when a stranger told her he had jacked off to her poster as a teen. *Sex thrills!*

She forced a tight smile. "Our transaction?"

"Right, right. Jackie said to take care of you." He paused. "Maybe you'd be more comfortable without the shades?"

"Thanks, I'm good."

Ace shrugged. "Suit yourself."

Erin handed him a scrap of paper. "This is what I'd like."

Ace consulted the list. Then he stepped over to a rickety folding card table, pushed aside an old pizza box, and set down the briefcase. Unfastened the clasps and opened it, hinges squeaking. The case looked as if it contained the jumbled innards of an entire medicine cabinet—or three. He rummaged through the baggies, vials and pillboxes, pulling out various items and setting them aside, then checking the list and adding others, as if he were a stock boy at a Walmart warehouse.

Ace hummed a show tune Erin couldn't quite place as he filled her order.

When he finished, he double-checked the drugs he'd removed from the briefcase against her list. "All set. Anything else you need?"

Erin licked her lips and jutted one leg out through the dress' slit so Ace got a good glimpse of flesh, all the way up to her hip. "Actually, there is. Jackie said you had *everything a girl could want.*" She uttered the last part of the sentence breathlessly, as if she were Scarlett Johannson lying next to him in bed, ready to roll onto her back and give him a night he'd never forget. "So I was wondering if maybe I could purchase a gun?" She reached out and touched Ace's arm with her fingertips and practically felt an electrical charge crawling on his skin.

"A gun?"

She raked her fingernails up Ace's bare arm. "A gun," she whispered.

"Well, I don't know." He swallowed, but didn't pull his arm back from her touch. "Why do you need a gun?"

She inched closer to Ace, and he had to crane his neck upward to see her face. "Self- protection, of course."

"Of course." Perspiration beaded on his scalp.

Erin took both of Ace's hands in hers. "I may not be Erin Rose, but I never forget a favor. And if you sell me a gun, I'll owe you one, a big one. I get down to this neighborhood about once a month. Maybe we could go out for a drink next time I'm around." She moved closer until Ace's hands, still in hers, touched her chest. Playing a horny sap was like riding a bike, you never forgot how. "What would you think about that?"

"Yeah, yeah. Sounds great. I think I might just have something you'll like. Hang on."

Erin released his hands, and Ace scurried away again into the bowels of the squalid apartment. When he returned, he carried a pistol. "How about this?"

"Looks fine. Is it loaded?"

"Well, not at the moment."

"It's for self-protection," she purred, "so it needs to be loaded, right?"

He reached into his pocket, came out with a handful of bullets. "Here's some ammo."

"Terrific." Erin tipped her head at the gun. "Would you mind?"

Ace hesitated.

"Please?"

He exhaled. "Sure." Then he loaded the pistol. "But you need to be super careful with it."

"Oh, I will be." Erin opened the sequined purse draped on her shoulder and removed a thick roll of bills. "How much do I owe you?"

Ace gazed into the air, lips moving as he did the math in his head. With a final nod, he quoted her the price, and Erin peeled off enough Benjamins to cover her tab and handed them over. Then she peeled off an extra hundred, folded it, and stuffed it into Ace's front jeans pocket, deep. "For the exquisite personal service. Ace, you're a peach."

Ace's face reddened as he handed over the drugs and the gun, which she stuffed into her purse. "Pleasure doing business with you."

Erin pushed her sunglasses down her nose and stared Ace in the eyes until he finally blinked. Then she slowly moved her caressing gaze down his body, settling on his crotch. "Oh no, the pleasure was all mine," she said, once again in her throaty whisper. "All mine."

She left Ace with his hard-on and went downstairs to wait for her ride.

She thought of Sierra again. Her death *was* Erin's fault, undeniably.

But not entirely.

*

Her cab whisked her to an exclusive midtown high-rise condo building. She took the elevator up to the penthouse, where a bouncer, dressed all in black, met her at the door. "Name, please?"

"I'm not on the list."

"Sorry, then. Can't let you in."

Erin jutted her leg out. "I'm an old friend of Derek's."

He checked out Erin's leg, slowly, all the way up to the hip. "Sure. We're all old friends of Derek's. Half this town is old friends with Derek. Still can't let you in."

She peered over the rims of her sunglasses. "Used to be a pretty girl could get into any party. Especially one of his."

"Sorry, ma'am."

Ma'am! She had an urge to whip off her scarves and shades and embarrass the shit out of this guy with the gall to *ma'am* Erin Rose, but she managed to tamp down her irritation. "I won't stay long. I just need to speak with Derek."

"Please don't make me call my friends to escort you out."

Erin extended her arm and uncurled the fingers of her fist to reveal a packet of white powder and a hundred-dollar bill. "Would you mind checking again to see if I'm on the list?"

The bouncer palmed the bribe off Erin's hand, then pulled out his phone and pretended to scroll through the attendee list. "Well, there you are. My mistake. Have a nice time." He waved her through and turned his attention back to the elevator.

Erin dodged past a knot of people hanging around the entranceway and into the penthouse proper. Beautiful people everywhere. Young. Vibrant. Palpable excitement, air thick with the scent of sex.

Enablers, pushers, hangers-on, celeb sniffers, star fuckers, groupies, yes-men, yes-women. Governed by greed and lust. All grab-assing. All posing. All searching for something they'd never find, at least not where they were looking.

Glam and glib, shiny and sleek and sweaty, the hardbodies gyrated in the clubs, gyrated in their beds, putting enlightenment up their noses or down their throats or into their veins. What else would nubile supermodels—men and women—do for recreation?

In the twenty-five years since Erin first broke out as a seventeen-year-old "It Girl," she'd engaged in more than her share of outrageous behavior, with all manner of celebrities—athletes, movie stars, politicians. Nothing was too over-the-top. She'd kept the paparazzi busy while keeping her name in the tabloids. Because without fame—or even infamy—what was the point?

Back in the day, it seemed that Erin had *pioneered* the scene, and the irony wasn't lost on her that the *scene* had killed Sierra.

According to the bouncer, everyone in New York knew Derek. A decade ago, at the apex of her meteoric trajectory, *she'd* been the one with all the friends. Erin Rose, the Queen of the Scene.

So where were they now, all those friends?

Erin weaved her way through the crowd. She still wore her diva get-up, although in this place, even a diva wouldn't attract more than a passing glance. She spotted a few people she thought she knew, but if they recognized her, they didn't act on it. She pushed on, the anonymous Amazon in the shimmery silver gown.

Throughout the room, men and women danced to their own rhythms, no matter what song was playing on the sound system.

The penthouse was decorated in brass and glass, featuring ultramodern furniture that looked impressively uncomfortable. Thick white rugs underfoot, as if a herd of polar bears had been slaughtered and skinned, then spread on the floor like so much marshmallow creme. Erin searched every square foot of the main living area but didn't find who she was looking for.

The man himself. Derek. Sierra's former manager. And part-time lover. And drug supplier.

It was his party, his place, his *scene*. He had to be there somewhere.

Probably in a back bedroom, getting a blow job from a seventeen-year-old supermodel wannabe trying to prove her worth, trying to break into the biz. Erin knew the go-to move from vast experience. *Sex sells!*

At the back of the large living room, she noticed two people descending a spiral staircase. Did the penthouse have a penthouse?

One way to find out.

At the top of the staircase, Erin pushed open the door and found herself stepping out onto the roof. The night was warm, with a slight breeze, and the fresh air felt liberating on her skin after the cloying hormone-filled atmosphere of the party below. Derek had created a small rooftop oasis, a crown-of-the-city lounge, landscaped with dozens of plants and decked out with fancy furniture, even a hot tub. Tiki torches and portable lamps were strategically placed to beat away the darkness. In one corner, a tux-clad bartender concocted drinks behind a gleaming black-and-gold bar.

People milled about, mostly near the edges of the roof, taking in the city lights.

And what a spectacular view it was, forty-five stories over Manhattan.

Erin strolled along the roofline, gazing out over the city that never slept, keeping her eyes peeled for Derek. Her mind drifted back to the inevitable. What had Sierra been thinking during the moments before she died? Had she been in pain? Was she afraid? Did she call out for her mother? Did she *curse* her mother?

Erin deserved every bit of her daughter's anger.

She navigated through a grouping of potted shrubs and almost smacked into Derek. Two young ladies hung off him, both giggling at something he'd just said. Both were barely in their twenties, less than half Derek's age. Both were barely dressed. *Sex! Girls!*

"Hello, Derek," Erin said. Her purse still hung from her shoulder, and she was keenly aware of the added weight of the gun inside.

"Hello, there. Care to join our little party?" Derek had one arm around each girl, and he hugged them closer. "Always room for one more!"

The girls giggled again, and Erin wondered how much alcohol the trio had consumed.

Erin smiled, stepped closer. She towered over the others, so she bent down and whispered into Derek's ear. "I was hoping for a private party. I'll make it worth your while, that's for sure." She opened up her palm, where she held another packet of white powder. Currency of the party people. "This is primo stuff, but there's only enough for two, I'm afraid." She stepped back, awaiting Derek's move.

Derek didn't need more than four seconds to make his decision. "Ladies, if you'll excuse me, I have some business to attend to here. I'll catch up with you later." He shooed them away, as if he were helping two wayward baby ducks cross the road. "Enjoy the party."

He turned to Erin, swaying slightly. "Okay, then. The junior varsity is gone. What did you have in mind?"

Erin didn't say a word. She removed the scarf from her head, then unwrapped the one around her neck. Underhanded, she threw the scarves into the air, over the three-foot wall—the only thing keeping the partygoers safe from stumbling over the edge and meeting pavement, forty-five floors below. The scarves fluttered in the breeze before disappearing from sight.

Erin removed her sunglasses and tossed them over the edge, too.

Derek's smile vanished. "My God. What are *you* doing here? I'm—" Even in the dim light, Erin saw his face turn ashen. "I'm so, so sorry. I don't think I ever offered my condolences. In person, anyway. Sierra was a fantastic girl. Such a tragedy."

Erin slipped her purse from her shoulder.

The awkward silence between them grew.

"So, uh, is there something I can do for you?" Derek glanced around her, as if he was expecting help. He seemed to have sobered up in a hurry.

"I came to talk to you. And you alone."

"I know things haven't been going well for you. Since...it happened. If there's anything I can do, please let me know."

"That's why I'm here."

He gave Erin a knowing nod. "I get it. I've heard the rumors. About you wanting to make a comeback. The mourning period is over, and you're ready to put it behind you, right? I applaud you. A terrible tragedy, but what's done is done."

"What's done is done. But sometimes things aren't really finished, until they are, you know?" Erin opened her purse.

Derek tilted his head. "Not sure what you're getting at, but if you *are* contemplating a comeback, I think it might work. Maybe a Jenny Craig campaign. A before-and-after kind of thing." He examined her, as if she was just another blond slab of meat auditioning for a gig. "Yeah, that might actually work. You've still got it mostly going on. If anyone can pull off a phoenix-rising-from-the-ashes thing for you, it's me. We could make Sierra proud."

"You have no right to say what Sierra would think. Or feel. Or do." Erin pulled the gun from her purse, pointed it at Derek's chest.

"Whoa, there. Settle down." He slowly raised his hands, fingers splayed. "What's going on?"

"I failed Sierra. I wasn't around when she was growing up, when she needed me. And even when I was present, I wasn't really *there*, you know? The drugs. The booze. All those men. And she was just a little girl. She followed in my footsteps all right."

"You did okay. She was so sweet."

"Yeah, she was, at least before…." The gun wavered in her hand. "Before she got involved with you. At first, things seemed great. You got her jobs, her career blossomed. She was *happy*. But then what? You started fucking her? Pumping her with drugs?" *Sex! Pills!*

"That's not how—"

"Don't bullshit me! You used her. She was found dead in your bed, a needle in her arm. Why? You could have had any girl you wanted. Why did you destroy *mine*?" Her hand tightened on the pistol's grip.

"I cared for Sierra. What happened to her was tragic, but it was an accident."

"That's what your crooked lawyers claimed. But I know better." Erin gestured with the gun. "*You* know better. Everyone around knows better."

"What are you trying to say?"

"I'm saying you're guilty of killing my baby."

Derek nodded at the weapon in Erin's shaking hand. "Why don't you put that away?"

"You mean this gun?"

"Yes," Derek said. "The gun."

Erin recalculated. She'd come here ready—eager—to shoot Derek right through the heart. But now that she was standing here, she had a different take on things. He didn't deserve to get shot. Too easy. Too quick. Too painless. He needed to suffer. Derek was guilty of killing Sierra, undeniably.

But not entirely.

Erin turned and dropped the gun, then spun on one sexy stiletto heel and lunged at Derek. She engulfed him in a lover's embrace, then drove him back, back, back, using every ounce of her strength. She barely felt her hips brush the top of the retaining wall as she launched herself over the side, into the void, still clutching Derek in a bear hug.

In a few seconds, she would be free from guilt. Free from pain.

At peace.

At last.

Fifteen blocks away, in Times Square, the electronic billboards flickered for just a moment, before blazing back to life to sell more jeans.

Last Chance Lost
by Sherry Harris

Stew Davis almost sobbed when he crested the hill and spotted the Last Chance Saloon down below. The gray wood building looked about ready to fall over. Tumbleweeds, for God's sake, were piled against one side. The hill behind the building shimmered in the heat like a moonscape. But at least a neon "Beer Here" sign was blinking sporadically in the window. The blinking reminded him of the fiancée he'd dumped this morning. She blinked just like that every damn time she put her contacts in.

Stew stopped and emptied a rock from his shoe. He'd been walking this road for the past four hours. Except it wasn't much of a road—barely more than a cow trail. Getting lost this morning and having his beloved 1966 Mustang stolen with all of his belongings was just the effing froth on the beer of his life. Stew still couldn't believe it. He'd been out of his car maybe two minutes. On a deserted road. Relieving himself behind a boulder because God knows there wasn't a bathroom or a sign of civilization anywhere around. Next thing he knew, his car was roaring off. How was that possible, when he hadn't seen another car or person for miles?

His Italian shoes had rubbed a blister over a mile ago. His designer suit and silk tie were coated in a fine dust that wouldn't brush off. And the wind blew with a fury. Dark clouds hung on the horizon. Stew trotted forward, twisted his ankle in a rut, and cursed. *Patience, buddy,* he told himself. In a couple minutes he'd be in the saloon, calling for help and drinking a cold one. *Last chance, my ass.* He had dumped the old ball and chain and would begin a new life in Nevada, once he finally got there. This would be a new *first* chance for Stew.

*

The air conditioner hiccupped like it always did when someone came into the Last Chance Saloon. The regulars turned to squint into the late afternoon sun to see who had broken their peace. Lily lifted her head from her worn paperback, pages yellowed, spine cracked. It didn't take long to see this guy didn't belong here. He wore a suit. His fancy shoes were covered with dust, but his hair was as pretty and shiny as an ad in a grocery-store magazine. Tousled, just like you saw on the movie stars.

"Help you?" Lily asked.

"Somebody stole my car. And I'm lost." A smile lit his cheekbones. Cheekbones that looked like God himself had hewn them.

A man who can smile in the face of adversity. Now that's something. "You got to be lost if you ended up here," Lily smiled back. It had been a while since anyone had brought a smile to her lips.

"I'm Stew. Stew Davis." He held out his hand to shake. "I need to call the police to report my car."

Lily took his hand, warm and soft against hers. He seemed to hold on a second longer than necessary, sending some tingles around parts of her that hadn't had a lot to tingle about lately. "I'm Lily. And it'll be the sheriff out here, not the police. I'll call for you."

Lily walked over to the wall phone, putting a little more sway in her hips than usual. It had been a long time since a stranger had shown up, and a handsome one at that. She winked at old Luke as she swished by. Luke looked cockeyed at the stranger, ignoring Lily completely. The locals didn't take to strangers out here. Lily would have to be on her guard. She didn't want any trouble.

She made the call and went back to Stew. "Might as well make yourself comfortable. Harry's on the other side of the county. It'll be a couple of hours before he can get here."

"Is there anyone else you can call?" Stew asked.

A snort came from the back corner of the room. Belle. Lily hoped she'd behave herself. She was already three shots of whiskey in, and even on her best day Belle wasn't one to hold her tongue.

"Sorry," Lily said. "There's a reason this place is called Last Chance. Harry'll make sure everyone's keeping an eye out for your car, though." She smiled again. Glad she'd washed her hair and left it loose, tumbling around her shoulders. She'd even put on a pair of clean shorts and a tank top that showed a little more cleavage than normal. Almost like Fate had told her something special was going to happen today, and she'd better be prepared. "Can I get you something?"

She watched Stew check himself out in the mirror behind the bar. He ran a hand through his hair and brushed at the lapels of his suitcoat. His shoulders went slack as he sat on the round barstool. "Sure. A beer. Something local, if you have it."

Lily opened the cooler, grateful she'd picked up some local beers last time she drove to Laramie. The bottle cooled her hand and made a satisfying *whoosh* when she opened it. She tipped a glass and poured the beer smoothly, so only a skiff of foam sat on top. She set it in front of Stew, and, when he reached for it, she saw he wasn't wearing a wedding ring. Didn't even have a white mark or indentation showing he'd *been* wearing one recently. Lily opened a Coke for herself and drank it straight out of the bottle.

"How'd you end up this far from the highway?" she asked.

"I get tired of highways. I like the back roads. But this might be a little too backroad, even for me."

Lily laughed. "I hear you."

"But you stay here anyway?" he asked.

"Family. They need me. I'm their last chance." She winked before moving off to check on the others. Gave them all warning looks. Don't be rude to the stranger. Maybe, if they were friendlier, more people would come in. And then Lily wouldn't be so lonely.

*

An hour later, when Stew went back to the bathroom, Belle raced up to the bar.

"Who is he?" She tossed her red curls with a practiced motion. Belle was a couple of years younger than Lily and had rodeo-queen looks. Hell, she had *been* the rodeo queen, and she never let Lily forget it.

"Leave him alone," Lily said. "You owe me." It was amazing she could even stand having Belle in here, what with Belle having stole the very first boyfriend she'd ever had. But Lily was a forgiving sort. And, with a little distance, she had realized she could never have lived with a man so deadly earnest, anyways. She shook her head, thinking about the way he had talked about love, yammering on how it was all about sacrifice and compromise. That boy could suck the fun out of any situation. But that hadn't made it right for Belle to steal him away before Lily had the satisfaction of breaking up with him.

"Come on. It's always cowboys and old men in here. It's been a while since somebody swept me off my feet." Belle gave her the sad look she always used. But Lily had become immune to it.

"Not this time," Lily said.

The bathroom door rattled open, and Lily shooed Belle away. The rodeo queen slunk back to her seat, tossing a come-hither look over her shoulder at Stew.

Lily was pleased—more than pleased, she was downright excited—to see Stew ignore the look and settle back onto his stool. Time for the charm offensive to start.

"What are you doing out here in Wyoming?" Maybe he was moving to the area, though he didn't look the part. No matter. It might just be time to shut this place down, ride off with a handsome man to somewheres else.

"It's a sad tale," Stew said with a half grin.

Lily opened another beer and refilled his glass. "I'm used to sad tales. Goes with the territory when you own a bar." She cocked her head to one side. "Let's hear it."

"My mom's not doing so well, so I'm heading out to Nevada to take care of her."

"I'm sorry to hear that." Her heart fluttered a little at the thought of a man who cared about his mother.

"And I had to dump my fiancée this morning. It's been a hell of a day."

So he was a free man. Although the word "dump" was a bit disconcerting. On the other hand, it didn't sound like he was nursing a broken heart. She'd mopped up enough of those with other men, foolishly hoping for the beginning of something but winding up with just a night or two on the rebound. "Breaking up is hard to do," Lily quoted the old song. Belle loved to play it on the rare days the jukebox was working. Another dig at Lily.

"Tell me about it. But getting rid of her was for the best. She was a total shrew."

Lily stiffened. She'd been called that once. But maybe his fiancée really *was* a shrew. Lily decided to give him the benefit of the doubt. After all, he loved his mama.

"How so?"

Stew took a long pull at his beer. Lily watched his Adam's apple bob, checked out the slight stubble of beard, flushed with embarrassment when Stew noticed her looking.

"Lily, have you ever tried to be the best partner you *could* be, and it just didn't work out?"

"Sounds like every damn relationship I ever had." She leaned forward a little to give him a shot of her cleavage. He took a quick glance and turned away. Lily relaxed. He'd passed another test. Stew was a gentleman. "I guess we have that in common."

"I love too much. Give too much." Stew shook his head sadly.

"And then they don't appreciate it," Lily added. She knew how he felt.

"Exactly. The nagging starts. The questions if I stay out too late or don't come home at all one night." Stew took another long drink. "A man needs respect."

Lily grabbed a towel and wiped at a spot on the bar so he wouldn't notice her agitation. She looked around. All the regulars were openly watching them now.

"But surely a woman has the right to ask a question if her man stays out all night?" She was throwing him a lifeline. That was pure Lily.

"Does she, Lily? Shouldn't she just trust me? Let me be the head of the family? Make the decisions?"

A couple of the regulars got up and left. *Chickens.* They were afraid of a woman who asserted herself. Belle stayed, though. Lily knew she had always enjoyed a good show.

"How much longer till the sheriff gets here?" Stew asked.

"Let me give him another call," Lily said. She dialed the phone and talked, then sauntered back over to Stew. "Bad news. They have a hostage situation on the other side of the county. Every resource they have is there."

"Damn it."

"You worried about your mom?" Really, maybe his love for his mother was redemption enough.

"No, that's not it. I've got a couple of days to get out there and stick her in a home. Then I'll make my fortune at roulette. My luck is changing, Lily. I can feel it."

A home? Lily had taken good care of *her* mother. Wiped her brow. Spoonfed her, when she grew too weak to feed herself. That's how you do for your loved ones. But not everyone's cut out to be a caretaker.

"I wanted to get to a pawn shop in Rock Springs to cash in this ring." He pulled a dark velvet box out of his pocket and flipped it open.

Lily almost gasped. It was at least two carats, as sparkly as the sun on raindrops. "You didn't let her keep it?"

Another regular got up and left. Lily glanced at Belle. Even *she* was starting to look pissed. And for Belle to get mad at a good-looking man was a rare thing. But Lily was starting to think he wasn't all that good looking, after all. His eyes were a little narrow, his forehead a bit broad. His recently dumped fiancée was probably better off without him.

"Why would I?" he asked.

Thunder rumbled, shaking the building.

Lily smiled. "Why, indeed?"

*

By the time Stew finished his fourth beer, he was obviously feeling no pain.

"It gets a little boring around here," Lily said. "I've got a shooting range out back. Want to give it a try? Or are you one of those city boys who's afraid of guns?"

It was the boyfriend with the earnest eyes who had taught Lily to shoot. All his love nonsense had eventually turned to bickering. But Lily would always be grateful to him, because the gun range had shown her a talent she hadn't known she had.

"I'm not afraid of guns," he said. "It's been a while, but let's go shoot."

*

Lily opened the bar the next morning. The regulars drifted in. Stew came, too. He looked a little the worse for wear. But then they always did. The sheriff had yet to show up. Lily expected him to come soon, though. Somebody always came by to check on her after a storm like the one they'd had last night. She wasn't sure if they'd be happier if they found her safe or if the building had been washed away.

*

Deputy Sheriff Tom Jerkins bumped down the road to check on Lily. He worried about her, out here all alone. Last night there'd been one hell of a storm, with flooding from Cheyenne west to beyond Laramie. Tom came over the rise to see the building still standing. *Barely* standing, but then that had described the place for years, according to his parents.

A neon sign winked at him: "Bee Her." A couple of the letters had burned out since the last time he'd been out this way. He parked, hitched up his belt, and opened the door. Inside, he had to wait a minute for his eyes to adjust to the dim light. Cobwebs hung from every corner. Dust lay thick on the tables. He really hated coming in here. But at least the bar was polished and clean. The lights dangling from strings above it reflected in its scarred surface.

"Lily?"

A door swung open, and she came out. *Good lord, she's wearing a tank top and Daisy Duke shorts.* The skin on her arms sagged in an alarming number of wrinkles. Age spots marred her face. The altitude and sun were unforgiving in Wyoming. Tom would reapply some sunscreen when he got back to the patrol car. Lily had dyed her thin hair a bright shade of blond. It clumped around her shoulders. She looked like one of the creatures at the haunted house in Laramie he'd taken his ex-girlfriend Molly to last fall. *Not very charitable,* he told himself. *She's just an old woman.*

"Hey, Lily. Thought I'd check on you after the storm last night."

She batted her eyelashes, what was left of them. Tom repressed a shudder.

"Why, that is so sweet of you," she said. "That storm was something. Want a beer?"

"Nice of you, but I'm on duty."

"A Coke, then?" She gestured toward an old cooler that clunked and choked and sputtered.

"Sure."

Lily got out two Cokes, opened them, and passed one over. She wore a large diamond ring on the fourth finger of her left hand. Tom leaned on the bar. The stools looked so rickety, he didn't trust them to sit on.

"You seen any strays out here?" he asked. "The sheriff found a '66 Mustang all smashed up over in the Vedauwoo Recreation Area, near the campground. There's no sign of the owner. Registration says it belongs to a guy named Stew Davis."

"You don't say. I haven't seen anyone. Just me and the regulars."

Tom wondered who the hell the regulars were. It was like a ghost town in here.

"How's that sweet girlfriend of yours?" Lily asked. "What's her name again? Mary?"

"Molly." Tom took a long swig from his icy bottle of Coke. "We broke up."

"I'm sorry to hear that. Getting dumped is never easy."

"I was the dumper, not the dumpee."

"How come?" Lily asked. She'd known Tom a long time. His parents, too. He put his life on the line every day for the folks who lived in this county. Well, more often than not he wasn't in any danger, but you never knew. Maybe that was enough for redemption. Everyone deserved a last chance—until it was lost.

She looked around at the regulars. Stew glared at her from a table in the back with Belle.

"So you *didn't* call the sheriff yesterday," Stew said. Belle had tried flirting with him earlier, but Stew had taken no notice. He was a changed man.

Lily gave him a quick shrug in reply. She didn't want to answer out loud, lest Tom think she was nuts. She wasn't. It was just that she could see and hear folks other people couldn't. Ghosts. Her regulars. Each of them had a bullet hole through the forehead and another one through the chest.

Some might disapprove, but Lily happened to have a heightened sense of right and wrong. She wasn't afraid to set things right. That's why folks in town thought the boy with the earnest eyes and Belle had run off together. Lily might have helped that myth along when she "found" a note she said Belle had written.

She'd given every last one of them a chance for redemption. Even her sister Belle.

Tom set down his Coke. "She told me last night she wanted to get married, but I'm not ready to settle down."

That didn't sound so bad. Tom couldn't be much over twenty-five. Young for settling down. "Well, that's a shame."

Tom looked down for a moment. "Not really. Besides, I met somebody else a few weeks ago. She had car trouble out on I-80. We hit it off. I've been working up the courage to break up with Molly. Trust me, dating two women at the same time isn't as fun as people make it sound."

Well, that was a shame, too. He should have had the courage to end the relationship right away, instead of leading the poor thing on.

"You got time for a little shooting at the gun range out behind the bar before you head out?" Lily asked Tom.

"Sure," Tom said. "I've got time."

"Run," Stew shouted. "Run!"

He waved his arms frantically, but they didn't even stir the air.

Lily looked at him and then at Tom.

She smiled.

Last chance lost.

Taming the Tiger
Released September 1998

"Harlem in Havana"
"Man From Mars"
"Love Puts on a New Face"
"Lead Balloon"
"No Apologies"
"Taming the Tiger"
"The Crazy Cries of Love"
"Stay in Touch"
"Face Lift"
"My Best to You"
"Tiger Bones"

All songs by Joni Mitchell
except "The Crazy Cries of Love" (by Joni Mitchell and Don Freed)
and "My Best to You" (by Gene Willadsen and Isham Jones).

Harlem in Havana
by Alison McMahan

It was my job to protect Julio Mella, but on the tenth of January, 1929, the Cuban journalist was assassinated. Shot in the street in Mexico City as he walked arm-in-arm with his woman. Point-blank to the chest.

I was making a delivery for Mella when he was killed. The police accused the woman at first, but no one had to tell me that Gerardo Machado, the Cuban dictator, was behind Mella's assassination.

It wasn't enough for Machado to banish us from Cuba. Now he was sending goons after us to cut us down on the street.

But you know what? Two can play at that game.

I packed away my white suit and white straw hat. Hopped a ship to Santo Domingo. Then I went undercover as an agricultural worker.

From there I charmed a fisherman into taking me to the eastern side of Cuba. Made my way to one of Machado's plantations, found the foreman, and joined the farmers cutting sugarcane.

The first morning, they piled us into wagons. We were all wedged together, our legs dangling over the sides, as two oxen pulled us out to the sugarcane fields.

The wagon topped a slight rise. Below us, and stretching as far as I could see, hectares and hectares of cane.

I sucked in my breath and went still, my mind blank, mesmerized by the waves of yellow, violet and green featherings of the cane's inflorescence rippling across the fields. For a moment I breathed in beauty. I forgot about my exile, about my murdered friend, about the ruler I'd come to kill.

The wagon jolted to a stop. I dropped off the back with the others, took up my cane knife and went to work hacking away at the dark green stalks, the feathered tassels high up where I could no longer see them.

Nothing I'd done before, even my stint as a guerrilla soldier in the jungle, prepared me for the life of a cane cutter. I wasn't bad at it, but the work was relentless. It was a relief when Sunday came. By then I'd made friends with some of the regular ranch hands. I followed one of them into a tavern and bought a round. Soon enough, I found out that Machado was supposed to spend Easter at the ranch, but had changed his mind at the last minute. My new friend groused about all the work to prepare for the presidential family, all for nothing.

I didn't just cut cane and wait. I also found men who I thought might help me in my task, members of the local resistance. They followed a radical socialist named Guiteras, a calm but charismatic leader.

Machado was again supposed to visit his ranch in May, but again cancelled. The sugarcane harvest ended, the migrant workers moved on.

I'd have to kill the dictator in Havana.

But first I got my foreman friend good and drunk. After he passed out, I brought in my other friends, the migrant sugarcane workers. We slaughtered all of Machado's cattle. Everyone helped themselves to meat and went home to feast.

I stayed behind and set fire to the ranch house. When the flames reached the roof, I started out for the capital.

In Havana, I put on my white linen suit and straw hat, the brim pulled low over one eye. I looked like any other bourgeois out for a stroll under the shade trees of the Paseo del Prado. I admired the mansions that could have been in Madrid or Paris or Vienna, such a contrast to the beggars on the corners and the ragged urchins playing ball on the promenade.

I walked around the Presidential Palace, pretending to admire the dome, but really assessing the windows, noting entrances, counting the guards. One thing was clear: it was nearly impossible to get to Machado as long as he was in the palace.

But why rush? One pull of the trigger, one thrust of the knife, and it would be over.

I preferred to take my time. Dismantle everything Machado had, piece by piece. Make him watch his riches wither while wondering who was after him.

Then kill him.

Machado ruled through fear. His main weapon was *La Porra*, the thugs paid to beat protestors into submission. The mercenaries were easy to spot: other men avoided them on the street. Cops let them pass thru barricades.

Across the street from the *Capitolio* was the National Federation of Labor. There must be a meeting taking place inside, based on the demonstrators outside. From the picket signs and chanted slogans, I gathered members of the Federation were meeting with union representatives, hoping to resolve the longshoreman and rail workers strike.

I recognized a few members of *La Porra* amongst the demonstrators. Their slogan-chanting was almost drowned out by a chorus of women singing a bolero, "Lagrimas Negras."

> *Gypsy, I'll follow you*
> *Even if it means my death.*

The lyrics inspired me. I wove my way through the crowd, pushing and prodding. "They can't hear us!" I yelled. "Let's *make* them hear us!"

The protestors didn't need much encouragement. They followed me into the Federation of Labor offices. We shoved our way up the stairs, turned in an instant from a motley crowd to a mob.

I recognized two of the men next to me as members of *La Porra*. "This way!" I instructed them. They followed me up the back stairway, moving quickly, and for a moment we were ahead of the crowd.

As soon as we reached the third floor, I turned. "Where is the meeting?"

I waited for them to look around, confused, then pulled out my revolver and shot them.

The sounds of gunfire turned the mob behind us into a screaming, bloodthirsty horde. I didn't wait for them. Goal accomplished, I moved quickly out of the building through a back door, then circled around to the front and blended with the crowd watching the singers. Incredibly, they were still singing "Lagrimas Negras," the pace of the bolero fast now, the girls swinging their hips and shaking their hand-painted maracas made from dried gourds.

One of them caught my eye.

I sucked in my breath and went still, my mind blank, mesmerized by her full, red, sensuous lips, her dusky face, the otherworldly expression in those immense emerald-gray eyes. I closed my own eyes and glimpsed the sea of sugarcane, ripples flowing through the yellow and violet flowers on the sea of green.

I opened my eyes. She was still there. Still real.

> I don't want to suffer. I'll go with you
> My hero, even if it means my death.

Her eyes met mine. I lifted my right hand and stretched out my left and she stepped into my dance space as if she had been born for it. We rumbaed around, I twirled her under my arm, and she turned me as I corkscrewed down to the ground and back up in an even, steady, perfect movement.

We danced, while inside the mob attacked the union men and the government men and the talks were disrupted and the *La Porra* mercenaries rammed home their blows and the stars came out and the women sang and swung their hips in time with their maracas.

"You are a vision," I told Emmy. We'd finally introduced ourselves and were strolling leisurely along the Paseo. I put my arm around her waist and squeezed. "You dance divinely. Are you in a show?"

She looked at her feet, demure. "I would love to be in a show. But my auntie won't let me. She's afraid...with *La Porra* and everything. She says it's not safe."

I heard the cane rustling again. I stopped and pulled a newspaper out of my back pocket. I showed her the ad I'd circled. "Look. At the Hotel Nacional. An American show is looking for singers and musicians."

It was the worst thing I could have done. I needed to get into the Hotel Nacional to pursue my other agenda. To bring a girl—that was just crazy.

I rubbed the back of my neck. My head pounded. Part of me wanted her to listen to her aunt and tell me no. *Don't go with me. You could be jailed. Tortured. Killed.*

But like the girl in the song, instead of cursing me, she threw her arms around me. "Oh, that would be wonderful!"

*

The Hotel Nacional was built by Americans for Americans. There was only one way to get in, if you were Cuban, and that was to work there.

The ad in the paper named one Leon Claxton, a black show entrepreneur extraordinaire from someplace called Memphis in the US. He wanted dancers, singers, musicians. Claxton was short, already nearly bald, though I thought he was close to my age, that is, just over thirty.

My original plan had been to get a job as a waiter in the hotel, but meeting Emmy had changed things. I'd had trumpet lessons as a kid, played in the school band. Emmy lent me a relative's silver trumpet and we practiced "Lagrimas Negras" a few times. That was our audition piece.

Claxton cast Emmy right away, as I knew he would. He was doubtful about my trumpet playing, but Emmy insisted he take us both or none. I watched him struggle mentally. He really wanted Emmy. He knew something was off about me. Emmy won. Finally, he shrugged. "Well, she's a beautiful girl. Make sure she doesn't get into any trouble."

"Yes, sir." I saluted him.

Claxton shook his head and went on with his auditions.

Emmy threw herself on me, wrapping her legs around me and kissing me deeply. For the first time.

I took her up to our room and made love to her, hearing the rustling of cane beneath her sighs.

*

Claxton made us rehearse, and rehearse, and rehearse. The whole show lasted only an hour, but we'd be doing it many times a day. There were sixteen singers and dancers, some of them black girls from America, most of them Cuban like Emmy. The jazz band had more than twenty musicians. There was a clown, and a belly dancer, and, at the end of every show, a chorus line.

Emmy loved it.

I loved the rehearsals, loved watching her dance. I loved our long nights of lovemaking in my hotel room. I loved Emmy.

But I had to get back to my real work.

Through the grapevine I'd learned that the last person to meet with Mella before Mella had gone out on his date was a so-called activist named Pepe Magriñat. And Pepe, a few *La Porra* men told me before I silenced them forever, was hiding out in Havana.

The resistance to Machado's dictatorship was growing. More Cubans went on strike: the truck drivers, the taxi drivers, the harbor workers. Protests, with the help of some "operators from New York," as the newspapers referred to agitators like me, turned into insurrection. Soon the whole country was on strike.

Chaos and anarchy are the best environment for a wet worker. I knew my chance to kill Machado would come soon. But I had to do it before things got so out of hand that the dictator would have to impose martial law.

So I did what I do best. Cornered the right people in bars, bought them drinks, spread a rumor that Machado was about to resign. The rumor spread like a relay torch from word-of-mouth to pirate radio station to newspaper, from Havana to Matanzas to Santiago de Cuba, from fishermen to sugarcane workers: Machado had promised to resign but then refused to follow through.

Inevitably, the wrong people died. The night Claxton's "Harlem in Havana" revue was to open to a paying public, a mob formed and marched on the *Capitolio* and the Presidential Palace. The police and the army took potshots. Later, I heard that over twenty people were dead.

I wasn't there. There were too many police, too many soldiers, for me to reach Machado. But while everyone was distracted, I made my way to Pepe's hiding place in a funeral home. The doors were locked—the owners probably marching or hunkered down in their homes—but picking the locks was easy. The curtains were drawn. I flipped open my lighter.

The first room was a sitting room. Then an office.

And in the back, a light.

The lit room was a showroom, with coffins arranged on platforms, shiny black or lacquered wood or plain pine.

And there was Pepe, dressed as if he was an employee. "We're closed. How did you get in here?"

"I'm sorry, the door was open." I smiled sadly. "I have an emergency. I came here from Venezuela, and the friend I was with was shot. I need a coffin to take him home."

"I'm sorry for your loss," Pepe said mechanically. He picked up a clipboard with a blank form and went to a desk in the corner. Probably had a gun in the drawer.

I stopped next to an elaborate heavy black coffin, surely the most expensive in the place, and slid my hand across its surface admiringly. "I think something like this. What's it lined with?"

Pepe paused by the coffin, unsure now, torn between the possibility of a big commission and his sense that I was not who I said I was. "This one is lined with padded satin."

"Padded satin." My voice was filled with wonder. "What's your name, by the way? I was told to speak to someone named Pepe. I was referred, you see."

Pepe relaxed, nodded. "That's me." He still had his hand on the rim of the coffin.

I slammed down the lid and bashed his shooting hand. "My name is Carlos Aponte." I grabbed his arm so he couldn't remove his fingers. "And the name of my dead friend is Julio Antonio Mella."

His eyes widened, and his mouth fell open. He tried to step away, but I slammed the lid on his fingers again, made sure they were broken.

I grabbed his shoulder with my other hand, swung his head down. My knee came up and struck his face, repeatedly.

Pepe hardly resisted. He'd been in hiding, going soft, while I'd spent months harvesting cane.

When he bent over, heaving, I hammer-fisted him on the back of his neck.

I could have killed him with my bare hands. But I needed to know, so I let go of him. His face was bloody. He cradled his crushed fingers, whimpering.

To get his attention, I took out my pistol, clicked off the safety, and pointed it at him. "What I really need is information." My tone was friendly now. "Who ordered you to shoot Mella?"

"I didn't—"

"Don't lie. Even the Mexican police knew it wasn't the woman. And you had a meeting with him at a bar just a few minutes before he was shot."

Pepe frowned, gazed painfully at his crushed fingers. "If I tell you, you'll let me go?"

"Sure." I handed him my handkerchief. "Tell me who ordered the hit. Who paid you to kill Mella?"

Pepe confirmed everything I knew, and more.

As soon as I had my answer, I shot him twice in the chest. At his look of surprise, I said, "Had to do it, Pepe. For Mella."

*

I made it back to the Hotel Nacional and took my place as second trumpet just in time for the first public performance of the "Harlem in Havana" revue. Claxton had set up an elaborate outdoor stage on the grounds of the hotel, with two sweeping flights of stairs and fancy backdrops, all brilliantly lit with electric lights that glinted in the dancers' platinum-blond wigs and made our costumes shimmer as we moved. All the chairs on the lawn were occupied, and people stood all around to watch the show.

Emmy was not the main attraction—that was a well-known dance pair—but I only had eyes for her.

I did my best to keep in time with the rest of the musicians, but from the dirty looks I got from the first trumpet player I guess I wasn't too successful.

When we finished our first performance, we got a prolonged standing applause.

Emmy came running up to me. "Where were you? I was afraid you weren't going to make it. I thought—I thought—"

She collapsed against my chest, weeping.

I pushed her away from me, gently. "Darling, you are going to mess up your hair and your makeup. Please don't cry. I'm here."

She pulled off her wig. "I thought you'd finally gotten yourself killed."

She knew.

The audience was filing out toward their rooms or the hotel bar, laughing and chatting. The musicians retuned their instruments for the next show. A group of giggling young women came towards us.

Emmy read the surprise on my face. "Carlos, I find spots of blood on your clothes. I found your gun. You should hide it better than that. My brother is a—"

I grabbed her arm and pulled her close. "Shh. Don't say anything else. If your brother is a—then you know, just being with me can get you jailed. Tortured. Even killed."

The giggly girls were all friends of Emmy's. She introduced me as her boyfriend, stopped short of telling them my name when I tightened my grip around her waist. I smiled, let them play with the trumpet, and flirted with them, just enough to make Emmy happy but not jealous.

At the same time, I watched the people milling around on the lawn. Mostly Americans, including the US ambassador. More soldiers than usual. I spotted Colonel Sanguilly, from Cuba's Officer Corps.

Something was up.

And then I saw Guiteras.

Something was definitely up.

Emmy's friends finally said their good-byes, thanked her for getting them good seats.

It was time for the last show of the night. We played "Lagrimas Negras." I kept my eyes on Emmy.

A gardener of love sows a flower and leaves
Another comes and cultivates it, which of the two will it be?

Halfway through the show, the lights went out. We kept playing, but Claxton silenced us with a tap of his baton. "Ladies and gentlemen, it appears that the workers at the electric plants are now on strike. But no need to worry. Give us a moment, and we will have torches set up."

I set down my trumpet and helped move the torches that provided a romantic atmosphere on the hotel garden paths closer to the stage.

On one of my trips out to the lawn, I saw a hotel guest pause and light a cigarillo. When the match flared onto his face, I recognized Guiteras.

"Machado has fled the palace," he said without preamble, shaking his match until it went out. "He's gone to ground somewhere. By tomorrow, he'll be in the Bahamas or Miami."

I swore. "Didn't we see this coming?"

"Don't worry," said Guiteras. "We'll get him eventually. But if there is more to you than a desire to avenge Mella, you will listen to me."

"I'm listening."

"Getting rid of Machado was only the first step. Our real problem is the Americans. You saw those four warships in the harbor, right?"

"Of course. But there's only so much a man like me can do."

"Nothing we can do about the warships. But the American ambassador is already talking about a 'New Deal' for Cuba."

I looked over at the stage. The musicians were going back to their stands. I'd be needed there soon. "What does that mean, a New Deal?"

"It means they want to smooth over the contradictions between American imperialism and Cuban capitalism. That can only happen at the expense of the workers."

"But the workers are on strike already. They won't let that happen."

"They are confused and disorganized. The strikes erupted out of an instinct for revenge."

"Well, that plus a little help." I thought back to the sugarcane harvesters who had helped me destroy Machado's eastern plantation, remembered their glee as they slaughtered Machado's cattle.

"Yes. Plus a little help. Imagine if they had *more* help."

"Guiteras, I have to get back on stage. What is it you want from me?"

"We have a long fight ahead of us. We have to make sure the same old officers don't take control of the army, that the *La Porra* doesn't remake itself under some other name. There is a lot of housecleaning still to do. And then we have to make sure the workers get a democracy and their rights."

I looked back at the stage. There was Emmy with the other dancers, ready to go on again.

"Think about it." Guiteras stamped out his cigarillo.

After one more look at Emmy, I went back to my room, changed my clothes, got my gun, and went to the palace. I hoped Guiteras was wrong, that I would still get a chance to kill Machado. I should never have indulged myself, taken my time, savored it.

I found Machado's palace surrounded by a mob lusting for revenge. The soldiers had disappeared.

So Guiteras was right. Machado was gone.

The mob broke through the portico entrance. I went in with it, but instead of going to the main halls I slid away and ran down to the pantries. I found a set of locked drawers and shot off the locks, loaded all the silver into a tablecloth and snuck out.

Emmy was waiting for me at the hotel. She searched my face and then my shirt.

I raised my hands as if in surrender. "No blood on me this time, Emmy. I promise."

I set the bundle at her feet.

She unwrapped the tablecloth. The silver spilled out, glinting in the candlelight. Her shoulders drooped, her radiant smile dimmed.

"What is this?"

"Machado is gone." I sat on the bed, put my arms around her, and buried my face in her neck. "The people are trying to get justice, and they started by looting the palace. I got this for you."

She tried to pull away and look at me, but I held her tight, breathed her in. "Listen," I said into her hair, "just listen. Claxton is going to take the show to America. Go with him. I hid an envelope full of dollars at the bottom of your makeup case." I whispered a New York City address and made her repeat it. "That's my mother's place. She'll love you. Anytime you have any trouble, go to her. My sister will be jealous of your beauty, but she will help you anyway." This got a little smile out of Emmy, but still she clung to me. "Make sure they know where you are, and I will find you."

Emmy pulled away sharply. "What? No! We have to go together."

I kissed her, long and hard and deep.

"I still have a job to do." I held her tightly. "But I can't do it unless I know you are safe."

Emmy wept. I wept, too, black tears, just like the song. I could hear shouting and pounding outside the hotel. But even with all that noise, the loudest sound in my head was the silence left behind by the fading breeze in the sugarcane.

Taming the Tiger
by Mindy Quigley

Catherine Carson hefted her secondhand suitcases from the trunk of the rental car with an inelegant grunt. Evening was falling, and the Big Dipper twinkled faintly in the darkening sky. In front of her sprawled the Victorian mansion of her new colleague, Anna-Sophia Lafarge. *The* Anna-Sophia Lafarge. Lafarge's most recent bestselling novel, *Mango Sweet*, depicted in sensuous detail the Victorian-era lesbian relationship of a buttoned-up British woman and an Indonesian pearl diver. Critics had clamored over one another to heap praise on the book, and now it smoldered on the nightstand of every fashionable liberal from Miami to L.A.

The University of Iowa was already two weeks into the fall '82 semester, and the maple trees on either side of the house's front path were tinged with burnt orange. Catherine's grip on the handles of her suitcases tightened. Before Catherine got the call from Iowa, she'd been staying with friends and friends-of-friends, eating bologna sandwiches and reusing her tea bags. She'd come to Iowa to take a last-minute semester-long adjunct professor gig, the first steady work she'd had since she received her MFA degree the year before.

Luck had brought her here. Luck and the unbridled alcoholism of George Younas, one of Iowa's poetry faculty. A few days before, when the man was saddled with a court-mandated stint in rehab, Jack Legg—department head and two-time Pulitzer nominee—had placed a few calls, looking for a warm body to show up the following Monday and take over the poet's classes. Legg had been a fraternity brother of Catherine's MFA advisor's husband, a connection that had proven useful when the all-points bulletin had gone out for a poetry teacher who could get to Iowa on very short notice.

Thus had Catherine found herself with an unexpected—and to her mind undeserved—opportunity to join the faculty of the Iowa

Writers' Workshop. And thus she stood gelled to the pavement, almost melting under the blazing shame of her inferiority.

"I thought I heard a car pull up," Anna-Sophia Lafarge said, stepping off the front porch. Her plummy voice carried across the distance between them, like a ventriloquist's trick.

Catherine hurried up the path. "Oh, yes. Hello. I'm Catherine Carson. Your new tenant." Catherine's heel caught on the edge of a paving stone, and she let go of one of her suitcases. Anna-Sophia caught it with a deft sweep of her long arms. She shifted it to her hand and snatched the other suitcase as well.

"Tenant?" Anna-Sophia repeated. "How ludicrous. 'Tenant' sounds as if I'll have you locked away in some drafty garret, paying me two shillings a week and an extra sixpence if you want hot water for your bath. No, no, no. Jack's told us all about you. You were a folksinger before becoming a poet, right?"

"Yes. Singer-songwriter, street busker, waitress, typist, cigar girl—I've failed at it all," Catherine replied with a mirthless laugh.

"Well, approaching poetry with a songwriter's mentality is bound to make your work all the more fascinating," Anna-Sophia said. "And so I won't have you called my tenant. You shall be a blisteringly talented up-and-coming poet and colleague who lives with me. If we're lucky, the whole town will assume we're engaged in a scandalous Sapphic affair." Anna-Sophia tossed a wink over her shoulder.

A deep blush stained Catherine's cheeks. "It was very kind of you to invite me. Nothing was available on such short notice."

"We couldn't have you homeless. Besides, you're doing me a favor. This big old beast of a house can get terribly lonely, especially once the winter sets in." The front door—carved mahogany with a stained-glass inset—stood open. "There's the cat, of course, but you'll never see him. Terribly skittish and comes out of hiding for no one. Rather more of a phantom than a pet."

Catherine's gaze flitted around the entrance foyer, to the two reception rooms that opened on either side, and up the wide, sinuous staircase. Every splendid detail her eyes alighted upon deepened her sense of dysphoria.

It didn't seem real. Catherine had somehow failed her way to an offer of steady work and a room in a famous author's mansion. Yes, she'd shown early promise as a singer-songwriter, and for a year or two after high school the gigs had been steady. But talk of a record deal floated and sank, floated and sank again, until the undertow of rejection almost pulled her down entirely. Her self-doubt developed into a paralyzing stage fright, dealing the final blow to her musical ambitions.

Eventually, she'd scraped together the wherewithal to pursue an education and a writing career, hoping that her gift for lyrics and melodies might translate onto the page. So far, though, literary jobs had proved as tough to come by as music gigs, and no more lucrative. Just that morning, Catherine had had to sneak out of the walk-through she shared with three other refugees from the record biz. She hadn't had enough cash to cover her share of the rent.

One false move and you're a goner. You'll fail at this, too. Catherine closed her eyes against the whispering doubts, as the familiar taste of bile crept into her throat.

"You're wondering why I bought this monstrous house, since it's clearly far too big for me, but you're too polite to ask," Anna-Sophia said. She raised an eyebrow, daring Catherine to contradict her. "For one, it's the only really interesting piece of architecture in this town. The university job is wonderful—and I absolutely adore teaching—but *Iowa*, darling. I-owe-ah." She emphasized each syllable as if she were describing some newly discovered tropical disease. "I simply couldn't picture myself living in a shabby little split-level with a chain-link fence. Life's too short to be boring. Frankly, after *Mango Sweet*, I could afford to indulge myself, so I did." She pulled a small silver case off a side table and snapped a cigarette free. Anna-Sophia offered one to Catherine, who demurred with a tight smile. "You can call me Feef, by the way. Everyone does."

"Feef?"

"A childhood nickname. In England, the posher one's family is, the more ridiculous one's nickname. I've got friends called Boffy and Tuppy. Absolutely everyone has a nickname." Feef paused, taking a thoughtful drag on her cigarette. "I lie. Francesca Browne is as posh as they come, and she's never been anything but Francesca, not even at school."

"Who's Francesca Browne?" Catherine asked.

Feef blew a thin stream of smoke through her nostrils. She turned toward a full-sized taxidermy tiger glowering from an alcove under the stairs. "That," she said, aiming the burning end of her cigarette at the beast, "is Francesca Browne."

*

As the 1982-1983 academic year began in earnest, Francesca Browne grew to occupy an outsized space in Catherine's psyche. Each Thursday afternoon, Feef hosted an informal wine-and-cheese gathering for the program's students and faculty at her home. Catherine attended every one of them, though she rarely could muster even a syllable to contribute to the conversation. For her, it was all impossibly glamorous, like a seventeenth-century Parisian salon. To be included in such company, treated as a peer by people who conversed in pearl-perfect witticisms—it was beyond anything she'd ever hoped for. Her happiness was cut through with a *frisson* of anxiety, though, knowing that, in a few short weeks, it would all be over.

One Thursday, a package from Burma arrived while the group was assembled, and Feef disgorged its contents for them: a necklace made of carved wooden beads and a small jade sewing needle.

"More tokens of Francesca Browne's love?" asked Lucinda Garett, whose first chapbook had sent the highbrow elite into a collective paroxysm in the mid-seventies.

"Hardly love. She's got a girl in every port," Feef replied archly, passing the beads and pin around for the others to admire.

Catherine had learned that Francesca wasn't, as she'd initially been told, the stuffed Bengal tiger in the foyer. Francesca was Feef's erstwhile school friend and fly-by-night lover. Almost daily, Feef would casually mention that Francesca had been the first woman to scale X or sail solo around Y. Her list of accomplishments seemed almost superhuman. Or Feef would point out some token jumbled among the treasures that decorated her home—some shell, tribal mask or ornate weaving—that had been a gift from Francesca.

The tiger, affectionately called Big Pussy, was the standout of the collection. Francesca Browne had shot and skinned it herself while climbing near Kathmandu.

"No," Feef continued, "Francesca's like Livingstone or one of those pith-helmeted chaps. She sends back the spoils of her conquests to the homeland. And this"—she opened her arms to encompass the whole space—"is a convenient homeland. She doesn't have a house, you see. At least not one where she'd be welcome. So she sends things here."

"No house?" Richard Lewis asked, swiping fig paste onto a wedge of brie. Richard was in the final year of the MFA program, and his poignant explorations of Caribbean culture already had New York agents salivating.

Jack, the department head, picked up on Richard's thought. "I always believed her to be royalty, or near as dammit to it. Surely she can afford a storage shed somewhere in East London?" Even among the glittering literati of eastern Iowa, it seemed, Francesca Browne was a source of fascination.

"Her maternal great-grandfather was indeed the Viscount Bolingbrook," Feef said. "She's full-blooded toff on both sides. But Francesca hasn't set foot in England for a decade. Her mother is a stodgy old goat, and doesn't think much of having such a flagrant queer for a daughter. Made things rather tough for her at home."

There was a lull as everyone sipped their drinks.

"Does your family mind?" Catherine probed delicately, her voice barely loud enough for those sitting next to her to hear. Before she'd meet Feef, she wouldn't have dreamed of asking such a personal question, especially not in public. But the way Feef so casually inhabited her sexuality, and indeed her whole life, had emboldened Catherine.

"That I fuck women, you mean?" Feef allowed the question to linger in the air as a few peals of nervous laughter pinged around the room.

"Oh, no. I mean, I just meant, the novel you published." Catherine could barely form the sentence. She held a napkin to her lips, fearing she might vomit.

Feef directed an imperious stare at Catherine for a beat or two before a suppressed trill of laughter danced from her lips. The others joined in. "I come from a family of equestrians and politicians. Of course they mind. I'm known to all their friends as the writer whose work made the *Times Literary Supplement* mention cunnilingus and digital penetration in a book review."

She reached out for Catherine's hand and squeezed it. "I'm sorry I teased you. You look like you could go up in a puff of smoke." She pulled Catherine's hand to her lips and kissed it. "You darling thing." Feef turned her attention back to the other guests. "Catherine won't like my telling you this, but she has quite a gift with Little Pussy."

"Beg your pardon?" sputtered Jim DuPont, one of the recent entries into the MFA program. Jim had grown up a Midwestern Methodist, and he, along with Catherine, often made convenient targets for the others' tang.

"My cat, Little Pussy," Feef said coolly. "I've hardly seen him for five minutes since I brought him home from the shelter last March. He hides, you see, and only comes out to swipe at my houseguests when they try to walk up the back stairs at night. I'd almost given up on the little demon, but our Catherine has managed to tame him." She turned a fond, almost maternal gaze on Catherine. "You should see Catherine in the dining room while we sip our morning coffee, stroking my Little Pussy. Purrs like a Ferrari engine in her hands."

*

That evening, after their guests departed, Catherine and Feef sat at what had become their usual 9 PM stations, a pair of matching brocade chairs next to the fire. Little Pussy cozied his lithe body into the crook of Catherine's arm, purring serenely.

Feef rose to add more wood to the fire. She knelt down and nudged the logs with a poker. Gray smoke billowed forth for a moment before retreating into the fireplace. "Must get this flue seen to," she said, coughing into her sleeve. "You'll have noticed by now that I'm terrible about keeping up with all the maintenance on the house. Plumbing's fractious, brickwork's a state, Big Pussy needs a proper dusting, painting constantly wants attention—the list is positively Sisyphean."

"Why don't you let me call and get some people in?" Catherine said. "I have more time than you."

"Would you? Oh, you're an absolute lifesaver," Feef said, getting to her feet. She paused and pressed steepled fingers to her lips. "I'm not supposed to tell you, but I've never been any good with secrets." She wiggled her fingers conspiratorially. "When we were in the kitchen earlier, Lucinda told me that Younas isn't coming back, at least not anytime soon. Can't seem to dry out properly, the poor old sod."

When Catherine didn't reply, Feef leaned down and gently took hold of her shoulders. "That means the job's yours for at least another semester, silly girl. Maybe longer. I know Jack's quite pleased with the way you've stepped in."

Catherine had heard talk among the students that Younas had been seen stumbling around Iowa City in broad daylight as recently as last week.

"Do you think so?" Catherine asked. "I thought that, now that Jack has time to look, he'd find someone more qualified than me to take over."

"We're all championing your cause. Me, especially," Feef said, giving Catherine a pat on the knee. "You fit this place like an old sock."

*

Catherine awoke a few nights later to the rhythmic thumping of a bass beat. She pulled the clock close to her face: 2:16 AM. She tugged on her flannel robe and crept down the hall in slippered feet.

The source of the music was Feef's bedroom. Her door stood ajar, an orange-hued light percolated into the hallway. Catherine opened her mouth to call Feef's name, but the sound of voices from inside the room trapped the utterance in her throat.

"This song is utter rubbish. It's junk food for juveniles," a woman's voice, creamy as butter, purred.

"Don't be a snob, Francesca darling," said Feef. Her voice was slow and sticky. There was a sound of rustling and a long moan.

"Formula music," Francesca said, spinning the radio dial until it landed on "Eine Kleine Nachtmusik."

Catherine leaned forward, just far enough to see inside the room. At the edge of her vision, two female bodies were interwoven, bathed in the glow of a scarf-draped Tiffany lamp. Though she couldn't see their faces, she knew it was Feef who reclined on a mound of pillows—freckle-specked skin, soft waist, and wide, welcoming hips. Threaded through her legs were another pair, muscular and bronzed.

So this was Francesca Browne.

Catherine tried to tear her eyes away. She forced her gaze back out to the hallway, where an oil painting of the poet William Blake hung on the opposite wall. Years ago, she'd set some of his poems to music, performing them at a festival outside Greenwich. She'd always thought of him as residing in the canon of dead white men, but on that dark night, his eyes locked on hers. She felt a strange urge to lick the moist bow of his mouth.

"Catherine would agree with you, I daresay," Feef replied languidly. "She was a folksinger for a few years, thinks disco and pop are DDT for the brain."

"Catherine? Your new pet, you mean?"

"Pet?" Feef asked, rolling toward her lover.

"The lodger," Francesca said. "'Her singing voice is like silk pajamas and she's pretty in a timorous sort of way,' I believe you said?"

"Did I?" Feef asked. She grabbed her cigarette, which had been smoldering in an ashtray next to the bed.

"You did. And apparently she's worked an absolute miracle with your neurotic cat." As she spoke, Francesca took hold of Feef's wrist and squeezed until she dropped the cigarette onto the bedcovers.

"You'll start a fire." Feef nipped at Francesca's hand, and they both laughed. "You jealous old thing, do you expect me to pine for you all the time you're away?" Feef asked, kissing her way over the tops of Francesca's breasts.

Out in the hallway, Little Pussy vaulted silently from atop the large armoire at the top of the back stairs, one of his favorite haunts. The cat pawed his way toward Catherine and figure-eighted around her legs. A minute shift in Catherine's weight caused the floorboard to creak, and, for a moment, she was sure the two women would look out into the hallway and she'd be exposed. She leaned back slowly, pressing her body against the wall. Catherine hunched over in panic, biting her lip and squeezing her palms between her thighs until the muscles stiffened and ached. She couldn't move, could hardly breathe.

"Yes." A series of fleshy slaps followed, and then a muted, sensual whimpering. "I do."

*

Feef was an early-to-bed, early-to-rise type, and, over the months, she and Catherine had developed a set morning routine. Catherine always came downstairs first, a little before 6 AM, to grind coffee beans using an old copper hand crank. She boiled water in the kettle and set the French press to steep. Just at the moment the coffee was ready, Feef would bound downstairs, fresh from the shower, her dark curls dripping, her cheeks scrubbed pink.

Catherine would open a can of tuna for Little Pussy and bring the coffee through to the dining room, where the two women would read the newspaper, sitting quietly.

The morning after Francesca arrived, though, 6 AM brought no sign of Feef and 6:30 came and went. The streetlights glowed outside, and only the barest hint of dawn pierced the late November sky. Catherine paced the room, stopping to stare at her distorted reflection in the glass of the dining room's large windows. The woman mirrored in the old leaded panes looked like a wavy wisp, hardly substantial enough to be human. She crossed the room and perched on the edge of her usual chair, taking nervous sips of now-cold coffee.

The floor above them creaked, and Catherine heard the sound of a faucet running. Little Pussy emerged from some hidden nook and curled unto her lap. She pressed her face into the cat's fur, inhaling the animal scent of him.

"It's going to be okay, Puss," she whispered. "She'll be gone soon, and everything will go back to normal." Anxiety zipped up and down Catherine's legs in an uncontrollable jiggle, but the cat somehow stayed put.

The footsteps moving down the hall overhead were unbearable. They hit the back stairs like peals of thunder—heavy, unlike Feef's bouncy stride. Even before Francesca had fully entered the dining room, Catherine felt a change in the air. Her nose twitched, and a spume of bile rose in her throat.

When Francesca finally came into view, Catherine popped out of her chair like a coiled spring, practically launching Little Pussy across the table. She hadn't gotten a clear look at Francesca's face the previous night. All these months, she'd been picturing someone mannish—dark and swarthy as Barnum's bearded lady. The woman who stood before her, though, had choppy reddish hair and knife-sharp cheekbones. Her body was long and sturdy, her face defined by a hawkish nose and a slack, pillowy mouth.

Francesca held the rough green pottery mug that Feef always used. "You must be the new roommate," Francesca said, extending her free hand.

Catherine took it, too frightened to speak. Those same fingers had spent the previous night exploring the recesses of Feef's body.

Francesca held Catherine's grip a few seconds longer than was necessary or comfortable. "Cold hands, cold heart, so they say," Francesca quipped. "You must have ice in your veins."

"Oh, sorry," Catherine stammered. "I must've forgotten." She scurried over to the thermostat and adjusted the dial up to seventy. "Feef usually turns up the heat in the morning when she comes into the room."

"Yes, she does," Francesca said.

"And it's so drafty in this room. We're getting someone in to have a look at the windows," Catherine continued.

Francesca's nimble lips curved into a smile. "So glad *we* are getting that taken care of."

"Is Feef feeling okay?" Catherine asked. "Should I bring her a tray?" When Francesca didn't reply, she continued. "It's just that she usually comes down by now. I thought maybe she was sick."

"'Bring her a tray,'" Francesca imitated Catherine's concerned tone. "How very sweet you are. No wonder Feef finds you so amusing. No, dear. I think she'll be just fine without a tray. Let her sleep." She crossed behind Catherine and leaned close, until her warm breath grazed Catherine's ear. "We had a rather happy reunion, you see."

*

Catherine walked the length of her bedroom, pivoted, and repeated the circuit. It was 6:30 on Friday night. Francesca has been there for six days.

The repairman she'd contacted had come earlier about the necessary maintenance on the chimney. "Good you called when you did," he'd said. "You're lucky you haven't already burned the place down. Probably hasn't been serviced since before you were born."

He quoted what was likely a high estimate, but Catherine agreed to pay. She knew Feef would want the work done as quickly as possible, and wouldn't want to be troubled with the details. The man had left more than an hour earlier, agreeing to come out first thing Monday to begin the repairs, but Catherine had been so distracted that she'd somehow come up to her room still holding onto the fireplace poker.

Her dilemma was serious. On alternating Fridays during the semester, Catherine and Feef met Lucinda in town to see the 9 PM show at the arthouse cinema. The three of them had been talking for weeks about *Sophie's Choice*, the new Meryl Streep movie. Catherine had overhead Feef and Lucinda discussing it after their department meeting that morning.

"Are you still planning to come tonight?" Lucinda had asked. She knew Francesca was visiting and wondered if it would change their usual plans.

"Of course," Feef had replied. "We wouldn't miss it."

Catherine had been on the far side of the table from them, and it seemed rude to insinuate herself into their conversation. Jim DuPont was distracting her, anyway, with his effusive congratulations about her reappointment for the spring semester, which Jack had officially announced during the meeting.

Feef had said nothing to Catherine directly about the movie plans, and now she was left to parse the semantics of what she'd overheard. Did the "we" mean all three of them—Catherine, Feef and Francesca Browne? The thought of sitting in the dark next to Francesca made Catherine shiver.

Or could Feef's reply mean that she and Catherine would come as usual, meet Lucinda in their customary Italian bistro for dinner beforehand and see the film as planned? Or was the "we" who would attend Feef and Francesca only?

Francesca had disrupted the whole routine of their household. In the mornings, Francesca and Feef came down to breakfast after Catherine had already left for campus, and in the evenings, Francesca and Feef drank Australian wine in the kitchen while Catherine sat alone by the cold, empty fireplace. Little Pussy had even gone back into hiding.

If only Catherine had plucked up the courage to interrupt Lucinda and Feef while they were still on campus, when Francesca wasn't around, she wouldn't be in this hopeless plight. If only she had Lucinda's phone number to clarify plans herself. But she'd never needed it before. Feef was the conduit to their shared social life, an arrangement that had worked perfectly until Francesca arrived.

From down the hall, Catherine heard Feef's laughter, pure as Christmas bells, followed by the harsh, animal-like braying of Francesca. Catherine tried to picture herself walking down to the bedroom and simply asking them whether they planned to go. Francesca's eyes would appraise her as if she were bait twisting on a hook. Francesca would say something to Catherine that would probably sound witty to Feef, but that Catherine would know was meant to be insulting. Maybe Francesca would choose that moment to announce that she wasn't going to return to her travels, but was instead moving into the house forever.

Catherine gripped the poker and twisted it until it caused her physical pain. Perhaps it would be better to go to the theater alone, to prove she could do things independently. But what if the others all showed up together and she was sitting alone in the dark? How foolish and pathetic she'd look. Worst of all, what if Lucinda decided not to come, and then Feef showed up hand in hand with Francesca? Even thinking the thought made her feel like her body might contort itself inside out.

Catherine lay down in the middle of her bedroom rug and curled into a tight ball. How could she bear the stress of this? She had to sink her front teeth into bones of her knuckles to keep from screaming.

From the quicksand depths of her anxiety, she heard something. An almost imperceptible, gentle scratching. The sound repeated, and then again. She uncoiled her body, rose and opened the door. Little Pussy turned the small triangle of his face up toward her, but he didn't come into the room. His eyes darted back and forth, and he stayed perched on his toe tips.

"What's the matter, Puss?" she soothed, crouching down to his level. "Feeling skittish?" She stepped into the hall so the cat could launch himself into her arms. Instead, he allowed her to stroke his soft fur but then glided away and disappeared down the back stairs. "Oh, do you want your numnums?" she asked after him. The poor cat, like Catherine herself, had hardly eaten since Francesca's arrival.

She padded quickly down the hallway after Little Pussy, but was stopped in her tracks when the door to Feef's bedroom flew open.

"Creeping around at keyholes again?" Francesca said, stepping into her path.

"I wasn't...Little Pussy...I only...." Catherine stammered.

Inside Feef's room, the bedcovers were askew and the radio thumped gently. The shower was running, and a vapor of steam escaped from the partially open door of the adjoining bathroom. Feef's sunny voice burst forth, matching the lyrics of the song, "And the last known survivor stalks his prey in the night, and he's watching us all with the aaaaah of the tiger."

Francesca followed Catherine's gaze. "Did you like what you saw the other night?" Francesca continued. "When you were spying on us?" She pulled the bedroom door shut behind her. "You seemed ever so interested." She stepped toward Catherine, forcing the smaller woman back against the wall. "Did you like the way she writhed when I licked her?"

Catherine cast her eyes down to the Oriental rug that spanned the second-floor hallway. A cocktail of fear and shame turned her blood from liquid to solid. "Or maybe it was me you wanted to see?" Francesca growled.

"I was only passing by," Catherine mewed. "To feed the cat." She pressed her fists to her lips to keep the contents of her stomach from spewing forth. Without looking up, she slid along the wallpaper toward the stairs.

"Oh, yes," Francesca said, shadowing her movements. "You're ever so dutiful. Seeing to this and that, doing her dishes, tidying around. She told me you'll be staying on in Iowa for another term." She paused. "You know, I gave her the poker you're holding." She reached out and took hold of Catherine's hand, peeling her fingers away from the poker one by one. When Catherine at last relinquished her grip, Francesca ran her fingertip up and down the length of it. "Pretty, isn't it? I forged it myself in Hungary. This house is practically mine, it's so full of my things."

Catherine took another step toward the back stairs, but again Francesca blocked her path.

"Where's the fire, Little Miss?" she asked. "Why don't you stick around? I think Feef and I will have time for one more quick shag before we go, if you want to get your jollies peering through a crack in the door." She rested her finger on the sharp tip of the poker and observed Catherine through her fan of blond eyelashes.

Francesca leaned her weight into Catherine, sandwiching the smaller woman against the wall. Francesca's lower thigh pressed into Catherine's crotch, and her breasts hit Catherine just below the chin. Catherine turned her head sideways and shut her eyes, releasing the tears that had pooled there. When she opened her eyes, they fixed on the portrait of William Blake.

Tyger Tyger, burning bright, in the forests of the night. The first line of Blake's most famous poem ran through Catherine's mind like a protective incantation.

"I think it's time you left," Francesca sighed into her ear. "Be gone before we get back from the film tonight."

The curved prong of the poker dug into Catherine's abdomen. She gripped it with shaking hands, and gave it a forceful shove. Surprised, Francesca stumbled backwards. Unseen, Little Pussy had been standing sentry there. When Francesca stepped into his domain, he gave an almighty screech and swiped wildly at her legs. Catherine found herself holding the poker as Francesca tried to regain her footing. The tight knot of fear inside her unwound in an instant, and before she could even form a thought, her hands stabbed the poker into the center of Francesca's chest, and Francesca flew backwards down the back staircase.

There was a series of sickening thuds. A barely audible whimper. And then nothing.

*

When Catherine walked into January's department meeting, a collective hurrah rose up from those around the faux-wood table. Even though this was their first gathering since the fire, they'd all heard the story many times. Throughout the holiday break, the campus had talked of nothing else.

A malfunctioning flue, only days away from being repaired. Francesca Browne igniting the flames that would spread out of control and reduce her legendary body to ash. The fabulous Lafarge mansion—stuffed as it was with the detritus of Francesca's globetrotting exploits—burned to a smoldering ruin before the Iowa City fire department could even mount their engines. Meek little Catherine risking her life, rushing straight into the flames to pull Feef to safety. And of course Feef's cagy cat, which had found his way to safety utterly unscathed, as cats somehow seem to do.

Feef was missing from the department meeting that day, still recovering in the hospital. Catherine, meanwhile, was staying with Jack Legg and his wife and finalizing the purchase of a new house— nothing as grand as Feef's former home, just a tidy Cape Cod with a well-kept garden and a view over the river.

Catherine took a chair next to Lucinda, who pulled her into a tight embrace. Catherine winced.

"Oh, sorry. I forgot about your burns," Lucinda said. She gently took hold of Catherine's arm, which was still bandaged from elbow to fingertips, and quoted, "'What the hand, dare seize the fire?'"

"What?" Catherine said, pulling back as if she'd been burned anew.

"'What the hand, dare seize the fire?' An apt quotation," Lucinda said with a quizzical expression. When Catherine continued to regard her warily, she added. "William Blake, dear."

"Of course," Catherine replied, returning Lucinda's smile. "I've gotten bored with the classics, though." She arranged the papers on the table in front of her. "For my next project, I'd like to do something that combines poetry and music, like Andrew Lloyd Weber."

"Oh, I love *Cats*," Lucinda said. "I haven't seen it yet, but I got a cassette of the cast album for Christmas. The lyrics are practically verbatim quotes of the Eliot. I'd never have thought *Old Possum* could work as a musical, but the songs are so catchy."

"Feef and I were just talking about it when I visited her yesterday," Catherine said. "We're thinking of organizing a trip to New York for the students once we close on the new house."

As they gathered their things and filtered out of the room, Catherine cradled her bandaged hand and hummed her favorite stanza from T.S. Eliot's feline-centered work:

Macavity, Macavity, there's no one like Macavity,
He's broken every human law, he breaks the law of gravity.
His powers of levitation would make a fakir stare,
And when you reach the scene of crime—Macavity's not there.

Shine

Released September 2007

"One Week Last Summer"
"This Place"
"If I Had a Heart"
"Hana"
"Bad Dreams"
"Big Yellow Taxi 2007"
"Night of the Iguana"
"Strong and Wrong"
"Shine"
"If"

All songs by Joni Mitchell
except "If" (lyrics adapted from Rudyard Kipling's "If").

Bad Dreams
by John M. Floyd

9:15 AM

Eddie Harmon sat on the side of his bed, fully dressed, elbows on his knees, eyes on the leaves of the sweetgum tree outside his second-floor window. Thinking.

He had a lot to think about. His job, for one thing. He was a web designer, or had been until recently, when over the course of two days his struggling printer finally broke, his computer's screen began fading to black, and his hard drive started making sounds like a blender full of gravel. Now he had deadlines approaching, and clients getting restless. He was also worried about his mother. He'd moved in with her six months ago, after the death of his father, and although she was a strong person—stronger than Eddie, for sure—she was having trouble adjusting, not only to widowhood but to sharing her house with a forty-year-old son who had depression issues of his own.

The funny part was, these weren't the things Eddie was thinking most about, at the moment. He was thinking about a phone call he was about to make.

For the tenth time Eddie rehearsed the words he would use. Then he crossed the room to his computer desk, picked up the telephone, punched in the number, and waited.

When he heard the voice on the other end of the line, he felt himself relax a bit. That voice always had a calming effect on him. Jake Lansdale was Eddie's oldest friend.

"I need a favor," Eddie said to him.

Jake groaned. "Just what I wanted to hear, this morning. Are you in jail?"

"This is serious," Eddie said. "Remember when I used to have those dreams, when we were kids? When I could see things nobody else could?"

"I remember." There had been several of those premonitions, some minor and some not so: a flat tire on a road trip to Memphis, the unannounced arrival of relatives from Georgia, a tornado that blew away the Baptist Church. Somehow Eddie had seen and predicted those events, days before they happened.

"Well, I had one last night," Eddie said. "Or maybe this morning, I don't know—anyway, I woke up with it still in my head."

"And?"

Eddie drew a long breath and let it out. "Something bad's going to happen."

"What do you mean, bad?"

"I mean like a blast. An explosion."

"What kind? An accident?"

"A building. And no accident—this is a bomb. Terrorism, I guess."

A silence passed. It was so quiet Eddie could hear the ticking of the clock on his night table.

"You *are* serious," Jake said.

"I am. I think it'll happen sometime today."

"Where?"

"Here in town. A strip mall on Robinson called Ridgewood Mart."

"Where you used to work?"

"Yep. But the building I saw is a post office, sort of a satellite branch, a few doors down from where I was."

"I know the place. I filled in there a couple days last month."

"Yeah, you told me you did," Eddie said. "That's one reason I'm calling you." Jake Lansdale was a mailman, and as a postal worker he had especially strong feelings about incidents of workplace violence. That was the other reason.

"So you really think there's a bomb there? In that post office?"

"I saw it, Jake. In my dream. I didn't see the blast, just the device. It was hidden under a pile of junk in a back room."

Another silence.

"Did you see who put it there?" Jake asked. Dead serious now.

"No. I just saw the bomb."

A long, shaky sigh came down the phoneline. "Well, what are you waiting for? Call the cops. Call 9-1-1. Tell 'em a building's about to blow up."

"I can't do that. There's been a dozen bomb threats at all kinds of places in this town in the past six months. All of them were false alarms."

"So?"

"So the cops are probably getting used to it. They might not take it seriously."

"But this isn't a hoax. You said so yourself. You know it's there."

"Well, I'm pretty sure." Eddie leaned back, stretching his neck as well as the phone cord, and looked up at his ceiling. "If you recall, the things I used to see in these dreams of mine—well, they weren't always right."

"Then you'll have to make them believe you."

Eddie felt himself nod. But he said, "There's another problem. If I call them about this, and they believe me, and send a bomb squad—they wouldn't know exactly where to look. It'd take too long to find it."

"What do you mean?"

"I mean I don't think they'll have a lot of time." Eddie sat up straight in his chair and stayed quiet a moment, looking for words. "In my vision, I saw a back room, in the building. I know that because I saw an outside window, and none of the businesses in that strip have windows on either side or in front. And I saw late-morning sun coming in. I know it was morning because the back of the complex is the east side, and I know it was almost noon because the rectangle of sunlight on the floor was so close to the window."

"So?"

"So I know the bomb hasn't exploded yet, because right now it's 9:30. Midmorning. I think this'll happen today, by noon."

When Eddie paused this time, he could hear his mother moving about, downstairs. Heard the voices on her TV, one of the morning talk shows.

"Okay," Jake said finally. "You think they need to locate this thing in the next couple hours. Fine. Call the cops, and let 'em get started looking."

"I told you, I have to be careful. One, if I don't convince them they might not respond. Two, if they believe me but I don't say *where* it is, they might take too long to find it. And three, if I do tell them exactly where it is…they'll think I planted it."

Both of them stayed quiet a moment, as that sank in.

"*Do* you know exactly where it is?"

"No," Eddie said. "But I know what room it's in. And they'll wonder how I know. They'll assume I'm the suspect. I sure can't tell them I saw it in a dream."

This time Jake's voice sounded far away. "No. I guess not."

"So what's the answer?"

More seconds passed. Then: "Make it anonymous. Spell out where the bomb is, but block your caller I.D., so they won't know who you are."

"How do I do that?" Eddie asked.

"Key in *67 before you key the number. Then hit the 1, then the area code, then the number—all ten digits. That works whether it's a landline or a cell. And they can't trace the call unless you talk too long." Jake paused. "But how do you convince them it's a real threat, and not just a prank?"

After a moment's thought Eddie said, "What if I point 'em to a suspect? What if I describe the bomber?"

"The guy who planted it? I thought you said you didn't see him."

"I didn't. But I could make up a description. I'll say I noticed him lurking around, carrying a duffel bag or something, then I saw him sneak into the post office, and found out later he'd placed a bomb inside. That's it. If I tell 'em what he looks like, they'll believe me."

"How do you figure that?"

"Because you'll call in," Eddie said, "and give them the same description."

"What?!"

"You won't have to say you know anything more—just that you saw somebody sneaking around outside with a bag, acting suspicious. When they realize it's the same guy I told them about, it'll be enough to tip the scale."

"But—"

"No buts, Jake. I need you to do this. You said yourself, there's no risk. Key in the *67 to block your I.D., disguise your voice somehow just to be extra safe, and make the call. We'll space it so I call it in a few minutes before or after you do."

For a long moment neither of them spoke. "Jake?" Eddie said. "You there?"

"I'm here."

"Will you do it? We're wasting time."

Eddie could hear him breathing.

"Yeah," Jake said. "I'll do it. How do we describe this imaginary bombardier?"

"Well...we need to try to make sure the description doesn't match a real person. You remember the folks who work in that P.O. branch, right? Describe them to me."

"Let's see...unless somebody's quit or transferred out since the two days I spent on site...there were six workers, besides me. An old dark-haired white guy, a gray-haired white lady, a blonde in her forties, and three skinny black guys, two of them middle-aged and one young. Some wore uniforms, some didn't, but all six wore those metal name tags."

"How's this, then?" Eddie thought for a moment. "Our perp will be white, thirtyish, red-haired and tall. Western shirt, jeans, ponytail. And no nameplate. That sound different enough?"

"Yeah. That should work."

"Write it down," Eddie said. "If we both report this, in slightly different words so they don't suspect we're together, the cops'd be crazy not to check it out."

"And what if they *do* find somebody who looks like that?" Jake asked. "In one of the nearby stores or something?"

"Are you kidding? A tall redheaded cowboy with a ponytail?"

"Well, maybe somebody who matches *part* of the description."

Eddie shrugged. "Then I guess they'd make his life miserable for a while. But we gotta describe him or the threat won't sound believable."

Half a minute dragged by, while both of them mulled it over.

"This is just to push them into investigating it, Jake. Hopefully, in the long run, we're saving everybody in that office."

After another wait Jake said, "If they do find a device and disarm it, they'll probably catch whoever did it, right? Security cameras in the buildings, and such."

"Maybe. Or maybe whoever did it checked out the cameras beforehand and disabled them somehow, or sprayed the lenses with black paint. Wouldn't be that hard to do."

Again both men fell silent. Eddie could hear, somewhere outside his window, a truck rumble past, could hear birds singing in the trees that lined the sidewalk. He leaned over and looked out at the yard. A dog was standing in the middle of his lawn, watching two cats in the flowerbeds. It was, for most people out there, a normal day.

"Are you with me, Jake? Will you do this?"

Eddie could picture his old friend thinking about it. Probably at the cluttered worktable in his cluttered garage.

"Okay," Jake said finally. "I'm in. When should I call?"

"Now. I'll wait ten minutes and then I'll call, too. And congratulations—you've done your good-citizen deed for the year."

"You'll let me know what happens?"

"I won't have to," Eddie said. "We'll hear about it on the news."

*

Eddie waited twenty minutes, just to be sure, and at exactly 10:05 phoned in the tip. He made his voice higher than usual and didn't talk long—just enough to pass along the necessary information—but he could tell from the responses he got from the 9-1-1 operator that she was more than a little alarmed, and he knew that was because Jake Lansdale had made a similar call and described the same suspect only moments earlier. By the time Eddie disconnected, he felt sure the plan would work.

He'd been sitting there for several seconds, staring at the telephone, when he heard slow footsteps on the stairs and then a knock on the door of his bedroom.

He took a long breath and said, "Come in."

His mother, who was almost seventy now, stuck her head into his room. She smiled at him despite the tiredness in her face. "I just wrote my monthly newsletter for my sewing group," she said. "Can you scan it for me like you did last time, and email it to the other members?"

Rewind to the real world, he said to himself. And the real world was a sad one, for both of them. Eddie's father's final health problems—triggered, as is sometimes the case, by financial problems—had taken him down fast. And now, months later, neither Eddie nor Nora Harmon could bear to think about it.

Eddie was just glad to see her involved with her ladies' groups. That, at least, seemed like old times.

He cleared his throat. "Sorry, Mom. My system's still down—I can't print, scan, *or* email." Which was true. "But I can drive to the library and make copies for you, to mail out."

"How kind of you, son. Hang on, I'll go put it in a folder you can take with you."

As soon as she left, Eddie ran a trembling hand through his hair and opened the bottom drawer of his desk. Carefully he took out a baseball cap, sunglasses, latex gloves, a cheap metal door key and a can of black spray paint. He stuffed everything into a backpack, then looked all around, taking stock. He was ready.

He checked the clock and forced himself to wait another ten minutes. When he was fairly sure the events he had set in motion were under way, he rose, pocketed his car keys, walked to the kitchen, picked up the folder from his mother, and headed out the door to the garage.

High above, as he pulled out into traffic, a red hawk was riding the sky.

*

Eddie Harmon returned home two hours later. He'd been to the library and had copied his mom's newsletter, but before that he had driven to Ridgewood Mart, and—amid the growing confusion and chaos there—had done what he'd planned to do. His old key to the back entrance of the store three doors down from the post office had worked perfectly, as he had known it would. He'd checked it out yesterday, before making a stop at a sporting-goods store and the county co-op, just to ensure the lock hadn't been changed since his days of employment there. No one had seen him. All the activity was in or around the P.O.

He stopped now in the living room, where his mother was watching TV. The noon edition of the news was reporting the aftermath of a bomb threat at a strip mall five miles away, on the east end of town. The threat itself had been groundless, the grim-faced anchor informed them; over the past hour or so, the Robinson Street branch office of the U.S. Postal Service at Ridgewood Mart had been thoroughly searched and declared safe and explosives-free. It appeared to be only the latest in a string of such hoaxes phoned in to the authorities in recent months. The two shops immediately adjacent to the post office had been evacuated and all the stores in the shopping center had been visited in search of a suspect who'd been described by two witnesses who had called 9-1-1. One computer-store manager who fit the description—there was a quick video of him being led away by cops—was instructed to close and lock up his place of business and was taken in for questioning. The good thing, the announcer repeated, as cell phone zombies milled around behind him, was that the threat had turned out to be a false alarm. No reported injuries, no damages, no loss of property.

That, Eddie knew, wasn't exactly true.

He wondered if Jake Lansdale was watching the same report.

"Didn't you work at a computer store in that shopping center a while back?" Eddie's mother asked him.

"I did. It's pretty close to where everything seems to be happening."

"Funny thing," she said, her eyes on the TV. "That man they showed earlier, with long red hair, being taken in for questioning…."

"What about him?"

"I don't know. He sort of looked like the guy who ran that store where you worked." She turned in her chair and gazed up at him. "You know, the guy who…." She trailed off, her eyes straying to the photo of his father, on the end table beside the couch.

"The guy who talked Dad into that investment deal?" Eddie said.

She nodded, adrift in her thoughts. They both remembered the aftermath of that financial decision, the loss of what Arthur Harmon had hoped would be his and his wife's retirement nest egg. Everyone agreed that the stress of that failed "business" arrangement had led to his fatal heart attack. As luck would have it, the man who'd lured Arthur into the crooked deal had evaded prosecution and wound up managing the local computer store where Eddie was working at the time. Since then, there had been rumors of embezzlement there, but—again—nothing ever came of it. Red had remained in charge, and the accusations were forgotten.

At least by some.

"You think that was him?" Eddie's mother asked. "In the news video?"

"I don't know, Mom," he lied. "Doesn't matter anyway. Sounds like there was no bomb." He took a seat in the chair next to her and, after hesitating a moment, said almost the same words he'd said to Jake three hours ago: "Remember when I used to have those dreams, those visions of things nobody else could see?"

"Vaguely." She grinned and added, "You were a smart boy, I remember that. All your card tricks and magic shows. I do recall you telling your dad one of our tires would blow out on that trip we made. He checked them, and all was well, but it still happened...."

Eddie leaned closer to her, and took her hand. "Mom, it was just a guess. I know now that all those visions I had, those predictions I made—they were dreams, and no more real than my magic tricks. It was just the law of averages. When some of my guesses came true, everybody was amazed, including me, especially when it was something really bad or really good—but most of them *didn't* come true, and the misfires were conveniently overlooked." He smiled. "I wasn't psychic. I wasn't even smart. As any politician'll tell you, perception—what other people think—is what matters. Understand?"

He could see, from the look in her eyes, that she didn't. Probably because she didn't want to. What seemed to matter to her right now was that he was sitting here, holding her hand. And he loved her all the more for it.

His mother gave his fingers a squeeze. "What I understand is that you *are* smart, Eddie, and you work hard, and you're good to me. Which reminds me," she said, glancing at the folder in his other hand. "Thanks for the copies. It's time I got one of the other ladies to handle our newsletter. One of the *younger* ladies."

He stood up. "No need. Next time we'll send 'em out the usual way." He pointed to the garage door. "I got a carful of boxes out there to unload. New computer, new printer, scanner, the works."

A smile lit up her face. "New computer? My, my. Business must be good."

"It will be," he said.

She gave him a sly look. "You sound sure of that. Did you have a vision?"

"No." He smiled back at her. "No visions today. Good *or* bad." Or last night, either. He'd lied to his best friend about that. For good reason, he hoped—but it was still a lie. There had been no dream, no premonition, no bomb.

Eddie wasn't a prophet. Nobody's a prophet.

Eddie was a planner.

That's why he'd stopped yesterday at the co-op for a bag of fertilizer and the sporting-goods store for a target-range kit before going to Ridgewood Mart today. When the cops received a second phone tip this afternoon, and discovered ammonium nitrate and Tannerite in the redheaded manager's office—well, possession of bomb-making materials would be a little hard to explain, wouldn't it? And when the cops were then told that a lot of electronics merchandise was missing from the store....

Burglary, Eddie had found, was a simple matter if the burgled store's been evacuated. And so was revenge.

He handed his mom her copies, kissed her on the forehead, walked back to the garage, and began unloading his new equipment. He had a business to run.

On his mind, as he worked, was a final thought: *Bad dreams are good, in the great plan.*

Acknowledgments

My thanks to the authors who enthusiastically contributed stories: to Martin Edwards, Barb Goffman, Donna Andrews, and Kathryn O'Sullivan for suggesting possible contributors; to Peter Riva for his encouragement and able representation; to Jay Hartman and K.D. Sullivan at Untreed Reads for shepherding *The Beat of Black Wings* through the process of publication; to my wife Laurie Pachter and daughter Rebecca Jones for putting up with me for all these years; to the letter *K* for setting everything in motion...and, most of all, to the incomparable Joni Mitchell, whose music and lyrics inspired this book.

About the Contributors

DONNA ANDREWS was born in Yorktown (VA) and now lives in Reston (VA). *Owl Be Home for Christmas* and *The Falcon Always Wings Twice* are the most recent titles in her Agatha-, Anthony-, and Lefty-winning Meg Langslow series. She's a former executive vice president of Mystery Writers of America and is active in Sisters in Crime. *www.donnaandrews.com*

ABBY BARDI is the author of the novels *The Book of Fred*, *The Secret Letters* and *Double Take*, and her short fiction has appeared in *Quarterly West*, *Rosebud*, *Monkeybicycle*, *The Bellingham Review*, and the anthologies *Reader, I Murdered Him*, *High Infidelity*, *Grace and Gravity* and *New Stories from the Midwest 2018*. She has taught in Japan and England and now lives in Ellicott City, Maryland, the oldest train depot in America. *www.abbybardi.com*

MICHAEL BRACKEN is a novelist and prolific short-story writer. He has received the Edward D. Hoch Memorial Golden Derringer Award for lifetime achievement in short mystery fiction as well as two additional Derringer Awards. He is the author of the private-eye novel *All White Girls* and several other books. More than 1200 of his short stories have appeared in *Alfred Hitchcock's Mystery Magazine*, *Ellery Queen's Mystery Magazine*, *Mike Shayne Mystery Magazine*, *The Best American Mystery Stories*, and many other anthologies and periodicals, and he has edited six anthologies of crime fiction, including *The Eyes of Texas* and the *Fedora* series. He lives and writes in Texas. *www.crimefictionwriter.com*

CAROL ANNE DAVIS is a Scottish writer who has lived in England for over twenty years and has written twenty crime books as well as contributing to numerous anthologies. When she isn't working, she loves to dance, walk and play Scrabble—albeit not all at the same time. She is about to take a break from writing to look after elderly, isolated patients in the community, though she will have to build an electric fence between them and her psychotic rescue cat.

DAVID DEAN has been a regular contributor to EQMM and to various anthologies since 1990. His stories have been nominated for the Shamus, Barry and Derringer Awards; "Ibrahim's Eyes" won the EQMM Readers Award for 2007, and "Tomorrow's Dead" was a finalist for the Best Short Story of 2011 Edgar. He is a retired New Jersey chief of police and once served as a paratrooper with the 82nd Airborne Division. His novels *The Thirteenth Child, Starvation Cay* and *The Purple Robe* are all available on Amazon.

BRENDAN DUBOIS is the author of 24 novels and over 180 short stories. He's currently coauthoring with bestselling novelist James Patterson, with the novels *The First Lady* and *The Cornwalls Are Gone* published in 2019 and *The Summer House* coming out in 2020. His stories—which have appeared in *Playboy, The Saturday Evening Post,* EQMM, AHMM and many anthologies—have won him three Shamus Awards, two Barrys, a Derringer, the EQMM Readers Award and three Edgar nominations from the Mystery Writers of America. He is also a *Jeopardy!* champion. *www.brendandubois.com*

JOHN M. FLOYD has contributed to more than 250 different publications, including AHMM, EQMM, *The Strand Magazine, The Saturday Evening Post* and two editions of *The Best American Mystery Stories.* A former Air Force captain and IBM systems engineer, he is also an Edgar nominee, a three-time Derringer Award winner, a recipient of the Short Mystery Fiction Society's lifetime achievement award and the author of eight books. *www.johnmfloyd.com*

BARB GOFFMAN loves writing, reading, air conditioning and her dog, not necessarily in that order. She's won the Agatha, Macavity and Silver Falchion awards for her short stories, and she's been a finalist twenty-eight times for national mystery short-story awards, including the Anthony and Derringer. Her book *Don't Get Mad, Get Even* won the Silver Falchion for the best collection of 2013. Her stories have also appeared in AHMM, EQMM, *Black Cat Mystery Magazine* and a number of anthologies, including *Crime Travel,* a time-travel crime anthology she edited that came out in December 2019. Barb lives in Winchester, Virginia, and works as a freelance editor and proofreader. *www.barbgoffman.com*

SHERRY HARRIS is the Agatha Award–nominated author of the Sarah Winston Garage Sale mystery series and the Chloe Jackson Seaglass Saloon mystery series. She is the immediate past president of Sisters in Crime and a member of Mystery Writers of America and International Thriller Writers. In her spare time, she loves reading and is a patent-holding inventor. Sherry, her husband and their dog Lily live in Northern Virginia. *www.sherryharrisauthor.com*

GREG HERREN is an award-winning author and editor, with over thirty novels and over twenty anthologies to his credit. He has been shortlisted for Lambda Literary Awards fourteen times and won twice, is the recipient of an Anthony Award and two medals from the Moonbeam Children's Book Awards, and has been shortlisted for the Macavity and Shirley Jackson awards. He lives in New Orleans. *www.gregherren.com*

EMILY HOCKADAY is the author of *Space on Earth, Ophelia: A Botanist's Guide, What We Love & Will Not Give Up* and *Starting a Life*, as well as the forthcoming *Beach Vocabulary* from Red Bird Chaps. Her poems have appeared in a number of journals, most recently *Parks & Points, Harpur Palate* and *Isacoustic*. She is the managing editor of *Analog Science Fiction & Fact* and *Asimov's Science Fiction*, and coedited the horror anthology *Terror at the Crossroads* with Jackie Sherbow. *www.emilyhockaday.com*

MATTHEW IDEN is the author of a half-dozen books in the Marty Singer detective series and several acclaimed stand-alone novels, including the psychological thriller *The Winter Over*, a thriller set in a South Pole winter, and *Birthday Girl*, featuring Elliott Nash, a homeless former forensic psychologist recruited to save a young girl from a serial kidnapper. His latest is the seventh book in the Marty Singer series, *The Bitter Fields*. *www.matthew-iden.com*

TARA LASKOWSKI is the author of the novel *One Night Gone* (Graydon House, 2019) and two short-story collections, *Modern Manners for Your Inner Demons* and *Bystanders* (which won the 2016 Balcones Fiction Prize). Her stories have been published in numerous places, including EQMM and AHMM, and in 2019 she won an Agatha Award for Best Short Story. She was a longtime editor of the online flash-fiction magazine *SmokeLong Quarterly*. "Both Sides Now" is her first literary collaboration with her husband, Art Taylor—although they previously collaborated on their son, Dash. *www.taralaskowski.com*

EDITH MAXWELL is the Agatha- and Macavity-nominated author of the Quaker Midwife Mysteries and the Local Foods Mysteries, as well as award-winning short crime fiction, which has appeared in EQMM as well as in Malice, Bouchercon and Level Best Books anthologies. As Maddie Day, she writes the Country Store Mysteries and the Cozy Capers Book Group Mysteries. An ardent Joni Mitchell fan since 1974, she lives north of Boston with her beau. When she isn't wasting time on Facebook, she gardens, cooks and contributes to the Wicked Authors blog. *www.edithmaxwell.com*

ALISON McMAHAN is the author of *Alice Guy Blaché, Lost Visionary of the Cinema* (Bloomsbury, 2002) and the YA historical mystery *The Saffron Crocus* (Black Opal, 2014). She has contributed short fiction to *Fish Out of Water* (Wildside, 2017), *Busted: Arresting Stories from the Beat* (Level Best, 2017), the Sisters in Crime anthology *Fatally Haunted* (Down & Out, 2019), and the Mystery Writers of America anthology *Scream and Scream Again* (HarperCollins, 2018). *www.alisonmcmahan.com*

ADAM MEYER is a screenwriter and fiction writer who has published many short stories, most recently in the anthologies *Crime Travel, Chesapeake Crimes: Storm Warning* and the Malice Domestic anthology *Murder Most Theatrical*. He's the author of the YA novel *The Last Domino* and recently finished a new novel, *Missing Rachel*. His TV credits include *Deadly Ransom* for Lifetime and several true-crime series for Investigation Discovery. *www.adammeyerwriter.com*

ALAN ORLOFF won the ITW Thriller Award for Best E-Book Original for his 2019 thriller, *Pray for the Innocent*. His debut mystery, *Diamonds for the Dead*, was an Agatha Award finalist; his story "Dying in Dokesville" won a 2019 Derringer Award; and "Rule Number One" was selected for *The Best American Mystery*

Stories 2018. His first P.I. novel, *I Know Where You Sleep*, was released from Down & Out Books in February 2020. *www.alanorloff.com*

KATHRYN O'SULLIVAN is author of the Colleen McCabe series (*Foal Play, Murder on the Hoof, Neighing with Fire*) and the Mae West short story "He Done Her Wrong" (in *Malice Domestic: Mystery Most Historical*). Her plays are published in *The Best Ten-Minute Plays of 2014* (Smith & Kraus), *The Best Ten-Minute Plays of 2011* (S&K) and *Plays of the Dramathon* (Theatre Lab). She is a Malice Domestic Best First Traditional Mystery winner; creator and writer of *Thurston* (Amazon); college professor; and member of Mystery Writers of America, Sisters in Crime and the Dramatists Guild. She is currently working on a documentary film. *www.kathrynosullivan.com*

JOSH PACHTER is a writer, editor and translator. Almost a hundred of his short crime stories have appeared in EQMM, AHMM and many other periodicals, anthologies and year's-best collections. *The Tree of Life* (Wildside Press, 2015) collected all ten of his Mahboob Chaudri stories; he collaborated with Belgian author Bavo Dhooge on *Styx* (Simon & Schuster, 2015); and he coedited *Amsterdam Noir* with Dutch writer René Appel (Akashic Books, 2019) and *The Misadventures of Ellery Queen* with Dale C. Andrews (Wildside Press, 2018); and edited *The Man Who Read Mysteries: The Short Fiction of William Brittain* (Crippen & Landru, 2018) and *The Misadventures of Nero Wolfe* (Mysterious Press, 2020). *www.joshpachter.com*

CHRISTINE POULSON is the author of the Katie Flanagan medical mysteries. The latest, *An Air That Kills*, came out in January 2020. Her short stories have appeared in *Ellery Queen's Mystery Magazine* and numerous anthologies and have been shortlisted for the Derringer, the CWA's Short Story Dagger and the Margery Allingham Prize. Before she turned to writing crime fiction, she taught art history at Cambridge and was a curator of ceramics at Birmingham Museum and Art Gallery and curator for the William Morris Society in Hammersmith, London. *www.christinepoulson.co.uk*

MINDY QUIGLEY is the author of the Mount Moriah cozy mystery series. Her short stories have won awards, including the 2018 *Artemis Journal*/Light Bringer Prize, and her non-writing career has taken her from the US to the UK, where she worked as the personal assistant to the scientist who cloned Dolly the sheep and as project manager for a research clinic founded by J.K. Rowling. She now lives in Virginia with her husband, their children and their idiosyncratic miniature Schnauzer. *www.mindyquigley.com*

JACKIE SHERBOW is the author of the poetry chapbook *Harbinger* (Finishing Line Press, 2019). She is the managing editor of *Alfred Hitchcock's Mystery Magazine* and *Ellery Queen's Mystery Magazine*, the editor of *Newtown Literary* (the literary journal dedicated to the borough of Queens, NY) and, with Emily Hockaday, the coeditor of *Terror at the Crossroads: Tales of Horror, Delusion, and the Unknown* (Dell Magazines/Eris Press, 2018).

AMBER SPARKS is the author of *The Unfinished World and Other Stories* and *I Do Not Forgive You: Revenges and Other Stories*, both from Liveright. Her fiction and essays have appeared in *Tin House*, *Granta*, *The Cut*, *The Paris Review* and other places. You can find her most days at *@ambernoelle*.

ART TAYLOR is the author of *The Boy Detective & The Summer of '74 and Other Tales of Suspense*. His previous book, *On the Road with Del & Louise: A Novel in Stories*, won the Agatha Award for Best First Novel. His short fiction has won an Edgar, an Anthony and several Agatha, Derringer and Macavity awards. He teaches at George Mason University. "Both Sides Now" is his first literary collaboration with his wife, Tara Laskowski—though hopefully not their last. *www.arttaylorwriter.com*

RICKI THOMAS is a British scriptwriter and the author of seven novels, as well as many articles, short stories and biographies. After living in numerous countries, she now enjoys a peaceful life in Hertfordshire, England. Her interests include true crime (particularly cases involving serial killers), criminal psychology and film comedies. *www.rickithomas.com*

MARILYN TODD is the award-winning author of nineteen historical thrillers, three anthologies and nearly a hundred short stories. She was also nominated for a Private Eye Writers of America Shamus Award. Her latest series kicks off with *Snap Shot*, featuring Britain's first crime-scene photographer—"a fabulous new historical crime series, which brilliantly evokes the darker side of Victorian London." Born in London, Marilyn now lives with her husband in France, and when she isn't killing people, she enjoys cooking…which is much the same thing. *www.marilyntodd.com*

ELAINE VIETS is the author of thirty-five bestselling mysteries in four series—the hardboiled Francesca Vierling novels, the traditional Dead-End Job books, the cozy Josie Marcus Mystery Shopper series and the Angela Richman, Death Investigator, books—and has won the Agatha, Anthony and Lefty Awards. Reviewer Cindy Chow called *A Deal with the Devil and 13 Short Stories* (Crippen & Landru, 2018) "a stunning collection." *www.elaineviets.com*

STACY WOODSON is a U.S. Army veteran, and her time in the military is often a source of inspiration for her stories. She made her crime fiction debut in EQMM's "Department of First Stories" and won the magazine's 2018 Readers Award. Her story "Armadillo By Morning" was a shortlisted finalist for the Bill Crider Prize for Short Fiction in 2019, and "The Hail Mary Play" was featured on the cover of *Mystery Weekly*'s July 2019 issue. Since her debut, she has placed work in ten anthologies and publications. *www.stacywoodson.com*

Made in the USA
Middletown, DE
27 April 2020

92057191R00215